THE
CHOCOLATE
CONNOISSEUR

FOR EVERYONE WITH A PASSION
FOR CHOCOLATE

Chloé Doutre-Roussel

HOME

A HOME BOOK
Published by the Penguin Group
Penguin Group (USA) Inc.
375 Hudson Street, New York, New York 10014, USA
Penguin Group (Canada), 90 Eglinton Avenue East, Suite 700, Toronto, Ontario M4P 2Y3, Canada
(a division of Pearson Penguin Canada Inc.)
Penguin Books Ltd., 80 Strand, London WC2R 0RL, England
Penguin Ireland, 25 St. Stephen's Green, Dublin 2, Ireland (a division of Penguin Books Ltd.)
Penguin Group (Australia), 250 Camberwell Road, Camberwell, Victoria 3124, Australia
(a division of Pearson Australia Group Pty. Ltd.)
Penguin Books India Pvt. Ltd., 11 Community Centre, Panchsheel Park, New Delhi—110 017, India
Penguin Group (NZ), Cnr. Airborne and Rosedale Roads, Albany, Auckland 1310, New Zealand
(a division of Pearson New Zealand Ltd.)
Penguin Books (South Africa) (Pty.) Ltd., 24 Sturdee Avenue, Rosebank, Johannesburg 2196,
South Africa

Penguin Books Ltd., Registered Offices: 80 Strand, London WC2R 0RL, England

While the author has made every effort to provide accurate telephone numbers and Internet addresses
at the time of publication, neither the publisher nor the author assumes any responsibility for errors, or
for changes that occur after publication. Further, the publisher does not have any control over and does
not assume any responsibility for author or third-party websites or their content.

PRINTING HISTORY
Previously published in Great Britain in 2005 by Piatkus Books Ltd.
Jeremy P. Tarcher/Penguin hardcover edition / February 2006
Home trade paperback edition / December 2006

Home trade paperback ISBN: 1-55788-503-6

The Library of Congress has cataloged the Tarcher/Penguin hardcover edition as follows:

Doutre-Roussel, Chloé.
   The chocolate connoisseur : for everyone with a passion for chocolate / Chloé Doutre-Roussel.
        p.   cm.
   Includes bibliographical references and index.
   ISBN 1-58542-488-9
   1. Chocolate.   2. Chocolate candy.   I. Title.
   TX767.C5D68   2006   2005055980
   641.3'374—dc22

PRINTED IN THE UNITED STATES OF AMERICA

10   9   8   7   6   5   4   3   2   1

PUBLISHER'S NOTE: The recipes contained in this book are to be followed exactly as written. The
publisher is not responsible for your specific health or allergy needs that may require medical super-
vision. The publisher is not responsible for any adverse reactions to the recipes contained in this book.

Most Home Books are available at special quantity discounts for bulk purchase for sales promotions,
premiums, fund-raising, or educational use. Special books, or book excerpts, can also be created to fit
specific needs. For details, write: Special Markets, The Berkley Publishing Group , 375 Hudson Street,
New York, New York 10014.

For Marlies and Roger

Contents

Images and illustrations   VI

Acknowledgements   VII

Introduction: A passion for chocolate   1

A brief history of chocolate   7

1. *Chocolate past and present*   9

2. *Building your own chocolate profile*   30

3. *Bean to bar*   48

4. *Tasting, tasting …*   76

5. *Chocolate to share*   101

6. *The cream of the crop*   115

7. *Bars and bonbons*   130

8. *Chocolate: friend or foe?*   157

9. *Becoming a connoisseur*   175

10. *The future of chocolate*   187

A last word…   205

Glossary   206

Bibliography   209

Resources   210

Index   212

Images and illustrations

Line drawings of chocolate bonbons, cocoa pods, chocolate bar, ballotin of chocolates and chocolatière scattered throughout © Amanda Loverseed.

Illustrations on pp: 23, 53, 55, 58, 85, 86, 87, 116, 192 by Rodney Paull.

Images on pp: 11, 57 © The Bridgeman Art Library.

Images on pp: 15, 59, 120, 140 © Mary Evans Picture Library.

Images on pp: 18, 114 © Corbis.

Acknowledgements

I WANT TO THANK MY dear friend chocolate, who has been my best friend (sometimes a she, sometimes a he), my companion for more than 25 years, and the source of much of my joy. As with people there are the good and the bad chocolates, the elegant and the vulgar, the honest and the cheats, and the jewels you keep as close to you as possible for the rest of your life. My best friend chocolate is always there for me, supporting me even when things go wrong.

Chocolate has shown me a path in life, a philosophy for living. Discovering the world of chocolate has given me the opportunity to learn about myself: what inspires me, what hurts and delights and surprises me. I am driven by an inner fire of curiosity and chocolate has helped me to know who I am and what I want my life to be.

Chocolate has enabled me to meet my best friends, the people who crossed my path thanks to chocolate. Even those who crossed my path and left remain with me, among my greatest treasures.

Chocolate is a magic wand for me, often a more powerful means of communication than words, because people drop their defences before chocolate and become like children again, vulnerable, open, and receptive.

In thanking chocolate I am also thanking all the people who helped me to discover this brown gold – my mother for putting melted chocolate on my lips when I was a few weeks old, my friends who accepted my obsession and didn't try to limit my passion (and refrained from stealing my chocolates!).

Thank you to all the professionals who, over the past ten years, looked beyond this obsessive girl and saw my passion, commitment and curiosity. Thanks to Karen Evennett for her help with writing the book and Anna Crago for her impressive work and perspicacity. Deepest thanks to Steve de Vries, the most humble, generous bright chocolate connoisseur I have ever met. And thank you to my choco dream team, Jack and Hilary, for their constant cocoa-obsessive enthusiasm and support.

Introduction:
A passion for chocolate

WHENEVER I ASK someone about their favourite chocolate, I see their face light up and their eyes start to sparkle. I know then that my simple question has transported them to happy times, and happy chocolate memories. I know, from the look on their face, that they love chocolate.

This is hardly surprising – most people love chocolate (certainly few people hate it!). But to my mind, chocolate lovers fall into two categories:

- Those who are so wedded to their current favourites that nothing anybody says to the contrary will change their mind. They know what they like!

- Those who want to learn more. They either thank me for introducing them to a new friend, or decide they hate what I have given them – but set themselves the challenge of discovering why it is deemed so 'special'.

This book is for all chocolate lovers, but perhaps particularly for those in the second category – innate connoisseurs who are always on the lookout for the best.

I believe chocolate has reached a turning point in its history. All over the world, we are seeing the rise of chocolatiers (chocolate makers, melters and sellers) who are truly passionate about chocolate, and perfectionist about their work. These people are quietly revolutionising methods of producing chocolate, seeking out the best-quality cocoa beans, and making chocolate that may well taste *entirely* different to the chocolate that you currently know and love.

What I want to do is guide you through this chocolate revolution. You'll learn how chocolate is becoming a gourmet foodstuff, ranking alongside the finest wines, coffees, teas, cheeses and olive oils. You'll see how chocolate tasting is becoming as advanced an art as wine tasting, with connoisseurs discerning flavours such as 'mushroom', 'berry' and 'floral' in chocolate, and using wine terminology like 'cru', 'vintage' and 'terroir'. And you'll discover that as fine chocolate is taken more and more seriously, the market for it grows exponentially.

In my former job – as chocolate buyer at Fortnum & Mason, London's famous department store – I increasingly saw people coming in and asking for chocolate from specific plantations or made with a unique and sought-after variety of cocoa bean. This would have been unheard of in the early 2000s (though the revolution was already well under way in France). But now, even supermarket brands of chocolate are changing the way they package their product, so word is spreading fast.

I love the fact that chocolate is such an important part of so many lives, because this is fuelling the chocolate revolution. When someone tells me they 'love all chocolate', my heart begins to dance because I know that, as a chocolate lover, this person will be willing to give all chocolate a chance – and discover what the very finest chocolate has to offer.

In this book, I will explain how chocolate is made, tell you about good chocolate and bad, and most importantly, teach you how to taste chocolate, so you can begin to decide for yourself what the best chocolates are and which ones suit you best. True connoisseurs prefer bars or blocks of plain chocolate to filled chocolates, and I'll tell you why. Along the way I hope not only to introduce you to a few new favourites, but to open your eyes to a whole new way of seeing chocolate.

In my case, I 'saw the light' at a very early age. I was a fussy eater, growing up in Mexico with nothing but Nutella and dark chocolate thins (Lindt) to tickle my taste buds. While you learned it at school, I learned it the hard way: the poor countries that grow many of our most basic crops – rice, tea, coffee, tobacco, and cocoa – do not process them. And although Mexico is a cocoa-producing country (not to mention the birthplace of cocoa cultivation!), the only chocolate we could find was the over-processed, sugary type produced by multinational companies.

Even our Nutella and chocolate thins were imported treats that we either squeezed into our suitcases on our return from our annual trip to France, ordered from a European mail order catalogue, or implored overseas visitors to bring us. Chocolate was literally the 'sweetener' that made up for the fact that we children had to surrender our bedrooms to our overseas guests. As the whole family welcomed arriving visitors at the airport, we children would wait anxiously, our hearts racing, eager to see how much precious chocolate they had brought with them.

On one occasion I remember waiting for my mother in the arrivals hall at Mexico's international airport as she returned from a trip to Europe, her suitcase laden with precious Nutella. We watched as a customs officer interrogated her – and became gradually more horrified as we saw my mother spread Nutella over her face. When she reached us, we greeted her with admonishments for wasting precious milligrams of our favourite food. 'But it was the only way I could get it through customs,' she explained. 'The officer said I couldn't bring a food product into the country. I had to pretend it was a beauty mask for my face!'

At the age of 14, I moved to Paris and was suddenly exposed to a much wider range of chocolate. As far as my pocket money would allow me, I bought every new bar I came across, saving the wrappings, and comparing each new taste with those I already knew. From this early age I began writing my comments and primitive tasting notes about each different bar. At the start these were very simple. For instance, I might describe a bar as 'too sweet, light brown, strong artificial vanilla flavour, grainy'. But my notebook gradually filled up, and eventually I had the beginnings of a database that I added to daily, tasting and comparing chocolate each day before breakfast when, in my opinion, the palate is at its most fresh – a ritual I still practise today.

I bought up to 20 bars a week, and gained notoriety among my friends for my obsession. For my 20th birthday, my friends arranged a surprise party. At one point they blindfolded me and formed a circle around me. A voice instructed me to open my mouth, but before I did so my nose had already sensed the beloved smell of chocolate. So I opened wide and, one by one, 25 tiny pieces of chocolate were popped into my mouth with a request for me to identify the percentage of cocoa (the total percentage of cocoa butter *and* beans in a bar). I not only gave the percentage but also the name of the chocolate, its brand, and my opinion of it!

You may never have thought of chocolate in this way before. I hope that in this book I'll be able to share my passion for chocolate with you – and expand your chocolate horizons in the process.

THE PRICE OF PASSION

When I landed the job of chocolate buyer for Fortnum & Mason in 2003 I found myself catapulted into the media limelight as 'the girl with the best job in the world'. Every reporter who met me started their interview with the same words: 'You're so lucky!'

I can see why people think that... After all, I ate all the chocolate I liked, and I was paid to travel around the world looking for the very best chocolate available. To anyone who loves chocolate, it must look as if I was permanently lodged on a chocolate-mousse cloud nine!

However, I firmly believe that luck has nothing to do with it. It wasn't pure chance that put me in this position. I have had a true passion (or some might say obsession) for chocolate from childhood, and over time this kind of passion becomes the air you breathe, the energy that motivates you, an everyday quest.

It's comparable to a passion for music or literature. Just like connoisseurs of either art, I cannot stop fighting to learn even more. I want to know about every new development about chocolate as it happens. I do not wait for the press to publish the conclusions of a symposium. I try to attend the symposium myself, or find a close friend who shares my chocolate passion to do so. I do not wait for a company to ask me to visit a plantation, all expenses paid. I use my holiday quota, pay for my own ticket, and find my way to the cocoa plantations to see, ask and learn.

It's a lot of work, but it is endlessly fascinating. To me, this is what passion is all about.

In this book I'll take you through a brief potted history of chocolate, from its beginnings as currency to present-day trends. I'll dispel a few popular myths and give you my vision of the future of chocolate. In between, there are lots of exercises, games and questions aimed at helping you to build up your own chocolate likes and dislikes. Ultimately, you'll be able to pick the chocolate you feel like according to your mood, or the time of day, or whether you feel like milk or dark, a bar or a filled chocolate, something flavoured or plain, sweet or savoury.

So tuck in, and enjoy!

A BRIEF HISTORY OF CHOCOLATE

1000 BC Cocoa trees are growing wild in the Amazon and appear in etchings on Classic Mayan pottery.

600–1500 AD: The Mayas and Aztecs use cocoa beans as currency, and the elite make a spicy drink from them.

1517: The Aztec Emperor Moctezuma introduces Spanish explorer Hernán Cortés to his favourite drink, *chocolatl*.

1528: Cortés returns to Spain with cocoa beans and the equipment needed to make the chocolate drink.

1620–1650: The Spanish slowly introduce their secret ingredient to the rest of Europe – where it continues to be consumed as an expensive and mostly 'medicinal' drink, and a treat for the elite.

1650: The chocolate drink reaches England.

1652: London's first coffee house opens. Here, people could drink coffee, tea... and chocolate. Coffee was by far the cheapest of the three, so chocolate remained a luxury for the rich.

1693: A form of solid chocolate is developed for making the drink at home – but it's nothing like the smooth chocolate we eat today.

1765: Chocolate arrives in the American colonies and the first chocolate factory opens in Dorchester, Massachusetts.

1815: It becomes possible to separate cocoa butter during the production process (and the by-product of this is cocoa powder!).

1831: John Cadbury begins manufacturing drinking chocolate and cocoa in the UK.

chart continues

1847: A new process makes it possible to manufacture an edible, solid form of chocolate – and the first chocolate bar is created.

1866: Chocolate is used in France for medicinal purposes.

1875: The world's first milk chocolate is created in Switzerland.

1879: Conching (see page 16) is invented – leading to much smoother, more aromatic chocolate.

1894: The American company Hershey makes the first mass-produced, affordable chocolate bar.

1913: The first filled chocolates are created, in Belgium.

1925: Cocoa beans are traded for the first time as a commodity at the World Trade Center.

1930s: Famous candy bars such as the Mars Bar and Kit Kat are invented.

1920s–1980s: Chocolate remains largely static and although the products do not change, marketing becomes increasingly important.

1985: Brands like Valrhona start to create chocolate made from selected high-quality beans and regions – the revolution is beginning.

1989: Lindt launches a 70% bar – the first supermarket brand to promote cocoa percentage.

2004: Chuao in Venezuela becomes the first cocoa-growing region to be legally protected as a producer of named-origin beans.

2004: About 600,000 cocoa beans are eaten in a year. Only *five per cent* are used in quality bars.

The shaded areas are periods of major change in the world of chocolate.

CHAPTER 1

·

Chocolate past and present

*O*NCE UPON A TIME in a faraway land, there was a magic bean that could transform the life of anyone who came into possession of it…

The poor used it as money to pay for food and cloth, while the rich made it into an exotic drink that boosted their energy and put a spring in their step. Then, the precious bean was carried thousands of miles across the sea to Europe, where it remained an aristocratic drink for centuries before finally being turned into a chocolate bar in the 1850s.

Today's chocolate retains its fairytale aura. Yet it's also abundant – accessible magic, if you like.

It is also coming into its own as a gourmet food – and when future chocolate historians look back, the start of the twenty-first century will be known as the chocolate revolution, when the quality of chocolate started to matter more than the quantity.

Becoming part of this revolution – developing the connoisseur's nose that will help you sniff out quality chocolate – does demand a bit of work. But don't let that put you off.

A huge part of it is chocolate tasting, so it's hardly a tortuous business. Moreover, the knowledge and pleasure you'll gain really will make it all worthwhile!

Let's start by going back to basics, and looking at some ways in which the humble cocoa bean gained its rightful place in history.

Chocolate as a drink

For nearly all of its 3,000-year history, chocolate has been consumed as a costly drink or as a health food – a far cry from the bars and filled chocolates we associate the word 'chocolate' with today.

The Mayas and Aztecs both traded with cocoa beans – such was their value – and the rich, who could afford to literally drink their money, used the beans to make a form of hot or warm chocolate flavoured with spices (vanilla and chili peppers were popular, but other spices were also used) and enjoyed for the sense of well-being and energy it gave. Hot chocolate was the champagne of society weddings, and the drink was prohibited to commoners.

As today, the drink was best served frothy and, to achieve this (for the froth was considered a sign of quality), it was poured back and forth between two jars.

A sixteenth-century Mayan image of hot chocolate being poured between jars

To both the Mayas and the Aztecs, drinking chocolate was thought to work some kind of magic – and it was treated with the utmost respect.

The Mayas had a cocoa god, and the drink was used in many of their rituals. A bride and groom would exchange it in their marriage ceremony, and children were often 'baptised' with cacao water.

The Aztecs, who used to make an annual sacrifice of their most beautiful slave, would serve chocolate to the elected victim to temper his melancholy in the final week before his execution.

When the Spanish invaded the New World in the sixteenth century, they too got to sample the drink – but its bitterness was a shock to the Western palate (in his *History of the New World*, published in 1575, Giralomo Benzoni described it as 'a bitter drink for pigs'), and it became the fashion to sweeten it with honey. It was this version of the drink that became a particular hit with the upper classes.

The Dominican friar Thomas Gage (1600–1655) tells a story of ladies living in San Cristobal de las Casas, Mexico, who claimed they couldn't get through a high mass at the cathedral without a fortifying cup of hot chocolate (brought to them by their maids). The bishop, outraged by the tea party going on in the congregation, banned the drink from the house of God. The ladies left his church – and the bishop was later killed … by drinking chocolate laced with poison.

When chocolate reached Europe, it remained a drink for the elite as it had been in South America. In these upper echelons of society, however, it began to take on the kind of simple social associations we recognise today – friends chatting over a cup of chocolate. In France during the time of Louis XIV, for example, it was a great honour if you were invited to drink hot chocolate in the bedroom at around 10 am, while your host remained in bed!

In Spain today you can still buy grainy, sugary drinking chocolate in blocks, probably relatively unchanged since 1600. The country has retained its chocolate-drinking tradition and it's common to find it served midmorning with churros, straight-shaped doughnuts coated with sugar.

MEXICAN STREET CHOCOLATE –
A TASTE OF HISTORY

If you have the opportunity of travelling to Mexico, go to the colourful street markets. You will find Indian women selling fist-sized tablets made from cocoa beans which have been pan-roasted at home, peeled by hand, roughly ground on a *metate* (a slab of volcanic stone used for grinding foods) and flavoured with cinnamon and a lot of sugar.

It is a far cry from what developed countries call chocolate. It doesn't melt, it is grainy, and it crunches with sugar crystals. It is, not surprisingly, very sweet. But these tablets are intended to be grated and then dissolved in hot water or milk to make a drink that hasn't changed much from the old recipe used by the Spanish in the sixteenth and seventeenth centuries. I grew up in Mexico, and when I return to visit my family, I still seek out the women selling their chocolate tablets in the market. I buy them for the simple pleasure of steeping myself in another culture, even though the flavour, to me, in no way replicates chocolate.

Although I really concentrate on pure chocolate bars and suggest that, as a budding connoisseur, you do the same, hot chocolate is a wonderfully soothing, pleasurable drink, and I have often served it at themed chocolate evenings for my friends. For my favourite recipes, see page 105.

Chocolate as medicine

The Aztecs had taught the Spanish colonials that chocolate was healthy, and the drink was esteemed as a medicinal remedy when it reached Europe. Philip II of Spain's personal physician, Francisco Hernandez, recommended chocolate to cure fevers, cool the body in hot weather, and relieve stomach pains. People started to use it to aid digestion and, in 1650, when the drink reached England, it was advertised as 'curing and preserving the body of many diseases'.

In 1866 chocolate entered the French pharmocopia and apothecaries developed chocolate lozenges which they sold for their mood-enhancing or digestive properties. These were available in two flavours: plain, or with ingredients such as vanilla, pepper and cloves (which had their own medicinal qualities).

Today, chocolate is being heavily promoted as a health food – for its antioxidants and brain stimulants. (More about that in Chapter 8.) In the future, I'd like to see chocolate – that is, *real*, good-quality, high cocoa-content chocolate – being recommended by doctors for its pleasurable, anti-depressant qualities, just as they might recommend a glass of red wine to fight heart disease. Why? Because when you're happy, you're stronger in the face of illness. And I really believe happiness and chocolate go hand in hand!

Chocolate as a food

Today we associate chocolate with bars and filled chocolates, but as you have seen, these products only emerged relatively recently. Chocolate was a drink for most of its history, and the first (gritty) bar wasn't made until 1847.

During the time of the Industrial Revolution, chocolate bars became the product we know and love today – cheap and accessible to the vast majority. The key events were these:

- In 1815 a Dutch chemist called Van Houten started looking for a way to remove much of the fatty cocoa butter from chocolate, and eventually reduced it to a 20 per cent fat 'cake' that could be pulverised into a fine powder – what we call 'cocoa powder'.

- With this breakthrough, in 1847, Fry's in the UK found a way to mix a blend of cocoa beans and sugar with melted cocoa butter (the by-product of the defatting process) to make a viscous paste that could be cast into a mould. Voilà – the world's first chocolate bars!

DID YOU KNOW?

The Fry, Cadbury and Rowntree families of British chocolate fame were all Quakers. Many Quakers set themselves up in business and manufacturing, and chocolate seemed a good option. At the time it was viewed as a healthy and revitalising drink, and the Quakers wanted to make it available to people as an alternative to the more morally dubious alcohol.

- In 1867 Henri Nestlé, a Swiss chemist, discovered a way of evaporating milk to make a powder. In 1875 Nestlé and chocolate-maker Daniel Peter added this milk powder to chocolate to make the world's first milk chocolate bar.

- In 1879 Rodolphe Lindt invented a machine for 'conching' (a process by which chocolate is mixed for up to three days at a minimum of 10°F and a maximum of 167°F), which vastly improved the quality of chocolate confectionery: it helps aromas develop, acids to evaporate and the texture to become finer and smoother.

- By the 1920s, much of the world's chocolate was being made from cheap, reliable, but not very tasty beans called Forastero – a fact noteworthy mainly because it con-tributed to lower production costs. To improve the flavour of the Forastero bean, ever-increasing amounts of sugar and vanilla flavouring were added to the mix. Most of the chocolate we know today is made from this combination of workhorse beans and overpowering flavourings.

All these technological advances and other changes meant chocolate could be cheaply mass produced. From being a drink for the elite, it was now a readily available and affordable sweet. In 1893, a Belgian labourer would have had to work for 24 hours straight to afford a 7 oz block of chocolate – but by 1913 the price had come down so much that he'd only have had to put in 24 *minutes*. And today's mass-produced chocolate is even cheaper.

STILL GOING STRONG...

Van Houten is still a famous name for hot chocolate powder.

- Fry's Chocolates – perhaps now most famous for Fry's Turkish Delight, invented in 1914 – still steams ahead today, albeit as a subsidiary of Cadbury.
- Nestlé is now to Switzerland what Coca-Cola is to the US: a symbol of the Swiss way of doing things.
- Lindt still exhibits an early conching machine in its Zurich headquarters, and now manufactures and sells chocolate in 39 countries. What a success story!

So, amazingly, many of the key players in the nineteenth-century revolution of chocolate are still around today – and are still some of the best-known supermarket brands.

All these companies have done a huge amount to promote chocolate – but their products, while enjoyed by billions, will never be in the top league that is of interest to the connoisseur. They tend to be what I call 'candy' (a term used by

A 1893 poster for Van Houten by Adolphe Leon Willette

prenez du Cacao
Van Houten

Americans for their 'chocolate', which contains very little cocoa), heavily flavoured with sugar and artificial vanilla ('vanillin'). Unfortunately, this is a taste the world has come to associate with chocolate, but you may start to reject it once you have discovered what I call *true chocolate*.

Chocolate as a commodity

When Christopher Columbus encountered the cocoa bean six centuries ago, it was being used as currency to pay for everything from household groceries to domestic slaves.

A BEAN'S WORTH

Chocolate historians are fond of regaling their readers with stories about what one could buy with cocoa beans. According to Hernando de Oviedo y Valdez, who went to America in 1513 as a member of Pedrarias Avila's expedition, ten cocoa beans could buy the services of a prostitute – or your own slave. Four beans would get you a rabbit for dinner.

Reports about exactly how much things cost differ, but Michael and Sophie Coe, whose book *The True History Of Chocolate* I recommend to anyone interested in the intricacies of cocoa's past, found the following in a list of commodity prices in Tlaxcala, Mexico, in a document dated to 1545:

A small rabbit = 30 beans
An avocado, newly picked = 3 beans; a fully ripe
   avocado = 1 bean
One large tomato = 1 bean
A fish wrapped in maize husks = 3 beans.

It wasn't only as ancient currency that cocoa had any worth. Once chocolate gained mass popularity during the Industrial Revolution, cocoa beans were again worth their weight in gold, metaphorically speaking, as manufacturers couldn't get enough of them. At this time, as we've seen, many of the big names we know today began to emerge, and chocolate began to become a highly marketable commodity.

Today we hold continental chocolate-makers in high esteem – but we've forgotten why. Several Swiss companies made important technological advances and were once at the forefront of the industry, but have made no great strides since their heyday in the nineteenth century. In fact, their efforts have mainly concentrated on streamlining processes, creating cheaper, poorer-quality chocolate. Furthermore, how often have you heard people say that Belgium has the best chocolates? In my opinion, the country has earned its reputation mainly through marketing breakthroughs.

A brief history of Belgian chocolate

- Neuhaus developed the first chocolates with soft centers (the famous Belgian moulded chocolates) and his wife invented the gift box, or 'ballotin', to sell them in.

- Leonidas leapt in with a much cheaper version of boxed chocolates, causing the quality and price of all chocolates to drop as everyone tried to keep up with them.

- Godiva (which despite its swanky image has been owned by the American food giant, Campbell's Soup, since 1974), simply marketed itself as selling 'The best chocolates in the world!' – and the slogan was enough to convince the public, who flocked to buy their chocolates.

When I took up my job as chocolate buyer for Fortnum & Mason, I introduced myself to my new staff by holding a chocolate workshop. I always start these sessions by asking the people gathered to reveal their favourite chocolate. More than one person volunteered that they loved Godiva, 'because it's the best chocolate in the world!' Some even added, 'I've never tried it, but I know.' That's what I call effective marketing!

Godiva is now perceived as one of the leading luxury brands. But Godiva isn't the only company with an effective marketing plan. My favourite example of the power of marketing is the Cadbury Creme Egg, probably as close to chocolate as a chicken's egg as far as I'm concerned!

Cadbury's marketing genius goes back a long way. In 1868 they produced the first decorated chocolate box. The attractive branded boxes could be kept long after the chocolates, and became one of the first chocolate marketing campaigns. Cadbury is still one of the world's biggest producers of chocolate, and remains the most popular bar in most of the English-speaking world.

The message I'd like you to take away from this is: the bigger the company, the bigger the marketing budget. Think of the best, tastiest and priciest olive oils or cheeses and they tend to come from 'boutique' companies – small groves or dairies that concentrate on quality ingredients and production values. I believe the same goes for chocolate.

Chocolate today

The world now consumes 42.2 billion dollars' worth of chocolate products – but most of this is milk chocolate or candy, satisfying a sweet tooth rather than a gourmet one. And most is now from the less flavoursome, but more robust, Forastero trees.

Because they are such big business, cocoa beans are exchanged as a commodity on the stock market. They're bought many years in advance to safeguard against fluctuations in the market price, and to maintain the ability to meet demand whatever unpredictable event occurs – be it a war, an economic crash, a cyclone or a disease.

The figures opposite show how much chocolate we eat, per head, per year in different countries. These figures take into account all chocolate, good and bad (including candy bars and other chocolate confectionery) – but lower-quality beans account for the lion's share. Think about how much chocolate you've eaten…did you know it's possible you have never tasted the best varieties of beans?

When you consider that 85 per cent of all harvested cocoa beans are Forastero, and look at the world's top ten selling brands, it is no surprise that most people have not yet encountered fine chocolate. In fact, the top sellers don't include anything that's 'real' chocolate – the list below is mainly candy with a thin milk-chocolate coating, except for Cadbury Dairy Milk. In fact, even that only contains 20 per cent cocoa – which, according to the EU, is not enough to make it officially chocolate!

The world's top ten chocolates

1. Mars Bar
2. Twix Twin
3. Snickers
4. Maltesers
5. Kit Kat (four-finger)
6. Cadbury Dairy Milk
7. Kit Kat Crunchy
8. Crunchie
9. Bounty Milk
10. Twirl

Once you've checked out the list above, it's hardly surprising that when chocolate lovers come to my workshops and

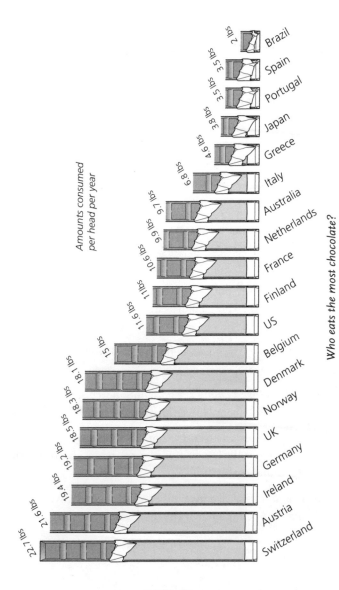

Amounts consumed per head per year

Who eats the most chocolate?

Brazil — 2 sq lbs
Spain — 3.3 sq lbs
Portugal — 3.5 sq lbs
Japan — 3.8 sq lbs
Greece — 4.6 lbs
Italy — 6.8 lbs
Australia — 9.7 lbs
Netherlands — 9.9 lbs
France — 10.6 lbs
Finland — 11 lbs
US — 11.6 lbs
Belgium — 15 lbs
Denmark — 18.1 lbs
Norway — 18.3 lbs
UK — 18.5 lbs
Germany — 19.2 lbs
Ireland — 19.4 lbs
Austria — 21.6 lbs
Switzerland — 22.7 lbs

explain what they like to eat and why they like to eat it, most are still into candy, rather than 'real' chocolate. They eat it because the sugar makes them feel good, it cheers up a bad day, and it's a form of indulgence.

What we choose to eat is also often dictated by where we come from, as countries seem to have their own chocolate identities.

- *Belgium* is the country of big moulded chocolates, with creamy, soft fillings, and milk chocolate bars.

- *Austria and Germany* both favour chocolates filled with marzipan or hazelnut paste, and milk chocolate bars.

- *Scandinavians* are entrenched in their milk chocolate culture and also eat a lot of white chocolate.

- *France* is a mainly dark chocolate nation (in fact, dark chocolate is so popular in France that it's the only country in the world where Lindt's entire range of dark chocolate is sold!).

- *Spaniards*, true to their history, still prefer their chocolate in a cup.

- *Italians* love *gianduja*, a hazelnut and chocolate paste – Ferrero Rocher or Nutella are its most successful versions.

- *English-speaking countries* prefer above all milk chocolate (such is the legacy of Cadbury), white chocolate and big, round truffles.

- *The Japanese* also love milk and white exclusive chocolate, importing French chocolates in large quantities.

These tastes are dictated by tradition, and the taste of each culture runs the gamut of 'good' to 'bad'. What one generation enjoys is passed on to the next. It is a difficult cycle for those making 'real' chocolate to break. But it can be done. Anyone with a palate and the will to learn will find their way to appreciate fine chocolate.

Good chocolate in a nutshell

I've been talking rather a lot about 'real chocolate' – but what do I mean when I say this? You'll learn more in the next few chapters, but put very simply, there are a few basic criteria:

- High-quality beans and other ingredients, treated with care.

- Production methods aimed at extracting the most flavour from the bean.

- A reasonable level of cocoa content, so the cocoa is not drowned out by sugar or other flavourings.

'Real chocolate' is sold in two types of shops:

- In delicatessens, department stores, and some high-end supermarkets – bars and filled chocolates are mainly sold here.

- Own-name shops. Some of these have chains of shops (and their own factories). Others are less well known, have only one or a few shops, and have a lab out the back to create new products.

The difference is in their regard for quality. If you want to be ahead of the game, look out for small companies putting quality first and profits second. Their chocolates may be new to you now, but I promise that they will feel like old friends by the time you finish this book.

These companies care about the cocoa beans they use and where they are sourced and are prepared to pay more for good quality. Often, they use less high-volume machinery than the larger companies and spend longer extracting the aromas from the beans. And they are always on the look out for better raw ingredients and improved production methods.

All the fine brands mentioned below are distributed in specialist shops and department stores, and on the websites listed on pages 210–11. All produce their chocolate from the bean. I recommend you try each brand at least once.

- *Amedei* – an Italian chocolatier based in Pisa, Italy. In 1997, after visiting cocoa plantations in Venezuela, Amedei decided to produce chocolate only from beans personally selected at the plantations (rather than via bean-brokers). Their chocolate range has a wide choice of dark chocolate bars, and a few filled chocolates. They are the direct competitors of Valrhona (*see below*), but are a much smaller company. Amedei's Chuao and Porcelana bars are their jewels.

- *Bonnat* – a French company founded in 1884. Their first dark chocolate bars, made from beans from specific countries (Venezuela and Ivory Coast), were produced in 1911. They were the first to propose a range of bars at 75% cocoa, each one made with beans from a different country. Their initiative has now been widely copied by other brands. In 1994, they were also the first to launch the concept of vintage in chocolate, with their Hacienda el Rosario bar, made from beans from a specific plantation. Their distribution is very limited thus the brand not very well known.

- *Chocovic* – an old company from Barcelona, which has been revived to follow the model of Valrhona, focusing on the world of professionals working with chocolate. Chocovic's cookery school has an international reputation. Their dark chocolate range Origen Unico is available in department stores and supermarkets.

- *Michel Cluizel* – a French brand from Normandy, which offers several different chocolate bars from specific cocoa plantations and a variety of boxes containing assortments of milk and plain chocolate, enabling you to discover the influence of bean origin or cocoa content on the taste of a chocolate. Their range competes directly with much older fine chocolate brands such as Valrhona. Try their Mangaro and Los Ancones bars.

- *Domori* – a young Italian company from Genoa. They collaborate with a big plantation in Venezuela. The founder is a passionate young agronomist who decided to revive the high-quality Criollo cocoa bean and since 1995 he has grafted various pure Criollo trees into different root stocks. Every year, they increase their range of top-quality bars. Their gems are mini chocolates made with beans selected from specific areas of Venezuela, such as Esmeraldas, Porcelana and Carenero Superior.

- *El Rey* – Venezuelan; they were established in 1929 and in 1995 became the first modern chocolate plant in Latin America. Until 2004, El Rey chocolates were the only example of a relatively fine chocolate produced in the country of origin of its cocoa beans by a national company and distributed around the world. Colombia, with Chocolates Santander, has recently successfully reproduced the concept. The El Rey range is small, and their chocolates are made with beans from the reputed regions of Venezuela. The chocolate could be described as a cross between fine and mass-market chocolate.

- *Felchlin* – Swiss company founded in 1908. They produce an extensive array of 'semi-finished products' for professionals. Try their Gran Cru range (Maracaibo dark 65% and Criolait 38%).

- *Guittard* – a family-owned San Francisco chocolate manufacturer established in 1886. They mainly produce chocolate for professionals. In 2000 they launched a fine chocolate selection from small plantations around the world, which is distributed in specialty stores.

- *Pralus* – a French company from Roanne, founded in 1948, which makes finest-quality chocolate using small batches of carefully selected cocoa beans. Pralus chocolates are the best way to discover that chocolate aromas can be as intense and complex as those in wine. With the Java bar you will be surprised to encounter notes of wet wood, moss and wild mushrooms.

- *Scharffen Berger* – an American company that produces excellent cocoa powder and a wide range of chocolate bars; among the finest made in the USA. Try their limited edition Jamaica and Porcelana bars. Now owned by Hershey's.

- *Valrhona* – a French company founded in 1924. They introduced the Gran Cru chocolate range, first in 1985 to the world of professional chocolatiers, then, in 1990, to all of us. This range of chocolate is made from the finest beans selected from geographic regions (for example, Caraïbe is made from beans from the Caribbean region; Manjari from Madagascar). Reliable, good-quality chocolate from a successful French company. Try their Gran Couva and Palmira bars.

Remember: small is beautiful! Don't be afraid to try an expensive new chocolate simply because you don't recognise the name on the bar – it may be made by a small manufacturer who cares deeply about his product, and has done his best to perfect it.

These quality brands are not easy to find – you may have to hunt hard or order from the internet (see Resources, pages 210–11). But I do urge you to seek them out. Only by tasting them can you recognise and rule out any smartly labelled impostors – for the chocolate revolution will lead big manufacturers to try to cash in on chocolate's new gourmet status, with their own cheap versions. Novice connoisseur beware!

CHAPTER 2

Building your own chocolate profile

*Y*OU MAY LOVE chocolate…but how much do you *know* chocolate? To my mind, there is chocolate, and then there is *chocolate*. What you buy in the supermarket is a different proposition from the finest-quality bars you have to hunt for in department stores or delicatessens. Have you taken the time to sample good-quality chocolate yet?

To my mind, there are a few necessary ingredients that the budding connoisseur must possess. You need to be curious. And it's good to know what you like. This doesn't mean being closed off from trying new things – or stopping when you have found something you like. For me, being truly passionate about chocolate has been a lifelong quest. I like to explore new chocolate, give another chance to chocolate I have previously rejected as no good, compare different varieties, and question my own assumptions. I have a good idea of what I like, but I ensure that this doesn't close me off from trying anything new – although I do draw the line at boozy white chocolate truffles. Let's just politely say that these cause mutiny in my taste buds!

But what about you? If I were to offer you a new chocolate with the promise that it will taste unlike anything you have ever tasted before, would you be curious enough to try it?

If I were to tell you that there are chocolate bars that are as different from a standard bar as lemons are to mustard, or that some dark 75% chocolate bars are as smooth and mellow as milk chocolate, what would you think? Would you want to know more?

You may be about to encounter something wonderful that knocks spots off the chocolate you have loved for life. That can be daunting. This new chocolate may be more expensive or harder to find than you're used to. It may also cause you to reject a chocolate you've grown up with – a chocolate that holds all sorts of happy memories, and is your favourite comfort food... Nobody likes to say goodbye to an old friend, to explore alone an unknown path in life.

On the other hand, you may be about to discover that I am extolling the virtues of a chocolate you loathe. Will you wonder about the quality of your palate, or feel affronted that a so-called chocolate connoisseur chooses something you would not? Will you feel concerned at the new direction chocolate is taking?

I'd like to reassure you. Whatever kind of chocolate you're currently eating, and however you eat it – whether you snack on family-sized bars of milk chocolate, fantasise about Fererro Rochers, or selectively eat only 70% organic bars with your coffee – this book will help you to broaden your interest and expand your knowledge, and give you some tips on where to meet fellow choco-soulmates.

Knowledge, passion, curiosity, dedication – these are the steps along the way to becoming a chocolate connoisseur, even if you end up going back to your old favourite. You will at least know then why you stick to it and, having learnt to look at it in a new way, your pleasure in it will be much stronger. Your relationship with chocolate will have changed for the better!

Your next step is to start building your own chocolate profile. How far will you need to go in order to become a connoisseur? Are you halfway there already ... or do you still have a lot to explore?

Your chocolate profile: step 1

The table opposite will help you to see at a glance what kind of chocolate you love most. What it also does, though, is to provide you with some ideas for what *else* you might like.

Look at the names of the bars, and circle those that you like or usually buy. Do they fall into any one category?

So what does it all mean? The distinction I've drawn here is a very simple one. Column 1 chocolates come from large companies and are available almost anywhere that chocolate is sold. The chocolates in column 2 are (yes, the bad news) more expensive, and are from my list of companies to watch out for – that is, typically, small ones who are doing amazing things with superb raw materials.

My ultimate aim is to show you that in time you can learn to love the very best milk or dark chocolate. You may have always eaten a bar available in any newsagents' shop – but now find yourself going for an artisanal variety in a big way. Or you may never have imagined yourself eating dark chocolate, until you encountered a truly ambrosial bar of it

	1	2
Milk		
	Cadbury Dairy Milk	Jivara (Valrhona)
	Galaxy (Mars)	Milk (Amedei)
	Milka (Kraft)	Lait Entier (Weiss)
	Milk (Lindt)	Latte Sal (Domori)
	Milk Organic	Milk 41% (Scharffen Berger)
	Hershey's Milk	Melissa (Pralus)
Dark		
	Lindt Excellence 70%	Palmira (Valrhona)
	Dark organic brands (70% or more)	Chuao, Porcelana (Amedei)
		Java, Indonésie (Pralus)
	Any dark bar from the supermarket	Porcelana (Domori)
		Los Ancones,
	Bournville (Cadbury)	Mangaro (Michel Cluizel)
	Côte d'Or Noir	Any 70% (DeVries)
	Duchy Originals	
	Hershey's	

from column 2. See Chapter 4 for more recommendations for each type of chocolate lover.

You might notice that a few of your favourite things do not appear in the table above. Where are Mars Bars and white chocolate? Where are filled chocolates? Well, they're not there for a simple reason. When chocolate connoisseurs meet to taste and discuss *real* chocolate, they usually choose bars. It's the pure, unadulterated form of chocolate. White chocolate (which only uses the cocoa butter from the cocoa bean) doesn't count – and neither does the milk chocolate wrapped around candy bars. These products are more about the sugar and vanilla than the chocolate. A filled chocolate, packed with cream or alcohol, is nice – but put it in your mouth, and is it really the *chocolate* you're tasting, or the sugar and the flavourings? For a connoisseur, the bar's the thing … just as a wine buff wouldn't spend too much time on a spritzer.

If your curiosity is piqued by all this, you'll find it leading you to seek out the best, and I suggest that you follow the recommendations given throughout this book at your own pace.

A CONSUMING PASSION

Compared with other gourmet pursuits – especially wine – chocolate is very affordable. This is a wonderful bonus, as I can think of nothing more frustrating than having a passion for something whose cost prohibits you from enjoying it to the full.

But this doesn't mean becoming a chocolate connoisseur is entirely without effort. You don't just waft into it: time, energy, imagination and a sense of adventure are all needed for this consuming passion.

Having a passion for *anything*, not just chocolate, is special. Many people feel that it has chosen them, rather than the other way round. It makes them feel alive: their passion is their oxygen.

Think of Ellen MacArthur, who at 28 broke the world record for sailing solo around the world. She began saving her lunch money to buy a boat when she was just eight years old. She was focused and dedicated, channelling all her spare time, energy and money into her passion. And it paid off.

My own passion led me to give up my well paid job as an agronomist and work unpaid for a chocolatier – but this was Paris's famous Pierre Hermé, the so-called 'Picasso of Pastry' (I didn't know this before I wrote to him, along with dozens of other chocolatiers). Working for Hermé at the renowned Parisian patisserie Ladurée, where he incorporated his wonderful chocolate into amazing cakes and pastries, was an honour, and the discoveries I made about chocolate were life-changing.

Through this job, I met people who shared my passion for the first time, much to my delight. M. Hermé introduced me to the finest chocolates, the raw materials used to make them, and the alchemy behind their combination. Not only did I learn a huge amount about what differentiates good chocolate from bad, I also found that the more I discovered, the more like minds I met, and the more my passion grew. There was, in short, no going back.

At this point in working out your chocolate profile, you might want to think about how big a part chocolate plays in your life.

Is it important, but a bit peripheral? No problem: even if you start by trying a new bar of chocolate once a week, or holding chocolate evenings with your friends every two months, your love for good chocolate will bring something special into your life.

If, on the other hand, you are like me, and chocolate is the main focus of your life, you may find you need to reassess your priorities to give it the space it needs.

But what if chocolate is definitely a passion – except it's got to be Galaxy, Mars Bars or Milk Tray? Don't worry. If you are keen to learn, you will. Remember, my own passion began with Nutella and Lindt chocolate thins all those years ago in Mexico. I loved them, and they became the springboard for my desire to explore every chocolate I could find.

Your chocolate profile: step 2

For fun, you could think back to your own chocolate history and palate development – and work out where you would like this book to take you. In my chocolate tasting courses, I always start with a round table, asking each person several questions to try and define their chocolate profile. How would you answer the following?

- What are your chocolate eating habits today? Do you eat filled bars, plain bars or filled chocolates?

- How do you eat chocolate – on its own, with coffee, after a meal?

- What brands of chocolate do you buy regularly?

- When do you eat chocolate? How often? Is chocolate a reward for you, a way to relax from stress, a way to fill boredom, or something else?

- Do you feel any guilt after you've eaten it, and if so, why?

- What kinds of chocolate do you like to get as a present (bars, or filled chocolates)?

- What chocolates did you have at home during your childhood? How have your chocolate choices changed since then?

- Can you eat a piece of chocolate without finishing the bar?

- What influences you when choosing chocolate?

- Do you make an effort to try new foods, or do you stick with what you know?

- Have you ever tried any of the brands on page 33? If so, what did you think?

I meet plenty of people through my workshops who have only ever eaten the 'column 1' chocolate from the chart on page 33. Usually, they'll stick to just a few brands. Yet these very people are often the ones who are most thankful for their discovery of real chocolate. They have discovered a new passion that changes their lives for the better.

I am always delighted to meet them later – for I feel quite evangelical about spreading the word about chocolate. I love to discover that I have given someone else the chance to experience the enormous pleasure I derive from chocolate.

Desert island chocolates

When I ask people *why* they like certain kinds of chocolate, their answers can be very revealing. Often a particular chocolate evokes special memories. It may be the first bar you ever tasted, or one you regularly shared with a brother or sister, bringing back warm feelings of love and connectedness. Taste (and, more importantly, smell, which makes up ninety per cent of what we taste) is powerfully linked with our unconscious mind, and the memories it revives can be quite amazing. To get to know chocolate, you need to understand your relationship with chocolate: what you like to eat, and why.

With this in mind, I love to get people to think about the different types of chocolate they would take with them if they were abandoned, Crusoe-style, on a desert island. What goes into *your* desert island suitcase?

Your list might contain anything from Cadbury Buttons (first encountered in a birthday party bag) to Galaxy – which you still indulge in when you need sustenance to get through a difficult project at work. Perhaps you've already discovered the intense pleasure of good-quality 70% dark chocolate, or the rich savour of nutty filled chocolates.

You may already have noticed that, when you take the time to taste chocolate, almost 'listening' to what each bar has to tell you, you learn that there is a lot more to it than 'milk' or 'plain'. Even 70% chocolate varies enormously. Once you start to notice these often very subtle differences, you are on your way to developing your own list of favourites or your 'survival kit' chocolates, and developing your palate as a connoisseur.

As an exercise, why not record your desert island list now? Can you think of ten different bars you'd take with you? When you've finished reading this book, go back to this list, and see whether it's changed.

In my survival kit…

People are forever asking me about my own favourite chocolate, as if I think that one bar alone is superior to all others. In fact, I always tell people that no individual's taste in chocolate is better or worse than anyone else's. My 'survival kit', or the list of chocolates that I love and can't do without, won't necessarily suit your tastes – and may not even fit mine in a few months' time.

As I have been a dedicated choco-explorer for many years, my kit is big and filled with bars you may not have come across, some of them not even sold over the counter yet. Column 2 of the chart on page 33 will give you an indication of some of the chocolates I return to again and again.

I keep a wide range of chocolates to match my different moods – and I actually couldn't choose one above all others! At any given time I'll have at least 25 different bars at home, all permanently opened and properly sealed to keep each future bite at its best. Although I would not have a bite from each one of the bars every day, there is not a week that passes without a reunion with each one.

But what matters is *your* taste – what special significance a certain chocolate holds for *you*. As you gradually try more and more of the bars mentioned in this book, some will resonate more than others. You'll find that a bar you try once and don't like suddenly hits you with a zing when you taste it again – perhaps you were just in the wrong mood for it the first time around. The more you learn, and the more you taste, and as you slowly build up your own 'survival kit', you will become able to match bar with mood, or clearly recognise when you hunger for a ganache (a chocolate filled with chocolate and cream), a nibble of Toblerone, or a few squares of something dark and challenging.

Your chocolate profile: step 3

To make the most of your discoveries, try to make notes about each new chocolate you encounter and how it made you feel. This will form the beginning of your own chocolate database.

- What did you feel when you put it in your mouth?

- How long did the flavours take to develop?

- What was your mood before you ate it? Were you happy and celebrating, or down and in need of comfort?

- What special significance (if any) did that new chocolate bring to your life that day?

The next time you taste the same chocolate, check back and see if you still feel the same way about it. This can be a very revealing exercise, because your palate will be developing without your realising it. For example, people who think they have learned something amazing when they discover a famous name in organic chocolate may later find that this chocolate gives them the kind of sweet and artificial-vanilla aftertaste and astringency in the mouth and the throat that they get from a much cheaper product. There's more about developing your chocolate database in Chapter 4.

Is your palate primed?

'Tell me what you eat, and I will tell you what you are,' said the nineteenth-century French gourmand Brillat-Savarin. This holds for chocolate, too.

As you proceed through this book you will be monitoring changes in the way you taste and appreciate chocolate. Your palate may already have been primed by a growing appreciation of other foods.

- Do you buy fine cheeses from the delicatessen or do you prefer the ease of vacuum-packed slices from the supermarket?

- Do you ever buy olive oil or tea from specialised shops, trying different origins or blends to discover their range?

- Do you pop into the coffee shop closest to you, or do you walk the extra block to a café that makes wonderful coffee?

- Do you avoid sandwiches made with white sliced bread?

- Do you prefer a full-fat yogurt over a low-fat one?

Most of us have certain expectations about food. You might worry that as you grow more discerning about what you eat, you are becoming a food snob. But I prefer to put it this way: you are discovering not only what you *really* like, but also the great pleasure that fine food can bring.

As a born chocoholic, I could never resist trying any new bar of chocolate I came across – and when I moved to Paris in my teens, I encountered enough new bars of chocolate to keep me going for months. My shopping expeditions yielded nuances of flavour I had never encountered before, and, with these discoveries, I started to develop a chocolate database where I listed my tasting notes and comparisons between different chocolates of the same cocoa percentage or country of origin.

Maybe this sounds like hard work, but believe me, it's not. It's all about pleasure – listening to your body, tasting new tastes, storing the memory of them. Brillat-Savarin wrote in 1826: 'The discovery of a new dish brings more to human happiness than the discovery of a star.' Except I substitute 'chocolate' for 'dish', of course!

Join the club!

Even if you relish buying different chocolate bars, and making notes on them, you may find this quite a solitary pastime. And although I actually recommend solitary chocolate sessions as a way of developing your palate (see Chapter 4), chocolate is also very much for sharing – and sharing with another impassioned soul is a way of learning. Just think of the number of times you have learned something new from chatting to a friend. You inevitably come away with a new bit of gossip, or a different perspective on an event in the news.

Coming together with a group of like-minded people is always a rich experience. Join a specialist chocolate club, and you will also learn who's making what, why it's deemed special, and where you can find it. You will get the opportunity to share your views on each chocolate, helping to further develop your database of information.

I have sometimes invited a curious friend to one of those meetings. Very soon they start laughing, finding it hilarious to see a diverse group of people discussing chocolate in the serious tones usually reserved for European art-house films or prize-winning literature. Well, to an outsider, maybe it does seem like madness! But it can be a life-changing experience. My own discovery of the Chocolate Society in 1991, when I was a student and living in London, had a dramatic influence on my development as a chocolate connoisseur.

I was visiting the chocolate shop Rococco on King's Road in London – an amazing Aladdin's cave of treasures – for the first time. In among the foil-covered chocolate sardines, parrots and rabbits for Easter, I saw a notice on the counter inviting customers to join the Chocolate Society. The leaflet read:

Chocolate not candy

The Chocolate Society was formed four years ago by three dedicated chocolate enthusiasts. One of the Society's first priorities is to draw attention to the difference between the complex delicacy the world's greatest cooks and gourmets recognise as chocolate, and the low grade, cloying confection which the British consume by the ton every week.

The principle ingredient of commercial chocolate bars and bonbons is not cocoa (on average a meagre 20% by volume) but sugar, saturated vegetable fat and powdered milk. These dietary villains are responsible for chocolate's undeserved reputation as a fattening, tooth-rotting, addictive indulgence.

True chocolate is a far purer, healthier product. A single square of Guanaja Noire (made by French manufacturers Valrhona, near Lyon) for example, contains 70% cocoa solids but only a tenth of the sugar of the typical so-called chocolate bar.

Strong words you may think, but if you are one of the growing band of chocolate enthusiasts who takes their chocolate seriously then why not become a friend of the Chocolate Society?

You will be in good company

The Chocolate Society is dedicated to elevating chocolate to its rightful status as one of the world's gourmet delights.

Fine chocolate, painstakingly produced from natural ingredients, is every bit as sophisticated as a great claret or single malt whisky. Each variety has its own distinctive character, aroma and flavour. Just like coffee, varying the origin, type and blend of cocoa bean opens an endless range of subtlety to the palate.

This couldn't have described my own beliefs and mission more accurately. I was overjoyed – and determined to become a member, even though the joining fee represented a week and a half of my student income at the time.

Through the Chocolate Society, my fixed ideas about chocolate were challenged and I learned to open up to new opinions – crucial if you really want to become a connoisseur. For example, through a chocolate tasting session hosted by the society, I met the Parisian chocolatier Robert Linxe, founder of La Maison du Chocolat. At the time I was one of those people I now come across all the time – the band of chocolate lovers who proudly claim they 'only eat dark chocolate'.

When Linxe offered me one of his chocolates, I proudly asked if it could be a dark one. He smiled and offered me a plain milk ganache, saying '*Goutez moi ça*' ('Taste this for me'). In front of *the* master of chocolate at that time, I swallowed my pride – and the chocolate, which turned out to be exceedingly good. From that day I have made it my policy to explain that I would rather eat a good milk chocolate than a bad dark one. And, if someone says they only like dark chocolate, I know they have not yet seen 'the light'.

All over the world, chocolate clubs exist. I am a founding member of the Academy of Chocolate, which will offer chocolate awards and guidance about quality chocolate.

A great site, dedicated to 'chocolate connoisseurs', is www.seventypercent.com, which sells itself as being interested in 'the pure stuff – chocolate bars – rather than products that are flavoured with chocolate or made with it, such as truffles or bonbons' (words that are music to my ears!). The Seventy Per Cent Club has a very good range of quality chocolate available by mail order, and, despite its name, you will find a wide range of milk chocolate as well as dark.

SHOPPING FOR CHOCOLATES

You will probably find as you read through these pages that you are encountering the names of many chocolates you have never seen in the shops. To find them, first search any delicatessens and fancy department store food halls near you. And if your search doesn't turn up all the brands you've read about, try the internet. There are many chocolate societies and chocolate suppliers who deliver all over the world – and many of my favourite chocolate makers also have their own websites. See Resources, pages 210–11 for some starting points.

And finally...

My father once asked what I would do if I ever became allergic to chocolate. His question stopped me in my tracks. From my scientific studies (I am a qualified agronomist) I knew it was possible to become allergic to practically anything at any time in one's life. But the thought of becoming allergic to chocolate was horrific. Then I realised I knew exactly what I would do. 'I would find another passion,' I told him.

Meanwhile, and thankfully, I'm not allergic to this intensely delicious substance. And once you have started to discover how very wonderful chocolate can be, you will, I am sure, be just as drawn to the taste of real chocolate – even though finding it won't always be easy. But if it was, we wouldn't need our desert island survival kits. We would know that we could walk into any chocolate shop and find the real thing.

Just why this should be the case is to do with the way that 95 per cent of the world's chocolate is manufactured. In the next chapter, I will take you through this long and complicated manufacturing process and help you to understand what it really takes to make good chocolate – and you'll begin to find it easier to distinguish the good from the bad.

CHAPTER 3

·

Bean to bar

*I*F I HAD MY WAY, chocolate bars (but only the very best, of course!) would grow on cocoa trees. Instead, what we have is a very ugly-looking fruit whose content has to go through a long and complex chain of events before it remotely resembles chocolate.

The good news is that, with human intervention, every stage of this process is an opportunity to maximise the quality of the chocolate and create a better bar.

The bad news is that quality is very often compromised in deference to profit. And if consumers seem to like the taste of the cheapened product, so much the better for the manufacturers!

Nowadays, the closest you can get to a chocolate factory tour is a *virtual* tour – in which trade secrets are firmly kept as trade secrets. I'm not going to show you how Cadbury, Hershey, or any other manufacturer makes chocolate, but in this chapter I will take you on my own virtual tour of the chocolate chain. And it begins at the very beginning, with the cocoa tree.

Tree of the tropics

Although you may fantasise about owning and nurturing one, the cocoa tree (*Theobroma cacao*) is fragile and fussy, and simply won't survive in an ordinary garden or conservatory outside the tropics. (You can visit one in the Palm House at London's Kew Gardens, however, and if you live near another botanical garden or a university offering tropical agronomy courses, look for one there.)

So what makes this precious little tree tick? Here's the lowdown:

- It grows only in tropical regions within the latitudes of 20° South and 20° North of the equator, where it is dependent on a year-round temperature of 70°F to 77°F (my ideal, too!). If you look at the map on page 53 you will see that the chocolate-producing countries form a belt around the equator.

- It is usually surrounded by other plants that provide shade (banana trees and leguminous trees). This is crucial when the tree is young, as it only needs to get 50 per cent of available light.

- It grows better between 1/4 mile and 3/4 mile above sea level, and requires at least 65–70 per cent humidity year-round.

- After three years, a typical tree measures 13–16 ft and at ten years it measures up to 26 ft.

The cocoa-producing regions

You will notice throughout this book that I often name the region where the beans used to make your bar of chocolate came from. Over a hundred years ago, it was possible – as it is now – to buy a 'single-estate' bar, made from beans from one specific region. In 1902, Bonnat did just this (his bars came from regions in Venezuela and Madagascar). Yet at that time, cocoa percentage was more important to chocolate-lovers than the origin.

Now, the origin of the cocoa beans used to make a bar is crucial information for the chocolate connoisseur. This is because the origin of the beans will dramatically affect the quality of the chocolate made from them. The well-established tradition in the wine world of indicating the region of the grape's provenance is becoming a growing trend in chocolate labelling. 'Single-estate' or 'single-origin' bar indicates that the cocoa beans used to produce a chocolate bar are from one region of a country (like 'Bordeaux' on a wine label). 'Plantation bar', or the specific name of a plantation (such as Michel Cluizel's *Concepcion* plantation in Venezuela), indicates that the chocolate comes from a particular plantation of a few acres, renowned for the quality of its beans – the equivalent of a *domaine* for wines. If you go to the most upmarket delis or department store food halls you will probably be able to find a few brands which already label their bars in this way.

The first wild cocoa trees are thought to have come from the Brazilian Amazon (though cocoa detectives have recently discovered DNA suggesting a separate line of trees originating in Venezuela), but they were first cultivated in Mexico and its neighbouring countries, and it's from here that they gradually spread to other continents. The Latin American beans came from the Criollo tree – the most fragrant, but also the most fragile, as we've seen.

Colonialism had a lot to do with the spread of the cocoa bean, as demands 'back home' for chocolate increased from 1650 onward, and plantations were started up in tropical colonies.

The map on page 53 shows the current growing regions.

WHERE IN THE WORLD? ...

Ivory Coast and Ghana: Forastero beans reached Africa in 1822, and by 1921 Africa had replaced the Americas as the major cocoa-producing continent. Today Ivory Coast and Ghana provide seventy per cent of world production – all Forasteros.

Indonesia: Cocoa from Mexico was introduced to Indonesia in 1515 by the Spanish, but commercial and intense exploitation only started in the 1970s. Most Indonesian cocoa is acidic and poor quality; only Java has very fine cocoa.

Brazil: Brazil was the world's second biggest cocoa producer until 1986, when disease decimated most of the trees. The country now produces only four per cent of the world's cocoa, and has to import beans to satisfy internal demand.

Mexico: The birthplace of manufactured cocoa, Mexico now produces mainly lower-quality cocoa. Interestingly, a few rare, fragrant Criollo trees grow wild in the jungle of Chiapas in the south. Attempts are underway to revive this precious species.

Venezuela: The country became a major cocoa producer at the beginning of the seventeenth century. But recession and cyclone damage in the early 1930s conspired to change all that and now Venezuela has just 0.5 per cent of the cocoa market. However, it is one of the world's top three countries in terms of quality. Venezuela is a special case as it is likely to be the first country in the world where specific bean-growing regions will be strictly defined and labelling regulated – thus protecting the special high-quality regional beans against copycats and false marketing. See page 134 for more details.

Equador: The country was the world's number one cocoa producer in 1850. Today, it has three per cent of world production and is the world's eighth biggest producer. Equadorian cocoa is genetically more interesting than anything produced in Africa, but I don't yet rate it very highly.

Madagascar: The country produces less than 0.5 per cent of world production, but most are fine-quality cocoa beans.

Jamaica: Jamaica also grows less than 0.5 per cent of the world's cocoa, and the beans are often poor quality or poorly fermented.

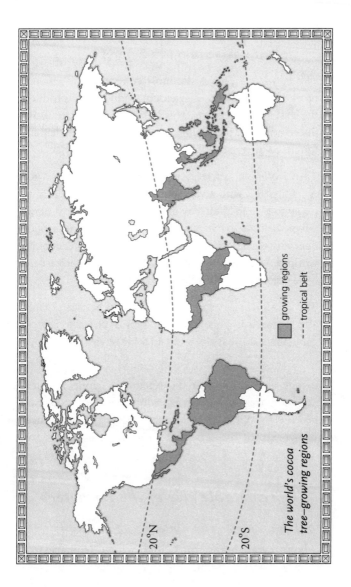

growing regions

tropical belt

20°N

20°S

The world's cocoa
tree–growing regions

The varieties

There are three main varieties of cocoa tree:

- *The Forastero*. This is the most common, and also the most robust and highest-yielding. Sadly, it also produces the least aromatic beans. This is the tree Europeans introduced into their plantations in the colonies when demand for chocolate grew in the early twentieth century.

- *The Criollo*. This variety is everything the Forastero is not. A fragile tree, with a very small yield, it is considered by many to give the best-flavoured bean. Today most books tell us that two to five per cent of cocoa trees are Criollos. Specialists in agronomy think less than one per cent of the world production is Criollo. Modern-day Criollos are not pure Criollo, but a Criollo/Trinitario hybrid.

- *The Trinitario* is descended from a cross between Criollo and Forastero. This tree has hybrid characteristics – robustness, aromatic beans, and average yield.

You may also hear about the Nacional, a fourth variety, which was once cultivated in Equador until plantations were wiped out by Witch Broom disease, a form of tree cancer. Only hybrids (of Trinitario and Nacional) remain.

The resistable rise of the Forastero

What makes good chocolate?

The fine, fragrant beans from Criollo or good Trinitario trees are the best starting point.

What makes bad chocolate?

Poor-quality beans from uninteresting Forastero trees.

Yet 85 per cent of the world's chocolate today originates from Forastero trees. So what went wrong?

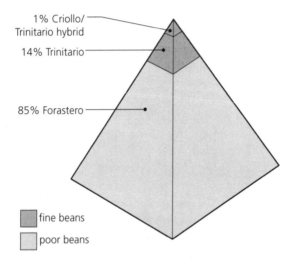

1% Criollo/
Trinitario hybrid

14% Trinitario

85% Forastero

fine beans
poor beans

Quality pyramid: world production of cocoa beans

In the nineteenth century, Criollo or Trinitario trees would only have been replaced with hardier varieties if disease or other natural disaster had destroyed the plantation. But in the early twentieth century, human greed for profits pushed many producing countries to destroy the Criollo trees and replace them with stronger and more productive Forasteros. I call it chococide – the genocide of good cocoa trees.

Why was this? The reason is that beans are sold at the same price per kilo, whatever their quality. And the vast majority of plantations are, in reality, small farms less than five hectares in size. If you were one of these small farmers, struggling to make ends meet and get enough money to buy basic necessities, and you could produce twice the quantity of beans by swapping your Criollo or Trinitario trees for Forasteros, you would have to be mad, suicidal or a masochist not to do so. Survival comes first. And most of the time producers do not even know that the weaker tree produces the more aromatic beans.

It takes seven years for a cocoa seedling to grow into a tree that is mature enough to produce pods. So, from the very start of the process, you can see why the poor farmers (for most are very poor) are reluctant to waste valuable time raising a fragile, aromatic tree when a robust but not so fragrant variety will thrive with ease.

But there is good news. This depressing situation is being turned around. Various growers and researchers are hunting for and planting the best genetic beans all over the world. In the next few years, we connoisseurs will experience unique aromas in chocolate that it is unlikely anyone has experienced in the last 100 years.

How it all begins: raw material

The pod

Cocoa trees, regardless of their variety, produce fruit all year round, although there are two main harvests in May and November. If you get a chance to see a tree, its mixture of blossom and pods at different stages of development is quite stunning. The cocoa pod grows straight out of the trunk, and I remember that the first time I saw them I thought the tree was diseased, with its gnarled and bulbous protrusions.

But the more familiar I became with the trees, the more I learned to love this characteristic. I am now fascinated by the variety of colours and hues of the different pods – golden yellow, orange, red, burgundy, brown. After one plantation trip

Cocoa pods growing on a tree

to Haiti, I took a lot back home hoping to build a collection, but they rotted. Since then I learned to gently dry them out at home on the radiator, but they shrink, become wrinkled and their wonderful colour fades.

Angoleto
Pods are long and ridged with wide shoulders and little or no bottleneck. The tip is usually somewhat pointed but not curved.

Cundeamor
Pods are long, warty, deeply ridged and furrowed, with either a pronounced bottleneck, or a suggestion of one, and a pointed tip which is sometimes curved.

Amelonado
Pods have melonlike shape, shallow ridges and furrows and tip is rounded, rather than pointed, with faint hint of a bottleneck. The skin is thick, and usually smooth with occasional wartiness.

Calabacillo
Pods are shaped like a small pumpkin and are round or oval with thick and very smooth skin. They have almost no ridges or furrows and no suggestion of tip or bottleneck. (Its colour is grass green changing to deep yellow as it matures.)

Four types of shape of cocoa pod (no link with genetics)

The bean

As soon as the pods are ripe enough, they are cut from the tree with a machete. They grow so close to the trunk that this is a delicate operation – the trunk can be easily damaged and is vulnerable to disease, so harvesting with machines will never be possible. The pods are then piled together for a group of workers to open by hand.

Split pod revealing cocoa beans

Within the pod, the beans lie wrapped in a thick protective coating of white mucilage, looking a bit like a bunch of grapes covered in soggy cotton wool. All this is emptied into large baskets or containers. The mucilage is juicy and fresh, with delicate aromas that vary from one tree to another. The flavour is honeyish, with a faint vanilla aftertaste, and plantation workers and their children love to suck this, and spit out the bitter beans.

RIPENESS IS ALL

What makes good chocolate?
Juicy ripe pods, from fine trees.

What makes bad chocolate?
Pods that have not been allowed to ripen fully, and have been cut off too soon.

This happens because poor farmers are living hand to mouth and want their bean cash as soon as they can get it.

First-stage processing

Fermentation and flavour

The mucilage needs to be removed from the beans before processing, so, most commonly, layers of fruity pulp are put in wooden boxes with holes at the bottom (which act like a colander), and covered with banana tree leaves which contain bacteria that enhance the fermentation process, liquefying the mucilage so it can drain away, leaving the beans.

This process also brings out the precursors of the aromas that the resulting chocolate will have – a crucial factor if you care about quality and full flavours.

COCOA LIQUEURS

The drained liquid may occasionally be reserved and used for cocoa liqueur that keeps all the aromas of the mucilage, tasting more sweet and acidic than chocolate. When buying cocoa liqueurs, check whether they're made from the bean, or from the mucilage; the latter is relatively rare.

By the book, fermentation should take five to seven days, although Criollo beans are faster to ferment and may be ready in three to four days. These lengths of time are needed to give the cocoa beans' aromas the best chance of developing. Unfortunately, co-operatives, like the small farmers who supply them, are often hungry for cash, and buyers from the big companies are not very interested in aroma. To all parties, there may seem little point in wasting precious time on fermentation when they can get the transaction over as soon as the beans have been sufficiently drained.

Down at the co-op...

Most farmers take their baskets of mucilage to their nearest co-operative, very often a neat little two-roomed house built with a grant from the cocoa programme of an international agency. Posters on the walls show pictures of different beans cut lengthwise so the farmer can see what 'faults' the co-operative wants to prevent ending up in the bags they will sell on to exporters or international companies. Fifty of each farmer's beans are placed on a flat metallic dish, with one hole for each bean. They are then cut in two, lengthwise, with a guillotine or knife and checked against the wall charts.

As we've seen, most co-operatives are not looking for quality, as they receive the same price regardless of whether the tree is a Criollo or a Forastero, or whether the pod is ripe or distinctly unripe. They are looking for size (100–150 beans 5 oz), a low humidity level (below six per cent), and minimal faults. Often, quality control is carried out by a group of women sitting on the floor and sorting the beans by their appearance (never the taste!). The 'bad' beans are used by the cosmetic companies for the cocoa butter, not the taste.

Drying

Once the beans are drained of mucilage, the next step is to dry them to the point where they contain less than six to eight per cent moisture. This will prevent them from going mouldy when shipped, and allows them to be stored for four to five years without going off – although most factories store only what they need for three weeks of grinding.

Some farmers dry their own beans and sell them to middlemen, rather than taking them to a co-operative. In these instances, the farmer may simply spread his beans onto a side-street and let the sun do the work of drying: the cement of the street may be the only hot, dry surface to which he has access. But, while it is better than the crude earthy floor of a typical farmhouse at keeping moisture away from the beans, the street leaves the produce open to crushing by cars or children at play, theft, and dirt.

The alternative is to take the beans to a co-operative, most of which have special drying areas. These are either basic cemented outdoor areas, where the beans can dry hygienically in the sun by day (but are brought in overnight to prevent the dew getting to them); or dedicated drying rooms where the beans are laid out on racks suspended about a metre above huge pipes containing hot air. The way that cocoa beans are dried can greatly affect the flavour of the chocolate. The aim should be to dry the beans slowly, softly caressing them rather than blasting them with the equivalent of a hair-dryer, which is sadly what happens in many drying rooms.

THE ART OF DRYING

Steve De Vries, one of the passionate chocolatiers who I believe is leading the chocolate revolution, has been experimenting with the drying of beans. He gave me two chocolates to sample – one made with beans that had been slowly and tenderly 'caressed' dry by the sun at its less-intense times (from 5 am to 10 am and from 5 pm until nightfall), the other made from identical beans which were sun-dried conventionally, in well-monitored drying rooms.

The difference in taste was spectacular. A fingernail-sized morsel just .1ocm thick of the specially dried chocolate was packed with fresh aromas of plums and tropical fruit that lasted a good five minutes. In the other sample I detected the same fruity aromas, but they were less intense, less clean, and swimming in the earthy, rustic aromas I associate with a typical African chocolate. The first sample was purity, elegance – in taste terms, a white cloud with angels dancing on it. The 'sun-bed', as I call the other one, was a beautiful orchid lost in the middle of a dirty, noisy city.

Off to the Factory

After drying, the beans are put in 130 lb jute bags and sprayed with chemicals to prevent damage from weevils, vermin or bugs. They are then sent on the long journey to the countries where they will be processed.

Roasting and shelling

To bring out the chocolate flavour and colours the beans are roasted. The temperature, time and degree of moisture involved in roasting depends on the type of beans being used and the type of chocolate being made. Thus, when the chocolate is made with a different blend of beans, beans are roasted separately and mixed afterwards.

A winnowing machine is used to remove the shells from the beans to leave what are known as the cocoa nibs – peeled beans transformed into chunks.

Many companies now sell pure cocoa nibs. Nibs, chopped into small chunks, even turn up in chocolate bars. The chocolate company Weiss kicked this fashion off in 1994 with its Noir aux Eclats de Fèves (dark chocolate with fragments of cocoa beans).

If you get the chance to taste a nib, I recommend you do so – if only for the shock it will give you. You may well expect the roundness and sweetness of chocolate, but you won't find it. It's an extreme experience ... and one that will leave you fully understanding why Europeans found the unsweetened Aztec version of hot chocolate so unpalatable.

It is only this year that I have begun to deeply enjoy eating nibs. I should say that these were very special, made from fine-quality beans fermented and dried with the utmost care. There are, I discovered, nibs and nibs. Most of the ones available at the moment are what you might politely call an acquired taste – and the fact that they can be transformed into such an exquisite concoction is due to the added vanilla and sugar, not the beans.

This is summed up perfectly in a quote from the French food writer James de Coquet: '*Il faut avoir goûté aux fèves de cacao pour mesurer toute la somme de génie que l'homme peut mettre au service de son appétit de volupté.*' In other words, what a genius man can be when he's motivated by his hunger for pleasure!

Cocoa liquor, cocoa butter and cocoa presscake

At the factory, the nibs are then milled to create cocoa liquor (peeled and ground cocoa beans). This paste has the consistency of peanut butter and is at last starting to smell something like chocolate. The cocoa liquor is pressed to extract the cocoa butter, leaving a solid matter called cocoa presscake. The machines used by the big companies to do this are based on the one invented by the nineteenth-century Dutch chemist, Van Houten. The machines eject the watery, yellow melted cocoa butter and leave a round cocoa presscake about 2 in thick and 1 foot in diameter.

Fat alternatives for fine or cheap chocolate

The process now takes two different directions:

- A. The cocoa butter is added to the cocoa liquor in the production of chocolate.

- B. Unfortunately, most cheap chocolate is made with a combination of cocoa powder (made from pulverised cocoa presscake) and vegetable fats, which are a much cheaper substitute for cocoa butter.

Before 2003, EU rulings allowed manufacturers in Britain and the Netherlands to add up to 5 per cent vegetable fats without declaring it on the label, and it was this which led EEC ministers in 1985 to suggest that British chocolate should be called 'vegelate' rather than chocolate! Ironically, in 2003 this was widened to include all EU countries, and now 'vegelate' is made throughout Europe.

Other Ingredients

Other ingredients such as sugar, milk, vanilla, and emulsifying agents such as lecithin, are added and mixed. The mixture then undergoes a refining process by travelling through a series of rollers until a smooth paste is formed. This improves the texture.

MIND THE ADDITIVES

What makes good chocolate?
Fine processing, and minimal additives.

What makes bad chocolate?
Cheap, poor-quality raw ingredients: cheap beans and artificial vanilla mixed with cheap vegetable fats. Start looking at the ingredients on your chocolate labels!

Conching

The paste is transferred to the conche, a machine which kneads and smooths the chocolate mixture for up to three days at a temperature between 140°F to 167°F, depending on the company. Some companies, such as Amedei, still use conches based on the original Lindt design, but the modern conches used by the majority of companies are very different and usually totally electronically managed.

The speed, duration and temperature of the conching affect the flavour. Conching also improves the texture, and allows any acidity to evaporate.

If you have ever read Roald Dahl's story *Charlie and the Chocolate Factory*, you will recall that the smell on approaching a chocolate factory can make you nauseated – in fact, a lot of people stop eating chocolate after two days of working in a chocolate factory. The reason is that the acetic fumes from the conching are the same as those in vinegar.

THE CONCH CONNECTION

What makes good chocolate?

Long conching. Conching should take at least two to three days, according to Lindt's instructions. I recently tasted chocolate at De Vries's factory that had been conched for three hours, nine hours, two days and three days respectively. The improvement with time was clear (although it would also be possible to over-conch a chocolate).

What makes bad chocolate?

Inadequate conching, which is done to cut costs. You can only be suspicious when a big company prides itself on conching for just five hours instead of the two to three days applied by Amedei, Valrhona, Pralus, Scharffen Berger and others. Yet at a major chocolate symposium in 2003, one expert presented his 'zero conching' theory. Lindt must have been turning in his grave!

Tempering

After conching, the chocolate mixture is 140°F to 167°F and needs to be cooled to around 104°F to allow stable crystallisation of the cocoa butter. Cocoa butter is basically made of six types of crystals which melt at different temperatures. By tempering, cocoa butter goes through a number of variations of temperatures and an inner grid of stable crystals is formed. The process produces a chocolate that is shiny and smooth, with a homogenous and silky texture. The melted chocolate eventually comes out of a tap – which must be every chocoholic's dream!

There's a lovely story about an American pastry teacher on a guided tour of the El Rey factory, near Caracas, Venezuela, who asked if she could swim in their tempering machine. The company explained that, unfortunately, this would not be possible for hygiene reasons. But they were able to accommodate her by providing a private room in which she could climb into a hot tub filled with melted chocolate. It took her two hours to wash it all off!

What makes good chocolate?
Careful tempering. To temper chocolate, you heat and melt it (around 104°F) and then cool it down very quickly, as the most stable of the six fat crystals in cocoa butter, used to prompt the crystallisation of the others, crystallises at the lower temperature. This is the reason why chocolatiers always work with chocolate on a marble slab.

What makes bad chocolate?
Careless tempering. When tempering isn't properly carried out the result is a grainy, crunchy chocolate with no shine, and possibly a grey or white film on the surface called 'bloom' (which is the fat coming to the top). If you have ever tasted a chocolate bar that crunches with crystals or has a powdery texture, it is because something went wrong with the tempering process.

Moulding

After tempering, the 90°F liquid chocolate is stored as a liquid for later use (see 'couverture', pages 118–20) or poured into moulds and placed in a cooling tunnel. The bars are then removed from the moulds and wrapped – usually by machines. After a very long and complex chain of chemical and physical reactions, the chocolate bar is ready to bring more pleasure to our life.

Storing up pleasure

Once they've left the factory, chocolate bars have an 18-month shelf life. Filled chocolates last just three weeks (unless they're packed with alcohol, sugar and artificial preservatives). Proper storage will keep chocolate in top condition within those time limits – but how do you manage it once you've got the chocolate safely home?

When I lived and worked in Jamaica as an agronomist, chocolate was not found in the shops (again, it's a case of the producing country rarely getting to enjoy the product it supplies), and I had to find a way of storing the huge supplies of chocolate I brought into the country. I still rely on this storage system today, and recommend it to anyone wanting to keep good chocolate for a long period – especially if you rarely get the opportunity to stock up on supplies.

In warm climates (above 80°F–86°F), store your bars in the fridge (never freeze them as you will kill their texture). Wrap them safely in a food bag (squeezing out all the air before you close it) to prevent them from becoming contaminated with the humidity and smells of the other food in the fridge. When you remove the bars, leave them in the bag until they reach room temperature. Then wrap them in a paper towel to absorb any condensation and prevent this from moistening and defiling the chocolate. They will be ready to eat when they have reached room temperature – normally within 20 minutes.

Only filled chocolates can be stored in a freezer (for up to six months). Package them in the same way as the bars, but plan 24 hours ahead before eating them. To defrost them, place them, still bagged, in the fridge for 24 hours, then remove and leave at room temperature for half an hour in a hot country or two hours in a cooler country (or in the evening in a hot country). Then open the bag, wrap the chocolates in a piece of paper towel (to absorb the condensation) and leave for another 10 to 15 minutes to get them to room temperature before serving.

If you are like me and like to eat three different types of filled chocolates every day, whatever your rations, you need to avoid storing each type separately. Instead, prepare daily assortments in separate bags, mini survival kits. If you can afford it, and want to store for a long time (for example, if you live far from a good supplier), invest in a machine for vacuum packing, and use this prior to refrigerating or freezing your supplies. Even better, store them in a wine cellar.

DIY chocolate

If you already make your own bread, ice cream and jam, if you love the control you get from making anything from scratch, and, if you are a true chocophile, it may have crossed your mind that maybe, just maybe, you could also make your own chocolate.

For you to produce your own chocolate from the bean, you would need to invest around $90,000 in machinery (and that's secondhand!). But, on a very small scale, you *can* make it happen at home.

If you need inspiration, look up stories about the child prodigy Amy Singh, who at 11, was exhibiting her own 56% blend of chocolate at international chocolate shows, which she had made herself with Venezuelan Trinitario beans. Amy uses two vegetable steamer baskets wired together, attached to the rotisserie rod of an outdoor grill for roasting. After husking and winnowing the beans, she grinds them in a coffee mill, then puts them through a pasta machine to refine them with powdered sugar and vanilla bean seeds. After a couple of passes through the pasta machine, the mixture is put into another type of pasta machine for conching. The heat source is a standard lamp.

Using these tools, made from household appliances, she has apparently been able to reduce her chocolate to particles of around 20 microns in size – well below what can be felt on the tongue – and in line with many of the best chocolates in the world that aim for 16 microns.

Even as a choco-connoisseur, I wouldn't aspire to such a thing. But, a few years ago, I had the privilege of making chocolate with Claudio Corallo – a truly passionate, perfectionist chocologist, and the man behind a special 'plantation' chocolate bar by the French company Pralus. Claudio and his family own a small cocoa plantation in São Tomé e Principé. They now have a small co-operative factory for their chocolate production. But at that time they made chocolate at home in their kitchen – to entertain the children and boost their morale and love for the product they are manufacturing. So, one day, as I was nearing the end of my stay, I asked them to show me how they did it.

We roasted some beans in the oven, peeled them by hand, carefully removing the acrid stem at the centre of each one, and then ground them by hand with some sugar in an old-fashioned coffee mill. The friction of milling causes the cocoa butter (50–55 per cent of the bean's content) to melt, and, out of the mill's spout came squidgy peanut butter–textured cocoa mass. Using our hands, we moulded this into bars. But these were nothing like the chocolate bars most consumers know.

The developed-country version is, as we've seen, highly processed to achieve its smooth texture – a process which Corallo says kills chocolate. He calls mass-market chocolate 'the corpse of real chocolate' because it has had all the life sucked out of it. The bars we made were grainy, with sugar crystals and crumbs from the nibs – far from perfect – but, for the connoisseur in search of the true taste of chocolate, this was closer to the real thing than anything you find in a typical supermarket. Today Corallo has developed a whole range of plain chocolates totally different from anything you can find in the supermarket.

Poor-quality chocolate is the equivalent of a ready-made meal, smothered in salt and sugar and artificial flavourings. People get used to that taste, and find it hard to enjoy real food when they are unaccustomed to it. The chocolate I made at

Claudio Corallo's had a somewhat crude consistency, some unpleasant smoky and cheesy notes, but its flavour was natural – not stifled by nasty additives. And of course there was the satisfaction of knowing we had made it ourselves!

And finally…

Three million tons of cocoa beans are processed worldwide every year, but ever since the 1900s, when chocolate production started to be widely industrialised, every step of the industrial development that has given us today's mass-market chocolate bar has taken us further and further away from the true taste of chocolate.

What drives me and my fellow 'chocologists' is a mission to bring about the changes needed to give the whole world, not just a lucky elite, the true, pure chocolate we all deserve. We know it is possible – but at a price.

- Manufacturers have to be prepared to devote more TLC to their plantations – growing the more fragile but more fragrant species of cocoa trees.

- Co-operatives must be encouraged to ferment their beans adequately to entice the delicious aromas out of them.

- More care must be given to drying, roasting and conching.

- Additives such as vanilla and cocoa butter should be taken out.

Now that the world is waking up to the fact that chocolate can be as fine as the finest wine – and prices will reflect this more and more – some producing countries are realising what a jewel they possess in their cocoa trees. These countries will help to force the changes that will bring more of us the gourmet bars of chocolate that I will be showing you how to taste in the next chapter.

CHAPTER 4

·

Tasting, tasting...

*M*OST PEOPLE ENJOY eating chocolate. But only a few make a habit of 'tasting' it in the same way that wine is tasted for its subtle notes of woodiness, spice, fresh fruit and floral bouquets (yes, all these flavours can be found in good chocolate too!).

But time and patience can, I believe, enable anyone with the right determination to become a chocolate connoisseur. Even if chocolate is merely a comfort food for you now, or just a small after-dinner treat, there is no reason why you can't also start on a connoisseur's tasting regime, choosing a time of day when you can sample chocolate in a studious way. The idea may be completely new to you, but it will ultimately enhance the enjoyment you derive from chocolate as you start to discover its secret aromas.

You won't need to throw away your favourite bars. But you will need to establish a new routine for your 'chocolate work', as this is the only way to give yourself the time you'll need to explore the world of fine chocolate. And it is a different world altogether.

- Good chocolate can evoke flavours you are not used to associating with chocolate – for example, mushrooms, flowers, berries, liquorice and even leather.

- It is like a symphony with many different notes – some come and go, others linger. Flavours may come in bursts, one after the other – and the aftertaste can be something completely different from the initial taste. Generally, as with wine, you should be able to distinguish a clear beginning, middle and end.

- The taste (not sweetness or vanilla) can linger for many minutes if the chocolate is of exceptional quality.

Once you discover the new kind of chocolate I'm talking about, there will be no going back. Moving on from sweet overprocessed chocolate is like giving up sugar in your tea, or cutting excess salt out of your diet. You will one day wonder why you ever liked it so much.

Learning to taste

If all of this sounds interesting, it may be time for you to move on to the next stage of tasting – trying chocolate in a more studious way.

To do this you will need to engage all five senses, but above all, you will have to work at developing your palate. You will also have to create exam-like conditions for your studies, and learn to tune into your body (it helps if you're used to doing this – perhaps through yoga or meditation, but it's not a prerequisite!). This will give you the confidence to trust your judgement on all matters chocolatey.

MUSHROOMS IN A WET FOREST?

I started tasting chocolate properly as a teenager but it took me years of hard work before people began to think of me as an expert. As I have already mentioned, I began by working, unpaid, in one of Paris's top patisseries, Ladurée. The interview with the head chocolatier Pierre Hermé (who now has his own bijou chocolate stores) was a humbling experience. In my application I had written that I believed I had 'a good palate', a point he was quick to challenge.

Soon after my arrival at 8.30 am, he pushed a pile of ten dark chocolate bars towards me, and one by one cut a tiny square from each one, and handed the first to me with the instruction, 'Tell me what you think!' The chocolates were a brand I had never encountered before, Pralus, and each bar was labelled with the name of an exotic country such as Venezuela, Equador, or Madagascar. All were 75 % cocoa.

I tasted the first one: 'A walk in the forest, a wet forest,' I said.

He put a square of the same chocolate into his own mouth, and added: '...with mushrooms on the ground!'

With the second, I tasted 'bread'. Pierre found 'biscottes!' (rusks).

And so we went on. At last – I'd found someone who spoke my language!

And the test? I had proven that I knew there was more to chocolate than simply dark or milk. But my

real success was understanding that ten dark chocolates with the same cocoa solid content could be
totally different from one another – and not only that,
but being able to translate into words what my body
was telling me about the flavour of each one. I used the
method that wine tasters do, of linking the tastes in
the chocolate to the environment around me. (See
page 87 for more about how to do this.)

If you enjoy dark chocolate, and pride yourself on
eating only those with 70% cocoa content or more, try
sampling different brands of fine chocolate of similar
cocoa percentages, from different plantations or
countries of origin – and see how much more than just
a dark chocolate taste you can detect in each one.

Your biggest hurdle may be your own self-
confidence. A lot of people find it difficult to form their
own opinions on anything because they are so used to
being led by what others think, or are worried their
opinion will seem stupid, or offensive to someone
who doesn't share it. Becoming a connoisseur does
take a degree of front. You have to be prepared to
accept that your own opinions are as valid as anyone
else's. And you also need to be prepared to revise your
view if you've misjudged something!

When I was in my late twenties, I formed my own chocolate
club, *L'Association Carrément Chocolat* (which, translated
literally, means the Fully/Squarely Chocolate Association), in
order to initiate others into the art of tasting chocolate.
Everyone who attended loved chocolate – but they had not

yet developed the ability to appreciate it in the way that they would a fine wine.

But chocolate can give as much pleasure (far more in my case!) as a wine whose alcoholic content is lost in the alchemy of wondrous aromas (and bad chocolate is just as ghastly as a wine in which all flavour is drowned by the liquor). When you learn to taste chocolate properly you will discover that each chocolate has its own uniqueness that can add to your personal chocolate database – the store of information to which you will refer frequently as you become a chocolate connoisseur.

If you are familiar with wine tasting, you will find that the methodology for tasting chocolate is very similar. If chocolate is your initiation into the world of tasting, you may be about to learn that you have a hidden talent for detecting the symphony of flavours waiting to be discovered – not only in chocolate but in other food products too. I have personally tested apples, yogurts, cheeses, teas, coffees and spices using the same methodology, and it really is an eye-opener!

The five-sense test

To taste – be it chocolate, wine, tea, coffee or cheese – you need to engage all five senses. The wine critic Jancis Robinson explains this methodology very clearly and entertainingly in her book *How to Taste*, which I thoroughly recommend to anyone who wants to become an expert. But here I will cover the basics.

1. Use your eyes

Look at the piece of chocolate you are about to taste, evaluating its texture before you put it in your mouth. The surface should be smooth and shiny, indicating that the cocoa butter is properly crystallised (tempered). Do not be swayed by the colour. There are few rules about what colour is best, and the shade of chocolate colour is influenced by many factors such as bean type and roasting time as well as milk content.

2. Touch it

Is it soft or hard? Sticky, grainy, sandy or velvety? Crisp or crunchy? Getting to know the feel of a chocolate will help you recognise it again in the future. It will also help you to identify quality. The smoother the texture, the more unctuous it will be in the mouth. The finer the chocolate's particles, the greater the aromas you will find in it.

3. Listen to it

Even your ability to hear affects taste – and loss of hearing can give the impression that a food has a strange taste. Tuning in to the sound that your chocolate makes when you break it is another way of familiarising yourself with the product, and assessing its quality. Did it break easily? Neatly? Drily? A chocolate that snaps without too much effort is a sign that the balance between cocoa and butter is right. Dark chocolate snaps more easily than milk because, unlike milk chocolate, it contains no milk powder.

4. Smell it

Taste is ninety per cent smell. Our sensing equipment seems to pick up subtleties in aroma or vapour that we cannot detect in solids and liquids. You will have noticed that food is more tasteless when you have a cold and your nose is blocked up. You may even lose your appetite for it because there is nothing to savour.

The vapour given off by food or drink and warmed up in the mouth has two routes to the brain. When we sniff it, with the aim of taking in its odour, the vapour travels up our nose to the olfactory receptors at the top. When we are tasting, the same vapour takes a back route, from the back of the mouth, up what's called the retro-nasal passage, to the same sensory organ.

To test the affect that smell has on taste, try holding your nose and chewing a piece of flavoursome food. Then repeat the same exercise with your nose liberated.

THE ODOUR OF QUALITY

I have occasionally been invited to taste chocolate 'live' on TV. On one occasion I shocked the presenter by categorising the unwrapped 'mystery' chocolates as either 'cheap and poor quality' or 'interesting and probably expensive' before I had even put them in my mouth. 'But how do you know?' she asked. 'You haven't even tasted them!'

'No, but I smelled them,' I told her, thrilled at the thought that the thousands of people watching would now know how much you can learn from smelling a chocolate! Cheap chocolate is easily identified by its overpowering smell of vanilla and sugar, and good-quality chocolate is all about wondrous aromas – the woody, spicy and floral smells I've mentioned.

Our sense of smell is a bit like a memory bank. You know yourself how the smell of freshly cut grass may bring back memories of your childhood, how the scent of freshly shelled peas can take you back to your grandmother's kitchen in the summer, and how the smell of perfume or aftershave can remind you of the loved one who wears it. (Eau Sauvage always brings back thoughts of my father, for example.) It takes practice to describe a chocolate's 'nose', but we do so by relating aromas to those in our past experience. 'The more we penetrate odours,' observed the great twentieth-century perfumer and philosopher Edmond Roudnitska, 'the more they end up possessing us. They live within us, becoming an integral part of us, participating in a new function within us.'

The problem is that, in today's world, we are so bombarded by artificial smells that many of us have lost our database of natural scents. Sadly, when a lot of people smell a fine chocolate for the first time, they do not recognise it as chocolate. For them, chocolate should smell of sugar and vanilla! But practice makes perfect – to coin a cliché.

Good chocolate smells often remind us of natural products – fruit, flowers, woodlands or spice. A chocolate that smells smoky may have been carelessly dried. One that smells mouldy has been damaged in storage. You can build up your database of smells by using your nose whenever and wherever you can – not only when you are smelling chocolate.

Experience the scents of wet weather. If you're in the woods, smell the soil and the leaves. Breathe in the odour of a tree trunk. When you go to the market, take a sniff of each basket of mushrooms, herbs, fruit and flowers. Do all this and you will rediscover the potential of your sense of smell. We all have the ability, but many of us have forgotten it.

5. *Taste it*

When tasting a new chocolate, try just a small, fingernail-sized piece. Put it on your tongue and chew for a few seconds to break it into smaller chunks. Then stop and allow it to melt so that all flavours are released. Make sure the chocolate is spread all around your mouth – this way you'll taste the flavours most intensely.

Flavours

When the taste of a wonderful chocolate reverberates long after we have consumed the chocolate, that indicates our olfactory system is going into overdrive. Our taste buds play a relatively minor role, picking up only crude definitions: sweet, acid, salty and bitter, but not the aromas.

When you start tasting truly good chocolate, you will find that its flavour can linger for many minutes. This is the best incentive I can think of to invest in an expensive bar. It may cost three times as much as your usual bar, but the pleasure you'll get from it is intense and long.

The flavour of chocolate comes from the combination of several of the basic tastes listed opposite. Sugar, and slightly acidic beans, can both act in the same way – in small quantities, they'll enhance the flavour but in larger quantites they drown it out. (Try a 99% bar once when you're feeling brave. Without the sugar, chocolate is a very different beast!) Fine chocolate has harmonious tastes – you'll need to concentrate to sense their presence. Look out in particular for bitterness, acidity and astringency. The first two are welcome, but astringency is a bad sign, often found in poor-quality chocolate. Next, I'll show you how to identify these tastes.

Sweetness

Sweetness is tasted at the tip of the tongue. My simple rule with sweetness is this: if you notice the sugar, if it annoys you slightly, there is too much of it in the bar. Excess sugar is used to disguise poor-quality or uninteresting beans, covering up the burnt, metallic or mouldy flavours you might otherwise taste.

sweet

Each time you taste a new chocolate, think about the sugar. Is it noticeable? Does it override the other flavours?

Bitterness, sourness and acidity

When I introduce novices to real chocolate, many use the word 'bitter' to describe it. (And it's the same word that often springs to people's lips when tasting tea or coffee, interestingly.) It is their way of qualifying a new taste that is a bit more intense than they are used to. Nine times out of ten, it is not the most accurate word to use. Poor-quality chocolate may be astringent (drying or puckering – like chewing a grape skin).

acidic

Alternatively, what you're tasting (if it doesn't seem sour) may be acidity. Try sniffing something very high in acidity, like vinegar, and notice how the edges of your tongue curl up in anticipation of how it will taste in your mouth. Acidity has a very strong effect on the sides of the tongue. Start smelling things routinely and you will realise how important a component acidity is in everything from milk to fruit.

True *bitterness* is felt in the middle at the back of the tongue. Test it in foods like chicory or grapefruit, to see how your mouth responds. Guanaja from Valrhona is rather bitter, but in such a mild and elegant way you'll hardly feel it.

With some training, you'll even detect chocolates that begin with one flavour (sweetness, for example) and evolve to another (say, bitterness) with a hint of a third (salty) e.g. Lindt 99%.

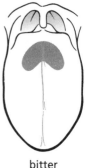

bitter

Saltiness

Saltiness is one of the first tastes you notice, and it lasts longer than sweetness. To familiarise yourself with the effect it has on your tongue, swill some salty water around in your mouth.

Salt is unusual in chocolate but you can find it in some filled chocolates (it enhances the nuttiness in pralines) or in bars like Domori's Latte Sal or 99% Lindt. Here it would be used to reveal particular aromas from the beans or the nuts – in the same way that a little salt brings out the flavour in food.

salty

Describing aromas and flavours

The last part of tasting consists in trying to find the words to describe the aromas and flavours you detect. This is very hard as we are not used to associating a word with a taste sensation. Bite any square of fine dark chocolate, and try to describe the aromas and flavours, not whether you like it or not. You might not be able to find the words to describe it.

I understand this completely. I've felt it myself, and I've seen it many times in my tasting workshops: you end up with a blank notepad. To make it easier, I suggest you proceed as for a wine tasting: try to find associations with the world around you. When you taste, close your eyes and think, 'What does this remind me of?'

In the beginning, try at least to work out which 'family' the chocolate reminds you of. Use the entries on the inner ring of the chart below as guidance or inspiration.

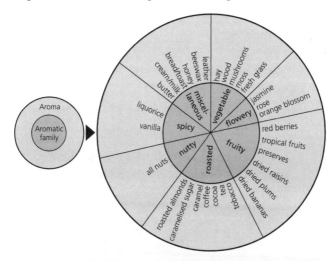

This tasting wheel will help you develop your own choco-vocabulary

Try it yourself! Take a square of Valrhona's Manjari. Pop a small piece into your mouth, and once the initial burst of acidity lowers, see if you can notice the clear red fruit notes.

In the beginning, if you can at least identify 'fruity', this is excellent. Later on, as your ability to identify flavours and aromas grows, you'll be able to fit more specific words to tastes. You can move from tasting Java from Pralus as 'vegetable' to something more accurate, for example, wood or even better, a wet forest.

Find words that sum up what *you* taste, not what you think you should taste, or what someone else has tasted. On a graph, you could draw up one curve for the 'intensity' of the flavours: in their initial attack, in their development, and in their finish. You may taste 'flowery' followed by 'woody' and then 'woody flirting with spicy'.

CHECKLIST FOR TASTING

Try doing the following exercise with a square of chocolate:

1. Look at it: what do you see? Colour? Shine? Texture? Blooming or discolouration?

2. Touch it: what do you feel? How does the broken surface look: smooth or rough and bubbly? Sticky?

3. Listen to it: what do you hear as you snap a square in half?

4. Smell it: what do you find?

5. Taste it: analyse only the texture. Notice its effect on your tongue. How does it feel in your mouth?

The simple approach is a good one to start with, and is what I use in my tasting workshops. If you want to take it further, here is the most traditional tasting method:

1. Put a tiny piece in your mouth, chew it, then stop and allow it to melt.

2. Concentrate on what you feel, and if there is any change in flavour or what your tongue feels over time.

3. Look for flavours:
    a. Do you recognise them?
    b. Do they evolve over time?
    c. Do they interact with each other, or do they seem to come in separate phases? Is one more present and clear than the others, or do they combine?
    d. Rate their intensity.

4. Do you feel any bitterness, acidity or astringency? Do you find it mild? Annoying?

5. A good chocolate has three distinct phases. Try to distinguish them:
    a. What you feel in the first seconds
    b. What you feel while it slowly melts
    c. Now swallow: what do you feel now? This phase is called the 'end of mouth'.

6. Rate it: How would you score it globally out of ten?

Remember: all the tastes that you can identify are valid. There's no right or wrong – and nobody is trying to test you or catch you out. No other person has your palate and therefore nobody but you can know what you taste in a chocolate!

Creating the right conditions

I started my analytical tasting regime at the age of 13, when, in Paris, I discovered chocolate was a treasure that deserved the respect and attention of an empty stomach and a clean palate. The longer I left it after eating, the more I could taste in my chocolate, so doing my ritual tasting before breakfast made total sense to me – and I still do my tasting for work at 6 am.

However, I am not suggesting that you have to eat chocolate so early in the day to appreciate it. Everyone has his or her own 6 am – a time in their day when they are at their most sensually alert, and have also gone several hours (I recommend a minimum of two, more after a meal) without eating, or drinking alcohol, juice, fizzy drinks, tea or coffee, or smoking. You will know what time of day would best suit you and your body: early morning, mid-morning (before a late breakfast), early evening (after a light and early lunch), or late at night (if you tend to eat a light early evening meal).

As I've indicated above, a successful tasting needs 'exam conditions': no smoking, no drinking (except water), silence, paper, pen, an organised table, and a clear action plan in your head. This sounds a bit intimidating, but it will simply facilitate the intimate conversation between you and the chocolate. And nobody is going to mark your paper or judge you!

Before you start, make sure there is no smell or noise to distract you; and be sure that you will not be interrupted for at least half an hour. Your tasting room should be at room temperature (68–74°F), and your body and mind should be calm and comfortable. Ideally, you shouldn't be wearing any perfume or other scent, as this can influence what you taste. A good way to start is to do a bit of yogic breathing, inhaling slowly through your nose and exhaling for the same slow count. Focus on the point between your eyes, empty your mind and relax your neck and shoulders.

ARE YOU READY TO TASTE?

- Is it the right time of day? Do you feel you have left a reasonable period of time since your last snack, meal or hot drink?
- Is it the right place? Are you comfortable and unlikely to be disturbed?
- Is the room at a comfortable temperature?
- Do you have peace and quiet?
- Are you free from interfering smells?
- Are you in the right state of mind – calm, but alert?
- Are you alone or with friends who will work to the same tasting criteria?

Changing tastes...

I meet a lot of would-be chocolate connoisseurs, and I pride myself on my ability to 'bring the choco-light' to anyone willing to discover and enjoy the finest chocolate – whatever their current level of consumption. However, your journey may not be straightforward. Rarely does anyone make a swift move from cheap, sugary milk 'chocolate' to fine dark chocolate. Moreover, I don't recommend that you taste the most unusual chocolates first – it should be a progressive discovery. Your tastes and feelings need to adapt gradually! So, be prepared to give this your time and dedication.

If you have children, remember how long it took them to adjust to each new flavour you tried to introduce when they were babies. You had to keep on giving them tiny tastes before their palate would even begin to accept some foods (some say it takes an average of 12 attempts at tasting something new for a child to begin to find it acceptable, so we should never give up!). Your palate is about to undergo the same shock therapy. What makes you pull a face today may one day become one of the most important bars in your chocolate survival kit (see pages 39–40).

Despite my years of experience, I am not completely beyond this stage myself. There is one company whose philosophy and bean-selection practices I greatly admire, but who make chocolate that I have never yet been able to enjoy, because its flavour is so new and challenging to me. But I won't reject it. Instead, I take a little bite each day, waiting for the time when the flavours start to speak to me.

Would I give every chocolate sample the same chance? Well, that depends on the sample. In my former job I received a lot of products containing ingredients that do not in my opinion qualify them to use the name chocolate. I also receive chocolates that I know, from first sniff, will never tell me anything about themselves other than that they are mediocre – and often, much worse. What many people call chocolate and what I call chocolate are not even close. When I eat a white chocolate truffle, any ganache made with liqueur, or any low-cocoa content (therefore fatty and sugary) 'chocolate' (and I have to eat a lot of these in my job), I am not even reminded of chocolate!

But have no fear. The chocolate bars I will recommend for your tastings are worth the trouble I am asking you to go to.

Choosing what to taste

Now that you know the methodology, you are ready to start to explore the world of chocolate. But if you walk into a shop, you'll be faced with a massive choice. How should you proceed? Where do you even start?

Look back at the chart in Chapter 2 (page 33). You might not have scaled the heady heights of what I would consider 'quality' chocolate yet, but I can give you a short-cut to the top by telling you what I recommend.

Start with your chocolate profile

When planning your first chocolate tasting session, be completely honest, and pick out the profile from those outlined below that most accurately describes you.

1. You love creamy milk chocolate – Cadbury, Lindt, Toblerone, Galaxy and so on.

TASTING SUGGESTIONS: Compare your very favourite milk chocolate bar with Jivara (Valrhona), Milk (Amedei) and Lait Entier (Weiss).

LOOK FOR: Intensity of sweetness, and taste evolution over time. Did you sense any aromas? For example, can you pick out notes of caramel, milk powder, nuts or fudge?

TAKING IT FURTHER: Discover the latest trends: Latte Sal (Domori), Hacienda Mangaro Lait (Michel Cluizel), Lindt Milk with cocoa nibs.

2. You have developed a taste for 'the good stuff', but generally buy the same bar.

TASTING SUGGESTIONS: Compare 70% Green & Black (or any fair trade or organic bar of similar percentage cocoa solids) with 70% Lindt, Porcelana (Amedei), Guanaja (Valrhona), and any supermarket-label dark (70%) bar.

LOOK FOR: Which ones smell of vanilla flavouring and/or sugar? Can you detect an aromatic palette, or is it mainly sugar that is standing out? Which have a feeling of elegance and harmony in the mouth? Which ones are acidic or bitter? Any astringency?

TAKING IT FURTHER: Chuao (Bonnat), Java (Pierre Marcolini), Trinidad (Pralus), Caraïbes (Valrhona).

3. You only like dark chocolate and sample a wide range of bars, but never milk.

TASTING SUGGESTIONS: In this tasting, you'll be sampling the worst end of the dark chocolate market with some of the most divine milk chocolate. Try a supermarket brand dark chocolate bar with Jivara (Valrhona) or Maracaibo 38% Criolait (Felchlin).

LOOK FOR: Pleasure.

TAKE IT FURTHER: Taste more slowly and compare the quality of the milk powders.

> You'll notice that the suggestions listed here all include some supermarket brands, and some of the artisan brands. Learning what you like is hard if you only taste things in isolation, and it is very important to compare a few bars at one time – varying qualities, but always tasting similar sorts of chocolate. This enables you to ask more questions of the chocolate and more easily come to your own, informed opinion about it.

4. You prefer filled chocolates, and when someone mentions the word 'chocolate' you immediately think of a truffle.

TASTING SUGGESTIONS: You have a sweet tooth – but there's no shame in that. Try the *crème de la crème* of truffles, made with top-quality chocolate and no added flavours. Find a good chocolate shop and ask for advice. Alternatively, if you don't have access to those, go online and order the chocolates I suggest on pages 149–50 for the four-chocolate test. You should make sure you try their best plain milk ganaches (chocolates filled with chocolate – does that make you swoon?!). Also try some fine milk chocolate bars: Jivara (Valrhona), Milk (Amedei) and Lait Entier (Weiss).

LOOK FOR: Does your pleasure mainly come from the sugar, or the flavours?

TAKING IT FURTHER: As for number 1, above.

5. You don't actually like chocolate – at least, you have never found a bar you can enjoy.

I assume that if you are reading this book you are not a chocophobe, but believe me, I have met them! If the reason is that you have more of a savoury than a sweet tooth, let me take you straight to my favourite plantation bars.

TASTING SUGGESTIONS: Palmira (Valrhona), Chuao (Amedei), Java (Pralus), Porcelana (Domori), Los Ancones (Michel Cluizel).

LOOK FOR: Flavours, as you would do for wine. Concentrate on the complexity and evolution of mouth-feel and flavour over time. *Don't* look for pleasure in your first tasting (but maybe in your second one!).

TAKING IT FURTHER: Taste together all Porcelana bars or all Venezuela bars from different brands.

FINESSE YOUR TASTING

- Try to compare a maximum of four chocolates in one sitting (each chocolate will influence the next, so by the time you get to your fourth, your taste buds will be approaching chaos). Drink water or eat bread to cleanse your mouth after each different chocolate.

- Try to compare chocolates of the same colour (all dark, for example, or all milk), and, within that colour, similar percentages (65–75%, for example). If not, the sugar content will prevent a fair comparison of flavours. For example, El Rey's 63%, 70% and 73% all have exactly the same blend of beans. The only difference is the level of sugar, and you will feel as if you are eating three totally different chocolates.

- Always include at least one supermarket bar you are familiar with as a reference. You already know your feelings about this, so it's a way of keeping your feet firmly on the ground when tasting lots of new bars.

- Look back systematically at the checklist for tasting on pages 88–9. Try comparing all the chocolates you are tasting according to these questions. As you become accustomed to different chocolates, levels of acidity and so on, this will start to come more easily to you.

Your tasting may remind you of wonderful or comforting memories from the past – or it may, as it does for me, create a whole story in your head (and the more relaxed and in tune with your mind and body you are, the more this will happen). When you become accustomed to tasting chocolate and articulating your findings, your database of choco sensations will become stored on your brain's hard drive. Not only will you find it easy to fill in your tasting sheet, but images will fill your mind. Your senses will take you to another dimension – even a kind of poetic ecstasy. When I taste Valrhona's Gran Couva Vintage 2003 I felt I was dancing among the stars and the angels are smiling at me!

This is a very personal, subjective state, and it's unlikely that two people will 'see' the same things. But, once you have created a chocolate image, it will return whenever you taste that particular chocolate.

SPEED TASTING: FIVE FAST WAYS TO DEVELOP YOUR PALATE

1. Start off slowly... chocolate theme parties are a good way to begin (see the next chapter). Invite friends who share your passion, and get everyone to bring along a new chocolate discovery, or replicate a chocolate dish. (Although, ultimately, only pure unadulterated chocolate will do for formal tastings, at a chocolate party it can be fun and interesting to see how differently people interpret a chocolate tart or cake recipe!) You'll soon find out who among your friends is keen to explore the world of chocolate with you!

2. Get into the habit of eating chocolate away from other food and drink. You know how strange a cup of tea tastes if you have just brushed your teeth, or how wine affects the food you eat, and vice versa. Tastes hang around longer than you may realise, and, to fully appreciate chocolate, I recommend leaving at least two hours after a meal and one hour after coffee, tea or cigarettes. (You can enjoy snacking on chocolate at other times – but, for the purposes of learning to 'taste', make this small sacrifice.)

3. Maximise the pleasure, don't develop cravings. If you tend to crave chocolate for the energy rush it gives you, ask yourself whether something else could satisfy that longing. Is it in fact the sugar rush you want, rather than the chocolate? One way to avoid cravings is to make sure you have a healthy balanced diet. Eating wholefoods (fresh vegetables, pulses, and wholegrains) should keep your blood sugar levels stable and prevent sugar cravings. If you can do this, it will be easier for you to eat chocolate for the pleasure of its chocolate content rather than the sugar it contains (and this is essential when you move on to fine chocolate).

4. Be prepared to pay the price. Good chocolate is expensive. But so is bad chocolate in pretty boxes. Don't get the two mixed up! A simply wrapped bar with a high price tag *and* a reliable name (see column 2 on page 33) will introduce you to the kind of chocolatey tastes that reverberate around the mouth long, long after you've consumed a tiny square.

5. Trust your intuition. Believe in your own opinions, and start forming them. Taste food like a critic. Think about the food you eat and its textures and flavours, and create your own tasting vocabulary. Good wine shops give customers labels with descriptions to alert them to the flavours to expect from selected bottles. Tasting notes are starting to

accompany chocolate sales too. But don't take that taster's word for it. Ask yourself what you think the bar tastes like. What does it remind you of? Does it conjure up an image? If it does, this image will return to you next time you taste the same bar! Also avoid fancy flavourings such as hot pepper, exotic spices or herbs when tasting a brand for the first time. Stick to plain bars until you know the brand well.

Now you know how to taste chocolate, and have a few ideas for tasting combinations, why not make it a social occasion? In the next chapter you'll be able to put your new knowledge to work.

•

CHAPTER 5

Chocolate to share

*B*UYING NEW CHOCOLATE is tough enough – there's so much to choose from, after all. We've already gone into the countries and regions of origin, and the brands to look for, and I know how daunting all this can be for the novice. So, as I indicated at the end of the last chapter, a fun way to develop your interest in chocolate is to start with themed parties. At these parties, you can invite other chocolate-loving friends, play simple chocolate tasting games with the skills you learned in the last chapter, and serve delicious chocolate dishes. Remember, one of the best ways to really learn and get excited about something new is to share your discoveries and passion with like-minded or interested people.

Chocolate tasting games

You do not have to aspire to becoming a chocolate connoisseur to enjoy the following party games – but you do have to like chocolate!

Here are the ground rules:

- Use all dark, or all milk chocolates, with similar percentages of cocoa solids (try not to have more than 15% difference. For example, if your darkest chocolate is 78% cocoa solids, do not use another in the same game with less than 64% cocoa).

- When setting up the chocolates, try to hide their identities by removing packaging and turning over any surface with a tell-tale sign on it.

- It is important that no participant has eaten in the last two hours, or had tea, coffee, alcohol or a cigarette in the last hour.

GAME 1: THE MYSTERY GAME

For some suggestions for which chocolates to use for these games, see 'Choosing what to taste' on pages 93–6.

This is very easy to organise and even young children can take part.

Give each participant their own plate with four squares of chocolate. Three are in their original wrapping, or three different colours of paper; one is a mystery square in neutral packaging.

- Cut each square into two pieces. The participants should be instructed to eat half of each of the non-mystery chocolates and then half of the fourth. (*The fourth chocolate is identical to one of three others, but which one? Can your friends work it out?*)

- Now participants should cut each left-over half into two pieces so that they have two-quarters of each on the plate.

- If they have not found out or are not sure which of the two chocolates are identical, start the tasting again, respecting the same order, but this time using only a quarter.

- If they still don't know, you should now reveal the answer and ask the participants to confirm it by tasting the last quarters.

- If they find the answer after the first half, they should use the first quarters to confirm their intuition and keep the last quarters to check the revelation. If they are right, they should just enjoy the last quarter without analysing anything. The aim is to let yourself go with the pleasure and enjoy the boost to your self-esteem!

GAME 2: THE MEMORY GAME

Take four chocolate bars and give each participant a sheet of paper divided into four columns. Allocate three squares of each chocolate bar per column. Using the tasting methodology (see 'The five-sense test' on pages 80–4), fill the columns with your personal tasting notes for each chocolate. The chocolates are then identified and you know which you liked the best and which you would want to add to your desert island suitcase (see pages 38–40). Share your findings.

Two months later … Take two of the same bars of chocolate as before and two new bars. In four columns on a sheet of paper make your tasting notes as before. Can you recognise the chocolates you tasted last time? And how do your new tasting notes compare with your old ones? Have you changed your mind about which chocolate you like best?

One of the ideas about tasting so intently is that you'll develop some clear ideas about your feelings for each chocolate. Gradually, you will build up a stock of information that you'll be able to refer back to. The next time you feel in a particular mood, and 'chocolate' springs to mind, your evolved choco-vocabulary and knowledge of the flavours and sensations each chocolate gave you may help you to pinpoint the exact chocolate you feel like.

At your chocolate theme party, and after your tasting games, why not serve hot chocolate and finish off with a truly sumptuous chocoholic dessert?

Tastes of heaven

What most people expect when they order a cup of hot chocolate is a sweet and milky chocolate drink, with whipped cream on the top. Here are two deliciously different recipes you can whisk up at home.

Ingrid's Spicy Hot Chocolate

MAKES FOUR SERVINGS

For the genuine experience, use exactly the kinds of chocolate and cocoa powder listed here. If you can't find them, do try and replace them with quality alternatives (rather than supermarket brands). It just won't taste the same otherwise! Valrhona cocoa powder can be used in place of Scharffen Berger, for instance.

2¼ cups whole milk
2 to 4 tablespoons mineral or filtered water
½ vanilla bean, split open
pinch ground ginger
pinch ground cinnamon
pinch finely ground black pepper
pinch ground anise
3½ ounces Pralus Trinidad chocolate, finely chopped
3 tablespoons sugar-free Scharffen Berger powdered chocolate
4 to 8 tablespoons sugar
3 tablespoons light cream

1. Heat the milk, water, vanilla bean, ginger, cinnamon, pepper and anise in a saucepan over low heat until hot.

2. Add the chocolate and cocoa, whisking vigorously to prevent the chocolate from sticking to the pan and developing a burnt flavour.

3. Add 4 teaspoons sugar and stir until dissolved. Add the cream and wisk again. Taste for sweetness and add more sugar if needed.

4. Remove from the heat and leave the chocolate to rest in a cool place for up to 45 minutes. Remove the vanilla bean.

5. Return the chocolate to low heat, whisking in air to make it frothy, and heat until hot. Serve immediately.

Hot Chocolate *à la* Chloé

MAKES 4 SERVINGS

If you are more of a traditionalist, and want to taste the ultimate hot chocolate, here is the way I make it.

3½ ounces Michel Cluizel Mangaro chocolate (see notes below)
2¼ cups whole milk
2 to 4 teaspoons confectioners' sugar
3 tablespoons Valrhona cocoa powder

1. Coarsely chop the chocolate and set aside.

2. Heat the milk and 2 teaspoons sugar in a saucepan over low heat until hot. Add the chocolate and cocoa to the milk mixture, and whisk until the chocolate pieces have dissolved. Taste for sweetness and stir in more sugar if needed.

3. Cool the mixture slightly, cover and refrigerate for five to six hours for the flavours to blend.

4. Reheat over low heat when you are ready to serve.

Notes:
If you can't find Michel Cluizel chocolate, use Valrhona Guanaja or Noir Gastronomie.

If you cannot wait six hours, try to give the drink at least one hour for the flavours to develop. However, six hours will give a much better intensity of flavour.

If you want an easy shortcut, use whole milk, cocoa powder (the best you can find – I recommend Scharffen Berger) and sugar to taste. The flavour will be at its best if you simmer over a low heat for one minute, whisking constantly.

Another truly delicious treat for your party is a chocolate tart. One of the most chocoholic desserts I know, this is almost like a big filled chocolate. But what makes it special is that, unlike a filled chocolate, you can share it.

A changing palate doesn't mean you have to give up on an old friend entirely. Before I became buyer at Fortnum & Mason, I used to eat a spoonful of Nutella each morning before I went for a swim – even long after I decided it wasn't equal in quality to other chocolate I loved.

I no longer eat Nutella, but it retains a special place in my heart. When I moved to London to start my job, my sister gave me the complete range of 14 oz Nutella jars. I haven't eaten their contents, but I must admit to taking the occasional sniff, for old times' sake. My new favorite is Guido Gobino's Crema di Gianduja.

DID YOU KNOW?

Nutella was created by Pietro Ferrero (a pastry maker and founder of the Ferrero company) in the 1940s.

- The spread started life as Supercrema Gianduja, and quickly became so popular that, in 1946, Italian stores offered a service called 'smearing' – which allowed local children to bring in a slice of bread on which they could have some Nutella spread.

- The spread changed its name to Nutella in 1964.

- Italy now makes 179,000 tons of it each year. That's 400 million 1lb jars!

- Its recipe, as secret as Coca-Cola's, has never been matched by any other chocolate spread.

- Even if the list of ingredients is long and a bit mundane-sounding – sugar, vegetable oil, hazelnuts, fat-reduced cocoa powder, skimmed milk powder, whey powder, soy lecithin and flavouring – its taste and smell are seductive.

- Nutella outsells all the world's brands of peanut butter put together – if you look in the luggage of any travelling Italian businessman, you're likely to find a jar of Nutella in there, a welcome reminder of home!

Nutella Tart

MAKES 12 SERVINGS

I came across my first Nutella Tart at my sister's 21st birthday party. It was delicious, and I quickly worked out a shortcut version. Simply buy a 9- or 10-inch graham-cracker pie shell and fill it with the contents of a 470g (about 17-ounce) jar of Nutella (double if you plan to lick the spatula!). A more sophisticated version of the Nutella Tart appears in Délices d'Initiés, a book of recipes using children's ingredients, written by Frédérick E. Grasset. The recipe was created with me and my passion for Nutella in mind!

FOR THE PASTRY
10 tablespoons (5 ounces) butter, softened
4 tablespoons ground almonds
¾ cup confectioners' sugar
pinch sea salt
1 teaspoon vanilla extract
3 large eggs
2 cups all-purpose flour

FOR THE FILLING
½ cup Nutella hazelnut spread
5 ounces dark chocolate (such as Valrhona Caraïbe), melted
1 large egg
2 large egg yolks
2 tablespoons superfine sugar
8 tablespoons (4 ounces) unsalted butter, melted and warm

1. To make the pastry: Whisk the butter so it's evenly blended. Add the almonds, sugar, salt and vanilla. Beat in the eggs. Stir in the flour, mixing just until the dough comes together. Wrap the dough in plastic wrap and refrigerate it for one hour.

2. Preheat the oven to 350°F. Gently press the dough into a 10- or 11-inch tart pan with a removable bottom. (This is a thick crust.) Line with aluminum foil and add pie weights or dried beans. Bake for about 25 minutes, or until edges are brown and center springs back when pressed. Remove foil and pie weights.

3. To make the filling: Combine the ingredients in the order in which they appear in the list. Pour the filling into the tart shell. Bake for about 15 minutes, or until the center of the filling is still soft but the edge of the filling is set. Cool until warm and serve.

Note:
This tart is best eaten on the day of cooking, but leftovers can be refrigerated for two to three days. It should be brought to room temperature before serving.

Ingrid's Tarte au Chocolat

This wonderful chocolate tart recipe is from my friend,
Ingrid Astier.

FOR THE PASTRY
6 tablespoons (3 ounces) butter, softened
5 tablespoons sugar
1 large egg
1¼ cups all-purpose flour
2 tablespoons cornmeal
2 tablespoons ground almonds
pinch sea salt
pinch ground cinnamon
seeds from ½ vanilla bean or 1 teaspoon vanilla extract

FOR THE FILLING
1⅔ cups heavy cream
pinch ground cinnamon
pinch ground ginger
1 Tahitan vanilla bean, split open
¾ cup confectioners' sugar
14 ounces dark chocolate (Ingrid uses half Pralus Ghana
and half Pralus Java, but use the best you can find)
1 ounce Jivara chocolate (a Valrhona milk chocolate)
1 tablespoon butter, in small pieces
2 tablespoons toasted, crushed hazelnuts

1. To make the pastry: Mix the butter (which should be quite soft) with the sugar. When this is well blended, beat in the egg. Add the flour, cornmeal, almonds, salt, cinnamon and vanilla seeds to the mixture. Work the dough into a ball, cover with plastic wrap, and refrigerate it for two hours.

2. Preheat the oven to 350°F. Gently press the dough into a 10-inch tart pan with a removable bottom. Line with foil and add pie weights or dried beans. Bake for 15 minutes. Remove foil and pie weights and bake about 10 minutes, or until lightly browned. Let cool.

3. To make the filling: Bring the cream to a boil with the cinnamon, ginger and vanilla bean. Turn off the heat as soon as the mixture boils. Let stand for 15 minutes to infuse and then remove the vanilla bean. Bring to a boil again and turn off the heat.

4. Make a caramel by warming the confectioners' sugar in a saucepan until golden (but being careful not to burn it). Return the cream to low heat and add the caramel, stirring to dissolve. Once the caramel is dissolved in the cream, take the pan off the heat.

5. Chop all the chocolate into pieces and place it in a heat-proof bowl. Slowly pour the hot caramel-cream mixture over the chocolate, whisking it in but without adding too much air. When the mixture is lukewarm, add the butter in batches, and mix carefully.

6. Place the hazelnuts in the tart shell. Slowly pour the filling over the hazelnuts. Cool for three hours, or until set, before eating.

Note: This tart is best eaten on the day of cooking, but leftovers can be refrigerated for two to three days. It should be brought to room temperature before serving.

An eighteenth-century French print of vanilla pods

Now that you know how good chocolate is made, and how it tastes, you are probably beginning to understand why I am so keen to introduce fine chocolate to as many people as possible, and why each little introduction means so much to me.

·

CHAPTER 6

The cream of the crop

*I*F YOU ARE READY to follow me in the discovery of 'real' chocolate – the cream of the crop – my advice is simple. Try new chocolates as often and as conscientiously as you can, tasting them (and not just 'eating' them), and following the methodology in the last chapter.

I truly believe that each one of us has gourmet potential, and that all you need is the opportunity to wake it up and educate it.

But first you need to understand what you are up against, and why, to a certain extent, you will have to turn detective to find the kind of quality chocolate I am urging you to taste.

To recap: the truth about chocolate

Here are the facts:

The world produces around 3 million tons of cocoa beans per year and Africa (Ivory Coast and Ghana mainly) provides seventy per cent of that total, using beans from

Forastero trees, the least aromatic of the cocoa family.

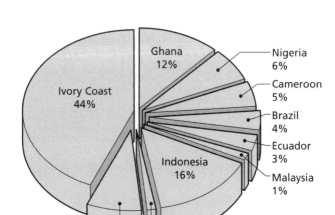

World cocoa-bean market 2002–2003 (ICCO)

The aromatic quality of the resulting chocolate depends on:

1. The bean that it is made from – its aromatic potential

2. How these beans are fermented

3. How the beans are dried

4. How these beans are roasted and conched

5. The quality and proportion of additives (vanills, cocoa butter)

An estimated 15 % of world production:
Good Beans (e.g. Criollo/Trinitario hybrid or
Trinitario) + good fermentation = good chocolate
Good Beans + bad fermentation = bad chocolate

An estimated 85 % of world production:
Poor Beans (e.g. Forastero) + good fermentation =
poor chocolate
Poor Beans + bad fermentation = terrible
chocolate!

The incredible truth ... most chocolate isn't great

Ninety per cent of the world's cocoa beans come from farms less than five hectares in size: that is to say, places where farmers ferment their beans in their backyard or take them to the nearest co-operative where, with no attention to ripeness or quality variations, all the local beans are mixed up and fermented together.

This fermentation process is usually too short for the proper development of the precursors of aromas to take place, because the co-operatives need cash fast.

Most of these poor beans are purchased and processed into chocolate by four main multinational groups, who supply the vast majority of the chocolate companies we know. When selecting their beans, they concentrate on size and lack of flaws rather than aromatic properties – the very same process that perpetuates the sale of those big, tasteless, ruby-red tomatoes you can buy in the supermarket.

The aroma-inducing conching process first used by Lindt lasted for three days. Only a few fine chocolate producers still conch for this length of time, as the multinationals push for 'more efficient' and shorter conching times.

You'll probably have a good idea where I am coming from now when I say that in my opinion, 90 per cent of the chocolate available to us ranges from uninteresting to horrendous (bad beans and/or bad processing)! The problem is that the majority of this poor chocolate is dressed up with marketing, labelling and packaging and presented as good chocolate.

I've recommended a number of top-quality chocolates. But what I haven't yet covered are the 'wolves in sheep's clothing' of the chocolate world. These have all the 'right' words on the label and aren't cheap. They are cleverly marketed – but they are an inferior product.

So how do you recognise friend from foe? Well, there is no other way than to taste. And taste again. *Think* as you taste … and learn to trust your taste buds. Only they can tell you if what you are eating is *true* quality or if it is a smartly marketed impostor. On the following pages I'll give you more information that will help you to distinguish between good, less good and bad.

COUVERTURE

Did you know that the vast majority of the brands we see in supermarkets, the Belgian chocolates Godiva and Leonidas, and Thornton's, as well as the small artisan chocolatiers, all buy the same raw material?

Most chocolatiers buy chocolate in bulk, called 'couverture', rather than grinding their own cocoa beans. Couverture can take the form of ready-to-melt chocolate in big blocks of 2 to 55 lbs. In addition, couverture can also be bought as liquid chocolate, which has been pre-melted and tempered. The liquid form is even easier for chocolatiers to work with as it is ready to be moulded. It is kept at 113°F and distributed in tank trucks. (Those trucks look so much like the ones used to transport milk or petrol that whenever I see one on the road, I end up imagining it filled with one of my favourite chocolates!)

So when you buy a few bars, say two single-estate bars from Madagascar, made by different brands, nine times out of ten the manufacturers will have had a choice of only two different couvertures. The two bars you've bought might actually have come from the same bulk chocolate! Chocolate makers do this because it's not cost-efficient to grind beans themselves. More than half the world's bean production is transformed into chocolate by just four multinationals: ADM, Cargill, Barry Callebaut and Nestlé. We all know Nestlé, but only professionals know the others – as these multinationals only sell to professionals. The bad news is that the groups who buy the beans have no real interest in aromas: when selecting the beans, they concentrate only on size and lack of flaws.

All the big companies that you've heard of offer a wide range of quality. But I find even their top of the

range 'single-estate beans' couvertures far less exciting than premium-quality ones from Valrhona, Pralus,
Cluizel, Amedei and Chocolaterie de l'Opera. The
problem is that chocolatiers would need to pay from
two to four times as much for these. And although
they want to keep their customers happy, they also like
to make money from their business.

Most customers enjoy and keep on buying chocolate that I would consider to be of inferior quality, thus
there is little incentive for the melters of couverture to
invest in a more expensive chocolate.

A 1929 advertisement from Nestlé for milk chocolate

Reading the ingredients list

As you know by now, the basic raw materials to make a dark chocolate bar are beans (*cocoa* on the ingredients list) and sugar. These were the ingredients used in the very first bar created by Fry's in 1847. Cocoa butter began to be added later that century, and lecithin after World War II. You also know that since Mayan times, vanilla was often added to the beans mixture. Today, most of the bars sold on the mass market have a much longer ingredients list – and reading labels of the bars in your local supermarket is an astonishing experience I recommend to any choco-explorer.

But what does cocoa percentage really mean? A 70% cocoa solids bar means that 70 per cent of the total weight comes from cocoa beans. For example, if you take a Pralus 70% bar, you will read 'cocoa, sugar, cocoa butter, lecithin and vanilla'. The 100g bar has been made by combining 2 oz beans, 1/4 oz cocoa butter and 1 oz sugar (the weight of the lecithin and vanilla are negligible).

In your mission to spy on as many labels as you can, do not forget that ingredients lists appear in decreasing quantities. You are not at the end of your surprises. The ingredients list of a very famous American milk chocolate bar starts with … 'milk chocolate'! Once you recover from the shock of discovering that milk chocolate is made with milk chocolate, I suggest you continue reading. Between a set of brackets you can then read: sugar, milk, cocoa butter, chocolate (finally we found you, dear beans!), lecithin and vanillin. *You* are expert enough now to know that 'chocolate' means 'cocoa'. But the fact that there is more sugar than cocoa is the final knife in the connoisseur's heart. In the US, you can legally describe as milk chocolate a product that has at least 10% cocoa content (that is, cocoa butter *and* beans). Our culprit here probably only contains 4% cocoa beans!

READ THAT WRAPPER

Take a look at the back of a bar you have at home. You will probably find most of the following words:

- Cocoa: ground cocoa beans (cocoa mass)

- Sugar.

- Cocoa butter: We know by now that most chocolate bars are made from ground beans and added cocoa butter. Usually the amount of cocoa butter is the equivalent of around 10 per cent of the weight of the ground beans.

- Lecithin: an emulsifier, added to ensure the ingredients are blended evenly.

- Vanilla/vanillin: Vanilla is the real thing. Any company using vanilla will probably announce it proudly as 'natural vanilla pods' or similar. Vanillin, on the other hand, is a cheap synthetic version of vanilla that pollutes the aromas the beans could have brought, or is added to hide the unpleasant bad aromas of cheap beans. In all cases, it means the brand decided to cut costs, and ultimately quality.

It is when you start reading ingredients such as lactose, whey powder, cocoa powder, malt extract, butter fat, emulsifiers (other than soy lecithin) that your alarm-bells should start ringing. Cocoa powder in a dark chocolate is very suspicious. Sadly, this does not prevent brands which include cocoa powder from pricing their product at a premium and calling it 'Finest dark chocolate' – and charging accordingly.

DID YOU KNOW?

There is a legal definition of chocolate related to the percentage of dry cocoa solids and the percentage of cocoa butter. They are not the same for every country. There are several different grades of chocolate, and these figures show the European Union and US regulations for standard (S) as well as fine (F) chocolate.

- Dark chocolate (S) must contain at least 35% dry cocoa solids (but 15% for 'sweet chocolate' in the US), while dark chocolate (F) must contain at least 43%.

- Milk chocolate (S) must contain at least 25% dry cocoa solids (but 20% in the UK, and 10% in the US), while fine milk chocolate must contain at least 30%.

Bars such as Cadbury Dairy Milk, Galaxy or Hershey must be labelled 'family milk chocolate' in the EU, as they don't contain enough chocolate to count as chocolate under these rules!

But what about the cocoa butter content? This substance is a commodity in its own right, used in cosmetics as well as chocolate. And it's expensive, at least ten times more than the vegetable fats used to replace it, known as cocoa butter equivalents (or CBEs).

Since a European ruling that up to 5 per cent of the total weight of a chocolate bar can be made of non-cocoa fats, many mass-market manufacturers are using CBEs. Do you want to know what they are? Take a deep breath ... palm oil, illipe (bomeo tallow or tengkawang), sal, shea, kokum gurgi and mango kernel. They don't sound very appetising or healthy to me!

Organic – is it worth it?

There is one final thing to be said about what to look for in chocolate. We live in an age when the word 'organic' makes people go weak at the knees. If a chocolate is organic, it is perceived as being healthier, less of a sin, and, therefore, more acceptable than the non-organic specimen next to it. Then there's the fact that organic and fair trade usually go hand in hand – so your money is helping to maintain a healthy environment *and* ensuring that co-operatives receive a good price for their product ... and many of us like to buy organic for just this reason.

The truth is that when you buy organic, you are buying a product certified to have been grown or made according to specific criteria: the beans, cocoa butter, and the sweetener (organic cane sugar or evaporated cane juice) have been grown without pesticides, are not genetically modified and are free from artificial additives. But I do wonder how organic bean brokers can afford *not* to spray their beans with pesticides when transporting them (and in all likelihood lose part of their shipment) when they sell them as cheaply as anyone else.

Whatever the criteria the ingredients conform to, the chain of production is no different to that of any old common or garden chocolate. It is not, as consumers believe, 'made by manufacturers who pick their own beans from co-operatives in producing countries'.

For a start, most organic brands do not begin with their own beans. They buy various couvertures (bulk chocolate) from big companies, selecting the ones they want to blend for each specific bar, melting, mixing, tempering and moulding them. They belong in the melters category.

The ingredients of the couverture they buy are, of course, organic, and the beans come from certified fair-trade co-operatives – but there are very few of these and producing a quality aromatic bean is not their priority. In fact, only two or three countries have had any of their bean production certified as organic – so you can imagine there's not much for the organic brands to choose from.

You may have noticed that within an organic dark range there are rarely more than two different types of plain bars (what I would consider 'real' chocolate). And this is the reason why – they just don't have enough beans to choose from. That's why most organic brands have a wide range of fancy bars, with various flavourings or mixed with orange, spices or nuts.

I have met a lot of organic 70% eaters on my chocolate courses. Some are 'exclusively organic products people', who usually indulge in the whole range, fancy bars included. But most of them are health-conscious people, who rejected supermarket milk chocolate long ago as too sweet and fatty, and moved to dark chocolate with a high percentage of cocoa solids. For them, when organic chocolate came on the scene it was another great boost for health.

I am always reminded of a 1997 meeting of the French chocolate society, the *Club des Croqueurs du Chocolat*, where we had a blind tasting of six samples of dark chocolate bars, all around 70% cocoa solids. None of us liked any of the chocolates we'd been given, unanimously describing them as 'astringent, acidic, harsh, grainy'. When their identities were revealed, it emerged that they were all organic.

I probably won't make any friends when I say this but every time I eat organic chocolate a little voice in my head says: 'Just let me give a cheque to the co-operative, but please don't make me eat this!' What I look for in chocolate is pleasure, and the day organic chocolate gives me the same thrills as fine chocolate, I will add it to my survival kit.

However, if you do really want to support these companies and like fruit and nut bars, the ones I recommend are Dagoba (an American brand), Valrhona and Vivani (Germany) and the quinoa and dark chocolate bar by Kaoka of France. Wherever you live, you can purchase them over the web (see page 211).

The future for organic

So what's the future for organic chocolate? As the demand for it increases, production is increasing too. Many medium-size bean producers all over the world sniffed a good opportunity two or three years ago and signed up for organic certification. Nearly all the producers I came across are about to be certified. This is very good news as it means that organic chocolate manufacturers will have more and more choice in terms of beans – so we can expect higher quality and more flavourful beans in the future.

But what I'm really interested in are the few companies that focus on the quality of the beans. Companies such as

Dagoba, aware of the quality gap in organic chocolate, are keen to improve the quality of their product right along the line, from fermentation to bar.

Pleasure and *profit*

Now that you have started to taste real chocolate, can you tell the difference between good and bad quality? Would you be prepared to pay more so that chocolatiers could afford to use the better-quality raw material that would push their prices up? They need to know you are on their side before they will take this risk.

But, as the revolution takes off, I am confident that more and more consumers will be aware of the quality it is possible to get, and will be more fussy. Eventually even the most profit-oriented chocolatiers will be pressed to demand finer ingredients from their suppliers – and more and more of us will be willing to pay for the pleasure.

And I hope that you will be there, to check who's producing the best chocolate!

CONNOISSEUR'S CORNER...

I eat more than a pound of chocolate a day, but none of it from the 95 per cent that makes up the majority of the world's chocolate. I only eat the best. When you have tasted quality, whether in food or wine, there's no going back.

Over the years I have created my database of 'chocopleasures', the same way one creates a music library. When I find a CD I like, I buy it and listen to it whenever I feel like it. My relationship with chocolate is similar but, as an expert, I try every new release, and take the time to analyse any that seems worth the trouble. I keep a track of all the chocolate that really deserves the name *chocolate* because of what I know about that company's production techniques, sourcing of beans, the chocolate's aromas, and, to some extent, whether I like them or not (I can't like everything – but I can recognise quality even if I do not like it!). I do this because I need to be able to refer to my database to check things I hear about different bars, or compare one bar with the sensations another one gives me.

Creating your database will open a whole new dimension in your journey in the chocolate world. The more attention you give chocolate when you taste it, the more you will be able to feel at any new tasting, the more you will be able to establish links with past tastings. A few examples of what you will be able to do as a connoisseur are:

- Recognise easily the brand of a chocolate tasted in 'blind conditions', even if it is the first time you've tasted that chocolate

- Be able to refer to other chocolates to compare them with the ones you are analysing (it has the same level of acidity as X but with a texture closer to Y and lingers much longer in the mouth than X or Y)

- Tell easily between 'good' and 'bad' – your taste buds are far more discerning than your wallet.

CHAPTER 7

·

Barʃ and bonbonʃ

*I*OFTEN TALK ABOUT chocolate and chocolates – to distinguish between chocolate bars and filled chocolates. As you know, the connoisseur concentrates on the bar. But perhaps, in *your* heart, you concentrate on the bonbon! There is nothing more thrilling for more than a few of us than a beautiful box of chocolates.

Let's look at the exciting developments bubbling away in the world of bars, and of bonbons.

Barʃ with a difference

I've been talking about the chocolate revolution. Now let's see how quality chocolate-makers are experimenting with new varieties of chocolate, and new labelling methods – along with some of the huge companies that supply the supermarkets.

In the last two decades we've seen startling changes in chocolate. The timeline opposite gives some idea of these seismic shifts.

As you can see, between the first ever bar and the 1980s, not a great deal happened. Once the technology was in place, nobody rocked the boat – but then when changes finally did begin to creep in (1985), everyone else followed suit. You can see the proliferation of fine-quality bars over the last 20 years. Also interesting to track is how the big brands have followed suit with similar bars, but not until five to ten years later! However, as the chocolate revolution speeds up, the larger brands have become much faster to copy successes.

1815: Van Houten isolates cocoa butter

1847: Fry invents the first solid chocolate bar: beans, sugar and cocoa butter

1879: Conching is invented, improving texture and coaxing more flavour from the beans

1911: Bonnat launch two foil-wrapped dark chocolates

1920: The first bar affordable for all is available

1984: Bonnat introduce single-estate bars

1984: Bonnat introduces a 50% milk bar

1986: Valrhona's first bar, Guanaja, is released

1989: Lindt's 70% Noir

chart continues

1992: Lindt's country-of-origin bars

1994: Weiss & Chaudun's dark bar with cocoa nibs
Bonnat's Hacienda el Rosario (the first plantation bar)

1998–9: Michel Cluizel's Nuanciers
Valrhona's Gran Couva (the second plantation bar)

2000: Michel Cluizel's Hacienda Concepcion (plantation bar)

2001: Lindt's dark bar with cocoa nibs
Bonnat's milk, 65%, country-of-origin bar
Lindt's 99% bar

2002: Michel Cluizel's Hacienda Los Ancones (plantation bar)
Valrhona's Amanpakia (plantation bar)

2003: Domori's Puertomar, the first pure Criollo bar

2004: Michel Cluizel's Hacienda Mangaro (country of origin)

Every year, the mass market brands launch bars with new and dramatic flavour combinations – so nearly every filling or combination of tastes you could imagine seem to grace the supermarket shelves. And there's another trend. Instead of just the traditional range of milk, dark and many different varieties of nutty, fruity, fancy, flavoured and filled chocolate bars, you might be seeing new additions on the shelves of your local supermarket or deli. They are plain and look very much, at least in terms of the labelling, like the ones we see at the more expensive end of the market.

What's on the label?

Once, 70% chocolate was the reigning favourite, and for many people it still is. But percentages are no longer the *only* way to distinguish between different varieties of dark and milk chocolate. And, in fact, there are more and more different types of plain chocolate bars creeping onto the shelves, with very different pieces of information on the label: country of origin, plantation, bean variety and vintage (but not, sometimes, the percentage).

You know, now, how much difference there can be between different varieties of cocoa bean. But it doesn't end there. Think of wine again. Many of the grape varieties that are grown to make wine have been planted in different wine-growing regions. For example, you might find the same grape growing in parts of Australia, California and France. The resulting wines, because of varying elements in the grapes' environment (the *terroir*) and treatment, are extremely different. The same goes for chocolate. So the region or plantation where the beans come from is quite important knowledge!

Origins

The different brands label their chocolate in several ways, giving more or less information:

- Plantation bars, such as Valrhona's Gran Couva – denoting beans which come exclusively from just one plantation (a few acres of land).

- Single-estate bars, such as Chuao, which is a region of Venezuela.

- Country-of-origin bars, such as Lindt's Ghana, Madagascar and Ecuador bars. These beans come from anywhere within the named country.

As far as I'm concerned, the more you know, the better. I can tell you from my own tastings that bars made from Venezuelan beans are better than those made from Ecuadorian beans, but the truth is that bad beans can come from Venezuela, and vice versa. (Just as you can buy cheap, horrendous French wine – the country or state alone is not enough to mean anything, in terms of quality.) If you look for labels with more information, rather than less, you will have a clearer idea of what you're actually buying.

As we saw at the start of this book, there are moves for wine terminology to be used more and more in the chocolate world. Some are for this, others against – but it is certainly true that some *ideas* from the wine world are useful, and being taken up by chocolate makers and plantation owners with gusto – for example, protecting the origin of the wine with legislation (in wine, it's called AOC, *Appellation d'Origine Controlée*), meaning 'guarantee of controlled origin'). The region of Chuao is a label of quality.

THE CHUAO BEANS

Chuao is a coastal region north of Caracas in Venezuela, well known for its quality beans. It is said that in the seventeenth century the Chuao plantation was given by an aristocratic Spanish woman to the Jesuits so they could make money from the cocoa to build schools and churches. Chuao, isolated by the mountains and the sea, has unique beans that have never been cross-pollinated with other varieties, and these are fermented and sun-dried according to specific local criteria. They are very sought-after. Several high-quality brands sell Chuao single-origin bars, but Amedei from Italy signed a contract a few years ago with the Chuao plantation, buying all their beans for the next few years. This means that legally, as with AOC in wine, Amedei are now the only company who can use the name Chuao for a chocolate. The first Amedei Chuao chocolate arrived on our shelves in 2004. Amedei pay above the odds for Chuao beans in order to ensure quality and you can be assured that if you buy an Amedei Chuao bar, it really will contain the wonderful Chuao beans!

In 1998 Valrhona took the associations with wine even further, and launched a bar whose label had the same layout and vocabulary as used on fine wine labels – including information on the plantation, the origin of the bean, the vintage and the type of chocolate. You will only find the percentage on the back – in small letters! Many other companies have followed suit since those days, and today you can often find this bean-related information on a label.

Vintage (or 'grand cru') is another wine concept that has been increasingly applied to specialist chocolates in recent years. Vintage denotes the year of the cocoa crop, and pays homage to the fact that cocoa beans (and therefore the chocolate made from them) can and should taste different from one year to another. Supermarket brands, on the other hand, spend years perfecting their formula – creating a recipe for chocolate that means the same bar will taste exactly the same at all times.

More and more, labels include tasting notes on them – a brief list of the flavours that you might be able to distinguish. Don't take them too seriously, but use them for inspiration!

Champions of the chocolate bar

I have wonderful contacts in the chocolate world, many of whom are hardly known so far – they are working behind the scenes to bring the best out of chocolate, to reinvent chocolate. Here are some of the most important.

Steve De Vries is a former glassblower who became interested in chocolate in 1999 after visiting Costa Rica. He returned home to Denver with 66 lbs of cocoa beans in his luggage! Steve made his first chocolate in his kitchen, using a grain grinder he'd had for 25 years. His first attempt was a crude, gritty product that was nevertheless swimming with flavours he'd never before come across in any industrial chocolate.

Since then he has worked relentlessly to learn more and more about chocolate. He's visited factories and plantations, experimented with new drying methods, and followed botanists round the Mexican jungle (hunting for 'wild Criollo genes'!). He follows the most advanced courses on the technology of chocolate and attends the latest symposiums. He is passionate about improving and optimising the flavour of chocolate, and is currently experimenting with different chocolate fermenting, drying and tempering methods to this end. He is even revising the traditional texture of chocolate.

He says: 'My approach is to try to make the best chocolate *possible* and a large part of that is to discover what is possible, with very little if any consideration for practicality. And that is why I will happily continue to do things like sun-drying cocoa beans in the manner I've seen in Venezuela, and try to make a chocolate with no added cocoa butter, or vanilla, and with a new texture, as in the 1890s.'

Steve works alone and his chocolate will not be on the market until 2005, but his discoveries will, I believe, be influential.

Claudio Corallo created, in partnership with Pralus, Pralus's plantation bar. Like me, Claudio studied tropical agronomy, and at one time owned a plantation producing coffee of an extremely high quality. But the political situation in Zaïre, where he was based, became so bad that he had to leave, losing everything. He went to São Tomé and started all over again with a new coffee plantation – but this one also had cocoa trees. He now has several plantations growing both coffee and cocoa. His approach is a perfectionist one, working with the locals, and running his business as a co-operative.

Claudio also makes his own chocolate, working miracles with beans that are generally regarded as not of the highest quality – São Tomé has only Forastero trees. He is taking a fresh look at the fermentation and drying process, just as Steve is, to see if different or more intense flavours can be created with different methods.

I got to see some of the process at firsthand when I was staying with his family. They left three plates out in the living room, each holding different cocoa nibs, coded and named. They were there to be tasted at random, and each time any one of us tasted a bean, we were to jot down notes on it. We would then gather to discuss our tasting notes and opinion of each. Claudio is putting his cocoa beans through the same painstaking selection process through which he discovered his superb coffee. (And the process? Each day for five days, he drinks coffee made from the beans of just one tree. After five days, he decides whether to keep the tree – or cut it down!)

He now has a range sold exclusively at Fortnum & Mason in London: three plain chocolates, two with nibs, and the fancy range with ginger, orange or coffee. Every week Claudio air-freights me different chocolates – he is constantly experimenting with processes or different ratios of ingredients, and his chocolate is very much a work in progress. But the improvements he is making, and the amazing results he gets, suggest to me that in years to come Claudio will be one of the biggest names in chocolate.

Domori: The Italian company Domori, founded by Gianluca, is reviving the pure Criollo bean in partnership with the owners of a plantation, grafting Criollos from a gene bank in Trinidad onto local Trinitarios. They plotted a planting schedule that will allow them to release a new bar from their plantation every year, made with a different variety of bean every time. Domori chocolates are much more easily

available than those of Steve De Vries and Claudio Corallo –
you can mail order them from anywhere in the world.

The path these three people have chosen to take perfectly
summarises what I believe will be the next trend in the
chocolate world, and as a connoisseur, you have to be up to
date with the latest!

Revolution…or revival?

Why are these revolutionaries so special, then? Do they also
use revolutionary machinery? To produce a chocolate they
want to be different to any they've tasted in the past, they
question each step in the process from bean to bar, rejecting
or revising it as they consider necessary. Bean varieties, fermentation, drying, the ingredients and even the type of
machinery used are all up for scrutiny.

Steve, for example, has travelled the world to buy
machinery that looks as if it's been stolen from a museum.
He is convinced that old machines were designed to get the
most of the bean's potential, and that industrialisation,
focusing on the speed and volume, doesn't pay enough
attention to flavour. Others look at the old machines for
inspiration – Domori and Corallo have both invented their
own machines.

And the reason for this old-is-new trend? A few vision-
aries realised there must be more to chocolate than the
mass-produced kind, and went about trying to create
chocolate that seems truly different to the smooth and
creamy, sugary and vanillin-enriched bars that are so
prevalent. Using old machinery, a producer is more likely to
be able to treat the beans with the respect they deserve, coaxing as much flavour out of them as possible, allowing them
some individuality in their texture.

The mélangeur is an old-style grinding machine

Along with this machinery comes the revival of various types of trees. Domori, Corallo, and Steve work on the quality of the bean from the plantations all the while. They are not alone – and growing numbers of chocolate makers are now going back to the source, either encouraging growers to revive old varieties, or also buying their own plantations.

In each case, these chocolate makers care more for flavour than for time or money, aiming to produce the best chocolate in the world. And what I have experienced so far is indeed totally new – the aromas, the flavours, the texture, often the pleasure.

The bars of the future, enriched by so much innovation and experimentation every step of the way, are likely to be even more amazing than today's. If you're like me, you might find it hard to wait!

The best bonbons

As a purist – and as you've seen – I tend to encourage people to taste chocolate rather than chocolates. Bars, instead of bonbons, in short. Chocolate contains the full array of flavours and is the equivalent of fine wine, coffee, or tea, while chocolates are a new and different product, of which chocolate is only one ingredient, and not even the major one.

A chocolate connoisseur is unlikely to eat many chocolates. For example, from the one pound of chocolate I eat a day, barely 1 oz is chocolates – the rest is either plain bars or bars with nuts. As far as I'm concerned, a bar of chocolate is the real thing, cocoa in its most concentrated form, and chocolates are just a diluted (or even polluted) form of chocolate.

If that sounds extreme, I hasten to say that a good filled chocolate *can* be a divine experience. You can probably guess my criteria by now. If the chocolatier is a quality freak, fuelled by real passion for their product, then yes, a wonderful filled chocolate is possible. Of course, as with chocolate bars, there are fine-and poor-quality filled chocolates. As a connoisseur, you need to know the tips to recognise glitter from gold.

Bonbon bonanza

There is no legal definition of chocolates as there is for chocolate (see pages 123–4). Almost anything sweet that has a filling and is coated with chocolate ends up being called a chocolate. Chocolates can, however, be separated into four main categories, based on the composition of the filling. Each of these may come coated in either milk, white or dark chocolate.

- *Ganaches:* these have a soft chocolate filling made with pure chocolate and cream (and many other ingredients when flavoured, or there's a need for a long shelf life).

- *Pralinés* (pronounced 'pralin-ey'): the filling of these looks like the texture of peanut butter, and is made from a mixture of caramel ground together with roasted almonds and/or hazelnuts. Cocoa butter, dark chocolate or milk chocolate may also be added to the filling, influencing the texture. If the filling includes only cocoa butter, it will remain the colour of the praliné. Beware of mistaking *pralines* for *pralinés*. The former is a Belgian word used for all filled chocolates. *Praliné* is the French word (adopted by professionals around the world) used to describe a chocolate made with the mixture described above. The word is also used to refer to the raw material of the praliné mixture.

- *Marzipan:* this filling is a mixture of roasted almonds or hazelnuts ground with sugar (not caramel this time – hence its whitish colour).

- *Others:* I call this category the choco-candies, as in most cases there is not a gram of chocolate in the filling.

Belonging to this category are nougat, Turkish delight, caramels, fudges and English creams.

These are the chocolates you'll be able to pick up at the counter of any chocolatier. Later in this chapter I'll give you a guided tour of a typical chocolates counter (see pages 149–50).

CHALLENGING CREAMS

As my chocolate education is mainly French, I find the ever-popular English rose and violet creams to be a major challenge! The first time I cut one in two and tasted the filling alone (a connoisseur tasting method – see pages 150–52), I had the feeling I had swallowed soap (albeit a fine one!). I guess that, as with Marmite, you need to grow up eating them to love them. Every year, Buckingham Palace orders sumptuous fabric boxes of chocolates for foreign presidents on official visits. I wish I could see the face of the French one biting his first cream!

Making chocolates great

Chocolate is a complex, wayward and fascinating ingredient to work with. Many French chocolatiers have fallen in love with chocolate and left the pastry world to devote their career to it. It is a wonderful arena for a creative mind – but it demands far more than just quality ingredients. This pursuit requires extraordinary skill.

So, when looking for fine chocolates, you need to look both at the quality of the ingredients the chocolatier or manufacturer is using, and how well they are used. You might call it looking for a spark of genius.

Cocoa butter, for example, which gives chocolate its high fat content and melting quality, is unstable at best. The chocolatier needs to understand the way it behaves when heated or when mixed with other ingredients.

But there is naturally more to a filled chocolate than just mixing up the ingredients. I call chocolatiers 'alchemists of pleasure'. Like a 'nose' in the perfume world, the chocolatier is always sniffing out different aromas, creating new pieces of art. How well the chocolatier masters the art of mixing chocolate with other ingredients determines to a large extent whether or not he stands out from the crowd.

Combining several perfectly matching or interestingly harmonious scents can create something sublime, even otherworldly, in the right hands. Take French chocolatier Jacques Genin. Jacques is one of the most talented chocolate makers I have ever met. Based in Paris, he sells only to people who 'get' his product – in fact, you have to pass his tasting test before you are allowed to buy from him! He also supplies the best hotels and restaurants in Paris (…but only once they have passed his test!).

Jacques' tiny workshop is almost impossible to find: there is no door handle, no sign, not even a number. And yet he is known as one of the world's best chocolatiers. He is a perfectionist, and loves chocolate deeply – not only its taste but also its feeling, its shine and its texture.

He is so familiar with the aromas of the chocolate he uses, he knows so well how each couverture will express itself when transformed into a ganache, that you could say that the aromas live within him. Like a perfumer, he intuits the flavour associations, the interactions and harmonies between them. When preparing a ganache, he knows the dance the aromas will perform.

Jacques has given me a huge insight into the world of the bonbon. His are the only mint or ginger ganaches I will eat. I hated all ganaches made with tea (Earl Grey, Lapsong Souchong, Jasmine, and so forth) before meeting him. But with Jacques as the 'scientific genius', and in collaboration with tea taster and expert Lydia Gaultier, we created a line of 'tea ganaches' using teas no chocolatier had used so far. These treated both the tea and chocolate ingredients with respect, so that neither flavours were stifled.

Lydia suggested the teas, I proposed the chocolates to combine with each one, and Jacques experimented, changing tea concentrations and infusion times, and tailoring the proportions of different chocolates in the blend. Together we created a mini-range of three ganaches, far more exciting and palatable than the tea ganaches found in most chocolate shops. Our ganaches flavoured with 'Butterfly of Taiwan', 'Qimen Imperial' and 'Bancha Hojicha' were a novelty and a delight. They became part of Jacques' signature range – and are also included in the chocolate box offered to VIP guests at Alain Ducasse's hotels and restaurants.

TEA, COFFEE AND CHOCOLATE

Now you know about tea and chocolate – they *can* mix, when done well! But what about drinking tea while eating chocolate – or that favourite combination, coffee and chocolate?

I know many people love the two together, but I don't feel that either can be fully appreciated when they're mixed. The sugar in the chocolate (and worse if there is a fruit or alcohol flavouring) will hide the flavours of the coffee. What brings you pleasure when having chocolate with coffee is the sugar content of the chocolate. The aromas of the chocolate are drowned out by the coffee. Coffee kills the chocolate.

But having said this, I have been spotted eating chocolate and drinking tea at the same time... If you love to combine your chocolate with a hot drink, it's not the end of the world. But if you want to taste *all* the flavours, I suggest you savour your coffee and your chocolate singly, rather than together.

The art of the chocolatier

When making a bar, a chocolatier has to intuit which blends will work together, selecting couvertures to combine and working out the ideal proportions to use. If they just melt a readymade couverture (as many do), there's no need for talent or creativity.

A chocolatier making filled chocolates has to follow the same path as those making fine chocolate bars, but the task is even more complex. By now you know the wide variety of flavours found in chocolate: flowers, teas, alcohols, spices, fruits, nuts and more. But to create a filled chocolate you must think how the filling will taste with the coating. What flavour filling, what flavour coating?

Smelling different teas, a top chocolatier will suddenly feel inspired and think, 'Hmmm, this Qimen Imperial tea is nice, it will go better with dark than milk chocolate. The tea has clear leather notes in the attack and spicy notes at the end of the mouth. I will use a mix of the Valrhona chocolates Guanaja (classical, slightly masculine, elegant chocolate to carry the leather note) and Manjari (its acidity will enhance the shy, spicy notes of the tea)'.

A chocolatier must, of course, know his basic aromas (he will have a choco-database just as I do) and concentrate on creating the right combination in the right proportions, without looking at cost. His goal is to create a delight, a masterpiece. But there are limits. Not all combinations of flavour are possible in a filled chocolate.

Choosing the right couverture to go with each filling means having a good variety of couvertures to play with. Although you have seen the care that a good chocolatier will put into choosing the right chocolate to go with each filling, the reality is that few chocolatiers will bother. A lot of them, along with the manufacturers, use at the most one or two different chocolate couvertures as a basic ingredient to produce all their range – which means that they have only one or two aromatic palettes to work from. This is a great loss, as making superb chocolates is much more complex a matter than just putting milk chocolate with one range of fillings, and dark with another. And there is no guarantee that they have chosen good-quality couvertures or flavourings.

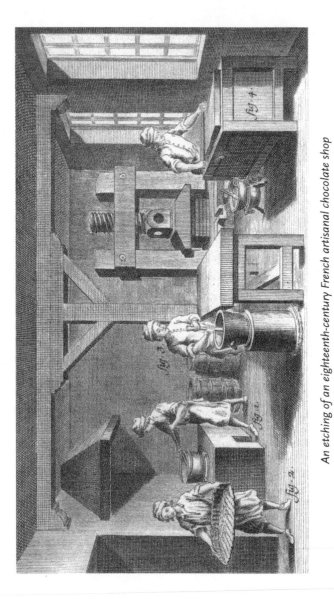

An etching of an eighteenth-century French artisanal chocolate shop

Becoming a chocolate connoisseur

And what about those fillings? A committed chocolatier views these as a fantastic journey into new worlds of aroma and flavour. Go into a chocolate shop and look at the filled chocolates counter, or open a pre-prepared box of chocolates. There's a whole world in there. But have the chocolates been made by a truly bold, creative chocolatier or one who copies others?

There are some basics that any chocolatier will have: plain ganaches, pralinés, marzipans. The creative ones usually have a wide range of combinations of flavours you are not used to seeing (and may not even have heard of!), such as Tonka beans or basil and yuzu ganaches. To see if a combination is pleasant, the only reliable way to test is to taste. Some combinations are really just marketing tools, used to cause interest (or horror): tobacco, cheese, or truffles for example!

Apart from looking at the range of fillings, though, how can you test the quality of a filled chocolate? Here is where my four-chocolate test comes into its own.

The four-chocolate test

When you find a new chocolatier, the ideal situation is to go into the shop armed with a list of questions. If you know what you want, this should prevent you from buying the wrong chocolates. Hunting down and selecting the right chocolates, the *best* chocolates, is far from a waste of time or money. When evaluating a chocolatier, you don't need to buy the whole range. A few carefully selected samples will tell you all you need to know about the entire range. Here are my tips...

Ask the person behind the counter to sell you one of each of the following. Use the exact words, to make sure that he or she understands that you know exactly what you want. (If the sales person doesn't know, ask for the chocolatier!) Don't accept any alternatives for this exercise. You will need:

1. **Ganaches.** A plain milk ganache (no alcohol whatsoever) and a plain dark ganache (no alcohol whatsoever).

2. **Marzipan.** A marzipan (not flavoured – ensure there is no pistachio or alcohol added – not even 'just a little bit'!).

3. **Pralinés.** A praliné (also not flavoured – you don't want chocolate added to the filling), plain.

4. **Specialities.** Two of their house specialties or two chocolates they are proud of (they usually carry their logo).

Go home, and prepare to taste your chocolates alone and in the right tasting conditions (see Chapter 4)… as what follows is *not* sexy to look at!

When you are ready for the tasting, proceed as follows.

First, you need to find out the quality of the raw material used (mainly chocolate, but also the nut-based ingredients). This will help you to determine the quality of the chocolate maker's whole range.

1. The ganaches
The chocolate used to make the fillings is usually different from the one used for the coating. To start with, take a dark ganache (it's better to taste the one with less sugar first). Scrape the filling out of the chocolate coating. Keep the coating for later.

The ganache filling is the closest you can get to unadulterated chocolate. In a proper ganache, you shouldn't be able to taste the cream – it's just there to give it a smooth texture. If you can detect it, go back to the shop and ask for a fresher version (don't erase that chocolatier from your database just yet!). If the ganache is grainy, it means the chocolate maker failed to tame the ingredients. But again, be lenient. It happens to everybody at times. Go back to the shop and exchange it. If the texture is fine, move on.

Look at the ganache as you do when tasting a chocolate bar (see Chapter 4). Evaluate its texture and the aromatic palette (its notes and evolution over time). As you progress, you will eventually (as I do now) be able to recognise the chocolate used to make the ganache, even if it is a blend.

And what about the chocolate casing of the ganache? This is one more sign of the quality choices a chocolatier makes. In many cases, as I've said, all dark coatings are made with the same chocolate, and all milk coatings with the same milk chocolate. A coating has to be as neutral and fine as possible, so it doesn't 'pollute' the flavour you want to savour! Of course, the vast majority of chocolatiers cut costs on the coating, and use poor chocolate. Sniff the casing… and then taste it on its own. Do you detect sugar or vanillin? If not, you may be dealing with a quality chocolatier. The casing should be as good as the filling, as in the end, they mix in the mouth.

2. The praliné

Again, taste the filling first without the coating. Are the nuts good quality? Are they burned or rancid-tasting? Is it too sweet? Too plain? If you answer yes to any of these, it means the chocolatier went for cheap praliné ingredients. And now you know: the rest of the range has most probably been created with the same inattention to quality.

3. *The marzipan*

Is it juicy, slightly grainy and quartz-like (this is a good sign) or dry, crumbly and shiny white? A good marzipan is made with a ratio of sixty per cent nuts to forty per cent sugar, but the vast majority are actually more like forty per cent nuts to sixty per cent sugar. Can you taste the difference?

4. *The signature chocolates*

Even the chocolatiers we have leniently described here as *traditional* have at least one chocolate they designed and are very proud of. For any chocolatier in the French tradition, it is likely to be a plain ganache carrying their logo in gold. For others, it might be a revived traditional recipe.

Taste the chocolates, looking for creativity. If the chocolate is a simple combination of a standard good quality 70% blend with cream, for example, it will probably be good... but not exciting.

DISTINCTIVE SIGNATURE?

What are signature chocolates, exactly? Let's take Fortnum & Mason as an example, where the signature chocolates are the rose and violet creams, and the champagne and finest truffles.

The creams are produced exclusively for the shop with the finest natural essential oils. The exclusivity makes them signature chocolates. The truffles, on the other hand, have become signature chocolates because they are bestsellers.

Appalled by the alcoholic truffles (a serious no-no

to a connoisseur), I decided to create some more signature chocolates to try and make the selection a little
more classy.

The 'Finest Selection' comprises four plain truffles, two milk and two dark. They contain only cream
and chocolate, no alcohol or preservatives, and the
finest chocolate couvertures. Each one of the dark
truffles is made with a different single-origin chocolate, Madagascar and Venezuela. The couvertures
used have the same cocoa solids percentage, but a
totally different aromatic palette. The two milk truffles are made with two fine and very different milk
chocolates, creating two elegant ganaches, one with
hints of fudge, and the other tasting of fresh full-fat
milk.

The four-chocolate test is a great (and inexpensive) way to
find out if you really want to commit yourself to a whole box
of this chocolatier's range, and it will tell you whether the raw
material your chocolatier is using is good enough to justify
further investment.

Don't hesitate to complete your test with some questions.
A good chocolatier is proud of his work, and will not hesitate to share with you which couvertures he uses, the story
behind the name given to one of his chocolates, or the choice
of a flavouring. Give him a few hints of your move into the
world of chocolate, and, if the queue is not too long, the
frankness of his answers and the quality of the time devoted
to your conversation should give you an indicator of whether
he is a businessman or an artist.

Finding your way around the chocolate shop

Perhaps you're a regular visitor already, buying up lots of filled chocolates. Or maybe you decide that it's finally time to pull open the heavy glass doors and step into the hushed interior of a chocolate shop you've never visited. Wherever you're coming from, you now know what to ask for on your first visit and how to taste what you've bought.

But of course there's a lot more on offer than just the few chocolates on your checklist. For example, if you come into Fortnum & Mason, you'll find the chocolates grouped by categories: nutty (plain chocolate and nuts), creams, marzipans, alcohol ganaches, fruity ganaches, pralinés, and Swiss, French and Belgian chocolates in separate cases – as often customers have a preference for one country's choco-tradition.

If you want to buy more than just the ones I've recommended to start with, here are a few of my favourite fruit and nut combinations – a delightful and healthy complement to chocolate bars.

- Milk chocolate with hazelnuts

- Dark chocolate and almonds

- Orange and dark chocolate

- Lemon or yuzu and milk chocolate

- Candied ginger marries well with either milk or dark chocolate – but only when it is made with fine ingredients.

Any other fruit pollutes the chocolate taste, in my opinion.

And what if you have been given a box of chocolates? Or what if your box doesn't have a menu? Well, you can do a blind taste test – you don't need to be told what the flavours are! Use the methodology outlined above. You might find that they're not all to your taste, though. Sadly, people tend not to give me boxes of chocolates as a gift – nobody is brave enough to buy for a professional chocolate buyer! A pity – as I love to discover new creations. On the bright side, though, a connoisseur will generally know what they want, and once you know your way around filled chocolates a little more, you'll be able to walk into a chocolate shop, look around, and know exactly what suits you best, just as I do.

Truffles

MAKES ABOUT 4 DOZEN TRUFFLES

As you can now buy fine chocolate couverture, you can make your own divine truffles, and present them attractively in gift boxes for your friends. This recipe comes from Cyril Prudhomme, a talented chocolatier I worked with at Ladurée in Paris.

20 ounces Valrhona Caraque chocolate couverture,
or other fine chocolate
10 ounces Valrhona Caraïbe chocolate couverture,
or other fine chocolate
2 cups light cream
¼ cup honey
1 vanilla bean, split open
2 tablespoons good-quality unsalted butter, diced
cocoa powder (the best you can find, such as
Valrhona or Scharffen Berger)

THE CHOCOLATE CONNOISSEUR

1. Finely chop the chocolate and put it in a bowl large enough to hold all the other ingredients, too.

2. Bring the cream, honey and the vanilla bean to a boil in a saucepan over medium heat. Remove the vanilla bean; pour the hot cream mixture, one-third at a time, over the chocolate, whisking each time to incorporate (but avoid getting air into the mixture). An elastic texture and shine show the chocolate mixture is ready. (Alternatively, place the chocolate in a blender and pour all the hot cream mixture over the chocolate and mix for 3 minutes.)

3. When the chocolate mixture is 95–104°F, blend in the butter.

4. Let cool to 72–75°F. Whisk the mixture lightly to add a little air, mold into about 1½-inch balls, chill until firm, and coat with cocoa powder. Eat immediately!

Note: The truffles can be refrigerated for three to four days, but for the best flavor, bring them to room temperature before eating.

Whether you stick to your beloved filled chocolates or prefer bars, the most important thing is to use the tips in this book to hunt for the best quality within your own preferences. This will mean that you'll have to look for the chocolatiers using fine ingredients and, consequently, will have to pay more than in the past – but believe me, the pleasure will be a concentrated one!

CHAPTER 8

Chocolate: friend or foe?

THE TASTING EXERCISES in Chapter 4 may have come easily to you. But if they didn't, one obstacle may have been the way that you think about chocolate. Is it your friend, or your enemy? Is it good for you, or bad? Do you love eating it, but hate yourself when you do so? Most people have mixed feelings about chocolate.

When I run chocolate tasting workshops, I always ask people about the feelings and thoughts they associate with it.

They love it, that's for sure. It makes them feel good because of the happy memories it nearly always revives (plus it contains chemicals that boost your happiness quota – see pages 165–7).

But it also makes them feel guilty, and bad – and that's because of the many myths and misunderstandings about chocolate that have built up over generations and still abound. Luckily, most of these are untrue. In this chapter I will help you to look at your own emotional relationship with chocolate and discover what is holding you back from becoming a connoisseur – and what you can do about it.

Chocolate on the couch...

If I asked you to close your eyes and imagine yourself biting into a piece of chocolate, your mind would immediately conjure up a bar with which you are already very familiar – and, as you love chocolate, the one you think of is bound to be a personal favourite. You can smell it, taste it, feel it in your mouth. You can even experience the warm sensations it will bring as you savour it, the aftertaste it will leave – and, more than likely, that awful sense of guilt after you've eaten it.

This simple exercise reveals a lot about the psychological obstacles that may be holding you back in your chocolate education. Firstly, you already have your favourite chocolates – your mind is made up about what chocolate should taste like. Secondly, you have preconceptions about chocolate that make you feel guilty when you eat it – usually that it is an indulgence that you don't deserve (because of cost, frivolity, calories, or the fact that it's a reward you haven't 'earned').

When I offer someone a new chocolate to try, I can tell immediately from their reaction whether they are weighed down with psychological baggage – associations they need to dump – or whether they are openminded, receptive and adventurous: ready to try something new.

Before any of us can move on, we have to understand why we feel the way we do about our chocolate, and much of this is to do with what psychologists call 'cultural references'. In the same way that we learn language and idiosyncrasies of dialect and vocabulary – according to where we were raised and by whom, and who we have mixed with as we've grown up – it is the influence of family and friends that leads us towards certain types of chocolate. This influence is so strong that whole nations have specific chocolate preferences.

In Chapter 1 I listed the favourite tastes of Europeans – mostly sweetened milk chocolate (except the French).

We like it because it's become traditional and it's the chocolate to which we are introduced at a very young age, but we are also biologically programmed to like this kind of chocolate. As babies our first food is our mother's milk (or a formula imitation) – which is fatty and slightly sweet. Most mass-market chocolate is also a combination of fat and sugar. So falling in love with it as a child couldn't come more naturally!

If, as you have matured, you have developed a more savoury palate, and are no longer so attracted to sweet chocolate, moving on from these early chocolate associations will come easily. If you have a sweet tooth, it's going to be harder – but a dark chocolate that's packed with flavours will take your mind off its lack of sugar and milky mildness.

On top of simply liking a certain type of chocolate are your own memories. So recognising that you like what you like 'because it's the chocolate I've always eaten', or 'it's the taste I associate with rewards – and it makes me feel good about myself' can help you to put these thoughts aside, in an imaginary locked box, while you get on with the job of tasting something new.

But there are still those feelings of guilt to tackle.

Take a moment to think about the three main thoughts you immediately associate with chocolate and write them down. For example, 'it gives you spots', 'it makes you fat', 'it's naughty but nice!' Now add another seven common beliefs about chocolate. For example, 'it's unhealthy', 'it's an aphrodisiac', 'it causes cravings', 'it causes mood swings', 'it's bad for your teeth', 'it's addictive', 'it's high in caffeine'. (Of course, you may have other ideas for your list.) Now write down the four main reasons you feel guilty when you have chocolate. Why does it make you feel so bad about yourself?

Some of the thoughts on your list have probably suggested chocolate is sinful in some way. It's nothing new – chocolate has always been controversial. Back in Chapter 1 we saw how the Spanish women of St Cristobal de las Casas were banned from drinking hot chocolate during high mass. But then, between 1650 and the late 1860s, it was recommended by doctors and pharmacologists as a health aid. Today the controversy rages on. We have people telling us it's healthy, and others telling us it's bad for us.

The media would not have to keep repeating the message that 'chocolate is good for health' if we weren't so severely handicapped by the myths that surround it. These myths are a major obstacle to becoming a connoisseur, as they present themselves as soon as you start to bite into a chocolate – and this actually 'pollutes' the palate with enzymes.

Close your eyes and remember the last time you had a chocolate for pleasure. Guilt probably flashed through your head as you bought the chocolate, possessed you as you took your first bite, and reminded you, while you were trying to enjoy your mouthful, that you were 'sinning'. Guilt spoils any sensual delight you hoped to derive, and normally gets worse when you have swallowed the chocolate – leaving you with just guilt and no physical pleasure.

We perpetuate these beliefs about chocolate by passing them from one generation to the next. From an early age our parents teach us not to eat too much chocolate, and to ask permission before helping ourselves to it. But they also use it as a reward, or a carrot to entice us to behave ourselves or do our chores... It is even the first culprit called to blame when, as children, we feel sick or have a headache ('You shouldn't have eaten so much chocolate!'). As a result, chocolate becomes a forbidden food, and something children are bound to try to sneak from the kitchen. I guess I was born to become a connoisseur as I had a quite exceptional mother who praised the yummy properties of chocolate – and she was the one who stole my precious stock!

DID YOU KNOW?

It is impossible to taste chocolate properly when negative thoughts about it are lurking in your mind. These negative thoughts provoke the secretion of enzymes that cause an acid environment in your mouth, so your taste buds will not be neutral and ready for analysis. Any conclusion you reach will be inaccurate. You may even eliminate from your choco database one that would have been worthy of your survival kit!

But what about all those myths – the spots, the weight gain, the dental rot? If we are talking about 'vegelate' – fat, sugar and flavouring – all those health risks may well be true. But real chocolate does not harm your health. Just look at the evidence … (and remember, we are talking about pure dark chocolate bars, not your fancy truffles or favourite milk bar!).

• It's good for your health

Back in the sixteenth century, the Spanish, who were as obsessed with health and diet as we are today, regarded chocolate as a health food. Chocolate bars are good for you – and here's why:

Chocolate fat is not all bad!

Cocoa butter – the fat that occurs naturally in cocoa beans – contains a lot of fat. The good news is that it is 'good' fat, as is found in olive oil. Typically, there's 1½ oz of fat in a 3½ oz 72% bar of dark chocolate. Of this, ¼ oz will be saturated fat. But the ⅕ oz of unsaturated fat are composed of oleic acid, which raises HDL cholesterol (the type that helps to protect your heart) and lowers levels of unhealthy LDL cholesterol. Of the saturated fat, more than half is composed of stearic acid, a fatty acid that is converted by the liver to more healthy oleic acid.

And, although a quarter of the fat in chocolate is palmitic acid – the dominant fatty acid in beef, pork, and dairy (and the fat believed to be most culpable in raising cholesterol levels and contributing to atherosclerosis) – studies show that its effect is neutral in chocolate.

It's packed with minerals

It's true! A 3½ oz dark chocolate bar provides the following percentages of your daily mineral requirements:

Iron 20%	Phosphorous 30%
Magnesium 33%	Copper 25%
Potassium 27%	Calcium 13%

It's a major source of antioxidants

In a US Department of Agriculture list of high-antioxidant foods, dark chocolate actually comes out on top – with 13,120 ORAC (Oxygen Radical Absorbance Capacity) units, nearly twice the antioxidants in milk chocolate, and more than double the ORAC units in the next best thing, the humble prune! These antioxidants are like a troop of bomb disposal experts, whose job it is to diffuse the free radicals that cause premature ageing and destruction in the body's cells.

Not only does chocolate contain high concentrations of antioxidants, it contains the highest quality of the lot – the same flavonoids (polyphenol antioxidants that are 100 times stronger than vitamin C) as red wine and green tea (credited with reducing heart attack risk and cancer), of which one, proanthocyanidin, is one of the few compounds that can cross the blood-brain barrier to protect brain tissue. The same compound also blocks the formation of enzymes in the body that cause inflammation and arthritis; and it acts as an antihistamine to protect against allergies.

A cup of hot cocoa (made with cocoa powder) has twice as many healthy antioxidants as a glass of red wine, and four times more than a cup of green tea, according to a study at Cornell University in 2003!

Of course, the health bandwagon is another useful marketing tool for big companies who want to promote chocolate (but may yet be uninterested in quality). Many brands have started to promote a new chocolate, even higher in antioxidants than normal chocolate. I would never suggest that chocolate should be your *only* source of antioxidants, so there's no need to sacrifice flavour for health. As I've said before, chocolate should be about pleasure!

• It's good for your teeth

Dental decay is caused by bacteria which accumulate in plaque on the surface of your teeth, especially in the absence of good oral hygiene. Chocolate, because of the sugar it contains, has long been associated with tooth decay in the minds of the public and some dentists. But studies show no direct evidence of a significant link. If anything, chocolate is *good* for your teeth, as cocoa contains fluoride, and the cocoa butter forms a coating in the teeth that protects against bacteria. However, the sweeter the chocolate, the less this is the case.

• It doesn't give you acne

The cause of acne is unknown, but contributory factors include hormonal changes around puberty and changes in the skin's bacterial status. No study has so far demonstrated a link between chocolate and acne, even though this link is often made. If a liking for cheap chocolate is accompanied by spots, it may more accurately be a sign that you are not taking care of your diet generally. For example, you may be eating too much junk food and not enough fresh fruit and vegetables.

• It doesn't make you fat (unless you want it to)

Having eaten more than a pound of chocolate a day for the last 15 years and still managing to maintain a weight of 100 to 105 lbs for my height of 5 ft 3 in, I am living proof of this. There are a few rules, however:

- It helps if you can try to eat chocolate on its own – not mixed with other foods. Give it a go, and you'll realise that your taste buds are more sensitive away from mealtimes. You should be able to derive a more intense pleasure from the chocolate, making it also easier not to overeat.

- You should also try to keep active. You put on weight when you consume more calories than you burn. I am a very sporty person. I sleep fewer than six hours a night and have been swimming for an hour a day over the last 20 years. This is also why I can get away with eating so much chocolate daily.

- Listen to your body. Try to tune into the right chocolate for your mood. Once you learn to find the chocolate that best fits your mood or moment, your body will also tell you when to stop. Of course, the larger your chocolate database, the finer-tuned you'll be to what you need. The danger, if you eat chocolate that is too sweet, is that the sugar will inhibit this internal regulator and trigger a demand for 'more'. Sugar is the evil in chocolate.

• It boosts the 'feelgood' factor

Have you ever tried this trick? Your post arrives in the morning, and you can see that there's an envelope you've been expecting. It contains the results of a recent job interview or a bank statement. You know it could be bad news. How can you make it less bad? By eating half a bar of chocolate before you open it! Of course it won't change the content of the letter... But it will change the way you react to the news, even if it isn't good.

Whenever I face a difficult moment, or bad news, I eat half a bar of chocolate. It has been scientifically proven that chocolate makes you feel good – or at least less bad.

Chocolate contains many psychoactive molecules which all contribute to making you feel better. It elevates your mood, reduces anxiety, and is probably the world's most pleasant antidepressant!

- Chocolate contains caffeine and theobromine, which stimulate the brain and central nervous system, giving you a burst of energy.

- Chocolate also contains phenylethylamine (PEA), a close relative to amphetamines, which increases attention and activity. PEA has also been shown to relieve depression and reduce anxiety. You get a surge of PEA when you fall in love, and it floods your brain during orgasm!

- Two other pleasure substances are also to be found in chocolate – N-oleoylethanolamine and N-linoleylethan- olamine – which have a make-up similar to the brain's pleasure chemical anandamide ('ananda' is the Sanskrit for 'bliss').

If this all sounds very scientific, let me explain. Imagine someone gives you a lovely box of chocolates (in my case, please fill it with a selection of plain dark chocolate bars!). Your brain interprets this action as 'someone cares for me'. This pleasant news triggers the production of natural endor- phins – feel-good chemicals – in the brain. It is a beautiful box (the aesthetic pleasure triggers more endorphins); and the delicious-smelling chocolates instantly remind you of past sensual chocolate experiences (your mouth salivates and your brain produces yet more feel-good chemicals). When you finally eat a chocolate (containing phenylethylamine), your pleasure is maximised. You are high on chocolate.

CHOCOLATE: FRIEND OR FOE?

So beyond the delightful experience of actually eating it, chocolate is also an elixir for mental well-being.

BUT IS IT AN APHRODISIAC?

Well, let's see... I've just told you how much chocolate I get through on a daily basis. How did I manage to hold down my job as manager in a traditional company if all that chocolate was firing up my sex drive? I'd be wearing lowcut dresses, baring my legs, trying to seduce my colleagues...

Seriously, the chocolate aphrodisiac myth is one that people like to maintain. It's a fantasy – albeit one with rather a lot of history behind it. The Aztec emperor Moctezuma is thought to have drunk 50 golden goblets of chocolate a day, allegedly to enhance his sexual prowess. So when chocolate was discovered by the Spanish conquistadors and introduced to Europe, it was natural for the Spanish and eventually the rest of the world to associate it with love.

The reasons for this can also be seen in the effects of chocolate on human behaviour. As I mentioned earlier, chocolate contains the same mood-lifting chemicals that rush in when we are experiencing feelings of love or lust. Chocolate also gives an immediate and substantial energy boost, thus increasing stamina. And although that could be credited with having boosted Casanova's sexual prowess (and he is said to have consumed chocolate as an aphrodisiac before frolicking with his conquests), recent

research suggests that women are actually more sus-
ceptible to the effects of phenylethylamine than men.
Casanova obviously didn't know this, as there's no
mention of him sharing his chocolate with the ladies.
Perhaps he thought his charms alone were enough to
guarantee success!

We turn to chocolate for comfort, but is it really any substitute for affection?

I like to quote the humorist Sandra Boynton on this topic.
She says:

> Clearly it is not the lovelorn sufferer who seeks solace in
> chocolate, but rather the chocolate-deprived individual
> who, desperate, seeks in mere love a pale approximation
> of bittersweet euphoria.

• It won't give you a migraine

Twenty to 75 per cent of migraine sufferers associate chocolate with migraine, although few actively avoid it. As I understand it, chocolate is implicated as a trigger only in less than
five per cent of cases. While some headaches are partly
chocolate-induced, probably related to chemicals such as
phenylethylamine, headache-inducing chemicals are also
found in aged cheeses, processed meat, coffee, peanuts and
red wine. It is the accumulation of various triggers that provoke headache, and only in people predisposed to regular
headaches. I really don't think poor chocolate should carry
all the responsibility.

• Its stimulants are no bad thing

Chocolate contains two stimulants: caffeine and theo-bromine. Theobromine's effects on the body resemble those of caffeine.

We all know that coffee, tea and cola contain caffeine. And we all hear that 'caffeine is bad for you'. But in actuality, a small intake of caffeine has positive benefits: it increases vigilance, and delays the symptoms of tiredness. A cup of coffee a day will not harm you, but like any food, and like anything in life, it becomes harmful if you have too much of it. The good news is that the caffeine content in chocolate is negligible. A teaspoon of cocoa powder carries 6mg of caffeine and a 1½ oz bar of dark chocolate carries 28 mg. Compare this to coffee and colas: a regular coffee (8½ oz) carries 65 to 150mg, and a 12 oz cola carries 40 to 50mg. So you would need to eat 3½ oz of dark chocolate – two and a half 1½ oz bars – all at once to have the caffeine effect of a regular cup of coffee.

Theobromine is found in the greatest quantities in chocolate; in fact, there is four times more theobromine than caffeine in chocolate. Luckily, theobromine is good for you: it stimulates the nervous system and boosts muscle performance.

• It doesn't cause cravings

When we get angry that we haven't managed to resist a chocolate, is it the chocolate's fault? I think 'chocolate' cravings are actually more often than not sugar cravings, resulting from the high sugar content in cheaper choco-lates. Chocolate is so much more attractive than any cake, biscuit or sweet: it is scientifically proven to contain the ideal proportion of fat and sugar. It is one of life's greatest pleasures.

Chocolate cravings have three main causes, and they are to do with us – not the chocolate, so they are something we can learn to control.

1. Chocolate is seen as a 'forbidden food'. A study at the University of Sussex in England looked at the effects of chocolate as a forbidden food, using a group of 30 women who were at their normal weight. Half the group were allowed free access to chocolate; the other half were told it was forbidden. After 24 hours, the latter group was allowed to eat as much of it as they wanted – and ate much more compared with those who had been allowed chocolate all along.

The message is clear. When we think of chocolate as a forbidden food, it becomes more tempting, and we are more likely to eat too much of it. The messages we have grown up with – chocolate is bad for you, it should be restricted, and so on, and those we impose on ourselves when we try to diet or curb chocolate consumption for some other reason – are the ones that are ironically causing us to eat more of it, and to crave it.

As you become a connoisseur, this kind of craving will be less of a problem. Chocolate will no longer frighten you. Once you understand your choco-psyche and discover quality chocolate, you'll instinctively eat more slowly and selectively. I believe if you listen to your body and reward it with what it asks for, you'll not only enjoy the chocolate more, but will actually eat less of it.

2. Chocolate is 'moreish'. The desire to eat more occurs during rather than preceding the eating episode, and it can apply

Chocolopolis

1527 Queen Anne Ave North
206-282-0776
www.chocolopolis.com

GOLDEN BAR GIVEAWAY

Two Golden Bar tickets will be hidden in chocolate bars available for purchase from Chocolopolis' extensive collection of chocolate from around the world. Whoever purchases a chocolate bar with a hidden Golden Bar ticket receives a free chocolate bar of their choosing every week for a year. The third ticket will be given away in a drawing on Saturday, July 18 at 5:00 pm.

Raffle tickets for the drawing will be based on purchases made during the week. Customers may earn raffle tickets for every $10 purchase made from July 12 until the drawing on July 18. For example, if a customer purchases $30 (pre tax) of chocolate during the anniversary week, he or she will receive 3 raffle tickets for the drawing.

The drawing will be held at 5:00 pm on Saturday, July 18 at Chocolopolis. The winner need not be present to win.

Chocolopolis

1527 Queen Anne Ave North
206-282-0776
www.chocolopolis.com

JOIN US FOR FREE EVENTS DURING OUR ANNIVERSARY WEEK

Bastille Day July 14 (Tuesday) 5:00 pm - 8:00 pm
Samples of French chocolate, 10% off all French chocolate bars, video of
Cluizel chocolate-making tradition in French and English.

DRY Soda and Chocolate Pairing July 15 (Wednesday) 6:00 pm - 8:00 pm

Customer Appreciation Party July 16 (Thursday) 7:00 pm - 9:00 pm
Snacks, chocolate samples and drawings for free chocolate.

A Day with Jeff Shepherd, Chocolatier Lillie Belle Farms July 17 (Friday)
1:00 pm - 3:00 pm: Tea, finger sandwiches & chocolate with Jeff
7:00 pm - 9:00 pm: Cheese, crackers & chocolate w/Jeff

Claudio Corallo chocolate tasting July 18 (Saturday) 3:00 pm - 5:00 pm

Golden Bar Giveaway July 18 (Saturday) 5:00 pm (see other side for details)

to any food you enjoy. It is most often experienced when you attempt to limit how much you will eat before your appetite is sated. Sugar is the main culprit behind the call for 'more'. As you begin to explore chocolate, trying darker and less sugar-laden varieties, you'll be less likely to become a victim of moreishness!

3. Cravings are often related to changes in mood. They affect the way we eat chocolate, but also the way we speak to other people, how well we concentrate, and so on. Premenstrual changes are often linked with chocolate cravings, but these have more to do with the sufferer's personal makeup (her sensuality, emotions and social values) than to the psychoactive chemicals contained in chocolate.

• It is not addictive

The word 'chocoholic' is often used to describe people who eat a lot of chocolate. I personally dislike this word: it's too close to alcoholic, and maintains the myth that chocolate is addictive. Which it is not. Addiction is generally associated with drug and alcohol abuse, or compulsive sexual activity. It's true that for some people, eating chocolate is a compulsive behaviour, but for people without disordered eating patterns, stopping the consumption of chocolate simply causes displeasure – not withdrawal symptoms.

In 1994, Professor Chantal Fabre-Bismuth, a specialist in toxicology, conducted a study at the hospital Fernand Vidal in Paris. She analysed the quantities and pattern of intake of 40 people eating more than 3½ oz chocolate per day (she had not met me!). The results showed that when the participants were deprived of chocolate, there were no withdrawal symptoms, they were just... less happy! They simply missed the pleasure. In no way were their physical and mental capacities affected.

> Despite the amount of chocolate I eat, I do not qualify myself as a chocoholic, at all. I am a choco-gourmet. I enjoy good chocolate more than anything else on earth, and I am also an epicurean. I eat a lot of chocolate. But you can lock me for days in a room full of poor-quality chocolate, *of any percentage*, and I'd rather starve. As you become a chocolate connoisseur, you will understand what I mean here. You will be able to look at some chocolate displays in shops or in a box proffered to you with total calm and control – even nausea in some cases.

But... and this is very important: remember that all the beneficial properties I've outlined above apply *only* to chocolate bars made of real chocolate with at least 60% cocoa content. Poor-quality, low-cocoa chocolate does not count. Beware of the following:

• Too much sugar

If you crave sweet milk chocolate, it's the sugar you are craving, not the chocolate: it will confuse your palate, and lead you to eat more than you need. And this is a big stumbling block for chocolate lovers who want to maintain a healthy weight. Don't try to cut down on the calories by going for so-called sugar-free chocolate (unless you really are diabetic). These bars are made with maltitol instead of sugar, and as this is a chemical sweetener, it brings its own chemical flavours and it is still moreish. Your chocolate not only tastes bad (or worse, depending on your starting point), but it is still calorific, at 450 calories per 3½ oz – if you eat the whole bar. So unless you're a masochist or diabetic, ban all sugar-free bars from sight!

• White chocolate

For me this is not chocolate; it is confectionery. White chocolate is made with cocoa butter, but contains no actual cocoa mass. In my opinion, it's about as tasty as eating a piece of paper coated with sugar and milk powder!

• Carob

Carob, also known as St John's bread, algarroba, locust bean and locust pod, is used by some as a substitute for chocolate. It has some similar nutrients (calcium and phosphorous) and, when combined with vegetable fat and sugar, it can be made to approximate the colour and consistency of chocolate. Of course, as writer and chocolate-lover Sandra Boynton puts it: 'The same arguments can persuasively be made in favour of dirt.'

• Price

There's no way round this: quality chocolate is more expensive than the cheap varieties – but so is luxurious wrapping. Don't be taken in by manufacturers who care more about the quality of their paper, boxes, gold lettering and ribbons than that of their raw materials!

• Percentage

People who say they only eat 70% cocoa chocolate need to realise that percentage is only part of the story. A high-alcohol wine is not necessarily better than a low-alcohol one. Nobody would judge a wine on its alcohol content. What matters is its bouquet of aromas, its symphony of flavours. In other words, it's all down to quality of ingredients and manufacture, *not* cocoa percentage all on its own.

Having said this, though, the higher the percentage of cocoa, the less sugar the bar will have. And the less milk powder a bar contains, the less fatty that bar will be. So there is a case for sticking to dark chocolate if you are concerned about eating too much sugar or fat.

And finally...

To start thinking like a connoisseur, you need to be open-minded, able to take what other people say about chocolate with a sceptical pinch of salt. You need to re-evaluate what chocolate means to *you*, forget all that you have thought about it to date (it is not something to feel guilty and bad about, it is to be enjoyed and esteemed!), and start with a fresh mind, a clean palate and a new page in your tasting notebook. You need to know that you can confidently eat chocolate without the fear that it will give you a headache, spots or excess weight. All these things will become possible, and, in the next chapter, I will show you how becoming a connoisseur can change your life – and even your career.

CHAPTER 9

·

Becoming a connoisseur

*I*F CHOCOLATE IS YOUR passion, then a job that pays you
to taste chocolate for a living must seem like heaven on
earth. Such jobs are, of course, few and far between. But it
may amaze you to learn that you do not necessarily have to
be a professional chocolate worker to achieve such dizzy
heights.

At the time that I applied for my job as chocolate buyer
for Fortnum & Mason, I was working for the cosmetics company L'Oréal – and the bulk of my chocolate career had so far
been amateur rather than professional.

As I've said, I had qualified as an agronomist. But alongside the scientific studies, I had, as you've seen, been secretly
studying chocolate for years. I would taste it and make notes
on it, sampling everything I could in the growing quality
market. When I left my job at the UN in Jamaica, I decided I
wanted a complete change from all that – and that's when I
wrote off to the chocolate companies, offering my services
for free in order to learn more about chocolate. And as you

know, it was Ladurée, the Paris chocolate shop, that finally gave me a chance.

I really have worked my way up from the bottom. I started on the production line, wearing a white gown and hat and doing everything from putting the delicious ingredients into the mixer to packing the finished chocolates into boxes.

During my first few days, I was putting a lot in my mouth along the way and the production manager said loudly, 'You will soon get tired of it – everyone does.' Four days later, he told our boss, chocolatier Pierre Hermé, 'In 18 years, I have never seen that!' I put another chocolate in my mouth, smiling at M. Hermé, my eyes sparkling with delight. He just laughed, knowing that he had met a true chocophile. By the end of my time at Ladurée I was managing the confectionary department.

However, that job would not have been enough to get me a look-in at Fortnum & Mason had the position been advertised when I was still at Ladurée. Ultimately, I believe, I got the job because of my passion for chocolate. After leaving Ladurée, I spent three years at L'Oréal, but continued to chisel away at the chocolate world in all my spare time – evenings, weekends, holidays. I founded a chocolate association in 1999 (Carrément Chocolat) and presented at chocolate conferences, gave tasting courses, and hosted special chocolate evenings for major companies. I was thirsty for knowledge and attended every chocolate conference or show I could, and visited as many factories and plantations as possible. Although it could be tiring, I was truly living my passion.

One day in August 2002, I switched on my computer to find 23 emails from friends, who had all seen a particular job advertisement. It went something like this:

CHOCOLATE BUYER

Are you looking for the best job in the world? Well, here it is! What could be better than being the Chocolate Buyer at Fortnum & Mason's world-renowned Food Hall?

Do you think you have what it takes to be this unique and innovative individual, able to inspire others with your passion for chocolate?

If you are this person then tell us why you believe that you can make a difference. We are looking for enthusiasm, creative flair and energy to develop the already divine range of products available.

Nearly every one of those 23 emails said, 'You were born for this'! And by this time, thanks to my extracurricular interests in the chocolate world, I had amassed enough experience to give me a decent chocolate-oriented CV – even though I had never attended a cooking or chocolate school. I sent my CV to Fortnum & Mason and was selected from a field of 3,000 – a turning point in my choco-life!

A day in the life of a chocolate connoisseur

People are always fascinated to know how a chocoholic who works with chocolate spends her day… 'So, do you really eat chocolate all day long?' many people ask. Well, I didn't need the excuse of working in the chocolate business to start eating a pound of it a day – I've been doing that for long enough. When I worked as a chocolate buyer, here's what my day looked like. As a chocolate consultant now, it is similar—and also delicious.

5 am: My stereo wakes me up with classical music. I stay in bed, eyes closed, enjoying the music.

5.15 am: Brush my teeth and prepare the tasting tray. I will wait until 30 minutes after brushing my teeth as the toothpaste would otherwise still be polluting my taste buds. I have normally decided on the theme of my tasting the night before, and a box of samples (many from suppliers wanting me to taste their chocolate) is waiting in the kitchen. (The rest of my personal chocolate stock is stored in a special cool, dark room.)

6 am: I have my first chocolate tasting of the day! This is the best time, when my palate is completely clean and fully receptive to the aromas and flavours I am about to encounter. (I spit out what I don't like.)

6.45 am: I head for the local swimming pool, where I swim for an hour a day nonstop (around 1¼ mi). Exercise is absolutely essential if you eat a lot of chocolate! The chocolate I eat provides an entire day's worth of calories, so swimming helps to make room for the other foods I need. I also do a lot of brisk walking and power yoga. Just as with listening (really listening!) to good music, these activities give me a sense of well-being, a harmony between body and mind, which I find essential. It helps me to eliminate any mental 'chatter' and listen fully to my senses while tasting.

8.40 am: Back on the Tube for the 20-minute journey to work. I take this opportunity to catch up on any chocolate-related reading.

9 am: I arrive at my office and go straight to my stock to pick myself an assortment of chocolate. The filled chocolates I like are mainly nuts with chocolate (hazelnut or almond bâtonnets in chocolate, the nutty pralinés, lemon peel in milk chocolate (one I introduced to Fortnum & Mason), a plain dark truffle using beans from Madagascar. Then I select three plain dark chocolate bars (generally two favourites, and one more that I want to rediscover). My morning kit weighs 12¼ oz, the bars represent 8 oz of it – and it will be usually be finished by lunchtime at 2 pm. I spit out everything I taste.

You're probably thinking, 'That's a *lot* of chocolate'! Well, it is, but I have to thank my taste buds for having a natural inclination towards nutty fillings rather than creamy ones. They're much less fattening, and the dark chocolate with nuts combination is actually pretty healthy. And, of course, ganaches are far more fattening than bars or pralinés.

9.15 am: I have breakfast at my desk as I check my work emails. If I start eating chocolate now, it will become an exclusively chocolate breakfast as I never mix chocolate with any other food – and I try not to do this more than twice a week. My regular breakfast is either fruit or a plain full-fat (full flavour!) yogurt.

9.30 am: The first phone call of the day from a potential supplier. 'My name is X. Our company sells outstanding confectionary products and I would be grateful if you could make some time to meet me...'

My response is standard. 'Thank you for your call, X; however, I would love to meet your chocolates first and I will leave it to my palate to decide if we shall meet. Please could you send me samples with the prices, shelf-life, ingredients list and availability over the year? I also need to know how long you take to deliver, who else in the UK sells your chocolate; and I would ask you to label your samples so that I know in advance what they are. Please also package those with alcohol separately.'

By then they usually say that they would like to see my reaction as I taste their wonderful chocolate.

'I totally understand and respect that. However, I taste at 6 am at home. If you wish to leave me your telephone number I will let you know when I plan to do the tasting and you may join me.'

Unsurprisingly, I haven't yet had a supplier take me up on this... and in fact, no one has even got as far as asking for my address!

10 am: I am called to the shop floor. A couple of Dutch tourists are looking for a bar I have never heard of, so I get them to describe it, then show them a few products I think they will find very similar. I also take the opportunity of introducing them to our range of plantation and single-origin bars. I know my eyes must be twinkling because I am very proud of this range, which is unique in the UK.

I have excited their curiosity and they decide to buy a set of four different bars. These two people make my day. I have somehow 'brought the choco-light' to them – it's a small thing, but, brick by brick, one can slowly construct a temple.

When I visit the chocolate counter, I watch the way customers select the chocolates and if I see any hesitation, I propose my assistance. Whether they are buying for themselves or as a present, I see it as an opportunity for them to discover a few different chocolates, close to those they like and are used to, but a step closer to the temple of fine chocolate!

10.30 am: Next, I systematically look at the filled chocolates in the fridges, spotting bloomed or damaged ones, which I then have removed. A bloomed chocolate, which looks grey or dull, has suffered from a too-fast change of temperature and humidity. It will still taste good but aesthetics are part of the pleasure, and in one of the finest department stores in the world, everything needs to be perfect.

Happily, there's no need for these chocolates to go to waste. Any bloomed chocolates go to the staff canteen – I love to see people's faces illuminated as they see the chocolates on offer. I feel like Father Christmas!

10.40 am: Back at my desk, my selection of chocolates by my side, I try to focus on the pile of paperwork – correspondence, orders, and complaints. When I bring a new product in – to refresh the range or to upgrade quality –I have to take one out to make space, and I then get letters from customers surprised and disappointed about the change. It is hard to please everybody, and I just hope that they will one day try one of the new ones.

11.30 am: We have a meeting to select the products we will present in the Christmas catalogue. This has to be started at least ten months ahead of Christmas.

2 pm: Lunch. After lunch, usually salad and a sandwich, I will not eat chocolate for at least two hours (or up to four if I have been taken out for a heavy lunch). If I do feel the urge, I go for a bite of Michael Recchiuti's 85% – I find this high-cocoa, good-quality bar the only pleasant chocolate to eat after a meal. Even 75% cocoa chocolate seems too sugary, and not sufficiently chocolatey, eaten close to a meal. Most of the time I go for cocoa nibs, though, which are perfect when you are not feeling like sweets but want to taste something that stirs your senses.

2.30 pm: Meeting with my assistant. We share information and tasks, and decide on products we wish to carry as Christmas novelties.

3.30 pm: I receive a call from the Italian chamber of commerce. I am invited to spend three days in Turin for their big annual chocolate show. I will have a series of meetings with the little-known small business confectioners who make Italy's best little chocolate jewels. I immediately make two more phone calls. One to book my flight, and the other to Domori, whose factory in Italy makes astonishingly expensive chocolate. This makes liking their bars a pricey pleasure, but I am nevertheless amazed by them, as they trigger a new set of feelings in my mouth.

Domori's brochures are so sophisticated and complete (they even created a chocolate quality code – which they have to stick to!) that I want to know more about the company. Furthermore, competitors tell me Domori don't work from the bean (which means they are buying their cocoa mass from another company, and just melt, blend, temper and mould). I am intrigued by this, because the chocolate tastes like no other I have tried, and I want to see with my own eyes what they are doing. Working for Fortnum & Mason opens almost all doors to me, and allows me to deepen my knowledge and the scope of sharing it.

5 pm: I feel like having a chocolate that's not in my box, so I pop down to the storeroom and examine the boxes. Hmmm. A good opportunity to check all the sell-by dates and stock levels. I remove any box whose shelf-life is too short to be sold – I need to make sure it doesn't accidentally end up on the shop floor.

6 pm: My assistant and I make a comparative tasting of raw materials such as candied ginger or orange. Improving our range also means encouraging the companies that produce Fortnum & Mason-branded chocolates to improve the quality of their raw material. I then negotiate prices and organise a delivery at their production unit – ensuring that everything goes according to plan.

6.30 pm: At the end of the working day, I will go to a yoga class, then return home to eat dinner, relax by listening to music, and then catch up with emails from my friends in the worlds of chocolate, perfume, tea and coffee, eager to get updated on the fight for quality elsewhere in the world.

What does it take?

Anyone can eat and enjoy chocolate, but you have to go the extra mile to develop your knowledge if you want to be taken seriously in the chocolate world.

- Acquaint yourself with chocolate, tasting every new bar on the market (but stick to the quality market – forget anything else!).

- Develop your own chocolate database, noting aromas, flavours and textures of new bars. Go back to Chapters 2 and 4 to find out more about how you should do this.

- Attend chocolate events – there are annual chocolate shows in London, Paris, New York, San Francisco, Tokyo, and even in Russia now! Here you will meet the names

behind the bars, and pick up all the news that only chocolate insiders are normally privy to.

- Join chocolate clubs, attend their meetings if possible,
  read the reviews on their websites, and hunt for tips and
  addresses. Write your own reviews on the website forums,
  but don't be influenced too much by what others say. Your
  own opinion is all you need, but these forums are valuable
  for information and ideas.

- Get some practical knowledge, too – is there anywhere
  where you could work alongside a chocolatier for free in
  order to gain more experience? You can also attend specialised chocolate courses. They exist in most cities of a
  reasonable size, and usually are a week long.

When you start to make a name for yourself in any area –
perhaps by writing articles on the subject, or hosting workshops (even if you have to invite an expert along to run
them), opportunities are more likely to come your way. The
American food writer Patricia Wells attended one of the tasting classes I ran at Ladurée and invited me to run chocolate-
tasting courses for her too. I became 'Madame Chocolat' at
her weekly Friday morning Parisian gastronomic classes.

HOW MUCH DO YOU KNOW?

You may have started this book as a mere chocophile, but already I hope you are beginning to feel more of an affinity with the product. How many of the following questions can you answer that you couldn't before?

- Where do cocoa trees grow?

- Which trees produce the most aromatic beans?

- What are the three main production steps from bean to bar that are crucial to the final aromatic quality of the chocolate?

- What are the ingredients of a dark chocolate bar? A milk chocolate bar?

- What are the ingredients you should not find/feel in a fine chocolate?

- What makes bad chocolate (make a list!)?

- What does 70% cocoa mean on a label?

- Why isn't white chocolate really chocolate?

- What is the best drink and food to go with chocolate?

- List at least five criteria for a good tasting session.

- What is the percentage of Criollo cocoa used in world production?

- Why should chocolate and coffee not be served together?

- How often do you try new chocolate?

- Do you attend chocolate clubs, and read about chocolate?

- Do you choco-surf on the web?

Feeling as if you have some level of expertise in any subject – particularly one about which you feel passionately – is great for your self-esteem. It can also change your life, introducing you to new people, and new activities (holding chocolate-themed parties, attending or hosting chocolate tasting workshops, and reading the news from international events, even if you cannot attend them in person) – and even if it doesn't turn into a career, as it did for me, it can only bring a new and special dimension to your everyday life.

For the ardent chocolate lover, I can think of no better time than now, when we are in the middle of a chocolate revolution, to further your knowledge and expand your interest. After years of living in the chocolate wilderness, we are seeing major changes that will make history, as happened in the 1850s with the Swiss and Dutch technological breakthroughs. There is much to learn and much to keep abreast of if you are to play an active role as a connoisseur and be part of this revolution.

CHAPTER 10

·

The future of chocolate

THE CHOCOLATE REVOLUTION isn't happening in isolation. We are in the middle of a quality revolution in all food and drink. Look around you. Quality ingredients – or at least labels that suggest quality – are everywhere. Suddenly everything is 'boutique'. Even supermarkets know their suppliers by name (or so they say). Farmers' markets are springing up for people wanting to buy direct from the producer. Boutique wineries are now on the tourist route in countries like Australia and Italy. The local continental deli still exists, but has competition from gourmet delis selling top-quality luxury products from around the world.

And chocolate is no different. People are, at last, waking up to the fact that variety of cocoa beans used, and the way they are treated after harvest and processed in the factories, can greatly influence the flavour and texture of a bar of chocolate. We are starting to see the difference, even in our supermarkets.

But, just as cosmetics manufacturers may seize on the fashion for ingredients like aloe vera or green tea and add these words (and perhaps a hint of the essential ingredient!) to their products, even the big, mainstream chocolate manufacturers have been quick to recognise the new trend for chocolates made with beans from a named country of origin. And they have also been quick to recognise the cachet associated with a label stating such information.

As a connoisseur, you can help to ensure that chocolates pertaining to be quality products really are just that, and not just the same old products in a new, trendy package. By buying selectively, and demanding the best, you can make a difference to the world of chocolate.

MAKING A DIFFERENCE

In my own way, I try to make the world of chocolate a more honest, and ultimately a better and more enjoyable, place. I try to show people how to distinguish poor from good quality by having them taste both at the same time, as you've learnt to do in this book. Often people find the difference so striking that it immediately triggers a change in their shopping behaviour.

And sometimes I see small changes that I may have helped to bring about in the chocolate world – as the result of a conversation with a manufacturer, or by having the idea to introduce a few people who could have a lot to offer each other.

One of the most touching moments for me came in 2004, with the release of a new bar that I had helped bring out. In July 2003 a man working for a company based in Papua New Guinea came to see me, bringing three bags of beans from his plantation. He wanted my opinion on them, as he'd been told they were of high quality, and had read about me in the press. I'm far from being a bean expert, so I suggested he contact a few companies that I know are always on the lookout for quality beans.

A few months later I received a long thank you letter and a cocoa-harvest sculpture. One of the brands I'd suggested had liked the beans so much they had signed a long-term contract for them, assuring the village they came from an improved income and secure future for the next few years.

And the brand? It was the French company Michel Cluizel, and they launched Maralumi, their fifth plantation bar, in September 2004. It felt wonderful to have helped not only the world of chocolate but also a small village.

Signs of the revolution

There are many important changes taking place every day, more signs of the choco-revolution. Let's look at a few of them now.

New flavours

Now that you are becoming aware of the different flavours in chocolate, you may be pleased to hear that some companies are reducing the often overpowering amounts of vanilla flavouring in their chocolate or replacing vanillin with real vanilla. In the future, I hope that the amounts used will be much more discreet, just as sugar should be – just enough to hold the aromas and allow them to express themselves with elegance, while maximising their potential.

The trend is in totally taking out the vanilla and lecithin. Michel Cluziel does not use lecithin. Domori is cutting back or not using vanilla for most bars. Others, such as Claudio Corallo and Steve De Vries, don't even consider using it in the first place.

Now that it has become compulsory to add 'artificial flavouring' after vanillin on labels, many companies are changing their couverture, replacing vanillin with natural vanilla or with no vanilla at all – and this is, contrary to what you might think, *not* good news! Vanilla or vanillin is often used to cover up the flavour of poor beans – so unless better beans are suddenly used in a couverture, we, the consumers, will be soon encountering chocolate that tastes *worse*!

In the future, people will not be so surprised when finding flavours of mushrooms, wood, prunes, jasmine and leather in chocolate bars. They will describe a bar as some do wine, speaking about aromas and flavours and their evolution over time. They will compare vintages, and be suspicious if, from one year to another, two different vintages have the same taste.

New style labels

The first thing to appear on our chocolate labels was its percentage of cocoa solids, then exotic words such as Criollo and Trinitario started to creep in – telling us what kind of tree the beans that made our chocolate came from.

Another change that has gradually been taking place is that percentages, once announced loudly on the front of a label, have been disappearing, or rather, have moved to the back of many labels, becoming just another item in the ingredients list. Now, instead, we are seeing the names of countries, regions or specific plantations, and sometimes even followed by the year of the bean's growth – similar to the 'cru 2004' (vintage) you would find on a wine label.

In the future the name of the particular bean used, such as Criollo, will only be legal on the packaging if genetically checked and crossed with an accurate location on the map of the plantation the beans come from.

As you know, pure Criollo disappeared a long time ago, and brands mentioning this bean are in fact talking about a hybrid of Criollo and Trinitario beans. Fine chocolate makers have tended not to use the word at all. But companies such as Domori, Pralus and others are planting pure Criollo (sourced from gene banks and grafted onto Trinitario roots), and waiting for their trees to mature. In 2003, the first bar made with pure Criollo beans appeared – Domori's Puertomar – and there will be many more to come.

The new labels, once you have become used to them, provide you with much more information – and the more you taste and try different bars, the more you will be able to pick and choose from the bars of the future exactly which ones you are likely to enjoy.

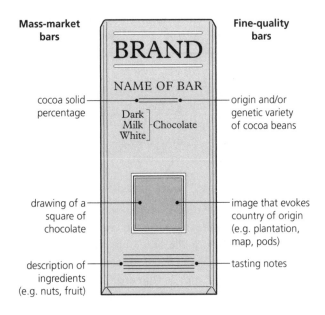

Mass-market bars

cocoa solid percentage

drawing of a square of chocolate

description of ingredients (e.g. nuts, fruit)

BRAND

NAME OF BAR

Dark
Milk ─Chocolate
White

Fine-quality bars

origin and/or genetic variety of cocoa beans

image that evokes country of origin (e.g. plantation, map, pods)

tasting notes

Characteristics of mass-market chocolate labels are on the left and those of fine chocolate labels are on the right

Tasting notes on bars

Now that you know that two bars of chocolate, both with 75% cocoa content, can taste completely different, you probably won't be surprised to know that more and more bars present tasting notes on the back of the packaging. I am confident that in the near future, this will become the norm!

Use these notes as a guide, but don't take what their authors say for granted. Use your own nose and palate to tell you what to add to your database. In fact, I suggest that you taste the chocolate first – and read the notes later. And don't feel bad if you didn't taste the same flavours!

In the future, labels will be clear and informative at the same time. The main focus is likely to be the tasting notes. At present these tend to be very simple (often only giving just the 'family' flavours, such as fruity, spicy or flowery, rather than more complex and detailed flavours). A new trend at the moment is to give a 'shopping list' of many different flavours. How can so many flavours exist within the one bar? My advice is to trust your own developing judgement.

CHOCOLATE IN THE NEWS

In January 2004, I discovered a revolutionary shop in San Francisco: Fog City News. In this narrow little newsagent, newspapers actually only occupy a third of the space, and the rest is packed with hundreds of chocolate bars – brands from all over the world, including many of those I cherish. Every taste was catered for, from top of the price range bars of Amedei and Valrhona, down to mass-market products such as Lindt and Cadbury Fruit & Nut. Amazingly enough, despite having a better range than many chocolate shops, and with two-thirds of the shop invaded by chocolate, it is still known as a newsagent!

What's even more astonishing is that when you buy a bar, you can ask for advice – all the sales staff are fully choco-trained! Not only this, but you can ask for a printout with a description of the product, its brand name, the percentage of cocoa and tasting notes. Wonderful!

Curious to compare with my own methods, I asked for a sample printout. I went for one I know by heart, Manjari from Valrhona. I read:

Flavour: Raspberry, faint pineapple, orange zest, balsamic vinegar, dried cranberry, vine, espresso, green olive, green bell pepper, paprika, nutmeg, oregano, cedar, spicy cinnamon, clove, condensed milk, sarsaparilla, walnut, rum, white raisin, oak, maple, rose, anise, vanilla, mint.

Aroma: Whiskey, pipe tobacco, tangerine, stronger cinnamon, honey, blueberry, cedar, fresh cut wood, lemonade, BBQ sauce, Worcestershire sauce, wheat bread, dried cranberry, candied ginger.

Phase 1:
White pepper, clove, sourdough, raisin, ginger, tangerine, lemongrass, lime, celery, apricot, nutmeg, cranberry, beeswax, cucumber, ginger, strawberry, cedar, marzipan, paprika, and a raisin finish. Aftertaste of orange marmalade, tangy blueberry, mocha, sourdough, raisin, long aftertaste of citrus-y fruit.

Phase 2:

Maple, clove, peppercorn, rose, cinnamon stick, vanilla, orange peel, sweeter this time, almond cookie, coconut, vanilla, pear, apricot, burned espresso, pear skin, ripe kiwi, finish of lime. After-taste of toasted vanilla bean combined with orange peel, molasses, pine cone, pine nut.

I was disappointed. Tasting is a very personal thing, and everyone will have their own way of describing a bar. Personally, I think it's better to have only a few short words to guide you on your way – but I do find this approach excellent. At the very least, these notes are suggesting a new way to look at and taste the bars. Use the suggestions as inspiration, and you might even agree with one or two.

New names

As in the fashion world, it is the true craftsmen who are always ahead of the game. The most creative artisans will always be taking risks and being more innovative than the largest companies, who will ultimately copy their ideas (although, in my opinion, only to produce an inferior imitation). But of course by the time they launch their copy, the creatives will already be working on new products. It's a familiar story – just think of the high-street knock-offs that hit the shops soon after the catwalk shows.

It is down to us, the consumers, to seek out the genuinely fine-quality products and not wait until a bar of Chuao is as easy to find as a Gap T-shirt.

In Chapter 1 I gave you my tips for wonderful chocolate brands. I've also suggested a few names to watch out for in the future on pages 26–29 – most of whom don't sell to the general public yet, or do so only in limited quantities. These artisans are not well known at the moment but they are likely to influence even the largest companies in time. Here's a reminder of those rising stars:

- Domori: you can already buy their chocolate, but now some of it is made from Criollo beans – with every year bringing more Criollo bars.

- Steve De Vries: Steve's chocolates are still in the experimental stage, but his 'experiments' have been so far the best chocolate I've ever tasted. He is one of those pushing the boundaries, and we are bound to see more of him.

- Claudio Corallo: his chocolates are becoming more readily available. Unusually, he both grows beans and produces chocolate – and so can control the whole process.

And in the world of bonbons, there is Jacques Genin. He is nothing short of a genius. His flavours and techniques again will prove hugely influential.

The price of quality

Next time you go shopping, pay attention to the changes. Look at the range of prices you find for chocolate bars. Yes, chocolate bars – not boxes. With the trend towards quality growing, it is becoming more and more accepted that, just as with wine, you can pay prices ranging from the rock bottom to the very top.

In the case of 'limited edition' chocolates such as Valrhona's plantation bar Gran Couva which was launched in 1998, the number of bars available for sale was directly related to the size of the harvest, and chocolatiers bought them in advance to ensure they'd have some for their customers.

And often, with rarity comes price. In 2003 the Belgian chocolatier Pierre Marcolini launched a bar labelled 'Limited Edition' in huge letters, selling for almost $16 for a 3 oz bar! An American radio station even put expensive chocolate on the news, reporting in 2004: 'In Hawaii, one factory owner is selling bars for $7 each – and they're flying off the shelves.'

But is it merely fashion? Not at all. I say get ready: things are just warming up. In the next few years I think that there will be chocolates available that are the result of years of intense research and a little bit of genius. And also during this time period most of the pure Criollo bars that Domori have planned to launch since 1995 will come to fruition (see page 27). I think it's likely that the prices of some bars will soar. For the most exclusive bars created from the most carefully selected beans, prices per 3½ oz may rise up to $90 to $150 according to scarcity. (You laugh, but it happened with olive oil and balsamic vinegar!)

Digging for gold

Now that there's this movement towards quality chocolate, governments are discovering the marketing potential of their cocoa beans – and this is good news for the connoisseur.

Venezuela was the first country in the world to wake up and smell the beans, supporting the creation of the El Rey brand. Until recently this made Venezuela one of the only bean-producing countries to also manufacture its own finer-quality chocolate onshore and export it successfully. But what of the others?

Colombia was swift to notice how successful Venezuelan bean-growing has been in recent years, and decided to revive cocoa growing in the state of Santander, eastern Colombia. They have been growing cocoa here for more than two centuries, with small and medium-size farms supporting 12,000 families. On the side of the Venezuelan border lies the highly regarded region of Lago Maracaibo. Both Domori and Amedei use beans from this region. In addition, Columbia also has its own chocolate producer – even if in my estimation, it is not yet quite up to standard. Look out for Chocolates Santander, though, as they are actively working on improving their techniques.

Ghana also boasts a rare manufacturer, Omanhene, which produces chocolate from beans grown in the country. Their bars are very popular in the USA.

I do hope that the example of these few countries will be copied by other cocoa producers, lest they lose all their beans to overseas producers. Most of the money is in the grinding and producing of chocolate, not in the growing of the bean. It is sad to see many quality brands using beans from Venezuela for their plantation bars, using names of the regions that have become synonymous with quality – and making profits that the Venezuelans don't see much of. (In fact, only around 17 per cent of the total price you pay for a mass-market bar comes from the cost of beans.)

Most of these chocolates are not great quality, but for many, a bar's origin will be their main criterion for buying it. This is a form of fair trade that will have more and more success. As soon as their aromatic and textural quality reach good levels, I will be happy, and proud, to promote them.

And what about my own country, Mexico? Currently, there is nothing exciting to report, but I am full of hope. As the country with the oldest and most interesting cocoa background, it has a ready-made, explosive marketing tool. Mexican TV was eager to showcase the Mexican chocolate buyer recruited by Fortnum & Mason, and a few months later a leading chocolate manufacturer sent me samples, asking for my advice on how to improve their range. Mexico may yet become a chocolate 'name' again, and I hope to see action taken to revive its plantations and support the development of a local industry.

Status-symbol chocolate

Ten years ago, almost no chocolate manufacturer or chocolatier had ever visited a cocoa plantation. Today, it is the trend. And some particularly adventurous ones such as Pralus, Domori, Amedei and Valrhona decided to buy land and grow their own beans. Rather than buying the finest-quality raw material, they will ensure that they have it – by growing it and caring for it themselves. And the great news is that many of those doing this are growing Criollos. It's wonderful for us – it means that the quality of chocolate as we know it now is likely to get even better in the future.

Now that chocolate is gaining status, its packaging is becoming more like that of fine perfume. Labels or brochures tell the story behind that product; a map shows where the beans come from. Tasting notes guide your tasting, and information on the brand's philosophy allows you to position them among the others.

ALL THAT GLITTERS...

Beware! As I mentioned in Chapter 6, where there is demand there is always a cowboy lurking around the corner, ready to lure you with a fake. An expensive-looking package, carrying all the right chocolate vocabulary, and backed by a strong advertising campaign, might look alluring – but inside the wrapping is the same old thing you have always been able to buy. The only difference is the pumped-up price.

Be ready for their fancy names and wrappings. When glitter and gold are sharing the same shelf space, you need to be able to spot the difference.

Just keep an eye on what pops up in the shops, and buy a bar here and there, as connoisseurs need to be up to date with the market. Trust me: just a sniff should be enough to make you realise you're on to something special – or that you should push that brand aside for the time being. For the next five years, stick to the brands on the right-hand side of page 33.

And if I have my own way...

Chocolate liquid, kept at 45°C (113°F) will be delivered door to door by big tank trucks. In the homes, sinks will have two taps: one for water, one for liquid tempered chocolate.

Restaurant menus will routinely offer, as they do for cheese or cakes, a trolley filled with a selection of the finest chocolate bars. The waiter, the chocolate equivalent of a sommelier, will suggest an assortment of five or six. Of course, this will be served as a starter, not at the end of the meal (when your palate is less fresh).

Shops will have a reduced range of bonbons to give more space to a wide choice of bars, classified by bean region and variety. Perfectly trained sales staff will guide you to your choice. In exclusive shops, you will be able to book an appointment with the chocolate expert to get a 30-minute choco-analysis session, at the end of which you will have a personalised list of bars to buy and a new appointment booked in a month's time.

Agrotourism will extend to the chocolate world. Imagine a week's holiday spent on a plantation, getting to know the harvest, seeing fermentation and drying, making your own chocolate and designing the label. Your friends will be impressed!

Coffee shops will no longer serve squares of chocolate with their coffee and if you are nostalgic and ask for one, they will look at you as if you asked for salt – or ketchup!

And by the vending machines at train stations, in offices, and public places, there will always be a selection of top-quality chocolate squares, milk and dark, for your daily fixes.

That may sound like a fantasy world, but look at the changes we have seen in cheese, wine, tea, coffee and olive oil. Thirty years ago, who would have predicted the range of produce to which we now have access? Chocolate is even more of a fantasy food, and it fires the imagination unlike anything else I know of. So are my ideas for chocolate really so offbeat? We shall see…

Ten things you really need to know about chocolate

1. To the Mayas chocolate was a gift from the gods (and this is reflected in the Latin name for the cocoa tree: *Theobroma cacao*, meaning 'food of the gods'). But since mass market production began in the nineteeth century, chocolate has not been treated with much respect. Little care is taken over its fermentation and drying, and processing has focused on changing its flavour rather than enhancing it.

2. Manufacturers quickly seized upon a sweet, vanilla-flavoured product that humans were programmed to like – and they rubbed their hands with glee, watching the money roll in. Today ninety per cent of the world's chocolate is produced by a few large companies. Even those chocolates that seemingly hail from bijou chocolatiers may, when you examine their ingredients, come from one of the big manufacturers.

3. Now the truth about chocolate has finally been re-discovered: when farmed and processed with lots of tender loving care, it is a fine and fragrant food. The world's most aromatic beans are now finding their way into exclusive bars, and experts are taking genetic material from fine trees to ensure a better future for the special varieties like Criollos, which had disappeared until a few years ago.

4. When you taste one of these chocolates it can spark a story or image in your mind – it is truly heavenly, and its aromas and flavours say far more to you than any marketing device ever will.

5. You won't find these chocolate bars in your average sweet shop or supermarket – not yet anyway – and will have to seek them out, looking for specialist shops and internet sites.

6. When you start to eat this chocolate, taking the time to savour it away from other food and drinks, you will gain more satisfaction from it, learning to eat it in moderation, and only consuming what your body needs – so you can eat all you want without guilt or fear of weight gain.

7. Your new chocolate regime will mean having to store different types of chocolate to suit different moods and times of day – you will now have the perfect excuse to go on a chocolate shopping spree!

8. As you become acquainted with more chocolates, you will become more selective, eventually rejecting the sweetest chocolates of your childhood.

9. As you become more selective, you will be better able to recognise the impostors as big manufacturers try to jump on the connoisseur bandwagon, with clever marketing to make their cheaply produced chocolates look more special to the consumer or to your local chocolatier.

10. As the demand for true quality grows, all manufacturers will eventually be forced to look at their processing techniques and see how they can improve their product. There will be more call for special beans, and buyers will be stricter about quality control. And, the best news of all? Chocolate will be back where it belongs – as a respected and revered food of the gods.

A last word...

*B*Y NOW YOU probably know that being a chocolate connoisseur is a matter of degree. You have learned a great deal about what chocolate is (and isn't), and what makes good-quality chocolate stand out from the rest. You know how to taste it, and quite a lot more about yourself and what you like.

You also know that being passionate about chocolate takes dedication, devotion and perfectionism. I have met experts in tea, coffee, perfume and wine; and, it is no accident that after just a few minutes together, we recognise each other as coming from the same planet. When we talk about our particular passion, we shine. And we are here to alight this passion in others. We are driven by the same values, the same mission: to lobby the world about our passion. For chocolate, the new revolution is underway.

Glossary

AOC (Appellation d'Origine Contrôlée): in English, meaning 'guarantee of controlled origin'. The French initiated the AOC system to safeguard the quality and guarantee the provenance of grapes used in certain wines. This concept is now being adapted for use in the world of chocolate.

Ballotin: the 'ballotin', a gift box for chocolates, was first invented by the wife of Belgian chocolatier Neuhaus in 1912.

Bloom: a condition affecting the surface appearance of chocolate (it looks dull or grey) due to migration to the surface of sugar (because the chocolate has been exposed to excess humidity) or cocoa butter (too rapid a change in temperature, preventing proper crystallisation). A sign that texture is damaged, but with little impact on taste.

Chocolatier: a French term for chocolate makers who either produce chocolate from the bean or melt bulk chocolate to make filled chocolates (the vast majority).

Cocoa beans: the beans inside cocoa pods, the fruit of cocoa trees.

Cocoa butter: 50–55% of a cocoa bean's weight represents cocoa butter. If kept below 18°F, this fat looks and feels like yellowy-white soap. Many chocolatiers add cocoa butter to increase viscosity and give chocolate a smooth texture. As it is expensive, in poor-quality chocolate it is partially replaced by other vegetable fats.

Cocoa liquor: when cocoa nibs are milled at the factory, cocoa liquor is produced. At above 104°F this paste has the consistency of peanut butter and is beginning to smell of something like chocolate. The cocoa liquor is pressed to extract the cocoa butter, leaving a solid matter called cocoa presscake.

Cocoa nibs: cocoa beans that have had their shells removed and broken into small pieces.

Cocoa pods: the fruit of the cocoa tree, containing around 50 cocoa beans.

Cocoa powder: is obtained by crumbling cocoa presscake.

Cocoa presscake: the solid matter that remains after cocoa liquor has been pressed and cocoa butter has been extracted.

Cocoa solids % (also referred to as cocoa content): represents everything that comes from cocoa beans – that is, ground cocoa beans as well as added cocoa butter. A high cocoa solids percentage does not imply strong choco-late. For example, a chocolate labelled '70% cocoa solids' could contain 2 oz ground beans + ¼ oz added cocoa butter. It could also represent 2 oz ground beans + ½ oz added cocoa butter. As cocoa butter has no taste, the latter would be weaker in aromas and would have a more fatty feel.

Conching: process that consists of a machine kneading the chocolate mixture for up to 3 days at a temperature between 140°F to 167°F. Acidity is reduced and aromas develop.

Couverture: most chocolatiers buy chocolate in bulk, called 'couverture', rather than grinding their own cocoa beans. Couverture can take the form of ready-to-melt chocolate, in big blocks of 2 to 55 lbs, or chocolate which has been pre-melted and tempered, delivered as a liquid.

Criollo: the finest and most aromatic of the three species of cultivated cocoa tree. As it is the most vulnerable to disease and has the smallest yield, it was replaced in the twentieth century. 'Criollo' on packaging, if not a lie, refers to the 'modern Criollo', a hybrid of Criollo and Trinitario. Since 2000, a demand for aromatic quality has triggered its revival in this form.

Dark chocolate: to be called 'dark' chocolate has to contain no milk powder and a minimum of 43% cocoa solids (35% in the USA).

Drying: once fermented and drained, cocoa beans are dried in the sun or with hot air. This reduces humidity to less than 6–8%, preventing germination and reducing risks of mould during storage and shipment.

Fermentation: a natural process which occurs when the cocoa beans, still covered in their fruity pulp or mucilage, are put in wooden boxes and mixed every 5–7 days. This brings out the precursors of the aromas which will be transformed into aromas at conching.

Forastero: one of the three species of cocoa tree (close to 85% of world pro-duction). They have the least aromatic beans but are disease-resistant with the best yield. Found mainly in Africa (but not Madagascar).

Ganache: mixture of cream and chocolate, found in all truffles.

Lecithin: an extract of soy beans. It is an emulsifier which is added to choco-late mixture to help achieve the right texture.

Mélangeur: this is an old-style grinding machine.

Milk chocolate: milk chocolate has to contain a minimum of 25% cocoa solids (10% in the USA). Its is enriched with milk powder and usually has more sugar than cocoa mass.

Nibs: *see* Cocoa nibs.

Percentage: *see* Cocoa solids.

Plantation bar: a bar made exclusively from beans selected from a plantation of a few acres, usually renowned for the quality of its beans. Similar to *Domaine* for wines. Plantation bars began in 1994 with Hacienda el Rosario from Bonnat. Aromas vary from one vintage to another and editions are limited.

Porcelana: a single genetic variety of cocoa beans, with more than 90% of Criollo genes, which comes only from Sur del Lago, Venezuela.

Praline: a Belgian word used for all filled chocolates.

Praliné: the French word used to describe a chocolate made with a mixture of roasted almonds and/or hazelnuts ground together with caramel.

Presscake: *see* Cocoa presscake.

Roasting: cocoa beans are roasted to bring out the aromas of the beans.

Shelling: a winnowing machine is used to remove the shells from the beans to leave what are known as the cocoa nibs.

Single-estate/Single-origin: a 'single-estate' or 'single-origin' bar indicates that the cocoa beans used to produce it are from a specific region of a country (like 'Bordeaux' on a wine label) or a single country.

Tempering: the process of careful heating and cooling that produces dark shiny chocolate with a sharp cut. The cocoa butter in chocolate has six crystal forms; tempering evenly distributes mainly the fifth form. Untempered ot poorly tempered chocolate is dull, streaky and often grainy.

Trinitario: the Trinitario is descended from a cross between Criollo and Forastero. This tree has hybrid characteristics – robustness, aromatic beans, and a fairly good yield.

Vanillin: a cheap synthetic version of vanilla.

White chocolate: this is not legally chocolate as it is not made from cocoa beans. The main ingredients are cocoa butter (often other fats are added), milk powder and sugar. The taste comes from the milk powder and the added vanilla (or vanillin), thus the quality of a white chocolate relies on their quality. White chocolate is confectionery, not chocolate.

Bibliography

Aftel, Mandy, *Essence and Alchemy: A Book of Perfume,* San Francisco, North Point Press, 2001.

Bailleux, Nathalie *et al.*, *Le Livre du Chocolat,* Paris, Flammarion, 1995.

Boynton, Sandra, *Chocolate: The Consuming Passion,* London, Methuen, 1982.

Coe, Sophie D. and Coe, Michael D., *The True History of Chocolate,* London, Thames & Hudson, 1996.

Khodorowsky, Katherine, and de Loisy, Oliver, *Chocolat et grands crus de cacao,* Paris, Editions Solar, 2003.

Prescilla, Maricel E., *The New Taste of Chocolate,* Berkeley, Ten Speed Press, 2001.

Robinson, Jancis, *How to Taste,* New York, Simon & Schuster, 2001.

Robinson, Jancis, *Jancis Robinson's Wine Tasting Workbook,* London, Conran Octopus, 2000.

Resources

$\mathcal{A}$s with any topic, the internet has become the easiest and fastest way to find out about chocolate. Over the last five years, chocolate-related websites have mushroomed. Although these are 'international', be aware that shipping constraints and costs, as well as the storage conditions of the chocolates as they wing their way to you, can make this an expensive option. So I strongly recommend that you surf websites of companies or organisations whose headquarters are in your own country. Below I have listed some useful websites, which I have divided into categories. You can subscribe to email newsletters through many of the websites, and try searching by brand of chocolate, including the brands in this book.

Research

www.icco.org – the website of the International Cocoa Organisation. It provides statistics and annual reports on cocoa-producing countries and all sectors of the industry.

www.retailconfectioners.org – is rich in information on legislation, retailers and brands in the USA.

Online Shopping (only a few of them!)

www.chocolateco-op.com (UK)

www.chocolatesource.com (USA)

www.chocolats-pralus.com

www. chocophile.com (USA)

www.chocolatealchemy.com (USA)

www.chocosphere.com (USA)

www.intveld.de/english.htm (Germany)

www.valrhona.com

Chocolate clubs

Do use your internet search engine and type in the words 'chocolate clubs' to look up others that may appeal to you more – or are simply closer to where you live.

www.chocolate.co.uk (UK)

www.croqueurschocolat.com (France)

www.passionnes-chocolat.ch (Switzerland)

www.berkeleychocolateclub.com (USA)

Index

Academy of Chocolate 45
acidity 84, 85
acne 164
addiction 171–2
additives 67
    see also flavourings
ADM 119
agrotourism 201
Amedei 26, 33, 67, 93–6, 120, 135, 193, 198–9
anandamide 166
anti-depressants 14
antioxidants 163
AOC (Appellation d'Origine Controlée) 206
aphrodisiacs 167–8
aromas 60–1, 147, 194
    describing 86–90
    factors affecting 63, 116–18
    sampling 81–3
Austria 23, 24
Aztecs 7, 10–12, 64, 167

bad chocolate 202
    aroma 82
    and health 172–4
    labelling 192
    marketed as good 118, 200, 204
    production process 55–6, 60, 68–9, 73
ballotins 20, 206
bars of chocolate 3, 130–41, 146, 179, 201
    early 8, 15–16
    mass production 8, 17
    plantation bars 50, 133, 189, 197, 208

single-estate bars 50, 133, 208
    tasting 33–4
Belgium 20–1, 23, 24, 28
bitterness 84, 85–6
'bloomed' chocolate 180–1, 206
body weight 164–5
Bonnat 26–7, 50, 131–2
boxed chocolates 20, 21, 206
Brazil 51

Cadbury 7, 16–17, 21–2, 33, 93, 123, 193
caffeine 166, 169
Callebaut, Barry 119
candies 8, 17–18, 21–4, 33–4, 36, 43–4, 142–3
careers in chocolate 175–86
    day-in-the-life of a chocolate taster 177–83
    tips 183–4
Cargill 119
carob 173
choco-gourmets 172
chocoholics 171–2
Chocolate Society 43–5
Chocolates Santander 198
chocolatiers 206
chocophobes 96
Chocovic 27
cholesterol levels 162
Chuao 134–5
Club des Croqueurs du Chocolat 126
clubs 42–6, 79–80, 126, 184, 211
Cluizel, Michel 27, 33, 50, 94, 96, 107, 120, 132, 189
co-operatives 61–2, 125
cocoa beans 7–9, 18–19, 21, 59–60, 121–2, 190

Criollo 27, 50–1, 54–6, 61, 117,
138, 191, 196–7, 199–200,
203, 207
definition 206
drying 62–3, 116, 207
fermentation 60–1, 116, 117, 207
Forastero 16, 22, 51, 54–6,
116–17, 137, 207
Nacional 54
organic 124–5
Porcelana 208
quality control 61–2
regions of origin 50, 133, 134–5
roasting and shelling 64, 208
sale 61–2
Trinitario 54–6, 72, 117, 138,
191, 208
world market 115–17
cocoa butter 7, 15, 65–6, 68–9,
121–3, 131, 144, 162, 206–7
cocoa butter equivalents (CBEs)
123–4
cocoa liqueurs 61
cocoa liquor 65–6, 206
cocoa nibs 64–5, 138, 181, 206
cocoa pods 56–60, 206
cocoa powder 7, 15, 105–7, 122–3,
169, 206
cocoa presscake 65, 206
cocoa solids (cocoa content) 121–4,
133, 174, 191, 206–7
cocoa trees 49, 50, 54–6, 202
cocoa-producing regions 49–54,
133, 134–5
coffee 138, 145–6, 169, 205
Colombia 198
commoditisation of chocolate 18–20
conching 8, 16, 67–8, 116, 118, 131,
207
continental chocolates 19–20
Corallo, Claudio 72–4, 96, 137–40,
190, 196
couverture 118–20, 125, 146–7, 153,
190, 207

cravings 99, 169–71
cultural references 158–9
curiosity 30–2, 34

Dagoba 126, 127
dark chocolate 32–3, 94–5, 123,
162–3, 207
databases, chocolate 128
De Vries, Steve 33, 63, 68, 136–40,
190, 196
delicatessens 46
dental health 164
department stores 46
diabetics 172–3
DIY chocolate 72–5
Domori 27, 33, 86, 94, 96, 132,
138–40, 182, 190–1, 196–9
drinking chocolate 7, 10–13, 64,
104–8, 163
drying beans 62–3, 116, 207

Ecuador 52, 134
El Rey 27–8, 69, 96–7, 198
endorphins 166
England 23, 24
European Union (EU) 22, 66, 123

factories 64–70
fair-trade 124, 125, 199
fats of chocolate 66, 162
    see also cocoa butter
Felchlin 28
fermentation 60–1, 116–17, 207
filled chocolates 33–4, 130, 141–56,
178–9
    invention 8, 20
    recipes 155–6
    storage 70–1
    testing 95, 149–53
flavonoids 163
flavourings 189–90
flavours 84–90, 190, 193–5
Fog City News 193–4
forbidden foods 170

Fortnum & Mason 2, 5, 20, 138, 152–4, 175–83, 190, 199
France 23–4, 26–9
fridges/freezers 70–1
Fry's 15–17, 121, 131
future of chocolate 187–204

Galaxy 33, 93, 123
ganaches 142, 145, 149–51, 155–6, 179, 207
Gaultier, Lydia 145
Genin, Jacques 144–5, 196
Germany 23, 24
Ghana 51, 198
ginger, candied 154
Godiva 20–1, 118
good/real chocolate 25–9
    aroma 82
    beans 54, 60
    distinguishing 115–29
    labelling 192
    production process 54, 60, 68, 69
    sampling 30, 77
Gran Cru chocolate 28, 29
Green & Black 94
Guittard 28

health, and chocolate 157–74
Hermé, Pierre 35, 78, 110, 176
Hershey 8, 123
history of chocolate 7–29
Hot Chocolate à la Chloé 107–8

Indonesia 51
ingredients lists 121–4, 143–4
Ingrid's Spicy Hot Chocolate 105–6
Ingrid's Tarte au Chocolat 112–13
Internet 45–6, 210–11
intuition 99–100
Italy 23, 24, 26, 27
Ivory Coast 51

Jamaica 52
Japan 23, 24

Kaoka 126

labels 191–3
Ladurée 35, 78, 176, 184
L'Association Carrément Chocolat 79–80
lecithin 121, 122, 207
Leonidas 118
Lindt 8, 16–17, 33, 67–8, 86, 93–4, 118, 131–2, 134, 193
N-linoleylethanolamine 166
Linxe, Robert 45

machinery 64, 139, 207
Madagascar 52
maltitol 173
Marcolini, Pierre 94, 197
marketing 20–1
marzipan 142, 149, 150, 152
Mayas 7, 10, 11, 202
medicinal chocolate 7, 8, 14
Mélangeur 207
Mexico 13, 19, 50, 51, 199
migraines 168
milk chocolate 16, 32–3, 94–5, 123, 159, 172, 207
minerals 162
modern chocolate 21–5
mood 165–8, 171
'moreishness' of chocolate 170–1
moulding 70
mucilage 59–62

Nestlé 16–17, 119, 120
Nutella 3–4, 108–11
Nutella Tart 110–11
nutritional value of chocolate 14–18, 162–7
nutty chocolate 154
    see also praliné

oleic acid 162
N-oleoylethanolamine 166
Omanhene 198

organic chocolate 124–7

palmitic acid 162
party games 101–4
passion 5–6, 34–5, 205
phenylethlamine (PEA) 166, 168
plantation bars 50, 133, 189, 197, 208
praline 208
praliné 142, 149–51, 179, 208
Pralus 28, 33, 68, 73, 78–9, 88, 96, 105, 112, 120–1, 137, 191, 199
price of chocolate 99, 173, 196–7
proanthocyanidin 163
production process 48–75
    conching 8, 16, 67–8, 116, 118, 131, 207
    drying 62–3, 116, 207
    fermentation 60–1, 116–17, 207
    moulding 70
    roasting and shelling 64, 208
    tempering 68–9, 208
psychological baggage 157–61
psychological health 165–8, 171

Quakers 16
quality control 61–2

Recchiuti, Michael 181
recipes 104–13, 155–6
restaurants 201
roasting 64, 208
rose creams 143, 152
Rowntree 16

saltiness 86
Scandinavia 23, 24
Scharffen Berger 28, 33, 68, 105, 155, 190
sense test 80–4
Seventy Per Cent Club 45–6
shelling 64, 208
single estate bars 50, 133, 208
smell, sense of 81–3

sourness 84, 85
Spain 7, 12, 14, 19, 23–4, 27, 167
speciality chocolate 150, 152–3
status-symbol chocolate 199–200
stimulants 166, 169
stockists 25, 46, 193–4, 201, 203, 211
    see also Fortnum & Mason
storage 70–1
sugar 99, 121, 165, 169–73
sugar-free chocolate 172–3
sweetness 84, 85

tartes 110–11, 112–13
tasting chocolate 2–5, 10, 76–100, 128–9, 203
    aroma 81–3, 86–90
    assessing your tastes 36–40
    changing tastes 92–3
    checklist for 88–9
    choosing what to taste 93–100
    clubs 42–6
    conditions for 90–1
    developing your palate 40–2
    filled chocolates 149–53
    flavours 84–90
    making notes 40–2, 128
    and memories 37–8
    and negative thoughts 161
    party games for 101–4
    personal profiles 30–47
    sense test 80–4
    speed tasting 98–100
    on your own 42
tasting notes 192–3, 194–5
tasting wheels 87
tea 145–6, 147, 205
tempering 68–9, 208
testing your knowledge 185–6
texture 66, 67, 80–1
theobromine 166, 169
Thornton's 118
Toblerone 93
truffles 95, 152–3

United States 23, 28, 29, 123

Valrhona 8, 26–7, 29, 33, 44, 68,
    86–7, 93–7, 106–7, 110, 112,
    120, 126, 131–3, 135, 147,
    155, 193–5, 197, 199
Van Houten 17, 18, 65, 131
vanilla 121, 122, 189–90, 202
vanilla pods 114
vanillin 121, 122, 189–90, 208
'vegelate' 66, 161
vegetable fats 66

vending machines 202
Venezuela 51–2, 134–5, 137, 198–9
vintage chocolate 27, 135–6, 190
violet creams 143, 152

Weiss 64, 93, 95
Weiss & Chaudun 132
white chocolate 33, 173, 208
wine 133–6, 174, 205
winnowing machines 64
world chocolate consumption
    22, 23

"Ha!" Reyna snorted.

"Go home, Wulf," Hagar said. "You and Reyna can sort this out tomorrow."

"I am not leaving without Reyna. My wife belongs in my hall, in my bed. Your son is cured of his illness, thanks to Reyna's skill, and she is no longer needed in your hall. Do not interfere in this, Hagar."

Hagar sighed. "I care naught about your marital problems as long as you confine them to your own hall. Please leave so I can return to my bed."

"Hagar is right," Wulf agreed. "It is wrong of us to air our differences in his hall, in the middle of the night."

So saying, he tossed Reyna over his shoulder and strode out the door.

"Wulf, put me down!" Reyna cried. "Your show of strength does not impress me."

"I know exactly what will impress you," Wulf growled. "I have been without the comfort of your body too many nights. 'Tis time you performed your wifely duties."

"I am sure Uma will be happy to take my place in your bed."

"I am sure she would, however Uma is not the woman I want or need in my bed."

When they reached Wulf's hall, he flung open the door and stormed inside. "You," he shouted, pointing to Uma, "leave. I have decided your fate. Henceforth, Hagar is your new master. I have just gifted you to him. Be thankful I will not sell you as I threatened."

Grabbing her coarse cloak from a peg, Uma left in a rush. Wulf carried Reyna to his sleeping alcove and tossed her onto his bed. She scrambled to her knees but he pushed her back down.

"Stay there and listen to me, you little wildcat. Think you I want Uma when I have you?"

Her chin rose in open defiance. "I am a Dane."

"I am aware of that."

"You never wanted to wed me; you were forced into marriage by my father and brothers. Once you tire of me, you will take Uma or another like her to your bed."

"I did not have to admit to your family that we were lovers. I could have left your farmstead without you and never looked back. Why can you not accept the fact that I wanted you in my life?"

"You are a lusty warrior, Wulf. Yes, we are good in bed together. But that is not enough for me. I want . . ."

"What do you want? Love?" He made a scoffing sound. "I had love once and lost it. Love is a fragile emotion; I have no wish to open my heart to that kind of pain again. Why can we not let what we have be enough? I do not hate you, Reyna. Far from it. I went against everything I believe in to keep you with me."

Reyna shook her head. "'Tis not enough, Wulf. What *do* you believe in if not love?"

"Honor, pride, vows, even though I broke mine when I wed you. Everything I swore I would not do I did, for you. Against all odds, you, a Dane, are my wife."

"Tomorrow I shall stand in the doorway and shout my intention to divorce you to one and all," she said.

Wulf's silver eyes narrowed to a smoky gray. "There will be no divorce. I will prove to you that we belong together, that the emotion you call love is but a word that means naught."

Chapter Sixteen

"Why do you want me?" Reyna cried. "Give me a reason I should remain your wife. A reason besides mutual lust."

Wulf sent her a bemused look before answering. "You are brave and fearless. You saved my life." A long silence fraught with tension ensued. "I believe you care for me."

"Caring for someone works two ways. I understand that you cannot love me, but I do not have to accept it."

"Reyna, you are being ridiculous. I am a warrior, a man of action, not of words. I can show you why I need you."

"Not good enough, Wulf."

"I can't believe you wish to return to Ragnar. He is not half the man I am."

Reyna sighed. She was getting nowhere with the stubborn Norseman. Perhaps she should accept what Wulf could give her and remain his wife. Mayhap Wulf would wake up one day and realize he loved her.

"You know I do not want Ragnar."

"Then why are you arguing with me? I miss having you in my bed, wife."

"Uma . . ."

". . . means naught to me. She will never crawl into my bed uninvited again."

Indecision bit deep inside Reyna. She lowered her head to ponder her options, but when she raised it a

dozen heartbeats later, she realized her options had been taken from her. Wulf's hands were already releasing the ties on her tunic. He stood over her, naked, a man aware of his virility and willing to use it to gain what he wanted. And from the scorching heat blazing in his eyes, it was obvious she was what he wanted. The sexual potency he exuded was magnetic. The scent of his skin filled her with longing.

Mesmerized, she offered no resistance when he grasped her arms, pulled her to her feet and pushed her against the wall. Shoving his pelvis against her, he effectively pinned her in place as he released the ties of her undertunic and pushed both garments past her waist to the floor. Immediately his mouth covered her right nipple, pulling and sucking while his loins pumped against hers, letting her feel the strength of his desire.

The wet heat of his mouth moved from one breast to the other, taking his fill of her sweet flesh. A moan slipped past Reyna's lips as she dug her fingers into his shoulders. She waited for him to carry her to bed to finish this and was startled when she felt his hands slide down her legs and then up again, clasping the taut globes of her bottom in his callused palms.

"Wrap your legs around my waist," Wulf whispered against her ear.

He lifted her bare bottom as her legs clasped his waist like a vine, her breasts pressed against his chest. Her pulse beat erratically. She felt weightless in his arms. She inhaled sharply when his sex probed between her thighs. When he found the slick place he sought, he thrust deep and hard, filling her with his burgeoning heat.

She clung to his shoulders, her back supported by the wall, as Wulf pounded into her, his breath grating harshly in her ear. With a cry of need she lurched against him,

meeting him thrust for thrust, thrashing her head from side to side until his mouth took hers in a blistering kiss. Her groans became cries of urgency. Her insides coiled tighter and tighter. Suddenly she shuddered, crying out as she dissolved in a pool of raw bliss, collapsing against him. Never breaking contact, Wulf carried her to the bed and lowered them both to the surface. He began to arouse Reyna again, kissing her breathless, teasing her nipples, nibbling her ear until her breath caught and she arched up in renewed invitation, fully engaged again in the act of love.

"I can wait no longer," Wulf gasped. "Come with me, love."

Reyna heard the word "love" but was too caught up in the moment to grasp its implication. Her violently aroused mind and body considered it nothing more than a meaningless endearment randomly uttered.

Fearing he would stop, Reyna grasped his shoulders and cried, "Do not stop! Not yet!"

A growl ripped from Wulf's throat. "You are killing me."

But Wulf didn't have to wait long. Heat filled her belly, shock waves buffeted her as she felt her insides contract and then explode.

"Thank Odin," Wulf muttered as he grasped her buttocks, pulled her hard against him and speared her with forceful plunges, over and over, the friction bringing him thundering to the edge. Reyna was still quivering from her own climax when his powerful body released, filling her with the life-giving heat of his essence.

Gasping for breath, he rolled to his back and pulled her hard against his side, as if fearing she might attempt to leave. Lulled by the sweet afterglow of intense love-making, Reyna had no intention of going anywhere.

Wulf was gone when Reyna awoke the next morning. She stretched luxuriously, a slow smile curving her lips as she remembered the previous night and Wulf's loving. Then the smile turned into a frown when she recalled finding Uma in Wulf's bed.

Reyna rose, deciding a long soak in the volcanic pool would ease some of her aches from the previous night's activities. She dressed quickly and left the sleeping alcove, stopping abruptly when she saw a woman bent over the hearth. The woman turned and smiled at her. Reyna recognized her and returned her smile. Her name was Gerta and she was one of Hagar's thralls. Gerta, who understood some but spoke little of the Norse language, had come from a Germanic tribe. Hagar had purchased her in Rika and, according to Thora, Gerta was an excellent cook.

Wulf had been as good as his word, replacing Uma with someone older and wiser. That small gesture pleased Reyna and made her less sure about leaving Wulf. Did she want love so badly that she would leave the man she *did* love to find someone who loved *her?* The answer became less clear.

"Mistress," Gerta said in a guttural growl. "Sit and eat." The thrall set a bowl of porridge and a pitcher of milk on the table and motioned for Reyna to sit. Since Reyna was hungry she sat down, poured milk on the porridge and ate until the bowl was empty. She had started to rise when Gerta placed a dish of eggs and ham in front of her.

"Oh, no, this is too much," Reyna demurred.

"It looks just right for me," Wulf said from behind her. He sank onto the bench beside Reyna. She pushed the plate of food in front of him. "Help yourself. Porridge was enough for me."

She rose. "Where are you going?" Wulf asked.

"Ask me."

"Come."

As winter fought its way toward spring, Lee came three more times. Each time was a godsend, a tiny respite from the routine. Robin had offered to do night duty, but until the very end I didn't want her to put so much of her own time into what really was my duty. Duty is such an intolerant word; I didn't want to shirk my responsibilities, and especially didn't want Robin to disrupt her own life. She had two young daughters to think of. Although, in the end, she did begin spending nights when her mother could take the girls.

When Lee came my father always rallied. Drawing on some strength he kept in reserve, Dad would keep talking for hours with Lee; no subject was excluded except illness. The two of them would wander over current events and sports. So fixed in the extremes of my daily concerns I had let the world slip away, promising to chase after it someday. Then, when Dad would doze off, Lee would make me tell him what I really needed to say. He offered me the comfort of an ear and gentle consolation.

No longer allowing him to slip away while I slept, I rose early on his departure mornings and we breakfasted together, most times discussing the night my father had passed, sometimes seeking neutral topics. Each morning he was a little ahead of me. I would waken to the light buzzing of his razor and then the scent of coffee brewing. I'd come down and often he would be in my studio, enticing embers into a blaze and lifting the sheet on my unfinished piece.

"You didn't do much on it since Tuesday—was it a bad week?"

"No, actually I stood in front of it for hours, playing

with it. Sometimes that's almost as much work as using paint."

"Hmm." He nodded over his mug. "Like sitting in front of the screen and playing with one sentence."

"Precisely."

The gray of dawn was just brightening when I walked him out to the station wagon. Our feet made disparate prints in the new snowfall. "See you Tuesday," he promised, ducking quickly into the car.

"Thank you." I rested my hand on his shoulder through the car window.

"For what?"

"Being here." I patted his shoulder. "Drive carefully; they don't always sand right away."

"I will." He started the car with an almost imperceptible shaking off of my hand. "Alix, don't hesitate to call me if anything happens. I can be here in two hours."

A lurch in my belly reminded me of why he was here, the need for his presence was my father's dying. There were, unbelievably, moments when I forgot, when his being here was unfettered by a reason for it. I walked back to the house in Lee's footsteps, marveling that my own fit inside of his.

Eleven

"Do you want to admit him?" Robin held my hand as she asked the question.

"No. No, we said we'd stick it out and we will."

Dad lay on the hospital bed, his clouded eyes lighting on me now and again, then drifting away to gaze blankly at the ceiling or the wall. I wiped a bit of saliva from the corner of his mouth.

Robin took the Kleenex from me and threw it away, then turned back to me to fold me in her arms. "Good. I'll stick it out with you. We just need to get Dr. Mulcahey to do house calls."

We laughed, Mulcahey being our least favorite physician on the short list of doctors who had been involved in Dad's case.

In the last three weeks the cancer had moved like an enemy army, stealing away strength and appetite and interest. The television sat silent, its blank gray eye sentinel over the quiet room. Instead I filled the room with

music, George Winston's *December* being Dad's favorite, calming him when he became agitated. Never
again could I listen to that tape without feeling the
emotions that daily trickled through me.

The Visiting Nurses came more frequently. In my
more whimsical moments, I thought of them as Crimean
War nurses, Florence Nightingales ministering to the
terminally wounded. Though neither wore uniforms,
their aura was so professionally powerful that the
image was undeniable. Strong, efficient, caring without
condescension. Tag-team nurses, they swapped shifts
and soon Dad and I were never alone.

"Come on, Alix, you've got to do this for me," Robin
chided when I declined her invitation to go out for
dinner.

"Robin, you know . . ."

"Alix, it's my thirty-fifth birthday and I'm depressed
as hell. You've got to help me get through it."

"Hey, I lived through that one, it's not so bad."

"The heck it isn't. Now I'm no longer in my early
thirties. Now I'm Old Widow Gates."

"You're as young as you feel."

"Bunk!"

While all around me the friends of my youth met
and married their husbands, had their children, and
drew a jagged chasm between our lives, I had continued to live the life of the independent woman, searching always for artistic success and looking down my
nose at the trifles of domestic life. Diapers and temperatures and teething became the topics of the conversa-
tions my friends had, and if two of them came together,
I might as well have dropped in from a foreign country
for all the comprehension I had of their concerns. The

SPOILS OF WAR

Scowling, Wulf sent her a dismissive look. "I suppose you are happy now that you can order me to do your bidding."

Reyna returned Wulf's scowl with a satisfied smile. "I am supremely happy. Give thanks that you are still alive. Being a thrall does not seem so bad when you consider the alternative. Now you know how I felt. Does it hurt your pride to serve me? Does it shame you? Make you feel less a man?"

Wulf felt all those things and more. Helpless. Enraged. Yet still hungry for the Dane vixen standing beside him, looking smug and far too lovely for his peace of mind. How would he manage an entire winter in her company without acting on his impulse to toss her to the ground and thrust himself inside her?

Other books by Connie Mason:

THE PRICE OF PLEASURE
HIGHLAND WARRIOR
A TASTE OF PARADISE
A KNIGHT'S HONOR
GYPSY LOVER
THE PIRATE PRINCE
THE LAST ROGUE
THE LAIRD OF STONEHAVEN
TO LOVE A STRANGER
SEDUCED BY A ROGUE
TO TAME A RENEGADE
LIONHEART
A LOVE TO CHERISH
THE ROGUE AND THE HELLION
THE DRAGON LORD
THE OUTLAWS: SAM
THE OUTLAWS: JESS
THE OUTLAWS: RAFE
THE BLACK KNIGHT
GUNSLINGER
BEYOND THE HORIZON
PIRATE
BRAVE LAND, BRAVE LOVE
WILD LAND, WILD LOVE

BOLD LAND, BOLD LOVE
VIKING!
SURRENDER TO THE FURY
FOR HONOR'S SAKE
LORD OF THE NIGHT
TEMPT THE DEVIL
PROMISE ME FOREVER
SHEIK
ICE & RAPTURE
LOVE ME WITH FURY
SHADOW WALKER
FLAME
TENDER FURY
DESERT ECSTASY
A PROMISE OF THUNDER
PURE TEMPTATION
WIND RIDER
TEARS LIKE RAIN
THE LION'S BRIDE
SIERRA
TREASURES OF THE HEART
CARESS & CONQUER
PROMISED SPLENDOR
WILD IS MY HEART
MY LADY VIXEN

Connie Mason

Viking Warrior

LEISURE BOOKS NEW YORK CITY

*This book is dedicated to my late husband Jerry.
Through 57 years of love and laughter, joy and
sorrow, our hearts remained firm and true.
Life ends but love is endless.*

A LEISURE BOOK®

November 2008

Published by

Dorchester Publishing Co., Inc.
200 Madison Avenue
New York, NY 10016

ISBN 10: 0-8439-5746-8
ISBN 13: 978-0-8439-5746-4

Visit us on the web at www.dorchesterpub.com.

Chapter One

A Farmstead on the Norwegian coast, 860 AD

Wulfric the Ruthless, son of the late jarl of Horgaland, Rollo Redbeard, rose gloriously naked from the fjord near his farmstead. Tall, golden and magnificently male, Wulf strode toward shore, water dripping down his powerful body in rivulets.

Wulf had earned his name and reputation because of his prowess in battle, wielding his sword, Blood-Seeker, and his battle-axe with skill and dexterity. During a raid by Danes on their farmstead two summers ago, Wulf had lost his wife and unborn child, and their deaths had turned him into a ruthless berserker. Skalds told and retold the saga of Wulf the Ruthless during long winter nights, embellishing his heroic exploits with each recital.

Wulf had just reached for his clothing when a shout brought him spinning around toward the fjord. Shading his eyes against the glare of the late autumn sun, he stared at the dragonship skimming across the water toward shore. Wulf's first instinct was to reach for Blood-Seeker. Then he recognized the square red-and-white-striped sail of his brother's dragonship and relaxed.

Hagar had finally returned. His arrival was expected though somewhat overdue.

The dragonship rode low in the water, laden, Wulf suspected, with silver, glassware, spices and silks from

the Byzantine, where Hagar had gone on a trading expedition. Wulf had also gone abroad but in a different direction and with different goals in mind. Wulf had spent the summer raiding the land of the Danes, seeking vengeance for the death of his wife, Astrid. Having had his fill of killing and plundering, Wulf had returned home to the farmstead earlier than usual.

Wulf pulled his fine linen breeches over his powerfully muscled legs, slipped into a sleeveless linen tunic and belted Blood-Seeker about his narrow waist. He wore no mail shirt this day for no enemy was expected to invade their farmstead so late in the year. Then he pulled on shaggy fur boots and turned to wait for Hagar's ship to reach the shore.

Hagar was the first to leap out of the vessel when it scraped against the sandy bottom of the fjord. As tall and broad as Wulf, Hagar was but two years older than Wulf's own twenty-eight. His generous beard was as red as the hair on his head.

"Ho, brother!" Hagar greeted as he splashed through the surf toward Wulf.

The brothers embraced. "Your ship rides low in the water, Hagar," Wulf observed. "Your voyage to the Byzantine must have been a profitable one."

Hagar threw back his head and laughed. "More profitable than even I expected. What about you, brother? When did you return?"

"Some days ago. Why are you late? Your arrival has been anxiously anticipated."

"Odin's blood!" Hagar exclaimed. "I would have returned sooner if Thor had not brewed a storm that sent us off course."

"Come, I will walk with you to the farmstead."

"In a moment," Hagar replied. "I bought you a special gift from Constantinople."

A frown darkened Wulf's rugged features. "You bought me a gift? What are you up to, Hagar?"

"You have become morose and overbearing of late. I thought you needed something to cheer you up."

Wulf's frown deepened. "I do not need cheering."

Hagar rolled his eyes, suggesting otherwise. "Do not look a gift horse in the mouth, brother. Enjoy it with my good wishes."

"Why am I suspicious of your largess, Hagar?"

"There was a woman with hair the color of moonlight on the auction block at the slave market in Constantinople. Her previous master could not tame her and was eager to sell her."

"What does this have to do with me?"

"I wanted to make life a little more interesting for you. All you've known since Astrid's death is sorrow and vengeance. Your grief weighs too heavily upon you."

Wulf slashed his hand through the wet strands of his golden hair. "Enough, Hagar, I have better things to do than talk nonsense with you."

Grasping his shoulders, Hagar turned Wulf toward the fjord, where men were unloading trade goods from the beached dragonship. The moment Wulf saw her, he whipped around to glare at his brother. "Thor's hammer, Hagar, what have you done?"

Hagar laughed. "Her name is Reyna. She is a Dane. I gift her to you. You can thank me later. I hope you have better luck taming her than her previous master." Then he strode off toward the farmstead, leaving Wulf with the terrible urge to kill his brother.

Reyna waded ashore, angry at the Norsemen and at the world. She hated men but Norsemen most of all. She wondered why the redheaded Viking had purchased her and what the future held for her. Fortunately she and

the Norseman named Hagar had been able to converse. She had learned the Norse language from a Norse-woman concubine in her master's harem. Hagar had refused to answer her questions, however, and had even laughed at some private joke when she asked about his plans for her.

Reyna had no idea what she was supposed to do when Hagar strode off, leaving her stranded on the shore. She started to follow, but stopped abruptly when she saw a man staring at her, his expression one of chagrin. At first she didn't recognize him and thought him the most impressive man she had ever seen. He was beautiful in a rugged, masculine way. With his blond hair ruffled by the wind and his clothing hugging his powerful muscles, he rivaled Odin, the great god of war.

Then, to her utter horror, she recognized him as a man she'd hoped never to see again. He was the Norse berserker who had raided her farmstead the summer before, ravished her in the heat of battle, and then taken her captive. Though he had not touched her again during the long voyage to Byzantium, she had lived in fear during those dark days. If the Norseman called Wulf the Ruthless had attempted to touch her, she would have jumped overboard. But he had simply brooded during the entire voyage to Constantinople, where he sold her to a slave trader without a hint of remorse.

Wulf stared through narrowed lids at the woman approaching him. With the setting sun behind her, obscuring her features, she might have been a seductive Valkyrie, one of Odin's handmaidens who carried a warrior's soul to Valhalla.

She was tall and slim and shapely, her head crowned by a coronet of braids so pale they gleamed like molten sil-

ver, her white tunic belted at the waist with a silver girdle. Her feet barely seemed to touch the ground as she floated toward him. A vague sense of recognition washed over him. Who was this woman Hagar had identified as Reyna the Dane?

Reyna reached Wulf and stopped in front of him, gazing with unleashed fury into his silver fire-and-ice eyes, her hands curled into fists. Her eyes dropped to his hard, flattened mouth, sculpted with harsh disapproval and bracketed by two sharp lines. Did he remember her? She certainly remembered him.

"Wulf the Ruthless, we meet again," she snarled, and spat on the ground at his feet. "You are the Norse berserker who destroyed my life. I hope you burn in hell."

Suddenly Wulf remembered the woman. He had scooped her from the ground and carried her aboard his dragonship after Rannulf Haroldson had climbed off of her. She had been curled into a ball and weeping. Though she had wept all the way to Byzantium, Wulf could find no compassion in his wounded soul.

Wulf laughed; a bitter sound that sent chills down Reyna's spine. "I already reside in hell. Your people made sure of that."

"Why was I brought here?"

"My brother purchased you and gifted you to me." Wulf had no intention of keeping Reyna. A Dane thrall with a body and face that would tempt a statue was the last thing he needed in his hall. To make matters still worse, apparently she was under the misapprehension that he had been the one to ravish her during the raid on her farmstead.

Reyna drew back in horror. "You are a rapacious beast. I refuse to serve you."

"You accuse me falsely. Rest assured that I do not

want you in my hall any more than you want me for a master. Follow me, I will take you to Hagar's hall. My mother can always use another thrall."

Wulf grasped Reyna's arm and pulled her along with him, trying to ignore the softness of her skin beneath his hand. Thank Odin, the trek to the farmstead was not a long one.

The yard was filled with activity. Thralls trod back and forth between the many buildings comprising the farmstead. The various structures were built of rough pine logs, their pitched roofs covered with turf. There were so many buildings it looked like a village. Beyond the farmstead, thralls and karls were harvesting crops such as oats, wheat and barley with curved sickles while others toiled in the garden. Cattle and sheep grazed on the nearby hillsides while pigs, hens and geese wandered around in the yard between the outbuildings.

Wulf headed directly toward the hall, where the family lived in a log and wattle longhouse more than eighty feet in length. The curved walls looked to be at least seven feet thick and the roof was supported on rows of posts.

"Do you live here?" Reyna asked, indicating the impressive longhouse.

"Nay, the hall was too crowded for my liking when I wed so I built my own hall on the farmstead. You will serve my brother and his family."

Reyna bristled. "I am a jarl's daughter, not a thrall. What you did to me and my family is despicable. You are a ruthless killer who took my innocence and then sold me to a foreign master."

Wulf regarded her with contempt. "Your people murdered my wife. I raided your farmstead in retaliation. I cannot even recall whether anyone was slain during the raid for I was half mad with rage."

Wulf opened the door and walked into the hall. Reyna

followed, stopping once she passed beneath the lintel to survey her surroundings. The hall was crowded with people, some clothed in rich fabrics and others wearing rough woolen tunics. Reyna decided the family must be a wealthy one for she saw several men and women wearing silks, brocades, silver jewelry and leather shoes. Once, she had lived in a hall such as this and dressed in imported silks and fine linens. Then she was assaulted and ripped from the bosom of her loving family. She thought of her brothers and Ragnar, her betrothed, and wondered if he had wed another.

Though plain on the outside, the interior of the hall was decorated with carved and painted woodwork touched with gilt. Wide wooden benches for sitting and sleeping lined the walls. The focal point of the hall was the central hearth, which provided not only heat and light but also the means of cooking. Even now cauldrons of iron were suspended over the fire from tripods, emitting mouthwatering smells.

Reyna's stomach rumbled. During the voyage from Constantinople she had eaten whatever the Vikings fed her, mostly dried meats, hard bread and cheese.

Hagar saw Wulf and hailed him. Wulf turned a sour look on his brother. "I am returning your gift. Let Mother put her to work."

A tall, richly dressed Norsewoman joined them. She was handsome rather than pretty, with dark blonde hair and a muscular build. She was also heavy with child.

"Who is this woman?" Olga asked.

"She is your husband's new thrall, Olga," Wulf said before Hagar had a chance to explain.

Olga glared at Reyna and then at her husband. "I will not tolerate this woman in my hall, and I am sure your mother will agree. She is too beautiful and will disrupt the harmony here. Your brothers will fight over her favors."

She sent Hagar a look that did not bode well for him. "What were you thinking, husband? If you intend to bed her yourself, forget it. I will geld you with my knife before I let that happen."

Hagar clutched his crotch protectively. "The thrall belongs to Wulf," he explained. "I purchased her for *his* bed."

"What?" Wulf and Reyna exclaimed at the same time.

An older woman dressed in sumptuous brocade strode over to them. "What seems to be the problem? Who is this woman?"

"Wulf's new thrall," Hagar quickly answered.

"I don't want her," Wulf replied heatedly.

"And I won't have her in my hall," Olga stated, folding her arms across her ample bosom. "Look at her. I won't have that kind of temptation in a hall where young girls and lusty boys live."

"Does she speak our language?" asked Thora, Wulf and Hagar's mother.

"Aye, she speaks and understands our language. Do not ask me how, but she does," Wulf replied.

"I found Reyna on the auction block in Constantinople and thought her perfect for Wulf," Hagar explained. "My brother is far too dour and lacks joy in his life." Hagar sniffed. "I thought he would appreciate my gesture to provide him with entertainment on the long winter nights to come."

"I find your humor perverse," Wulf returned. "Reyna is a Dane."

Hagar laughed. "I know. You cannot deny she is a rare beauty, however. Don't be so grim, brother. Perhaps one day you will thank me."

His face dark as a thundercloud, Wulf took a menacing step toward Hagar.

Thora stopped him with a single word, "Wulf!" Wulf

subsided, though the look he slanted Hagar promised painful retribution.

Olga made a gesture toward Reyna. "If this woman has lived in a harem in Constantinople, she doesn't belong with decent folk. Just imagine all the evil things she has done. If you don't want her, Wulf, sell her to my brother. Rannulf mentioned he was in the market for a new bed slave."

But selling Reyna to Rannulf didn't sit well with Wulf. All too vividly, he recalled Rannulf climbing off Reyna's body and walking away in search of another woman to assault.

Thora stroked her chin. "The woman is lovely. I agree with Olga, Wulf. If you do not need another thrall, sell her to Rannulf."

"I am a jarl's daughter," Reyna protested. "Your son raided our farmstead, did despicable things to me, carried me off and sold me to a slave trader. I will never consent to serve a Viking berserker."

"My brother purchased you. You belong to him," Wulf retorted.

"And I gifted her to you," Hagar shot back. He offered his arm to his wife. "Come, Olga, this is Wulf's problem. My brother is being surly and unappreciative. He no longer knows what to do with a beautiful woman. Shall we inspect the trade goods I brought back from the Byzantine? There are some particularly fine silks for you to choose from."

Wulf glared at Hagar's back.

"Wulf," Thora said, garnering Wulf's attention. "What are you going to do with her? She claims you assaulted her and I am inclined to believe her."

"Return me to my homeland, Wulf the Ruthless," Reyna pleaded. "My family had nothing to do with the raid upon your farmstead. They didn't kill your wife. My

father is a farmer and fisherman. He gave up raiding years ago. My brothers were away, trading along the Volga; they couldn't have been involved in the raid on your farmstead." Her green eyes sparkled with tears. "If you left them alive, eventually they will find me."

Wulf turned his icy gaze on Reyna. Why hadn't he noticed before how lovely she was? During the voyage to Constantinople, he had barely looked at her. She had been a pitiful sight with her torn clothing, matted hair and red-rimmed eyes, and he hadn't wanted to feel compassion for her. Filled with hatred and grief, he had seen her as the enemy instead of a great beauty.

"Thor's blood, Mother," Wulf muttered. "I did not assault Reyna. I am guilty of selling her but naught more. Are you sure you can't use another thrall?"

"Since your father's death, Hagar is the new jarl. He and Olga choose who is to live in the hall and 'tis obvious Olga doesn't want this woman here. She is increasing and we cannot upset her." She spread her hands. "There is nothing I can do."

For the first time in his life, Wulf wished he were the older brother instead of the younger.

Thora looked at Reyna. "What skills do you have? Can you cook? Do you weave? Are you skilled at brewing ale or mead?"

Reyna squared her shoulders. "I cannot cook. Nor can I weave or brew ale or mead. I am a skilled healer and knowledgeable in herbal medicines."

"At least that's a skill we can use," Thora said, nodding. "But you must deal with Wulf yourself—I cannot help you."

Reyna spared Wulf a withering glance. "I do not wish to belong to you, Wulf the Ruthless. Think you I don't remember the pain and degradation I suffered at your hands? Sagas of your nefarious exploits are sung far and

wide. You are a berserker. Your sword drinks innocent blood."

Thora threw up her hands. "She is a bold one, Wulf. Punish her, put her to work or sell her. The decision is yours to make. But before you take her to your hall, I will provide her with a garment more fitting to her station. The silk tunic she wears is too good for a thrall."

Turning, Thora strode away. Reyna folded her arms across her breasts. Her former master had provided her with the white tunic and silver girdle to display her assets while on the auction block. She loved the sensual feel of the silk against her tender skin despite the way it revealed her womanly curves.

"What is my fate to be, Wulf the Ruthless?" Reyna asked, chin jutting in defiance. "Will you ravish me again, sell me or punish me?"

Wulf surprised her by looking directly into her eyes. Their gazes locked, held. What Reyna saw in his eyes stunned her. She had expected an icy flash of hatred, or even lust; not the tiny flame of heat emanating from their frozen depths. Wulf was the first to look away.

"This should do," Thora said, her voice shattering the sexual tension building between them. She thrust a rough woolen garment at Reyna.

The garment felt coarse and unevenly woven. Reyna knew its rough surface would abrade her fair skin and hoped she could keep her silken tunic to wear beneath it.

Thora dismissed Wulf with a wave of her hand. "I have no more time for your problems, Wulf. I will see you tonight at the evening meal."

Thora turned her back on Wulf's pleading look. She had left him no choice but to install Reyna in his hall. "Come with me," he said gruffly.

"If you touch me, I will kill you."

"Go ahead if you think you can."

Turning on his heel, Wulf walked away. He walked so fast Reyna had trouble keeping up with him. He led her through the compound to a smaller version of Hagar's longhouse and stormed inside. Reyna followed. Her first glance revealed a modest hall richly decorated. Two thralls, a man and a young woman, looked up from their chores as Reyna trailed behind Wulf.

Wulf summoned the thralls and they came to him immediately.

"Uma and Lorne are Normans," Wulf explained. "Though their native tongue is English, they speak and understand our language well enough. Uma will show you where to change your tunic and assign chores to you."

Reyna shuddered. "Have you decided to keep me, then?"

"I have decided nothing." His gaze swept over her, settling on her breasts. "Perhaps," he mused, "I will make you my bed slave. You seem useless for anything else."

Reyna drew herself up to her full impressive height. "Hear me, Wulf the Ruthless. Touch me in that way again and you will find a dagger in your heart when you least expect it. I do not make idle threats. My former owner was smart enough to believe me; for your sake I hope you are too."

Wulf threw back his head and laughed. "Are you, a mere female, threatening me, a Viking warrior? I am called Wulf the Ruthless with good reason."

"I know that better than anyone." She drew back her hand as if to strike him. He caught her fist and pulled her against him. The allure of her femininity and her soft body made his cock harden. He released her instantly and stepped away.

"Never raise your hand to me again," he warned. "Though your family may not have killed my wife, your

people did." He raked her with a scornful look. "I would take you to my bed if I wanted you, but you do not appeal to me."

Wulf was lying through his teeth. He hadn't had a woman in a long time, and bedding Reyna would not prove difficult. Hagar had urged him countless times to buy a bed slave and even advised him to bed Uma, who was both young and attractive. Though Wulf had thought about it, he had yet to act upon Hagar's suggestion.

Wulf scarcely recalled the days after the raid on Reyna's farmstead, for he had been mindless with grief, but one thing he did know: He had not raped Reyna. That deed had been accomplished by Rannulf, Olga's brother. Wulf had a strong suspicion, however, that bedding Reyna would be no hardship for him, despite the fact that she was the enemy.

Reyna breathed a sigh of relief as she was led off by Uma to a curtained cubical, where she was told to don the rough woolen tunic. She prayed her words had discouraged the Viking berserker from bedding her.

Recalling the terrible day Wulf had carried her off, she distinctly remembered his blond hair, clean-shaven chin and iron helmet. He had taken her maidenhead, sold her, and then promptly forgotten her. She would never forgive him.

Reyna removed her silver girdle and prepared to don the rough woolen garment over her silk tunic.

"Remove the silk tunic first," Uma ordered.

"The rough wool will chafe my skin."

"You are a slave, and only the master can grant favors. He doesn't appear inclined to do so. Give me your silk tunic."

"Admit it, you want it for yourself," Reyna hissed.

Reyna was too surprised to react as Uma reached out

and ripped the fragile silk garment from her body. Aware that Uma was studying her naked form with pursed lips, Reyna slipped the woolen tunic over her head and belted it with the silver girdle. Then she followed Uma into the hall.

Uma eyed the silver girdle enviously. She pointed to it and demanded, "Give me your girdle. It is too grand for you."

"No, you cannot have it."

"Obey me—I am in charge here. Give it to me now or I will tell the master to beat you."

"Go ahead. I won't give up my girdle."

Reyna could tell that Uma was going to be neither friend nor ally. She acted as if she disliked Reyna on sight.

Uma flew into a rage. Grabbing a broom leaning against the wall, she began beating Reyna with the handle. Taller and stronger than the Norman woman, Reyna wrested the broom from Uma's hands and pushed her to the ground, looming over her like an avenging Valkyrie. Uma began wailing like a banshee, bringing both Lorne and Wulf running to her defense. Wulf tugged the broom from Reyna's hands and tossed it aside.

Lorne helped Uma to her feet. "What is going on here?" Wulf growled.

"Your new thrall is vicious," Uma wailed. "She turned on me for no reason."

Reyna pointed to the remains of the silk tunic Uma still clutched in her hands. "Uma tried to steal my possessions," she shot back. "She took my silk tunic but I will not give up my girdle. Am I allowed nothing of my own?"

Angry at Reyna, his brother and the world in general, Wulf yanked the girdle from Reyna's hands. "You belong to me, as does everything you own."

"I need something to gather the excess material about my waist," Reyna dared.

"Come with me. Uma, return to your chores."

Glaring at Reyna, Uma obeyed Wulf without question as he led Reyna to the other end of the hall, where he removed a coil of rope from a cabinet. He measured out a length, cut it with his dagger and handed it to Reyna. "This should serve." He watched while she tied the rope about her slim waist. Then he turned and disappeared inside a curtained alcove, taking the silver girdle with him.

"Stubborn Viking," she muttered as he walked away.

Uma appeared before her, holding a broom in her hand. She shoved it at Reyna. "Make yourself useful. The hearth needs sweeping."

Gritting her teeth, Reyna took the broom and headed to the hearth. Though her stomach was growling hungrily, no one had offered her food. Were they going to starve her? The cauldron bubbling over the hearth on a tripod gave off a delicious aroma, making her mouth water. Spying some crockery bowls, eating utensils and a loaf of bread on a nearby shelf, Reyna decided to help herself.

Setting the broom against the hearth, she cut a generous slice of bread, ladled out a portion of stew from the cauldron and dipped a hunk of bread into it. She dipped and ate with gusto, until Uma spied her and let out a shriek.

"What are you doing?"

"I am eating. I have put nothing in my stomach since yesterday. This is wonderful. You are a good cook, Uma."

Uma grabbed the bowl and tried to pull it out of Reyna's hands. "You cannot eat without permission! You must wait for mealtime like the rest of us."

A tug of war began. At first Reyna refused to relinquish her food, but then she thought better of making

another fuss and released her grip. Unprepared, Uma flew backward. The contents of the boiling hot stew splashed on her bare arm. Uma screamed, bringing Lorne and Wulf running for the second time that day.

Reyna hadn't wanted to hurt Uma; it had just happened. Now she knelt beside the thrall and picked up her arm to inspect the damage. The girl had suffered a superficial burn, painful but not life threatening unless it festered.

"What's happened now?" Wulf demanded as he helped Uma onto a bench.

Before Reyna could answer, Uma wailed, "The witch threw hot stew at me. She wanted to kill me. Sell her, master, before she kills us all."

"I did no such thing," Reyna scoffed. "I was famished and merely helped myself to the stew simmering over the hearth. I hadn't eaten since yesterday and no one thought to ask if I was hungry."

She paused, glaring up at Wulf. "Uma tried to tug the bowl out of my hands. I didn't want to cause trouble so I released my hold. The stew was hot. What you see is the result of Uma's clumsiness."

"Is that true, Uma?" Wulf asked.

"No," Uma denied tearfully, "the witch lies. She threw the bowl of stew at me."

Wulf turned to Lorne. "Did you see what happened, Lorne?"

Lorne hung his head, stammered a bit and then said, "Reyna lies. It happened just as Uma said."

"I do not lie!" Reyna vehemently protested. "Your thralls do not like me."

Wulf sent her a heated look. "We'll settle this later. First I must determine how badly Uma is hurt."

Reyna grasped Uma's arm and inspected the burn.

"The burn is not serious, Wulf the Ruthless. Fetch your medicinal chest."

"Lorne, go to my brother's hall and fetch the medicinal chest." The young thrall took off. To Reyna, he said, "Can you treat the burn?"

"Aye, it will be fine. I hope your mother keeps the chest well stocked."

Wulf sighed. "My aunt was the healer in the family. She died in the raid along with my wife. My mother isn't much of a healer so I cannot attest to the contents of the chest."

Lorne returned with the medicinal chest and placed it on the bench beside Uma. Reyna opened it and frowned. The herbal preparations inside were not as adequate as she had hoped. Searching among the neatly labeled jars and vials, she found the preparation she was looking for, opened it and sniffed the contents.

"Is something wrong?" Wulf asked.

"This salve will do, though it is not fresh." Cradling Uma's arm, she began slathering a thick coating of salve over the burn.

Apparently Uma didn't appreciate Reyna's efforts. "She is trying to kill me. Stop her, master."

"Are you sure you know what you're doing, Reyna?" Wulf asked.

Reyna sent him an affronted look. "I am a healer. Of course I know what I am doing. Tomorrow I will search the forest and hillsides for fresh herbs and roots."

"You do not have that freedom unless I give it to you," Wulf growled.

Reyna finished bandaging Uma's arm with clean linen cloths she found in the chest and slammed down the lid. Turning, she glared at Wulf. "If you wish for me to be useful, then let me do what I do best."

The fire in Wulf's eyes melted the ice as he pulled her aside and growled in a low voice, "I am beginning to believe that what you do best should take place in my bed."

Reyna stared up at him with huge green eyes slightly slanted up at the corners. Her mouth was beautiful, Wulf noted, her lips full and lush. A man could lose himself kissing that mouth.

His head lowered. But before he could complete the act his body demanded, Reyna pulled away. "No!" she cried. "Never again will you touch me with lust!"

Stunned by what he had nearly done, he glowered at Reyna. "Do not try to seduce me, wench." Spinning on his heel, he stalked off.

Chapter Two

Shaking, Reyna sank down on a bench, her heart pounding erratically. Had Wulf been about to kiss her or had she imagined it? Wulf was many things, magnificent, raw, primitive, ruthless, angry and exciting in ways that frightened her. But above all he was a Norseman, a man she must now call master, a man she hated for what he had done to her and her family.

"You shouldn't have angered him," Lorne warned.

Reyna turned to look at the thrall, anger simmering in her veins. "Why did you lie when you knew what happened wasn't my fault?"

Lorne shuffled his feet, as if too embarrassed to answer. Finally he said, "I feared the master would punish Uma if I told the truth."

"But it was all right if he punished me?"

"You do not understand. Uma and I are Normans. We come from the same village in England. We were taken in a raid by Wulf's father three summers ago, brought to this godforsaken land and given to Wulf the Ruthless as a wedding gift. I try to protect Uma from her own follies for I care deeply about her."

"I do not need your protection," Uma shot back. "My arm hurts," she whined.

Uma seemed to do a lot of whining, Reyna decided.

But if she was going to work with these people, they needed to be friends, allies, even.

"Since we are all in the same situation," Reyna began, "we should not be fighting one another. Why can we not be friends?"

"I have been doing the master's bidding for three years and not once has he looked at me the way he looks at you," Uma complained. "Why should I be friends with you when I do not like you?"

Stunned, Reyna asked, "Are you jealous, Uma? You have no reason to be. Wulf hates me and I despise him. My people killed his wife and he . . . he . . ." She stopped in midsentence, unable to say the words.

"I think we *should* become allies," Lorne agreed. "We are foreigners in this land of the Norsemen. They are vicious warriors, though at times they surprise me with their knowledge of farming and success at trading."

"You can trust Reyna if you wish, Lorne. You aren't the injured party. I am in great pain because of her."

Though Reyna didn't like Uma any better than Uma liked her, she couldn't bear to see her suffer. She returned to the medicinal chest and found some dried leaves in a little pouch.

"I will brew some marigold tea for you, Uma. It will relieve your pain."

Uma recoiled in alarm. "How do I know you won't poison me?"

Reyna drew herself up to her nearly six foot height. "I am a healer. My oath to heal was not taken lightly. Do you wish me to help you or not?"

"Go away," Uma sobbed. "Wulf chose you over me. We will never be friends and I refuse to accept anything from you, including comfort."

Shrugging, Reyna moved off. She was still hungry and

there was food in the cauldron. Once again she ladled out a generous portion of the stew into a bowl, cut another slab of bread and sat down to eat. A short while later Lorne joined her.

"You must forgive Uma," Lorne said as he ladled stew into two bowls, one for him and one for Uma. "Her lot in life has not been easy. She was snatched from her homeland at a young age and forced into slavery. Give her time—she will come around."

"Her story is no different from mine," Reyna huffed. "I suffered as well. I think Uma has feelings for Wulf."

Lorne considered Reyna's comment a long time before answering. "Uma wants to better her life. The master has no wife or concubine. Uma hopes to catch his eye."

"I wish her luck," Reyna said truthfully. "I have no interest in Wulf the Ruthless. If the opportunity arises, I will escape."

Lorne gave a snort of disbelief. "You are naïve if you think you can find your way back to your homeland. We are slaves, Reyna the Dane, and slaves we shall remain."

So saying, he carried the bowls of stew to Uma, offered her one and sat down beside her to eat his.

Reyna turned away. Was Lorne right? Was she doomed to a life of slavery forever? It might take a while, but Reyna truly believed that her brothers and betrothed, if they were alive, would eventually track her down and rescue her. She could not serve the man who had defiled her.

Wulf stalked through the compound toward his brother's hall. He couldn't believe how close he had come to kissing Reyna. How could that happen when the very sight of a Dane in his household brought back painful memories?

He still blamed himself for leaving the farmstead the summer invaders had struck. He should have been home protecting his wife and unborn child when she was so close to her time instead of going off a-Viking.

Wulf deliberately composed his features before opening the door and entering Hagar's hall. It wouldn't do for his family to suspect how thoroughly Reyna had turned his life upside down in the short space of one day.

"Come join us, Wulf," Hagar invited. "We have been waiting for you to partake of the evening meal with us."

Wulf glanced at the family members seated around the long table. Hagar sat at one end and his mother at the other. Olga sat at Hagar's right and Olaf, his younger brother, next to her. Eric, his youngest brother, sat beside Olaf. Across from them were his younger sisters Inga and Helga, two blond beauties on the brink of womanhood. Wulf took his place next to Helga.

Immediately thralls began placing platters of food on the table. A pig had been butchered in honor of Hagar's return and the hall was redolent with delicious odors. There were fish, mashed turnips, green vegetables, curd cheese and fresh bread and butter to complement the roasted pig. Ale was served to the adults, with buttermilk available for the younger members of the family. People ate well at the table of Hagar the Red.

Lost in thought, Wulf consumed his food with gusto, ignoring the table talk until Hagar addressed him by name. "Is your new thrall adjusting, Wulf? Is all well in your hall?"

Wulf glared at Hagar, aware that he was being goaded. His brother's perverse sense of humor annoyed him. "Reyna has disrupted my household, if you must know. There has already been an altercation between her and Uma that resulted in an injury."

"What happened?" Thora asked.

"I am not sure. According to Uma, Reyna dumped a bowl of hot stew on her."

"Ah, so that's why Lorne asked for my medicinal chest. As you well know, I'm not a healer and am glad for Reyna's assistance. I hope she found what she needed to treat Uma's burn."

"Reyna did not seem impressed by what she found," Wulf admitted. "She wants to roam about to search for fresh herbs and roots to supplement your supply."

"Do you believe she is a healer?" Hagar asked. "Perhaps she is merely looking for a means of escape."

Wulf thought a moment before replying. "I believe she does know about healing. But it appears that is all she is good for."

Hagar sent him a mischievous grin. "I doubt that's *all* she is good for. She told Mother that you ravished her during a raid."

Wulf bent his sisters a fierce scowl when they began to giggle, and an even fiercer one at Hager. Then he glanced at Olga, wondering if telling the truth about her brother's actions would upset her? He decided it might and chose to dissemble. "Do not believe everything Reyna says."

"Tell me more about your new thrall," Hagar goaded. "I find it a rather amusing coincidence that you two had already met. I had no idea who she was when I bought her. My own experience with her is that she has a nasty temper. Have you beaten her yet?"

"No, though Uma advised it. I decided to let Reyna come to terms with her situation before inflicting punishment."

"If you cannot tame her, Wulf," Olaf said, "perhaps you will let me try." At twenty, Olaf perched on the cusp of manhood and had been feeling his oats of late. He had gone a-Viking with Hagar for the first time this summer.

Hagar laughed raucously. "From what I hear, brother, you have half the girls in the village vying for your attention."

"But Reyna is . . . experienced, Hagar. Taming her would enhance my reputation."

"You would do well to spend less time thinking about your next conquest, and more practicing with sword and axe to prepare yourself for next summer's voyage."

"Enough of that kind of talk," Thora admonished in a stern voice.

The conversation turned in another direction, allowing Wulf's mind to wander. He thought about the simple stew his thralls were eating compared to the abundance of food served in the main hall. Hagar's thralls enjoyed a better board than he provided in his own hall. Reyna was a jarl's daughter and doubtless accustomed to richer fare than he provided.

Wulf told himself that Reyna was a slave and should not expect the same comforts family members enjoyed. Besides, she was the enemy. Unfortunately it was difficult to remember her lowly position in his hall when every time he looked at her he saw a great beauty of queenly proportions who acted nothing like a thrall. Proud, defiant, lovely beyond comparison, shapely: those were the words he'd use to describe her. There was nothing meek or submissive in her manner. And she blamed him for an act not of his doing.

Once Wulf had eaten his fill, he pushed his plate aside and prepared to leave. Thora sent him a speculative glance. "Will you allow Reyna out of your sight long enough to gather herbs and roots, son? The woods are dangerous, but we do need a skilled healer on the farmstead. I would be happy for her to take over that chore."

"Perhaps you should go with her, Wulf," Hagar sug-

gested. "I paid dearly for her; I'd hate to see her attacked by a wolf or bear. You need to protect your property."

Wulf knew Hagar was baiting him. "When I find the time, I will take her into the woods so she can gather what she needs." He stood. "Now I bid you good night." He kissed his mother's cheek and made a hasty exit.

"What do you think?" Hagar asked no one in particular once Wulf had left. "Did Wulf take Reyna's innocence as she claims? More importantly, will my dour brother fall victim to his new thrall's charms?"

Everyone seemed to have a different opinion. But the consensus was that Wulf wasn't as unaffected by the lovely Dane as he pretended.

Wulf approached his hall with trepidation. He had no idea what he would find when he returned and hoped it wouldn't be trouble. It had been a long time since he had found the need to beat a thrall and he wasn't in the mood to do so now. Since Reyna was the cause of dissension in his hall, perhaps he should take her to the nearby trading port of Kaupang and sell her. He frowned. Rannulf would probably be the first in line to bid for her and that didn't sit well with him.

Wulf opened the door and stepped inside. The hall was dark but for the dying fire in the central hearth. A quick look around revealed two distinct shapes sleeping on nearby benches, rolled up in the wolf pelts he had provided. There was no sign of a third person. He knew intuitively that the missing thrall was Reyna. Where in Odin's name was she?

A swift inspection of the sleeping alcoves proved fruitless. Reyna was not in the hall. He even searched the privy, a separate attachment to the longhouse. Growing angrier by the minute, Wulf was in a rage by the time he stormed from the hall to search the yard and

outbuildings. If Reyna had wandered into the woods, she wouldn't stand a chance against wild animals.

Wulf had no idea where to start looking for his missing thrall. He'd never find her in the woods in the dark. And since she didn't know about the hot volcanic pool located a short distance behind the longhouse, she couldn't have gone there. Nor would she know where to find the steam hut, used regularly by the family.

Spitting out a curse, Wulf was too keyed up to return to his hall and decided to take advantage of the full moon and walk down to the fjord. He could use a cold swim. Erotic thoughts of the blonde beauty had caused his body to overheat and his loins to swell. He definitely needed to go to the village soon and find a willing woman. Perhaps he should buy a concubine to fulfill his needs, or accept Uma's blatant invitation to bed her. It was certainly something to consider.

When Wulf arrived at the fjord, the sight that met his eyes stole the breath from his lungs. *He had found Reyna.* She rose naked from the surf, a goddess crowned with silvery hair that brushed her hips. The ethereal vision enthralled him.

Moonlight painted her naked body with gold as she walked from the water. Her breasts were round, firm, and tipped with prominent nipples. Her legs were long and shapely, her waist tiny, her hips gently curved. He wondered how those limbs would feel wrapped around his waist. The pale gold fleece on her woman's mound was thick and luxurious. Wulf found it difficult to hate so glorious a creature.

Mesmerized, he stared at her, unable to speak or move. Then, as if the devil was nipping at her heels, she snatched up her tunic and started running. Gathering his wits, Wulf stepped into her path, filling his arms with satiny smooth woman's flesh.

"Reyna, what is it? Has something frightened you?"

Reyna gasped, her arms momentarily clinging to him as she fought for breath. "Wulf . . . I saw . . ."

Sweet Freya, he could scarcely think with her naked curves molded against him. "What did you see?" His hands slid down to cup her round bottom.

Reyna appeared too frightened to note where his hands had drifted. "Sails!" she cried. "I saw sails in the fjord, where it curves to the left. Ships approaching at night always mean trouble."

It took a moment for Reyna's words to sink in, but when they did, he glanced over her shoulder. "You have a vivid imagination. There are no sails in the fjord."

"They were there a few moments ago."

"What you saw were dragonships returning home after a long voyage."

"Why would they sail into this fjord?"

He looked down at her. "They could be tying up for the night near the village. I'm sure there is naught to worry about."

As if suddenly recalling she was naked, she shrugged out of his arms and struggled into her tunic. Wulf watched her closely, suddenly aware of the angry red rash blooming on her skin. He grabbed her arm, inspecting it closely.

"What is that?"

"What do you mean?"

"Your skin is red and raw."

Reyna glanced down at herself. "Wool irritates my skin. I knew this would happen. That's why I wanted to wear my silk tunic beneath the wool. Uma wouldn't let me keep it."

Finding Reyna naked had severely taxed Wulf's control. He was rock hard; if they remained alone much longer, he would do what his body demanded. Just

thinking about Reyna's soft curves made his cock jerk with desperate need.

Reyna is the enemy, his conscience told him. *She is a desirable woman*, a much louder voice contradicted. *You are Wulf the Ruthless. She is yours, take her.*

Wulf grasped the hem of Reyna's tunic, raised it back over her head and tossed it to the ground. Then he pulled her against him. She stared up at him, her green eyes wide with fright.

"Stop! What are you doing?"

"Your lips . . ."

"What about my lips?"

"I've been wondering how they taste."

"Don't touch me! Let me go. I am cold and 'tis late. We should be abed."

"Aye, I am thinking the same thing. My furs are far more comfortable than the ground. I know now you are not a maiden. Your Byzantine master doubtless had you many times after . . . well, after."

"After you raped me!" Reyna shot back.

"No, it was not me, I swear it."

"Liar!"

With a groan, Wulf's mouth came down hard over hers, effectively stopping her words. His lips were demanding, his tongue probing against hers with fierce determination, forcing them open.

His tongue darted inside, exploring, savoring her honeyed taste. Wulf ached. He wanted to throw her to the ground and thrust his cock inside her sweet tunnel.

Reyna whimpered in fearful protest as Wulf's hard mouth plundered hers. When he paid her no heed, she flailed her hands against his rock-hard chest, to no avail. When his big hands kneaded her breasts, she knew she was just moments away from being ravished again by her Norse captor. She couldn't bear it. With-

out thinking about the consequences, she bit down hard on his lip.

He jerked his head back and touched his lip; his hand came away with blood on it.

"Thor's hammer! Why did you do that?"

Panting, Reyna stepped away from him, snatched up her tunic and pulled it over her head. "I won't let you ravish me again."

There was no mirth in Wulf's smile. "Though you accuse me unjustly, this time it is my right. You are my slave, to do with as I please, just as it was your previous master's right."

Reyna faced him squarely. "You are wrong about me. My previous master did not touch me."

Wulf threw back his head and laughed. "Am I supposed to believe that?"

"I speak the truth."

"Did you not reside in his harem?"

"Aye, but that was your fault. You tore me away from my home and loved ones and sold me to a slave trader." She smiled. "I proved to be too much trouble for my master. My threats to turn him into a eunuch kept him away from me. Besides, why would he risk his manhood to bed me when he had many beautiful women vying for his attention?"

"Had you harmed him, you would have died a horrible death."

She angled her chin upward. "I was willing to take that chance. Never again will a man take from me what I am not willing to give. That means you, Wulf the Ruthless."

So saying, she turned on her heel and stalked off.

Wulf took two long strides in her direction, then stopped. What in Thor's name was wrong with him? Reyna was the last woman on earth he wished to bed.

Her people had killed Astrid. He didn't know why he had carried her to his dragonship after Rannulf had finished with her. Perhaps it was because she had looked so pitiful lying there that he had felt an unexpected jolt of compassion. But once she was aboard his ship, he'd wanted nothing to do with her and had sold her to a slave trader.

Nothing had changed since that day. Nothing, not even his lusty appetites would endear Reyna the Dane to him.

Beauty was only skin deep.

Reyna stormed back to Wulf's hall. She had gone to the fjord for a bit of privacy after Uma and Lorne had fallen asleep. Though Reyna knew the water would be cold, she had been in desperate need of a bath and didn't think anyone would miss her.

Why had Wulf come looking for her? Why had he kissed her? What had happened tonight had convinced her that she wasn't safe from Wulf's lustful attentions. He was a Norseman, a man born to kill, rape and plunder. No woman was safe from him.

And yet . . . When he looked at her, there was no denying the spark of admiration that lit his icy silver eyes. She swore she would not return that admiration. She hated what he had done to her and her family and had no intention of falling prey to the handsome brute.

Reyna entered the hall, found a wolf pelt in a corner cupboard and curled up on a bench. Sleep eluded her. The bench was hard and uncompromising. In her father's hall she had slept in a real bed covered with furs. And in Constantinople she had experienced luxury she had only dared dream about.

Reyna was still trying to find a comfortable position when Wulf returned to the hall. She went still when he

stopped beside her bench. She could feel his eyes on her and scarcely dared to breath. Would he order her to service him in bed? She released her breath in a soft whoosh when he continued on to his sleeping alcove.

Before falling asleep, Reyna recalled the sails she had seen at the entrance of the fjord and wondered if she had made too much of them. She had been terrified when she'd first noted them. To Reyna, sails on the horizon meant the approach of raiders. She had lived in terror of Viking raiders her entire life. But since Wulf didn't seem concerned, why should she be?

Reyna drifted off to sleep with the image of sails floating through her mind.

Wulf tossed and turned on his bed of furs, aching for the soft, curvy body he'd held in his arms earlier. Reyna had to be a witch to enthrall him so thoroughly. For a moment he had forgotten who she was and what her people had cost him. In his mind's eye he pictured her as he had seen her, rising from the fjord, her body lithe and supple; her hip-length hair glowed like pale gold in the moonlight. Wulf's loins swelled just thinking about her.

His cock was still hard when sleep finally claimed him.

Reyna was shaken awake by Uma. "Get up, lazy! Thralls do not have the luxury of sleeping past dawn."

Reyna opened her eyes. "Is it dawn already?"

"Aye, long past. Fold your furs and put them in the cupboard. There's porridge left over from yesterday. You can break your fast after you carry water in from the well."

Reyna rose, stretched and folded her covers. As she replaced the furs in the cupboard, she noticed that Lorne was sitting at the table wolfing down a trencher of eggs and ham.

"I prefer what Lorne is eating," she told Uma.

"You will eat what you are served," Uma replied. "You have done naught to deserve eggs and ham. The bucket is sitting beside the door and the well is located in the yard. I'm sure you can find it. It will take several buckets to fill our barrel, so you had best get to work."

Despite Uma's glower of disapproval, Reyna took time to visit the privy and wash her hands and face before leaving to fetch the water. She found the wooden bucket beside the door and carried it to the well, prominently situated in the center of the yard.

She had taken no more than a few steps when she saw Wulf and his brother, Hagar, exiting a building she supposed was the steam hut. All farmsteads, even hers, had one. Though she tried to ignore the men, they saw her and came in her direction.

"Where are you going?" Wulf asked.

She held up the bucket. "I should think that would be obvious."

"Fetching water is Lorne's duty."

"'Tis mine now, or so I've been told." She continued on her way.

Wulf grabbed her arm, stopping her in her tracks. "There are other duties you can perform. Have you broken your fast?" Reyna shook her head.

"I haven't eaten either. Return to the hall; Uma can cook your food along with mine."

"But Uma said . . ."

"I am the master here," Wulf roared. "Do as I say."

"Tell that to Uma," Reyna muttered as she spun around and marched back to the hall.

"I see your problem, brother, and I am glad 'tis yours," Hagar said, trying desperately not to laugh.

Wulf glared at him. "Go ahead and laugh. 'Tis your fault, you know."

"I had no idea you had any history with Reyna when I bought her. I thought I was providing someone for you to sport with in bed. You needed a woman to spice up your life." Laughing, Hagar walked away.

Cursing beneath his breath, Wulf returned to his hall in time to see Uma strike Reyna.

"Witch!" Uma cried. "When I tell you to do something, I expect you to do it. Why did you return without the water? For disobeying me, you can go without food the rest of the day."

Neither woman knew Wulf was in the hall until he spoke. "Since when have you usurped my authority, Uma?" His voice, so cold, so menacing, sent a shiver down Reyna's spine. "I am the only one who can dispense punishment in this hall."

"I did not mean to offend, master," Uma whined. "Your new thrall is disobedient and must be dealt with harshly."

"That is for me to decide, Uma. And fetching water from the well is Lorne's duty." He sent a pointed glance at Lorne. Lorne took the hint, plucked the empty bucket from Reyna's hands and made a hasty exit.

"What would you have your new thrall do?" Uma asked. "She cannot remain idle."

"I will think on it," Wulf said. "Meanwhile, I am ready to break my fast. When you cook my food, make an extra portion for Reyna. She has not yet eaten."

"I warmed up some porridge for her," Uma said, reaching for a bowl.

Wulf glanced at the trenchers Uma and Lorne had been eating from, noting the remnants of eggs and meat. "I see you and Lorne have already eaten."

Reyna saw Uma swallow nervously and she suppressed a smile despite her smarting cheek. Uma had a heavy hand.

"Aye, we broke our fast while Reyna slept," Uma mumbled.

"I see," Wulf said. "What did you eat?"

"Eggs and ham, master."

"Reyna and I will have the same."

"There are no more eggs. I assumed you would eat with your family as you usually do."

"This time you are wrong." He turned to Reyna. "Go to the henhouse to fetch eggs while Uma prepares food for us."

Reyna didn't argue. Gathering eggs was far easier than hauling water.

The hens were generous this morning. Reyna easily found enough eggs to fill her basket and returned to the hall in quick order.

"You may sup at the table with me," Wulf said, as if granting her a boon.

Reyna sat as far away from Wulf as she could get. A few minutes later Uma placed a platter of eggs and ham in front of Wulf and a smaller trencher before Reyna. Then she served each a horn of buttermilk.

Reyna ate with gusto, savoring every bite. She preferred eggs and ham to porridge any day.

Wulf watched Reyna eat from the corner of his eye. She had a hearty appetite, he noted, and wondered if all her appetites were robust. He shook the thought from his head and concentrated on his food.

"May I begin my search for herbs and roots this morning?" Reyna asked.

"Not now. Perhaps later, when I can accompany you," Wulf replied.

"Do you fear I will run away?"

"I fear losing a valuable property to wild animals."

Reyna bristled. "Give me a weapon. I can take care of myself."

Wulf pushed his empty plate aside and rose. "Thralls are not allowed weapons. I will take you when I have time."

A commotion outside the door effectively stopped the verbal confrontation. "What is happening?" Reyna asked.

"I do not know. Stay here, all of you," Wulf ordered as he retrieved Blood-Seeker from where it leaned against the hearth, and he strode out the door.

The sound of agitated voices in the yard grew louder. Reyna's lively curiosity wouldn't allow her to sit idly by when she might be of help. She started toward the front door.

"Where are you going?" Uma called after her.

"To see what is happening," Reyna answered.

"But the master said . . ."

"I heard Wulf, but I refuse to take orders from the likes of him."

Reyna opened the door and stepped out into the morning sunshine. One glance at the crowd gathered around something or someone lying on the ground was enough to send her racing forward to investigate. No one seemed to notice as she pushed her way through the crowd until she saw Wulf kneeling beside a youth. The boy's head rested in Thora's lap while his life's blood drained from his body. Pushing Wulf aside, Reyna dropped to her knees beside the lad.

"What happened?" she asked, visually assessing the boy's wounds. "Who is he?"

"My brother Olaf," Wulf said. As if suddenly realizing whom he was talking to, Wulf ordered, "Return to the hall at once. You are not needed here."

"Your brother is wounded, I can help."

"Reyna is right, son," Thora agreed. "She is a healer; let her tend to your brother."

That was all the permission Reyna needed. "Carry him inside. Be careful not to jostle him. Someone fetch the medicinal chest from Wulf's hall."

Though some might have thought Reyna had overstepped her authority, no one countermanded her orders.

Chapter Three

Wulf scooped Olaf into his arms and carried him to his sleeping alcove in Hagar's hall.

"Lay him down carefully," Reyna admonished. Wulf obeyed without question. "Undress him so I can see how badly he is injured."

"Hagar and I will disrobe him," Wulf replied. "Step back, Reyna."

Reyna heaved an exasperated sigh. "You do know I'll have to see his body if I am to treat him, don't you?"

"I know," Wulf said through clenched teeth, "but let us do this for him. Gather what you need to treat him."

The medicinal chest arrived, and right behind it a basin of hot water and strips of linen cloth. By the time Reyna had everything laid out on a nearby table, Wulf and his brother had undressed Olaf and covered him with a sheet Thora had provided.

"Light more rushes. Then all of you leave except for Thora," Reyna ordered.

"We will stay until we learn how badly our brother is hurt," Wulf declared as Hagar hurriedly lit two more rushes, placed them in wall sconces and returned to hover over Olaf.

Just then Olaf opened his eyes and reached a shaking

hand out to his brothers. Wulf clasped his hand. "Do not talk. You are going to be all right."

"Listen to me," Olaf gasped. "You need to know . . ."

"Can it not wait?" Hagar asked.

"Nay, this is a matter of life or death. The village to the south of us was raided by Finns before dawn today."

"Raided? By Finns? Are you sure?"

"Aye, I bear the wounds to prove it. I went to the village after the evening meal last night to visit . . . a friend. I lingered too long and decided to spend the night, arise before dawn and return home. The Finns came ashore in wave after wave while I was preparing to leave. I . . . I had no choice but to fight for my life."

"The sails!" Reyna cried. "I knew they meant trouble."

Olaf was breathing hard now as he struggled to continue. "The raiders are coming here next. They will attack at dawn tomorrow."

"How do you know this?" Hagar asked.

"I heard them talk about it as I lay wounded on the ground. They thought I was dead. They want plunder and slaves."

"Enough!" Reyna said. "I beg you, if you care about your brother, let me treat his wounds."

Hagar and Wulf exchanged speaking glances. "Come, brother," Hagar said, "there is a great deal to be done before dawn tomorrow."

"Take care of Olaf," Wulf told Reyna as he ushered Hagar out the door.

Thora hovered over her son, wringing her hands. "Olaf has lost consciousness. Will he live? Is there anything I can do?"

Reyna spared Thora a glance. "His head injury is bleeding profusely but 'tis not life threatening. Dip a cloth in water and clean it while I tend to his more serious wounds."

Slowly Reyna slipped the sheet down Olaf's body, until she found the source of all the blood. Stifling a gasp, she stared at the gaping gash in his right side, just above his hip. Blood still oozed from it. Apparently a Finn had tried to cleave Olaf in half with his battle-axe.

"How bad is it?" Thora asked tremulously.

Reaching for a cloth, Reyna dipped it into the basin of hot water and pressed it against the wound. "It doesn't look good, but rest assured I will do my best to save him."

"You were right about my son's head injury, Reyna, it is not serious," Thora said. "A stitch or two will suffice. I can do it while you treat the more serious wound."

Reyna nodded as she concentrated on the work ahead of her. She continued putting pressure on the wound while Thora placed neat stitches on Olaf's forehead. After several long minutes, the bleeding from the gaping wound in Olaf's side slowed to a trickle. Very carefully Reyna removed the cloth, frowning when she saw just how many stitches it would take to close the wound. But first things first.

After washing her hands with soap, she carefully cleaned the wound. Then she asked Thora to fetch dill seeds from the medicinal chest. These she placed directly into the wound before stitching it up. The stitching was a slow process; Reyna was a skilled healer and would allow no mistakes. Before binding the wound, Reyna smeared salve made from yarrow root over it.

"That's all we can do for him now," Reyna said as she felt Olaf's forehead for fever. "He must be watched closely. I will brew an infusion of herbs to ward off fever and valerian root to help deaden his pain."

When Reyna turned to leave, Thora pleaded, "Do not leave. Olaf may need you."

"I won't be gone long. Do you know where Wulf went?"

"He left to summon warriors from nearby villages and farmsteads. We will need all the help we can get to defeat the raiders. We are too few to do it without help."

Reyna nodded and left the alcove, carrying the medicinal chest with her. She was surprised to see Wulf pacing just outside the curtain. "I thought you'd left."

"I waited to learn more about Olaf's condition. Is he awake? Can I speak with him?"

"He is still unconscious. I am going to brew an infusion of herbs to ease his pain, and then prepare a rich beef broth to replenish the blood he has lost. As for his condition, though he has lost a great deal of blood, I believe he will recover."

"Thank Odin for that. I must leave now. The more warriors we can gather, the easier it will be to crush the Finns when they attack. Though they are fearsome warriors, I have every confidence in our ability to defend our farmstead."

Reyna watched Wulf stride off. Armed to the teeth, he was an awesome sight. Shuddering at the memory, she vividly recalled her first encounter with Wulf the Ruthless. He had been so crazed and driven by bloodlust, she was surprised he had recognized her when his brother brought her to their farmstead. He had scarcely spared her a glance during the voyage to Byzantium.

Shaking her head to banish the memory, Reyna carried the medicinal chest to the hearth, where she asked a thrall to help her prepare what she needed for Olaf.

Reyna glanced around the hall, surprised to see the thralls going about their duties as if the farmstead weren't about to be raided. She supposed they had no choice in the matter.

While the tea was brewing, Reyna found a piece of newly slaughtered beef and placed it in a cauldron with water and herbs for the broth. She worked over the

hearth until Thora poked her head through the curtain and said, "Olaf is awake and in pain."

"The tea is ready," Reyna replied.

She poured the valerian tea into a horn, carried it to Olaf's sleeping alcove and handed it to Thora. "I will lift his head while you try to get some of it down him."

"Where are Hagar and Wulf?" Olaf gasped. "The Finns . . ."

"They know, you already told them," Thora soothed. "Your brothers will take care of everything. Drink this; it will ease your pain."

Olaf took several sips, then pushed the horn away, signaling that he had had enough. Thora glanced at Reyna. Reyna nodded, indicating that Olaf had consumed enough to dull his pain. Then Thora laid his head back on the pillow. A few minutes later, he closed his eyes and slept.

"If you have things to do, I can sit with him," Reyna offered.

"Thank you, I should see to the preparation of food for the warriors that will help defend us against the raiders."

"Where are your daughters?" Reyna asked. "I did not see them in the hall."

"I sent the girls inland to my brother's farmstead with young Eric for protection. The Finns have come for plunder and slaves." She drew herself up to her full height. "No daughters of mine will become slaves."

Reyna's voice was strangely calm despite the insensitivity of that statement. "My mother said the same, yet I was taken captive by your son and sold to a foreign master. Now I am Wulf's slave."

Thora had the grace to flush. Her words held a hint of pity. "I am sorry, Reyna. It may not be fair, but it is the way of life in our harsh lands."

"Some of us are unluckier than others. If there is

a change in Olaf's condition, I will summon you." Bitterness tinged Reyna's words; she did not want Thora's pity.

Thora nodded and left the alcove. Reyna pulled a bench up to the bed and sat down to watch over the wounded lad. Olaf slept most of the day, moaning softly in his sleep. Toward evening, the fever she had been expecting arrived.

Rummaging in the medicinal chest, Reyna found willow bark and left the alcove to brew an infusion to cool his fever. Thora saw her and sent her a worried look.

"Has Olaf taken a turn for the worse?"

"He is feverish. 'Tis no more than I expected. Can you boil some willow bark tea? It should help bring down his fever."

"Of course, and I will send a thrall to fetch cold water. I have found that bathing feverish patients with cold water helps." Thora searched Reyna's face. "You look exhausted." She led Reyna to one of the tables being set up in the hall. "Sit down—you need to eat and rest. I will boil the tea for Olaf and bathe him myself."

Reyna sank onto the bench. She was tired and worried. Though he might be her enemy, she didn't want Olaf to die. He was young and ought to have a full life ahead of him.

Thora placed a heaping plate of food before her. "Eat your fill; once the Finns arrive, there is no telling when we will eat again."

"Do you think they will prevail over the Norsemen?"

"Our men are strong and prepared. Fear not, they will defeat the enemy."

Reyna's stomach growled, and she dug into her food. She had been given a generous portion of roasted pork, cheese, vegetables, bread and freshly churned butter. While she ate, Wulf returned to the hall and strode over to join her. "How is my brother?"

Reyna pushed her empty plate aside and glanced up at Wulf. "Feverish, but I expect him to recover."

"Why are you not with him?"

"Your mother ordered me to eat and rest while she bathed Olaf with cold water and fed him willow bark tea to bring down his fever. Did you find the warriors you need?"

"Many of our kinsmen, kraalls and warriors from neighboring farmsteads have begun to arrive, armed and ready to defend our shores. Surprise is on our side. The raiders have no idea we have been warned, or that we plan to set up two lines of defense to protect our farmstead."

"What happens now?"

"After I look in on my brother, I intend to see to my weapons and then get some rest."

"Shall I return to your hall tonight?"

"No, remain here with Olaf. He might have need of you."

"Am I allowed a weapon to defend myself?"

"We defend our own," Wulf growled. "A weapon will be of little use to you." So saying, he strode into Olaf's sleeping alcove.

Reyna spent a restless night rolled up in a wolf pelt beside Olaf's bed. Except for those on guard duty, everyone had retired for the night, though Reyna had no idea how they could sleep with the prospect of a fierce battle looming over them.

Reyna awakened several times during the night to check on Olaf. He was still feverish. She fed him more willow bark tea and bathed his face and neck with cold water. When she awoke at dawn, it was to war cries and the clash of weapons.

The Finns had come ashore and the battle had begun. Reyna rushed from the sleeping alcove, surprised to see

Thora and Olga sitting on a bench, calmly tearing cloth for bandages. Olga scowled at Reyna as she joined them.

"What are you doing out here? You are supposed to be tending to Olaf."

Thora placed a calming hand on Olga. "Do not fuss at Reyna, Olga. She saved Olaf's life." To Reyna she asked, "How is my son? He was sleeping when I looked in on him earlier."

"Olaf's wound has not turned putrid and he seems to be holding his own. I am confident his fever will break today."

"His recovery is due entirely to your healing skills, Reyna. I thank you. The warriors ate hours ago but there is porridge in the cauldron. Please help yourself."

"I couldn't eat a thing while the fighting is raging, but perhaps we should try to get some broth down Olaf."

The din outside became louder. Reyna glanced toward the door. "What is going on out there?"

" 'Tis none of your concern," Olga snapped. "You are a thrall. You will either have a new master or keep the old one this day."

A commotion coming from Olaf's sleeping alcove brought Thora to her feet. Reyna cried out in dismay when she saw Olaf stagger through the curtains, a sword hanging from one hand. If Thora hadn't run to support him, he would have fallen.

"What are you doing up? Are you trying to kill yourself after Reyna worked tirelessly to save your life?"

"I want to fight," Olaf mumbled. "Dying a 'straw death' in my bed will not earn me the right to enter Valhalla. When I die, I want it to be with a sword in my hand."

The words had scarcely left his mouth before his sword clattered to the floor and he collapsed to his knees. Olga rushed forward to help Thora ease Olaf back into his

bed. Reyna glanced at the sword lying on the floor and without hesitation scooped it up. Though its weight felt heavy in her hand, the weapon reinforced her courage. The battle being waged outside reminded her of that fateful attack upon her farmstead, and her capture by a Norse berserker.

Reyna's natural curiosity sent her inching toward the door. She had to know what was going on outside. With shaking hands she unlatched the door and pushed it open just enough for a glimpse of the chaos outside. She covered her mouth with her hand at the sight of the bloody battle being fought with swords, battle-axes and spears. It was a scene straight from hell. It appeared that the Finns had gained substantial ground despite the carefully laid plans of the Norsemen. It didn't take a genius to realize why. The Norsemen were outnumbered two to one.

Reyna couldn't move, could scarcely breathe as she watched the raging battle in growing horror. Blood-soaked men lay on the ground, some wounded, some dying, some already dead. But despite the odds against them, Reyna was heartened to note that the tide appeared to be turning in favor of the Norsemen.

They were slowly driving the Finns back, toward the fjord and their dragonships. She looked for Wulf and saw him fighting for his life, using his sword and battle-axe to hack at the enemy. Wulf the Ruthless was upholding his name with fierce courage and a magnificent display of skill.

Then Reyna saw something that stole the breath from her lungs. While Wulf defended himself against a frontal attack from two Finns, a third crept up on him from behind. Wulf was very close to dying and she was the only one who saw it coming.

Without a thought for her own safety or a valid reason for reacting as she did, Reyna tightened her grip on Olaf's sword and ran out the door to Wulf's defense. Vaguely she heard Thora calling to her. Though the place where Wulf fought for his life was of no great distance, every step seemed to bring Reyna no closer to Wulf and the Finn attacking him from behind.

Sweat pouring down his face, bleeding from several superficial wounds, Wulf used his formidable strength to wield his weapons against the two Finns moving in for the kill. Wulf wasn't ready to die, even though a warrior's death would earn him the right to be carried to Valhalla by Odin's handmaidens.

With a forceful thrust of his sword he vanquished one of the warriors while jostling for position to deliver the killing blow to the second. But the Finn was a skilled warrior, nearly equal to Wulf in strength and skill. Nevertheless, Wulf was gaining the upper hand when he heard a strangled cry behind him. Not daring to turn his back on his opponent, he cut him down with a slash of his battle-axe and whirled to face the unknown enemy at his back.

Horror-stricken, he glanced first at the body sprawled on the ground and then at Reyna, who stood as if in a trance with a bloody sword dangling from her fingers. All color had drained from her face as she stared at the Finn lying at her feet.

Wulf was no idiot. He knew immediately that Reyna had just saved his life. How she'd found the strength or why she'd done it escaped him. But the danger was not yet over. Another Finn came hurtling at him with raised sword and a bloodcurdling war cry.

"Return to the hall, Reyna!" Wulf shouted.

As if coming out of her trance, Reyna turned and fled. Unfortunately, she ran straight into the arms of a massive Finn retreating from the battle. He scooped Reyna into his arms and fled with his captive to the fjord and his dragonship.

When Wulf saw the Finns fleeing, he knew the Norsemen had broken the attack. He tasted victory when his opponent ceased to defend himself and turned to flee. His sword held high, Wulf shouted a Viking victory cry and gave chase. That was when he saw Reyna being carried off by the enemy. Rage coursed through him as his protective instincts took over.

Reyna struggled fiercely in her captor's arms; her pale hair scraped the ground as the Finn flung her over his shoulder. Wulf's enraged war cry alerted Hagar, who was closer to the Finn than Wulf. Seconds before the Finn reached his dragonship, Hagar tackled him, sending both men and Reyna to the ground. Rising swiftly, Hagar put a quick end to the Finn with a wicked slash of his sword.

Reyna lay still as death on the hard ground, her glorious hair pooling around her. Wulf reached her in two long strides, scooped her up into his arms, leaving the fleeing Finns to Hagar and the Norse defenders.

Wulf carried Reyna to his sleeping alcove and placed her on the bed. Reyna moaned and opened her eyes. Wulf dropped to his knees beside the bed and stroked strands of matted hair from her forehead.

"What happened?" Reyna asked.

"You tell me. Why did you leave the hall? Whatever possessed you to place your life in danger?"

Reyna struggled to sit up. "A simple 'thank-you' would suffice."

Her words took the wind out of his sails. "Are you

saying you deliberately risked your life to save mine? A man you claim to hate?"

Reyna glared at him. "Now I wonder why I wasted my time. I should have let you die. And you would have died, you know. The Finn was within seconds of cutting you down while you fought off his comrades."

"You have not answered my question."

"Very well, if you insist. If your Norsemen were defeated I would have had to accept a new master. I prefer the devil I know to the one I do not. Are you satisfied?"

Wulf gave a jerky nod.

"Then let me ask *you* a question," Reyna continued. "Why did you rescue me? You could have let the Finn carry me off. You have been looking for a way to get rid of me."

Wulf gave her question due consideration. Why, indeed? At length he said, "You are part of my household now. What I own, I keep. You are mine, Reyna the Dane, whether either of us likes it or not. Besides, your healing skills are a valuable asset to the farmstead."

Reyna glared up at Wulf. "You may have physical possession of me, but you don't own my soul. You stole something irreplaceable from me and I will never forgive you. I don't know why I didn't let you die."

"I told you before, you accuse me unjustly. It was not I who took your innocence."

Reyna glared at him. "I know what I saw. Move aside, Wulf the Ruthless, I wish to leave. There are wounded who have need of my skill."

Reyna all but leapt from the bed. Wulf blocked her way, feet spread wide apart, hands on hips. "Is that any way to speak to your master?"

Her chin rose defiantly. "Would you let your wounded die for lack of care? You can punish me later if that is your wish."

Pushing Wulf aside, Reyna darted past him and through the curtain. She was relieved when he made no effort to stop her.

Punishing Reyna was the last thing on Wulf's mind. He'd rather join her in bed, caress her creamy breasts and push himself inside her.

If Reyna believed he had ravished her, why had she saved his life while placing her own in danger? He had heard her explanation but didn't believe it. She had stated clearly and often that she hated him. Any other woman in her position would have stood by and watched him die. Yet Reyna had killed a man who would have dispatched him to Valhalla with a single stroke of his sword.

Wulf followed Reyna out the door and into the yard, stopping to help an injured warrior into Hagar's hall, where the wounded had gathered to have their injuries treated. Hagar met Wulf at the door and together they eased the bleeding warrior onto a bench.

"How many dead and wounded?" Wulf asked.

"Three dead and seven wounded. All those able to return home have already left. The Finns slain in battle are being buried as we speak. They managed to carry their wounded with them."

"According to Olaf, the Finns took captives from the village. Were any of them rescued?"

Hagar grinned. "There were but six captives and they jumped from the dragonships and ran off when we surprised the Finns at the fjord. Setting up two lines of defense, one at the fjord and another at the farmstead, was a brilliant strategy," Hagar remarked.

"Aye," Wulf agreed. "They weren't expecting to be met at the fjord by armed warriors hiding in the brush. And those that broke through our first line of defense

were handily defeated by the warriors awaiting them at the farmstead."

Hagar regarded Wulf keenly. "What do you intend to do about Reyna? She saved your life, you know."

Wulf glanced at Reyna, who was across the room. Head bent, she was stitching up a nasty cut on a man's head. "What are you hinting at?"

"She deserves some consideration."

"Such as?"

Hagar grinned. "I am sure you will find a suitable reward. Apparently she does not hate you as much as she would have us believe."

"I carried Reyna off and sold her, remember? She has every reason to dislike me."

Hagar waved Wulf's words aside. "Apparently she came to no harm at the hands of her foreign master."

A shadow turned Wulf's eyes murky. "Reyna believes I raped her. I do not remember much about that raid, given my rage and frame of mind, but my mind was clear enough to know I did not ravage her. I know who did, however. It was Rannulf, Olga's brother. Reyna refuses to believe I am not her abuser."

Hagar clapped Wulf's shoulder in commiseration. "Ah, now I understand." A frown creased his forehead. "But if Reyna hates you, why did she save your life?"

"I have no idea."

"Nevertheless, honor demands you reward her. Set her free or . . ." His words fell off as he beamed a smile at his brother.

"Or what, Hagar?"

"You are not dull-witted, brother. Can you not guess what I am thinking?"

"Oh, I can guess, all right, but you would have to be out of your mind to suggest such a thing. Reyna is a Dane."

Turning on his heel, Wulf strode off to join his mother, who was tending the wounded alongside Reyna.

Thora smiled up at Wulf, her eyes carefully inspecting him for injuries.

"I am fine, Mother, truly. I've suffered but a few scratches this day. What you see on me is the enemies' blood."

Thora gestured toward Reyna and lowered her voice. "I saw what she did. I have yet to thank her for saving my son's life, but I will. Reyna is a jarl's daughter, Wulf. She deserves better than what life has dealt her."

Wulf groaned. "Not you, too, Mother. Reyna is a Dane; have you forgotten that her people killed my wife and the child she carried?"

Thora stroked Wulf's cheek. "Of course I haven't forgotten. But I seriously doubt either Reyna or her family took part in that particular raid on our farmstead. I urge you to do what is right concerning Reyna's future, Wulf."

Thora walked away, leaving Wulf to his own thoughts. Turning his eyes on Reyna, he gave her a long, slow look. As if sensing his gaze upon her, she glanced up at him. Their eyes met and held. Wulf was the first to break the spellbinding tension that flowed between them. He deliberately turned his head away and left Hagar's hall to return to his own.

Wulf spent a long time cleaning up and changing his blood-soaked clothing. He used that time to consider Reyna's future. What his family expected him to do was absurd, and Reyna would be the first to agree with him. He was the last man in the world Reyna would agree to wed.

When Wulf's stomach began to rumble, he walked to his brother's hall to share the evening meal. He hadn't eaten since early morning and hoped the thralls had had time to put together a substantial victory feast.

The family was already gathered at the table when Wulf arrived. The earlier chaos in the hall had been restored to order. The wounded were resting on benches and the thralls were engaged in normal activities. The delicious odors coming from the various cooking pots made Wulf's mouth water.

"You are just in time, Wulf," Hagar greeted. "Sit down and join us."

Wulf took his seat, suddenly aware that Reyna was not present in the hall. "Where is Reyna?"

"She is resting in Helga's sleeping alcove," Thora explained. "The girls and Eric will return tomorrow." She sent Wulf a meaningful look. "I do not know what we would have done without Reyna today. Thanks to her skill, we didn't lose any of our wounded."

"Do not discount your own skill, Mother Thora," Olga huffed. "I do not know why everyone is making so much over a thrall whose duty is to serve her master in whatever capacity is required of her."

Thora sent Olga a quelling look. "What makes you dislike the girl, Olga?"

"Am I the only one to see through her? Reyna will bring trouble to our farmstead, mark my word."

"If that is the way you feel, Olga, then send me home."

No one had seen Reyna leave the sleeping alcove. Nor were they aware she had overheard their conversation.

"I would have Wulf sell you, were it within my power," Olga snapped. "You are disobedient and far too bold. You should call me mistress like the other thralls. You are no better than the lowest slave in my household."

"Enough, Olga," Hagar commanded. "We owe a debt of gratitude to Reyna."

Olga's humph was loud and heartfelt.

Wulf paid scant heed to the conversation as his

heated gaze raked over Reyna. Apparently his mother had given her a new set of clothing. Instead of harsh, dun-colored wool, Reyna wore a soft linen undertunic and an overtunic of bright green velvet, belted with links of silver. Her shining pale hair had been combed out and fell loose to her waist.

"Your new clothing suits you, Reyna," Thora said. "Sit down and join us. You must be starving."

Reyna cast an uncertain glance at Wulf before sinking onto the bench. She was starved and wasn't about to deny herself the pleasure of a meal.

As the thralls began placing food on the table, Reyna felt a strange undercurrent she did not understand. From the surreptitious glances aimed at her, she assumed it concerned her future.

Did Wulf intend to sell her to another master?

Chapter Four

Wulf pushed his chair away from the table and rose. "It has been an eventful day and I am exhausted. Reyna can remain here tonight in case my brother has need of her."

"Reyna deserves a good night's rest," Thora replied. "Take her with you. I'd like to keep Uma and Lorne, however, to help our thralls tend the wounded. They may need water or assistance during the night. As for Olaf, I will look after him myself. Reyna can check on him on the morrow."

Wulf glanced at Reyna and gave a jerky nod. She rose immediately and followed him out the door. The night was dark, moonless, and completely devoid of stars. Wulf thought it was a fitting end to a day of carnage. Three of his friends had died this day and several others were wounded. His own life had been in jeopardy. If not for Reyna's quick thinking, he would be with his forefather in Valhalla this very night.

Wulf entered the hall and turned back to watch Reyna. She had followed him inside but stopped on the threshold.

"What is it?" His voice held a gruffness he hadn't intended. Or had he? Being alone with Reyna did things to his body he didn't understand. His blood pumped at a furious pace and his loins grew painfully tight.

"Am I allowed to use the steam hut?"

Her question sent Wulf's cock into spasms. He imagined Reyna naked, sweat beading her lush body as hot mist swirled around her.

"I suppose it would be all right. But there's a volcanic pool a short distance behind the hall that would better serve your purpose. I will accompany you, of course. You will find soap and linen drying cloths in the cupboard. Fetch them."

Reyna gave a defiant shake of her head. "I prefer to bathe in private."

When Reyna refused to move, Wulf asked, "Are you afraid of me?"

"Of course I am. I would be a fool not to fear the man who abused me."

"I did not do that to you, Reyna. Another warrior hurt you."

"Name him," Reyna demanded.

Wulf considered her request. Olga was fond of her brother. If Wulf named Rannulf, Reyna might confront Olga, and a confrontation between them could prove harmful to Olga. Wulf wanted no harm to come to Hagar's heir so he kept the name to himself.

"Believe me when I say that I was not the man who abused you."

"Liar!"

Wulf winced; her accusation affected him more than he cared to admit. He recalled how pitiful she had looked when he had scooped her from the ground and carried her to his dragonship. Fragile, bruised, defiled, her eyes empty. He no longer hated Reyna for who she was. He was beginning to understand that Norsemen were no different from Dane warriors. All those who fit the description of Vikings plundered, raped and killed, and he had joined in the carnage before he wed Astrid.

Wulf had turned to trading after his marriage, save for one or two retaliation raids into Dane territory after his wife's death.

Wulf glared at Reyna. Why was she being so difficult? How could she mistake him for Rannulf? True, they were both blond and had worn iron helmets that day, and they had been garbed nearly alike. But the similarities ended there. Wulf was larger and broader than Rannulf, and lacked the scar that marked Rannulf's left cheek. But he supposed a woman being ravaged wouldn't notice those differences.

"Go," Wulf growled, "I will not join you. If I have need of a woman, Uma will gladly service me."

"Uma fancies you, though I do not know why. Perhaps you are kinder to her than you are to me."

"You are treading on dangerous ground, Reyna. If you wish to go to the pool, I suggest you do so while I am of a mind to let you go. You do not wish to see me angry."

"I already saw you angry and still bear the scars," Reyna shot back.

Wulf took a menacing step in her direction. Reyna gave a startled squeak and fled out the door, taking neither drying cloth nor soap with her. Wulf followed her to the doorway and stopped, watching her disappear into the darkness.

Hands clenched at his sides, Wulf debated whether to follow her to the pool or seek his bed. His body was sore and stiff from wielding his weapons against the raiders. A hot soaking would ease his aching bones.

But that wasn't the only reason Wulf wanted to visit the volcanic pool. He imagined Reyna naked, standing in the water, steam glistening on her fair skin, and his blood ran hot. Though he willed his mind in another direction, it always returned to lusty thoughts of the blonde beauty.

He wanted Reyna. Why shouldn't he take her? He owned her. She was his thrall. But she was also afraid of him and he couldn't bring himself to force himself on her as Rannulf had done.

Wulf considered his choices. Should he fetch Uma or go to his bed alone, his lust unsatisfied? Did he even desire Uma? The answer was a resounding no. Had he desired Uma, he would have had her long ago. She had hinted often enough that she would be a willing bed slave.

Wulf had almost convinced himself to ignore his rampant lust when he recalled that Reyna had fled the hall without drying cloth or soap. A grin stretched his lips. He would be doing Reyna a service by bringing those items to her.

Pleased with his logic, Wulf fetched a drying cloth and some soap from a cupboard and left the hall. His cock twitched with impatience. He felt himself harden with each step closer to the volcanic pool and Reyna.

Reyna had no idea where to find the volcanic pool but she would rather stumble around in the dark than ask Wulf to show her the way. Though the night was black, she was fairly certain Wulf hadn't followed her. Her relief was enormous when she finally found the pool some distance behind the longhouse. It was surrounded by trees and foliage, providing a modicum of privacy.

Misty steam hung like a heavy cloud above the pool. Reyna found it immensely inviting. She undressed quickly, folded the clothes Thora had given her and placed them on a nearby rock. She tested the temperature with her foot, found it hot but bearable, and sank down into the water. Relaxing, she closed her eyes and rested her head against the rocky side of the pool. It felt like heaven.

The hot water soothed her frayed nerves but not her troubled mind. She couldn't purge Wulf from her thoughts. He could lie all he wanted, but she knew the truth. He had brutally stolen her innocence. She had lost consciousness during the assault and had woken in time to see Wulf leaning over her. Vaguely she recalled him scooping her up and taking her aboard his dragonship.

Reyna had learned a great deal from that terrifying experience. She had found inner strength and courage during her time in the Byzantine harem and learned that she could take care of herself. She might fear Wulf's vile plans for her future, but she didn't fear *him.* He had already done his worst to her; there was nothing left to fear.

Reyna had no idea why she had saved Wulf's life. Why hadn't she let him die? She believed she hated him with every fiber of her being . . . yet she couldn't bear to see him die a violent death. Even though he claimed to hate her, he hadn't treated her cruelly or ordered her to his bed. Wulf was an enigma she had yet to figure out.

Why did he have to be so handsome? Reyna mused. She pictured his face in her mind. High cheekbones, straight nose, well-formed lips and lean, hard jaw. His silver eyes weren't as cold and empty now as they had been during the voyage to Byzantium. He had barely looked at her then, scarcely acknowledged her existence. No one had bothered her as she huddled inside a small enclosure aboard Wulf's dragonship. Never in her wildest dreams had she imagined she would one day belong to Wulf the Ruthless.

"You forgot your drying cloth and soap."

Reyna nearly jumped out of her skin. Wulf had followed her after all. He was standing behind her, drying cloth in one hand, soap in the other.

"Go away!"

He sat on the grass and pulled off his boots and tunic. "What are you doing?"

"Disrobing, obviously. I decided to join you after all. My bones ache after today's battle."

"Why didn't you go to the steam hut?"

He stood, untied his trousers and let them drop. Reyna jerked her eyes away.

"I prefer the volcanic pool. I need a good soak."

The water surrounding Reyna rippled as Wulf eased himself into the pool. "Why can't you leave me alone?" she demanded. "You hate me; you can't stand my company."

Wulf let out a sigh as he settled in. " 'Tis difficult to hate the woman who saved my life."

Reyna gritted her teeth, almost wishing she had let Wulf die. "Forget what I did. I would have done the same for a dog."

Wulf's laugh ended in a strangled growl as the moon scooted from behind a cloud, dusting the pool with thousands of sparkling stars and turning the water translucent. He stared transfixed at the perfect white globes of Reyna's breasts bobbing in the water. His gaze wandered lower, past her slim waist and rounded hips to the golden fleece covering her plump mound.

Slowly his gaze traveled upward, taking in all the lush hills and valleys he had missed upon his first inspection. Thor's hammer! How had he missed Reyna's spectacular beauty the first time he had set eyes on her? Had his rage and thirst for revenge blinded him?

"I should leave," Reyna said.

Wulf reached behind him and retrieved the soap from the ledge above the pool. "Not until you wash. Is that not what you came here for?"

She started to rise. "The hot water has soaked the dirt away."

Wulf reached for her, holding her in place. "Turn around while I scrub your back. Then you can scrub mine."

Reyna cringed. "No, do not touch me!"

"Reyna, I am not going to hurt you."

"You already have."

"No, you mistake me for another. All I will admit to is selling you into slavery during a frenzy of revenge that I now regret."

"Tell me who hurt me if it was not you."

"A member of my raiding party; that is all I will say."

Reyna didn't believe Wulf. Admittedly she had been in shock after the attack, but she had seen Wulf looming over her as clear as day. She was jerked back to the present when she felt his calloused hand spreading soap over her back, and repressed a shudder. Since the raid she hadn't been able to bear a man's touch. But for some reason, Wulf's caress wasn't as repulsive as she had thought it would be. It actually felt rather soothing.

But when Wulf turned her around and spread the soap over her breasts, she made a valiant attempt to evade him.

"Hold still. Why are you so skittish?"

Deliberately she glanced down to where his hands rested on her breasts. "Your hands are on me."

Though his hands were gentle, Reyna didn't trust him. No man was trustworthy. She had to admit, however, that his touch sent subtle shock waves through her body. She felt . . . strange; her nerve endings tingled and her skin felt tight. When Wulf's hands continued their downward path, gliding over her stomach to settle between her legs, anxiety and fear made her stiffen.

"Do not touch me there!"

When his fingers slid into the folds of her sex, panic seized her. Then she realized what Wulf was doing to

her now was nothing like the first time he had assaulted her. His shockingly intimate foray into her private parts made her hot and shivery.

"I have done nothing yet."

She raised her hands to his chest in an age-old gesture of protest and felt downy hair curl between her fingers. She jerked her hands away as if scalded. The feel of his hair-roughened skin was too raw, too intimate. Then she felt his finger slide inside her and shock pierced through her.

"Stop that!"

He rested his head against her forehead. "*Now* I'm doing something. Do you like it?"

"No, I do not. Nor do I like you."

He wedged another finger in beside the first. "You are as tight as a maiden. Do you know how badly I want to be inside you right now?"

Reyna had a good idea and cursed her body's betrayal. She arched upward in an effort to dislodge him and realized her mistake at once. She could feel every hot, hard inch of him, his massive, powerful chest crushing the softness of her breasts, his long muscular thighs pressing against hers and his thick sex probing the place where his fingers now played.

Her terror dissolved into something she refused to recognize or name. She had to remind herself over and over that Wulf was the man who had abused her. She looked into his eyes and saw a flicker of something she'd never expected to see in the eyes of Wulf the Ruthless. She saw desire, compassion, and aye, admiration. She shook those thoughts from her head. Surely she was mistaken. Wulf the Ruthless knew no other emotion save brutality and lust.

"If you need a woman, I will fetch Uma for you."

"I do not want Uma, I want you."

Reyna was dissolving under his sinful manipulation, her mind spinning in confusion. She could scarcely find the breath to protest.

"I am going to kiss you, Reyna."

"Oh, no, I . . ."

He brushed aside her protest. The last thing she saw was the gleam of Wulf's white teeth as his mouth came down over hers. How could a man as hard and unrelenting as Wulf have lips so soft? Reyna wondered. His lips moved over hers with assurance, as if she was his for the taking, which indeed she was. She tried to push him away, but he was an immovable presence, bent on getting what he wanted. Unfortunately for Reyna, *she* was what he wanted.

When Wulf pushed his tongue past her lips, deepening the kiss, Reyna renewed her efforts to make him stop. But it was increasingly difficult with her bones melting and her head whirling. What this bold Norseman did to her body was beyond comprehension. Nothing in her previous experience compared to Wulf's kisses.

How could this man be the same Norseman who had taken her innocence without remorse? Even the rich, earthy scent that clung to him was not as she remembered. She could still recall the pungent odor of blood, sweat and something feral emanating from her attacker.

As if they'd happened yesterday, Reyna began to relive the events of that terrible day. Her body stiffened, terror settled deep in her stomach. She had to stop this now, for she couldn't bear that kind of hurt again.

Wulf seemed to recognize her fear and eased away from her.

"What is it? Did I hurt you?"

Tossing her head from side to side, Reyna began to beat her fists against his chest. "I refuse to let this happen to me again."

Understanding settled deep in Wulf's gut. Rannulf had hurt Reyna terribly and instilled in her a lasting fear of men.

"It does not have to be painful, Reyna. I can make it enjoyable for you."

"Like you did the first time?"

Wulf cursed Rannulf. Reluctantly moving a respectable distance away from the object of his desire, Wulf decided to bide his time until Reyna came to him willingly.

"You win this time, Reyna," Wulf said, "but I cannot wait forever for you to come to me. You belong to me and I *will* have you."

Suddenly the moon slid fully from behind a cloud, revealing Wulf's warrior's body in all its splendor. Reyna stared at him as he lifted himself from the pool and pulled his clothing on over his wet body. Despite her fear of men, she couldn't help admiring Wulf. He was a truly magnificent specimen of masculinity; large and hard muscled, broad shouldered, deep chested and narrow hipped. His legs were long and powerful and his body was tanned all over.

Reyna had to force herself to look away.

"Are you ready to return home with me?" Wulf asked once he was dressed.

"No, I intend to return to your brother's hall. Olaf might have need of me."

"My mother can take care of him. I know you are exhausted; you worked hard today to save lives." He placed the drying cloth within her reach. "I will wait down the path and escort you to your bed."

Reyna waited until Wulf walked away before leaving the pool and drying herself. She didn't want to return with him to his hall but had no authority to refuse. Wulf was her master, whether she liked it or not. Why did she feel a strange tug inside her when she looked at him?

The feeling was unsettling in light of their history, and she couldn't understand why she was experiencing these unwarranted sensations. Why was she attracted to the Norse raider? She should not have any feelings but hatred for Wulf the Ruthless.

"Are you ready?" she heard him ask, his voice resonating through the darkness.

"Aye," Reyna answered as she shrugged into her tunic and fastened her belt around her waist.

Reyna followed Wulf to his hall and stepped over the threshold. The hall was dark; no one had been there to tend the fire or rush lights. While Wulf added wood to the hearth and set a rush light into a sconce, Reyna removed a wolf pelt from the cupboard and prepared to curl up on a bench.

"No!" Wulf said, removing the wolf pelt from her hands. "You have earned the right to a real bed."

Reyna drew back in alarm. "I am *not* sharing your bed."

"There are other sleeping alcoves in the hall. You may choose one for your own."

"Uma will be angry; she was here before I arrived."

"Uma did not save lives today," Wulf pointed out. "Nor does she possess a skill as useful as yours. My mother wants me to reward you, and I intend to respect her wishes. As our healer, you shall have a real bed and wear clothing befitting your skill. 'Tis my way of thanking you for your services."

Emboldened, Reyna said, "Setting me free would be a more fitting reward."

Wulf's mouth flattened. "I have no intention of freeing you. Where would you go? What would you do? I am your master—no one else can protect you as I can."

"I will never call you master," Reyna stated.

"Go to bed, Reyna. I am weary of bandying words

with you. You are welcome to use the sleeping alcove or not. 'Tis your choice. Good night."

Reyna stood in the center of the hall, contemplating her choices. Could she trust a man like Wulf the Ruthless to leave her unmolested? Her bones ached and she was so tired she could barely stand upright. The bench was as hard and unyielding as it looked; she knew that from experience.

But if she chose to claim a sleeping alcove for herself, she would earn Uma's enmity. In Reyna's opinion, refusing the comfort of a bed and room of her own would be stupid, and she wasn't stupid. Reyna chose the sleeping alcove.

Wulf was too aroused to sleep. The memory of Reyna's naked body beneath the water in the pool haunted his thoughts. He was hard as stone and not likely to lose his erection any time soon. But he would not take her against her will; he wouldn't be able to live with his guilt or the accusation in her eyes if he did. Hurting her as Rannulf had done did not appeal to him.

What was he to do with Reyna?

Though Wulf should have been exhausted from the battle, his body refused to relax; most of his discomfort was due to unrequited desire for Reyna. There was no help for it. Since he wasn't going to have Reyna beneath him this night, he stripped off his clothes and climbed into bed, pulling the wolf pelts over him. He tossed and turned restlessly, his body too sore to find a comfortable position.

Finally, he rose from his bed and walked naked into the hall. His steps led him to Reyna's sleeping chamber. He pushed aside the curtain and stepped inside. Pale moonlight streamed into the chamber through the single

window, turning Reyna's hair to pure silver. She was sleeping soundly, her folded hands resting beneath her cheek.

Wulf had no idea why he was standing over her bed, but somehow looking at her seemed to ease him. He stretched out his hand as if to touch her and then drew it back. If he touched her, he wouldn't be able to stop until she was stretched out beneath him with his cock buried deep inside her.

Wulf had to force himself to leave the alcove and return to his own bed. The longer he lingered, the less likely he would be to leave her untouched.

Reyna had already left the hall when Wulf awakened the following morning. Before going to break his fast at Hagar's hall, he washed the sleep from his eyes and shaved the stubble from his chin.

The air had a definite chill to it, Wulf thought as he walked across the yard. Soon he and Hagar would put their ships up for the winter and spend their days and nights chopping wood, hunting and telling rousing Viking sagas around a blazing fire.

The hall was a beehive of activity. The wounded from yesterday's battle were up and seated at long tables, breaking their fast. Reyna was nowhere in sight. Wulf greeted his mother and found an empty spot at the table.

"Where is Hagar?" Wulf asked Thora.

"He went to fetch your sisters and Eric. You look tired, son. Did you not sleep well?"

"Ha!" Olga snorted. "He was probably up all night plowing his thrall."

"You are wrong, Olga," Wulf bit out.

"Show some respect, Olga," Thora reprimanded. "Reyna saved Olaf's life."

"Where is Reyna?" Wulf asked. "She left my hall before I awakened this morning."

"She arrived shortly after dawn to check on the wounded," Thora explained. "She is with Olaf now, changing the dressing on his wound."

"Speak of the devil and there she is," Olga said, gesturing toward Reyna, who had just left Olaf's sleeping alcove and was approaching the table.

"How is my brother?" Wulf asked as Reyna joined them.

"He is doing very well, considering the gravity of his injury. He was lucky."

"We are the lucky ones," Thora said, "for we have you. Your skill saved Olaf's life. Please sit down and join us."

"Oh, really, Mother Thora," Olga chided, "Reyna is a thrall and unworthy of praise."

Wulf glanced at Reyna's bowed head and could almost feel the anger emanating from her. Had she been looking up instead of at her plate, he would wager that her heated gaze would turn Olga to cinder.

Ignoring Olga, Reyna slid into an empty seat beside Thora and helped herself from a platter of eggs. She was too hungry to argue.

Wulf came to Reyna's defense. "Mother is right, Olga. Perhaps one day Reyna's skill will prove useful to you."

"I think not," Olga denied.

An uneasy silence reigned as everyone concentrated on their food. At length Reyna pushed her empty plate aside and rose. "Please excuse me. I have checked on all the wounded. May I go now to gather herbs and roots to replenish the medicinal chest? It must be done before the ground freezes." She sent a pointed look at Olga. "If I am lucky, I might find raspberry leaf to aid your labor when you deliver."

"I vow you will not touch me when I give birth," Olga swore.

Reyna ignored her. "What say you, Wulf the Ruthless? Am I allowed to journey beyond the farmstead for what I need?"

"You should address Wulf as master," Olga scolded.

Reyna glared down her nose at Olga. "I call no man master."

Wulf thought it a good time to intervene, before the two came to blows. What was it about Reyna that set Olga on edge? Did she fear Reyna might tempt Hagar to stray?

"If you wish to gather herbs and roots, I will accompany you," Wulf said. "Be sure to wear a warm cloak and bring a basket to hold your harvest."

"I have an extra cloak you can wear," Thora offered. "And there are plenty of baskets in yonder cupboard that should suit your purpose."

"I will fetch the basket and meet you outside," Wulf said as he strode off.

Thora left and returned momentarily with a fur-lined cloak. "Take this," she said, draping the cloak over Reyna's shoulders.

"'Tis far too grand for a walk in the woods, Lady Thora," Reyna protested. "Something older will suffice."

"The cloak is yours to keep, Reyna. Wear it in good health."

Reyna nodded her thanks and left immediately to join Wulf. As she strode away, she heard Olga make a strangled sound low in her throat. Pretending not to hear, Reyna walked out the door and joined Wulf in the yard. He handed her the basket and strode toward the woods that grew beyond the farmstead. Reyna lengthened her steps to keep up with him.

"Must you accompany me?" Reyna asked. "I am perfectly capable of finding what I need without you."

"Can you defend yourself against wild animals?"

She looked pointedly at the sword he carried in a sheath at his waist and the spear he held in his hand. "I could if I had a weapon."

Wulf snorted. "Knowing how you feel about me, I might find a blade in my back if I arm you. Besides, I have a mind to do a little hunting."

Since Reyna had no answer for Wulf, she followed him in silence, keeping her eyes on the ground in search of plants known for their curative powers. Occasionally Reyna would stop, point to a plant and watch as Wulf dug it up and placed it in her basket. By the time they entered the forest, Reyna's basket was half-filled with mallow, dill, mint, borage and comfrey.

Reyna felt a definite chill as she entered the forest. She should have realized it would be dark and cold with the sun blotted out by tall trees. Shivering, she pulled her cloak tighter about her shoulders and continued her search. Luck was with her. She harvested leaves from raspberry bushes, ripped off pieces of bark and leaves from willow trees and pulled up valerian plants, roots and all.

"Your basket is full," Wulf observed. " 'Tis time to leave."

"There is still more to gather, but I can return another time now that I know where to find what I need. I should gather as much as I can before the first frost."

Wulf started to take the heavy basket from her, then froze, his face a study of intense concentration. "Be quiet!"

"What is it?" Reyna whispered.

"Do you hear that?"

"No, I hear nothing . . ." And then she did. Something was rooting about in the tall underbrush to their left. She had opened her mouth to ask Wulf what it was

when a wild boar charged out of its hiding place, heading straight at her.

A scream erupted from her throat. Wulf drew back his powerful arm, preparing to throw his spear at the rampaging beast before it reached Reyna. Unfortunately, the boar swerved away from Reyna and toward Wulf at the same time Wulf released his spear, missing the animal by mere inches. Feet spread wide, his body braced against the impact, Wulf drew his knife blade. Reyna screamed as boar and man prepared to meet in a fierce battle of life and death.

Chapter Five

"Move out of the way, Reyna!" Wulf shouted.

Reyna obeyed immediately, seeking out the sturdiest tree to hide behind. She knew that getting in the way would hinder Wulf's movement and place him in greater danger. Peeking from behind the tree trunk, Reyna spied Wulf's spear and decided it was too far away for her to recover easily. But if Wulf seemed to be losing the battle, she would make a mad dash for the spear and try to save Wulf.

Reyna suppressed a scream when she saw the boar lower its head and aim the sharp points of its tusks at Wulf. Terror stricken, she watched as Wulf stood his ground, still as a pillar, his body tense and waiting. What was wrong with Wulf? Was he just going to stand there and let the boar gore him?

The quiet of the forest was rent with snorts, grunts and squeals as the beast bore down on Wulf. Reyna did scream then, for she was certain Wulf would die.

Reyna nearly fainted with relief when, at the last minute, Wulf stepped to the side, out of the boar's path. When the animal realized it had missed and came charging back, Wulf leapt into the air and landed on the beast's back. She watched with bated breath as Wulf drove the knife into the animal's tough hide, once,

twice, but the blow only appeared to further enrage the boar.

Reyna found it difficult to keep track of the action after that. First Wulf was on top of the boar and then the boar seemed to be gaining the upper hand. Reyna was on the verge of racing for Wulf's spear when she saw Wulf deftly avoid the boar's tusks and plunge his blade into its throat, ripping it open.

The noise the dying animal made was deafening, but finally it went still, its blood soaking the ground. Reyna's gaze flew to Wulf. He was standing over the boar, panting, his clothing covered with blood. His blood or the boar's, she couldn't tell.

" 'Tis all right now, you can come out," Wulf called.

Reyna had already left the tree and was walking toward him. Her anxious gaze slid over his body. "Are you hurt?"

He flexed his left arm. " 'Tis naught."

Reyna grasped his arm, saw the rip in his shirt and knew it was more than naught. "Let me see."

"Do not fuss."

Ignoring him, Reyna ripped open his sleeve, drawing in a sharp breath when she saw the long gash, from shoulder to elbow. "You were gored," Reyna exclaimed. "The wound should be treated immediately."

"This scratch? 'Tis naught to worry about."

"Nevertheless, we must take precautions against infection."

Wulf glanced down at the boar and then at Reyna. "Very well, we can leave now if you wish. I will send thralls back to fetch the boar. The meat should be rendered as soon as possible."

Wulf retrieved his weapons and turned toward Reyna. "Shall I carry your basket?"

Reyna was stunned to see the basket of plants and

roots still slung over her arm. "No, I can manage." She glanced at Wulf's arm, noting that it was still bleeding. "We need to hurry."

Wulf grinned. "Are you worried about me?"

Reyna refused to look at him. "I am a healer. 'Tis my nature to worry about the injured. Wounds like yours can turn septic and even kill."

Placing a finger beneath her chin, Wulf turned her face toward him. "Look at me, Reyna."

Reluctantly, she lifted her eyes to his.

"I am not your enemy. Do not fear me."

Reyna watched in growing panic as he lowered his head and covered her lips with his. Though she tried to evade his kiss, his persistence won out. Reyna fought against responding. She couldn't imagine feeling anything but revulsion for Wulf's kisses. But respond she did. He kissed her hungrily, his hands moving restlessly over her body. Her breath came hard and fast in her throat. She wanted to touch him and that frightened her. She could not credit the sensations inundating her body. How could she respond to Wulf knowing what he had done to her? It was wicked of her, she told herself, yet she could not escape the yearning for something more that twisted in her gut.

Wulf's kiss seemed to go on forever, his soft lips sucking the very will from her. His hands were turning her body into a tingling mass of nerve endings. She must put a stop to this now. Reyna began to struggle in earnest.

Wulf broke off the kiss and removed his hands from her body. Retreating a few steps, Reyna wiped her lips with the back of her hand and glared at him. "Do not do that again."

Wulf looked at her strangely, as if trying to understand what had just happened between them. What had

started out as simple lust had grown into something deeper. Shaking the unwelcome thought from his mind, he retrieved his spear from the ground, where he had dropped it when he'd kissed Reyna, and said roughly, "Time to go."

Reyna trotted after Wulf. Neither seemed inclined to talk as they walked back to the farmstead. At length, Reyna said, "My medicinal supplies are in Hagar's hall. We should stop there first."

Wulf nodded, rather grimly, Reyna thought, and continued onward. She wondered if he was in pain and then dismissed the thought. His discomfort shouldn't concern her. He had caused her pain in the past. The kind of pain one didn't forget.

Wulf's thoughts were as confused as Reyna's. She had responded to his kiss; he could feel it in the softening of her lips and the easing of tension her body. If he could convince her he hadn't harmed her the day of the raid, he knew he could coax her into his bed. Hagar had been right. He did need someone to spice up his life. He needed Reyna.

Desperately.

When Wulf and Reyna entered the main hall, they found various activities in progress. Most of the wounded had left for their own homes, but Helga, Inga and Eric had returned and their voices added to the din. Helga spied her brother first.

"Wulf! What happened to you? You are covered in blood. Are you injured?"

" 'Tis naught to fuss about, Helga."

"A wild boar took exception to our invading his territory," Reyna explained.

Thora arrived in time to hear Reyna's explanation. "Where are you hurt, son?"

" 'Tis mostly boar's blood, Mother."

"Wulf has a deep gash down his left arm," Reyna contradicted. "It needs disinfecting, and mayhap stitching."

"Helga, please fetch the medicinal chest for Reyna," Thora directed. Helga hurried off to do her mother's bidding.

"And a ewer of hot water," Reyna added. To Wulf she said, "Remove your shirt and sit down."

Though Wulf raised an eyebrow at her request, he obliged without objection, tossing off his blood-splattered shirt and subsiding onto a bench. Reyna tried to keep her gaze on his wound but it kept straying to the massive expanse of his chest. This man, her enemy, shouldn't be such a magnificent specimen of manhood. Nor should she be attracted to him.

Helga returned with the medicinal chest. Inga arrived in her wake with a ewer of hot water and clean cloths. Both girls set down their burdens and hovered over Reyna to watch.

"Mother, there is a dead boar in the woods that needs rendering," Wulf said. "Would you please send thralls to fetch it? It will provide welcome meat during the winter months."

"Where shall I tell them to look?" Thora asked.

"Tell them to follow the path into the woods and take the left fork. The boar is but a short distance down the path."

Thora hurried off as Reyna sprinkled borage, an antiseptic, into the hot water and began to cleanse the bloody gash in Wulf's arm.

"Stitches are not required," Reyna said after a thorough inspection of the injury. "The gash is not as deep as I first thought."

"I told you not to fuss," Wulf said.

Reyna placed a hand on his chest when he attempted

to rise. "I am not finished yet. You cannot leave until I apply marigold salve and a bandage. The boar's tusks are unclean; they could cause infection to invade your wound."

Wulf shifted impatiently while Reyna treated his wound. The moment she finished, he stalked off. "I am going to the volcanic pool to wash off the boar's blood."

"Try not to get your bandage wet," Reyna called after him.

Hagar met Wulf in the doorway. "I heard you were wounded. What happened? I thought you were helping Reyna gather herbs and roots."

"Wild boar," Wulf muttered. "Come with me to the volcanic pool and I will tell you about it."

They walked off together.

"Where is Wulf?" Thora asked when she rejoined them.

"He and Hagar went to the volcanic pool to bathe," Helga explained.

"Did you find what you needed in the forest?"

"Oh, aye, and there is more to be harvested before the first frost. But that will have to wait for another day. I must process the herbs and roots I gathered today before I look for more. I will need a place to hang the herbs to dry and somewhere I can make salves and antiseptics. Is there such a place on the farmstead?"

"My sister set up a stillroom in one of the outbuildings. There is a hearth, worktable, and various pots and kettles available for your use. Helga will take you there. I will send a male thrall along to build a fire in the hearth. The stillroom has not been used in some time."

Reyna picked up the basket she had placed on the floor while she treated Wulf and followed Helga out the door. A thrall trotted behind with a rush light. Soon Helga arrived at a small windowless building with a

pitched roof and opened the door for Reyna to enter. It was dark as night inside.

The thrall hurried past them, placed the rush light he had brought with him in a sconce and began to lay a fire in the hearth. Reyna looked around, finding the small outbuilding adequate for her purposes. There were even racks set up for drying herbs.

"This will do nicely," Reyna told Helga. "Thank your mother for me."

Helga made no effort to leave. She looked as if she wanted to say something but didn't know how to begin.

"Is there something you wish of me?" Reyna asked bluntly.

"Is it true you saved Wulf's life? Mother told us you slew a Finn who tried to skewer him. I . . . I admire your courage," Helga said. "I know of no thrall who would have acted with such bravery."

Reyna shrugged. She didn't want too much made of her spontaneous act. "I would have done the same for anyone."

"Call it what you will, but I still call it a courageous deed on behalf of our family. I could not have borne it if Wulf had died that day. Thank you, Reyna. I care not what Olga says, you deserve high praise. I am glad Mother saw fit to garb you appropriately. Your healing skills and courage have won over our family, except for Olga and mayhap Wulf."

"I wish no accolades, Helga. I do what I can to heal and save lives."

"You saved Olaf's life too."

"He is young and healthy. His body will heal of its own accord."

" 'Tis not what Mother says. We all believe Wulf should free you, but no one can tell Wulf what to do. It would please me if you accepted my friendship."

Tears prickled behind Reyna's eyes. "Gladly. How kind of you to offer, Helga, but I would not want you to get in trouble with Olga. She objects to my presence at the farmstead."

"I believe Olga's bad temper has to do with her fear of childbirth. Since our aunt's death, there is no midwife nearby to help her."

"Does Olga not trust your mother to see her safely delivered?"

"No, Olga had a dream about dying in childbirth and since then has been hard to live with. I am sure she will mellow once her child is born."

As soon as the fire in the hearth caught, the thrall scooted out the door. "I should get to work," Reyna said.

"May I help? I have a great interest in plants and healing. I often helped my aunt."

"You can start separating the plants by species, if you like," Reyna instructed, "while I fetch water from the well."

While they worked, Helga asked countless questions about Wulf's battle with the boar. She remained until Inga came to fetch her to help with chores. Reyna worked until late in the day. She was so excited to be working with her beloved herbs again that she missed the noon meal and would have missed the evening meal if Wulf hadn't come for her.

"Why are you still here?" Wulf asked. "It is time for supper."

Startled, Reyna looked up. "Is it that late already?"

Wulf walked into the chamber, glancing first at the drying racks hung with plants and then at various bowls lined up on the worktable, some filled with unidentifiable mixtures and others still empty.

"You have worked enough for today. Come join us; tomorrow is another day."

Reyna nodded and followed Wulf out the door. The family was already seated at the long table when they arrived. Wulf escorted her to an empty place and sat down beside her. Immediately thralls began placing food on the table. The delicious smell of roasted pork made Reyna's mouth water. It didn't take long for her to realize she was ravenous.

Wulf served her generous portions of pork, potatoes, turnips, fresh bread and butter. Reyna ate steadily, listening with half an ear to the conversation taking place around her. She didn't look up from her plate until she heard Thora speak her name.

"Olaf wondered about your absence today, Reyna. I think he feels neglected."

"I am sorry," Reyna replied. "I became so involved with my work I did not realize how late it was. I will look in on him after supper." Her brow wrinkled in concern. "Has he taken a turn for the worse?"

"He is healing well," Hagar assured her, "and anxious to leave his bed."

"Not yet," Reyna said firmly. "I will tell him when that day arrives."

"You assume responsibility that is not yours," Olga huffed. "How many times must I remind you of your position as a thrall?"

Hagar sighed and patted Olga's hand. "Can you not be kind to Reyna? She has done us a great service."

"Mayhap you have forgotten that her people killed Astrid, her unborn child and Aunt Freya, but I have not. I do not care how many times Wulf plows her, she is not family and should not be allowed special favors. Look at you, Hagar; you cannot stop staring at her. Mahap you would like Wulf to share her with you."

"Enough, Olga!" Hagar roared, startling Reyna. "Reyna belongs to Wulf. I bought her for him and him

alone. Tis none of our business what my brother does with her."

Wulf watched the color drain from Reyna's face and decided this had gone on long enough. "Are you finished eating, Reyna?" When she nodded, Wulf pushed himself from the table and rose. " 'Tis time we returned home."

"I promised to look in on Olaf before I leave," Reyna protested.

"I will accompany you."

They found Olaf sitting up in bed, looking forlornly out the window. He perked up immediately when he saw Reyna.

"I thought you forgot me," the young man said.

"We went to the woods to gather herbs for Reyna's remedies," Wulf explained.

"And to slay wild boars," Olaf replied. "I heard about it from Hagar and enjoyed my share of the meat tonight."

"May I look at your wound and change your bandage?" Reyna asked. Without waiting for an answer, she selected a jar of salve from a nearby shelf and brought it to Olaf's bedside. Then she began removing the soiled bandage. While she worked, Wulf and Olaf discussed recent events, including the raid on their farmstead.

"I am glad you are here, Wulf," Olaf said when the conversation waned. "I wanted to speak with you in private."

Reyna looked up. "Shall I leave? I am almost finished here."

"Stay," Olaf said. "This concerns you as well as Wulf."

Wulf eyed Olaf warily. "You wish to discuss my thrall with me?"

"Aye, Wulf. Reyna saved your life, did she not?" Wulf

nodded. "She also saved mine and treated the wounded warriors. I cannot imagine why you have not freed her."

"Reyna is none of your concern, brother. Her fate is mine to decide. Fear not, she will not be ill treated."

Olaf cleared his throat. "Will you allow me to wed her?"

"What!" Reyna gasped, startled by Olaf's unusual request.

"Are you feverish, brother? You are too young to wed. Besides, Reyna is unavailable."

"I appreciate your offer, Olaf," Reyna injected, "but I am too old for you. One day you will find a woman worthy of being your wife."

"I am twenty," Olaf replied, "old enough to know what I want."

Wulf's fists clenched at his sides. The thought of Reyna in Olaf's bed did not sit well with him. "Believe me, Olaf, you do not want Reyna. You are not man enough to handle her." He sent a guarded look at Reyna. "When I tire of her or she becomes troublesome, you can have her with my good wishes. However, I doubt that day will arrive any time soon, if ever," he added.

Reyna didn't appreciate being talked around, as if she were not there. As she tidied up, her anger grew by leaps and bounds. Having heard enough, she turned on the two men.

"You may argue about me all you like, but I will have neither of you. One day I will return to my homeland and my family."

Turning on her heel, she stormed off.

"What in Odin's name is wrong with you, brother?" Wulf scolded. "Why did you offer to wed Reyna?"

"She saved your life and mine. How can you ignore her courage? I appreciate her skills enough to wed her

and make her a free woman. If you refuse to let me have her, wed her yourself."

Wulf shook his head. "There is a great deal about our relationship you do not understand, Olaf. It goes back to the time I raided her farmstead. Suffice it to say, Reyna belongs to me, and I keep what is mine. Concentrate on getting well, not on my thrall."

Wulf left his brother's room in a thoughtful mood. Why was everyone concerned about Reyna? Did they think he beat her? Of all his family, Olga was the only one who didn't like her. And Wulf put Olga's emotional state down to her pregnancy.

As if his thought had conjured her up, Olga appeared before him. "Might I have a word with you, Wulf?" his sister-in-law asked.

"Of course, Olga. What is it you want?"

"Would you please keep your thrall away from Hagar? I do not like the way he looks at her."

"There is naught going on between Reyna and Hagar," Wulf assured her. " 'Tis your condition speaking."

Olga didn't look convinced. "I would feel more at ease if Reyna did not share meals with us. None of the other thralls are treated like family."

"You should discuss your fears with Hagar. He will be the first to tell you he has no interest in Reyna."

"I know my husband, Wulf. Believe me when I say he wants to bed your thrall." Tossing her head, she flounced off.

After Olga's unfounded claim, Wulf left the hall in search of Reyna. He found her in the stillroom, working with her herbs and roots. Helga was with her, their heads together in private conversation.

"What are you two whispering about?"

Reyna turned slowly, frowning when she saw Wulf. "I am teaching Helga about herbal remedies. She is inter-

ested in learning healing skills. Is there something you want?"

"No, I just wondered where you had disappeared to."

"Why? Have you decided to give me to your brother after all?"

"What?" Helga exclaimed. "Which brother would that be?"

"Olaf," Reyna said. "If you wish to know more, ask Wulf."

Refusing to elaborate, she turned back to her work.

Helga shooed him away. "Go away, Wulf, we are busy."

"What I see is a thrall I have no control over despite the fact that I own her. Very well, continue your work. Just remember, in the end I have final say over Reyna's fate, no matter what you and the family seem to think."

"What was that all about?" Helga asked after Wulf left.

"As a reward for saving his life, Olaf wants to wed me. Wulf denied Olaf's request."

Helga's eyes grew wide. "Do you want to marry Olaf?"

Reyna forced a laugh. "No, I do not. He is young and mistakes gratitude for something more. 'Tis growing late, we should retire for the night."

By the time Reyna arrived in the hall, Uma, Lorne and Wulf were all abed. Breathing a sigh of relief, she crawled into her own bed and fell instantly asleep.

The next day Wulf and Hagar left for the trading port of Kaupang, where they intended to sell or trade some of the goods Hagar had obtained in Byzantium this past summer. They took with them a list of commodities that Thora and Olga had requested, including iron pots, pottery, needles and various ribbons and threads. They planned to return within a fortnight.

Reyna spent most of the following two weeks in the

stillroom. Sometimes Helga joined her and once in a while Inga tagged along. Reyna was becoming fond of both girls. Olaf was healing well and now took his meals with the family. When Reyna saw him exercising in the yard, she knew he was well on his way to regaining his former strength.

Regrettably, Uma remained hostile to her, even more so now that Reyna had been given a sleeping alcove of her own. As far as Reyna was concerned, she had earned the right to a bed.

After watching Wulf's interaction with Uma and Lorne, Reyna realized that Wulf wasn't a cruel taskmaster, so she couldn't feel too sorry for his thralls.

Reyna had to admit that life was calmer without Wulf around to remind her of the past. Or taunt her with his handsome face and hard body. The last thing Reyna wanted to think about was Wulf's warrior's body.

Reyna was working in the stillroom late one afternoon when Uma came to fetch her. "The master wants you to attend him."

"Wulf has returned?" Why did Wulf's return make her feel giddy?

Uma's voice was sharp with jealousy. "Aye, he asked for you the moment he entered the hall."

"Tell him I will attend him after I finish what I am doing."

"You are a bold one," Uma huffed. "I would be punished if I disobeyed an order."

"Name one instance in which Wulf punished you."

Uma stared mutely at her.

"I thought not. Give Wulf my message and tell him if he cannot wait, he can come here."

Reyna never expected Wulf to take her words literally. She was putting the finishing touches on an elixir to

cure coughs and colds when Wulf stormed into the still-room, slamming the door behind him with enough force to shake the building.

"How dare you disobey me!" Wulf roared. "You may have forgotten that you are my thrall, but I have not. I could beat you and no one would interfere."

Hands on hips, Reyna faced him squarely. "I am not afraid of you, Wulf the Ruthless. I am no weakling. I survived the worst that can happen to a woman."

Wulf's voice was less harsh when he asked, "Why did you not come when I sent for you?"

"If I stopped what I was doing, the entire batch of elixir I was preparing would spoil. The remedy will come in handy this winter. I told Uma I would come when I finished here."

Wulf scowled. "That is not what Uma told me."

Reyna should have realized Uma would turn her words around to suit her purposes. "What *did* Uma say?"

"She said you told her you are not my slave, that you are not answerable to me and will not obey me. Is that not what you said?"

Reyna sighed. "I said I would attend you as soon as I finished mixing the elixir."

Wulf stalked closer, until he was standing within arm's reach. Reyna tried to retreat but the worktable was at her back. The way Wulf looked at her sent shivers down her spine. He had the look of a wolf eager to mate. His silver eyes had darkened to smoke and his face had a watchfulness about it that made Reyna's heart skip a beat.

He sidled closer. "Did you miss me?"

He was so close Reyna could feel his hot breath fan her cheek. "Why would I miss a man who stole my innocence and sold me into slavery?"

"I sold you because I was bereft over the death of my wife, but that is all I did. Believe it or not, I missed you, Reyna. All I could think about was your sweet body and how badly I want you in my bed."

"That will never happen," Reyna scoffed.

"It will happen sooner than you think."

"Could you find no woman in Kaupang to satisfy your lust?"

"I found plenty of willing women but they were not you."

He reached out and dragged her against him, his big hands circling her waist. And then he kissed her, his teasing mouth making her forget who he was and what he had done to her. When his tongue dipped into her mouth, she made a little mew of protest. To her dismay she felt her body softening, her will eroding. Without volition her eyes closed, and her hands slid around his thick neck. The kiss went on and on; his mouth was literally devouring her. Her mind spun in denial. She should hate Wulf's kisses. She should be struggling in his arms instead of melting into his hard body. She felt his muscles rippling down his firm abdomen and pressed herself closer, suddenly aware that his rigid sex was throbbing against her stomach.

Wulf broke off the kiss and grinned down at her. "Your body tells me you are not as opposed to me as you pretend."

"I hate you, Wulf the Ruthless," Reyna hissed.

"Do you?" He kissed her again, this time moving his hands from her waist to her breasts, cupping them and then tweaking her nipples until they became pebble hard. His touch was surprisingly gentle as his lips coaxed an unwilling response from her.

How could this man be the same brute who had ripped her innocence from her? Reyna wondered. This man was as different from that abuser of innocents as

night was from day. Wulf made her body feel things she feared. She shouldn't want to experience desire with Wulf, or with any man. And yet . . .

Reyna's cheeks burned. She broke the kiss and turned her face away. "This . . . cannot be happening. You are . . . You did . . ."

"I did naught, but I certainly intend to, and very soon."

Wulf was shocked by his unaccustomed lack of control. He had lusted after Reyna since she'd first come to the farmstead. Hagar had urged him to find a woman to bed in Kaupang but he hadn't wanted just any woman; he wanted Reyna. Her response to his kisses and the way she had melted into his body surprised him. He had expected much less but wanted much more.

Grasping Reyna about the waist, he flung her over his shoulder and strode toward the door.

"Stop! What are you doing?"

"My patience is gone. I have waited long enough for you to come to me."

The door opened before he reached it. Thora stepped inside and stopped abruptly, her face clouded with concern.

"What is going on here? Has my son hurt you, Reyna?"

"Mother," Wulf said with waning patience, "I have not hurt Reyna and do not intend to. Has everyone forgotten that Reyna belongs to me? Why are you here?"

"I came to fetch Reyna. I have not seen her since she broke her fast this morning and we are waiting for her to join us for the evening meal. I sent Helga to your hall to fetch you but here you are, Wulf."

"I am not hungry for food," Wulf said as he attempted to brush past Thora.

Reyna lifted her head and sent Thora a look of mute appeal. "I am starving, Lady Thora."

"If you are not hungry, Wulf, put Reyna down so she can eat with us," Thora ordered. "Before you protest, we have a guest, son, one you will wish to greet. He arrived a short time ago."

"A guest? Were we expecting company?"

"Rannulf needs no invitation. He decided to visit his sister before winter snow makes travel difficult. I invited him to spend a few days with us before he returns to his farmstead. I . . . I think he is interested in wedding Helga."

Wulf set Reyna carefully on her feet. Would Rannulf recognize Reyna, or she him? How would she react when she came face-to-face with the man who had ravished her? As much as Wulf wanted to shield Reyna from Rannulf's hurtful presence, he knew that bringing them together would force Reyna to recognize that she had accused him, Wulf, falsely.

"Very well, Mother, Reyna and I shall greet Rannulf. I do not want to keep Hagar's brother-in-law waiting."

Grasping Reyna's elbow, Wulf ushered her out the door. Thora fell in step behind them.

Chapter Six

Wulf and Reyna entered Hagar's hall together. The family was gathered around their guest, talking animatedly. Wulf watched Reyna closely, waiting for her to recognize Rannulf as the man who had ravished her. Rannulf saw them first and called out a greeting, a huge smile stretching his lips. They grasped arms and patted each other on the back.

Wulf glanced at Reyna. Her brow was furrowed and her cheeks were unnaturally pale. He waited for her to say something, anything, but her expression remained thoughtful as she slowly edged away from him and Rannulf.

As for Rannulf, he did not appear to recognize the woman he had abused two summers ago.

"I thought I would pay my sister a visit before winter closes in," Rannulf explained. "The farmstead is a lonely place without a woman's gentle touch."

He winked at Wulf and said for his ears only. "After both my sisters married and moved away, I find myself in need of a wife. Helga came to mind immediately. She is of an age to wed, is she not?"

Wulf frowned at Olga's brother. In his mind's eye he saw Rannulf climbing off of Reyna. Did he want a man like that for his sister? Then again, he had been no saint

in his wild youth. Would Rannulf change his ways as
Wulf did after he'd wed Astrid? From the way Helga
was staring shyly at Rannulf, Wulf assumed she wasn't
adverse to a match between them.

Hagar, who had been at the other side of the hall, approached Rannulf, eyeing him with speculation. "What
is the reason for your visit, Rannulf? Though you are always welcome in my hall, and your sister appreciates
your visit, have you a specific purpose in mind?"

"I thought to wait and discuss this with you and your
mother later but this is as good a time as any. With
your permission, I would like to wed Helga."

"What, no courtship?" Wulf challenged, hoping to
observe Rannulf's behavior toward his sister before
agreeing to the match.

"Wulf has a point," Hagar observed. "Perhaps you
should spend the winter with us. I am sure Olga would
enjoy your company. A long visit will give Helga time to
get to know you. If she wishes to wed you, you can join
with her in the spring. We will discuss this with Mother
later."

After Hagar departed, Rannulf spotted Reyna talking to Helga and sent Wulf a questioning look. "Who is
the woman, Wulf? Have you taken a wife? She is a
beauty."

Wulf shifted uncomfortably. How could Rannulf not
remember Reyna? "Reyna is my thrall. Hagar bought
her for me at the slave market in Constantinople this
past summer. He thought I needed a little excitement in
my life."

Rannulf slapped Wulf on the back. "I agree with Hagar. I would not mind a bed slave who looked like that.
She has the look of a Norsewoman about her."

"Reyna is a Dane. Does she not look familiar to you?"

Rannulf's gaze lingered on Reyna. "Am I supposed to know her?"

Wulf wanted to bloody Rannulf's nose and then knock him flat on his arse. Instead, he gritted his teeth and said, "Think on it. It may come to you."

"You seem protective of her, Wulf. She must please you in bed."

Wulf had his mouth open to spit out a reply when Thora approached them. "Come join us at the table, you two. You can catch up after we sup." She gazed at Rannulf, a twinkle in her eyes. "Hagar says you wish to court our Helga."

Wulf kept his reservations to himself as he took his place at the table beside Rannulf. Wulf regarded Reyna with concern when Rannulf sat across from her. The frown had not left her face since she'd first set eyes on Rannulf.

Reyna felt a strange buzzing in her head whenever she looked at Rannulf. Like Wulf, he was a handsome, clean-shaven man, tall and muscular but a bit shorter. His blond hair was tied at his nape with a piece of leather and his clothing was the same as that worn by most Norsemen.

There was something vaguely threatening about the man, Reyna decided. Though the family seemed to accept him into their inner circle, he made Reyna feel uncomfortable. Was there a reason she should not like this man? Rather than look directly at him, she lowered her eyes to her plate and tried to eat. All she succeeded in doing was pushing her food around on her plate.

"Is something wrong?" Wulf asked. "Is the food not agreeable to you?"

"The food is fine," Reyna answered. "I seem to have lost my appetite."

She glanced at Rannulf; he was listening to Olaf explain about the recent raid on the farmstead. As if aware of her gaze, the Norseman turned to her, looking directly into her eyes.

"I find it strange that a thrall eats at the table with her master," Rannulf said to no one in particular.

"Reyna has earned her place at the table," Thora was quick to explain. "She saved the lives of both Olaf and Wulf and treated the wounded after the Finns' surprise raid."

"Olaf has been telling me about the raid," Rannulf said. "I had not heard about it until now. Obviously you sent them fleeing."

"Aye." Hagar grinned. "They will not bother us again any time soon."

Rannulf's intense blue eyes returned to Reyna. Their gazes collided in startling recollection. Rannulf's eyes widened in shock and disbelief, and then an unexpected flush started at the base of the Norseman's neck and traveled upward.

Reyna's hand flew to her mouth, stifling the scream that threatened to erupt from her throat. It was as if a curtain had been lifted from her memory. This Norseman, this man named Rannulf, not Wulf the Ruthless as she'd wrongly assumed, had brutally ripped away her innocence and left her lying hurt and bleeding on the ground. Although Wulf had sold her into slavery, he had not physically harmed her.

Staggering to her feet, Reyna clung to the table's edge, trying to find the strength to stumble away. Beside her, Wulf lurched upward, grasping her about the waist to steady her. Though Reyna felt everyone's eyes on her, she saw no one save Rannulf.

Her conflicting feelings for Wulf, her desire for a man she should hate above all others, had plagued her. Now

that she knew the truth, it was as if a weight had been lifted from her.

"Are you unwell, Reyna?"

Wulf's voice released her from her shocked paralysis. She returned her gaze to the brutal Norseman sitting at the family table.

"I . . . want to leave," Reyna gasped. She released her hold on the table and backed away. Unfortunately the shock had been too much for her, and she started a slow spiral to the floor. She heard Thora call her name and felt Wulf's arms sweep her off her feet.

"What ails Reyna, son?" Thora asked, concern coloring her words.

"Do not worry, Mother. I will take care of her."

"What is wrong with her?"

He sent a pointed look at Rannulf. "I will explain later." Whirling on his heel, he headed out the door with Reyna resting securely in his arms.

Reyna regained her wits the moment the cold air hit her hot cheeks. She felt herself floating and opened her eyes. Relief swamped her when she saw Wulf's face close to hers and realized she was in his arms. She lifted her own arms, slid them around his neck and turned her face into his hard chest.

"What happened?" she mumbled.

"What do you remember?"

"I . . . sweet Freya, it was Rannulf! Why did you not tell me?"

"I tried to tell you I did not do what you accused me of, but you refused to believe me."

"What was I to think? You refused to supply the name of the man responsible."

"Rannulf is Olga's brother. I feared you might confront Olga about her brother's depraved act and upset

her. I worried that a confrontation might cause harm to my brother's heir. Olga is a volatile woman."

Wulf opened the door and carried Reyna inside the hall. Both Uma and Lorne came running up to them.

"Master, what is wrong with Reyna?" Uma asked.

"Reyna is fine, Uma. You and Lorne may take your ease in the volcanic pool; I have no further need of you tonight."

Uma sent a venomous look at Reyna. "Lorne can go; I will remain behind to assist you."

Wulf brushed past her. "I do not need your help. Do as I say, Uma."

Lorne grabbed Uma's hand and dragged her out the door. Wulf proceeded to his sleeping alcove, placed Reyna on the bed and pulled the curtain shut behind him.

Wulf stood over her, gazing at her with an expression Reyna found difficult to interpret.

"All these weeks I believed you a monster," Reyna whispered. "You should not have let it go on so long."

Wulf subsided onto the edge of the bed. Reyna moved over to make room for him. "I am not without guilt, Reyna. I did sell you to a foreign master."

"Why did you take me aboard your dragonship? Why did you not leave me behind?"

"If I had left you, others would have taken Rannulf's place. You looked so vulnerable, so hurt, that I could not think beyond removing you from the path of danger."

Reyna sent him a puzzled look. He had paid so little attention to her during the voyage to Byzantium, she could have been invisible.

"I know what you are thinking. Believe it or not, I did not see you as a desirable woman then. You were the enemy. I was still mourning my wife; my rage was so great that vengeance was all I cared about. The sooner I rid myself of the enemy the better."

"Yet here I am, with the very same man who wanted nothing to do with me. Do you not think it strange?"

"Beyond strange," Wulf agreed.

" 'Tis as if the gods preordained our meeting again. I did not know Hagar and he did not know me. We happened to be at the same place at the same time. And now I am your thrall."

Reaching out, Wulf smoothed a silken strand of pale hair away from her forehead. Reyna felt a jolt of awareness where his hand lingered, and then a surge of heat spread through her body.

"You are so beautiful," Wulf said, his voice low and strangely hoarse. "How could I have failed to see what I had in my possession? Had I not been wild with grief, I would not have sold you. I would have kept you for myself."

"How long will Rannulf remain here?" Reyna asked, trying to distract herself from the intense pull of Wulf's nearness, which was wreaking havoc on her senses.

"Hagar asked Rannulf to stay the winter. He has expressed his desire to court and wed Helga."

Reyna lurched upright in bed, her face a mask of horror. "No, never say 'tis true. The man is a monster. Helga deserves a man who will appreciate and love her."

Wulf's arms came around Reyna in an effort to soothe her. "Rannulf is not a bad man. 'Tis a Norseman's nature to lose control when his bloodlust runs high."

Reyna pushed Wulf away. "My father and brothers do not harm women."

Wulf sent her a look of disbelief. "Do you know that for a fact? Have you been with them when they raid?"

"My brothers are traders and my father is a farmer. They have never raided property belonging to another."

Wulf had the grace to flush. "We are Norsemen; we go a-Viking because it is our way of life. Some of us are

traders, like Hagar and your brothers. But many of us raid to acquire fertile land and for plunder and slaves. 'Tis a harsh life we lead."

Reyna remained mute, quietly digesting everything Wulf had told her. At length she said, "And what of your women? How do you treat them?"

"Norsewomen are strong and resilient. They can fight alongside their men when the need arises. They run our homes and bear our children. Norsemen revere their wives, mothers and sisters."

"I noticed thralls are not included in your list of those you respect."

"I have the highest respect for you, Reyna. You have won over my entire family."

"Obviously I have not won you over for I am still your thrall."

"I no longer think of you as my thrall. You saved my life."

"Then why have you not freed me?" she asked bluntly.

"Are you sure you wish to hear the truth?"

"I prefer it to a lie."

Wulf found her hand, turned it over and stroked her palm with the roughness of his thumb. "So be it. The truth is that I want to keep you for myself. I want you in my hall and in my bed. Letting you go would give you the freedom to leave and find a man more to your liking. I know you cannot like me, for I tore you away from your home and abandoned you in a foreign land."

Reyna touched his cheek, feeling the roughness of a sprouting beard. "In an odd way you saved my life. Being abused by countless men would have taken the will to live from me. During the voyage to Byzantium, I learned a great deal about myself. I was stronger than I realized. That introspective time on your ship lent me

the courage to face my new master with newfound confidence.

"I challenged him and he backed down. He never touched me during those months I spent in his harem. His decision to sell me was the best thing that could have happened to me. Now I am returned to my own part of the world."

"Now you are mine," Wulf whispered.

Grasping her shoulders, he pulled her against him. He felt her stiffen and wondered if it was every man's touch or just his she could not bear. Then he recalled her previous response to his kisses and smiled. Though Rannulf's assault might have made Reyna skittish with men, she had accepted his kisses eagerly before.

Wulf stared into her wide green eyes as he slowly brought his mouth down on hers.

Reyna allowed herself to relax as soft, full lips moved over hers, tasting her, letting her taste him. She felt surrounded by his male scent, his very essence, the power of his need. He exuded sexual musk as he deepened the kiss, his tongue stroking into her mouth, hot, fierce, determined. Then terror overwhelmed her. The memory of a hard body smelling of blood and sweat threw her into a panic and she began to struggle.

Wulf pulled back from the kiss and stared at her. "I am not going to hurt you, Reyna. I am not the ravishing beast you think I am. I want to make love to you. Though it has been a long time for me, I know how to be gentle. Are you frightened of me?"

Reyna regarded him for a long time. She *was* frightened, but not of Wulf. She hated the act that had torn away her innocence and couldn't imagine doing *that* again. But her body was in contradiction with her mind.

Her body wanted the same thing Wulf wanted. The raw, purely sexual need to experience fulfillment with Wulf nipped at her senses. Her body told her there was pleasure to be had if she could overcome her fright and embrace it.

"I do not fear you, Wulf the Ruthless. I may have at one time but no longer. That does not mean, however, that I wish to become your bed slave."

"Let me touch you, Reyna. I promise to do naught you do not wish me to do."

He was determined in this, Reyna realized, but in her heart she feared the pain and the degradation of being forced to a man's will. Yet some small part of her wondered what a sexual experience would feel like if she were a willing participant.

"What are you thinking, Reyna?"

She stared at his mouth, recalling the pleasure his lips were capable of giving. She had suffered so much pain, why shouldn't she allow herself a brief taste of pleasure?

"Kiss me, Wulf."

He inhaled sharply. "I might not be able to stop with just a kiss. Are you willing to accept my loving if I promise not to hurt you?"

Before Reyna could think about what she had agreed to, she nodded her head.

"Thank Odin," Wulf breathed. "It would have killed me to walk away from you. You won't be sorry, Reyna, I promise."

Reyna couldn't deny she wanted Wulf, wanted to know what it felt like to be made love to instead of being ruthlessly ravished. Dragging in a deep breath, she waited for the pleasure to begin.

Wulf seized her mouth, claiming her with a passion that made her flinch, but then his mouth softened,

coaxing her lips open and thrusting his tongue between her teeth. The kiss went on and on, softening at times then turning wildly savage as he took her deeply with his tongue.

She felt his hands working on the ties of her tunic, easing it down her shoulders along with her under-tunic. His mouth never left hers as he lifted her and skillfully swept away her clothing, tossing it on the floor. Her heavy woolen stockings and shoes followed. Before the rush of air could cool her body, he covered her with his own.

"Wulf . . ." She trembled as he took a nipple into his mouth and suckled her. A wave of pleasure hit her. She arched upward, pushing more of her breast into his mouth.

What she did next shocked her. She tugged at his leather jerkin, wanting, needing to feel his naked body against hers. One swift movement brought Wulf to his feet. He undressed swiftly, his clothing flying hither and yon. Then he stood naked before her, his body a flagrant statement of his masculinity. Reyna's avid gaze swept over him, gasping when she saw his swollen sex bursting from the thick blond forest between his thighs.

She gulped audibly. He would kill her if he tried to put *that* inside her. "Wulf, I do not think . . . You are so big . . . I am not sure."

Wulf dropped down beside her. "Don't think, Reyna. Our bodies are made to fit together."

Then he kissed her. Despite her frayed nerves, Reyna returned his kiss, and soon she was drowning in a sea of bliss. Her fears floated away as if they had never existed as Wulf's mouth found her breasts, his white teeth tugging on the succulent tips. A small cry of protest erupted from her throat when his mouth left her nipples and nibbled a path down to her abdomen. When his big

hand sifted through the soft curls above her sex, a lance of liquid heat pierced through her.

He palmed her mound, separating the damp petals of her sex and stroking her with his fingers. Raw, incomprehensible need flamed through her, and a yearning so intense she cried out his name. She began to tremble. This desperate woman she had become could not be her. The sex act was abhorrent to her. Then she gazed into Wulf's expressive silver eyes and knew she had nothing to fear from him.

She yelped in surprise when his mouth clamped on that tender place where his hands had worked their magic just moments before. "Wulf, what are you doing?"

Wulf lifted his head and grinned at her. "You will like this, I promise."

She didn't believe him. When his mouth returned to his succulent feast, she tried to push him away, but he was an immovable force, determined to have his way.

Then his tongue came into play, stroking her tender folds and dipping inside her melting center. Reyna felt something loosen inside her, felt fire lick over her body, and making him stop was the last thing she wanted.

She wanted . . . She wanted . . . Sweet Freya, she wanted something that had no name. "Wulf?" she cried out. "What is happening to me?"

He raised his head. "Let it come, Reyna. Don't hold back."

Her body burned, her skin felt as if it was stretched too tight over her bones. She arched and twisted, trying to escape the pleasure/pain of the unknown. Wulf's hands held her hips in place as he continued to torment her.

She was dying.

And then life poured through her in an explosion of sensation so intense she would swear later that she had glimpsed Valhalla. Wulf waited until her tremors ceased,

and then he parted her legs with his knees and came up over her. His engorged sex stroked her wet cleft before easing inside her, inch by excruciating inch.

"Am I hurting you?" he asked in a strangled voice.

She wrapped her arms and legs around him, holding him in place. "Nay, if you stop I could not bear it."

With a relieved groan he surged forward, driving his thick cock deep inside her. Reyna had prepared herself for the pain she knew would come, and when it didn't arrive she embraced the pleasure, shifting to accommodate the weight and size of him.

Wulf's massive body surged forward, driving him deep, his hips flexing, pumping his engorged staff in and out. Reyna felt herself stretching to accommodate his rigid length and reveled in the sensation he created inside her. Her nipples rubbing against the soft hair on his chest sent tongues of flame racing along her nerve endings, and a sweet fire began in that place where they were joined.

Caught up in the fierce sensations, Reyna met his pounding hips with wild abandon, each thrust bringing a delicious tightening to the very core of her being.

"Wulf, please!"

He grunted something unintelligible and picked up the tempo, driving her further and further into a kind of madness. And then something sweet and fierce gripped her insides, spreading liquid fire through her limbs. Tiny points of light burst behind her eyes. Powerful shock waves of pleasure shook her and she cried out his name.

She felt Wulf's muscles tense, heard his teeth gnash and felt his control slipping away seconds before the hot splash of his seed filled her womb. Moments later he collapsed against her, his breathing harsh against her ear. Replete, Reyna held him in place, but Wulf, mindful of his weight, lifted himself away from her and flopped

down beside her. Long seconds passed. Her heart was still pounding madly as his arms came around her. She could hear his pulse thumping in rhythm with her own.

"Are you all right?" he rasped.

"I . . . I had no idea it could be like that."

"It is when you are not being forced. I hope you enjoyed it as much as I did."

"It was . . . um . . . not what I expected."

"Was it better or worse?"

"I believe you know the answer to that."

"Go to sleep, Reyna. You have earned your rest."

Reyna tried to rise but Wulf's arm held her in place. "Where are you going?"

"To my own bed."

"This is where you will sleep from now on. In my bed and in my arms."

"Is that wise, Wulf? What will Uma think?"

" 'Tis not her place to think."

"Everyone will assume I am your bed slave."

"Everyone will be right." When Reyna objected, Wulf rolled on top of her, spread her legs and slid inside.

Wulf woke the following morning to the sound of voices coming from somewhere beyond his sleeping alcove. Glancing down at Reyna, he saw that she was still sleeping and he eased out of bed so as not to awaken her. Quietly he donned breeches and jerkin, parted the curtains and stepped into the hall. He was surprised to see Rannulf seated at the table, sipping a mug of ale.

"There you are," Rannulf greeted. "I have been waiting for you to wake up. We need to talk."

"Join me in the steam hut," Wulf invited. "We can talk in private there."

Rannulf accepted Wulf's invitation with a nod of his head and rose. Uma ran to fetch soap and drying cloths,

handing them to Wulf as he and Rannulf walked out the door.

"Master!" Uma called after Wulf, "shall I awaken Reyna and put her to work?"

Wulf stopped and turned slowly. "No one tells Reyna what to do but me. Let her sleep."

The steam hut was empty when they arrived, though someone must have used it earlier for steam rose thick and hot inside the small enclosure. Wulf undressed, then dumped a bucket of water on the hot rocks. When a hiss of steam curled around him, he lowered himself onto a bench beside Rannulf.

"What is this about, Rannulf?" Wulf asked.

"Reyna, of course. I did not recognize her at first. You know how it is when a man is blinded by bloodlust. You can imagine my profound shock when comprehension dawned. I think she knew me too." He paused, staring thoughtfully into the rising steam. "If I'd had the sense to recognize her beauty and value, I would have claimed her for myself before you carried her off."

"Did Hagar or Olga explain what happened? How she came to be my thrall?"

"Olga told me. My sister wants Reyna gone. She fears Hagar is too fond of her."

"Olga is wrong. Hagar bought Reyna for me; he never wanted her for himself. Your sister's jealousy is unwarranted."

Sweat poured off each man in rivulets. When the steam started to dissipate, Wulf dumped another bucket of cold water over the hot rocks and returned to the bench.

"Olga should not have to suffer Reyna's presence if it makes her uncomfortable," Rannulf said. "I am confident Hagar will agree with me. He has waited a long time for an heir."

Wulf slanted Rannulf a curious look. "What are you suggesting, Rannulf?"

"I wish to purchase Reyna from you. Name your price."

Wulf hissed out a breath. "I thought you wanted to wed Helga."

"I did . . . I do. I understand Helga and Reyna are friends. Doubtless my new wife would welcome Reyna in our hall."

Wulf fought hard to control his rage. "If I sell Reyna to you, do you intend to bed both my sister and Reyna?"

Rannulf shrugged. "Why should that bother you?"

"It bothers me that you intend to bed another woman under my sister's nose and feel no guilt about it."

"Hmmm, I suppose you are right. If you will allow me to purchase your thrall, I will wed her instead of Helga. After all, I was the first to have her. Did I ever tell you she was a virgin? Tight and hot as anything I've . . ."

Without warning, Wulf lunged. He picked up Rannulf and tossed him out the door.

Chapter Seven

Red dots of rage formed behind Wulf's eyes as he pulled on his leggings and stormed from the steam hut, stepping over Rannulf, who was still lying in the dirt.

"Wulf, wait!"

Wulf whirled at the sound of his name. He cursed beneath his breath when he saw Hagar hurrying toward him.

"What happened here?" Hagar asked, gesturing to Rannulf, who had apparently regained his wits and had staggered to his feet.

"Put some clothes on," Hagar ordered the dazed warrior. Rannulf returned to the steam hut while Wulf and Hagar continued their conversation.

"I hope you are not considering Rannulf as a brother-in-law," Wulf said.

"Why not? What has Rannulf done to offend you? I could not believe my eyes when I saw him staggering before the steam hut."

"The bastard wanted to buy Reyna."

Hagar's brow furrowed. "What is so unusual about that? Thralls are bought and sold every day."

"He wants Helga *and* Reyna, with the intention of bedding both women. When I flatly refused, he offered to wed Reyna."

Both men stared at Rannulf as he exited from the steam hut. Hagar motioned for him to join them.

"I brought your jerkin," Rannulf said, handing Wulf the rest of his clothing. Wulf snatched it from his hand. "I did not mean to upset you, Wulf. We have been a-Viking together too often. And you, Hagar, are my sister's husband. I meant no disrespect."

Hagar shook his head. "No disrespect? Did you truly intend to wed Helga, buy Reyna, and bed both of them?"

Rannulf shrugged. "I spoke without thinking. Helga deserves better from me."

"Wulf said you offered to wed Reyna instead of Helga."

Rannulf shot Wulf an exasperated look. "I thought it no more than right since I took her virginity during the raid on her farmstead."

Hagar held Wulf back when Wulf made a menacing move toward Rannulf. "I was not aware you were the man who assaulted Reyna during that raid. Now I understand why she avoids you."

"It took awhile, but Reyna finally recognized Rannulf as the man who had hurt her." Wulf glared at Rannulf. "Until she saw you, she held me responsible."

Rannulf huffed out a breath. "You are not entirely guiltless. You sold her to a slave master."

"I am well aware of that," Wulf replied.

"I see no reason to fall out because of a thrall. What say you, Wulf? I but tried to do the right thing, for I understand you and your family value Reyna. If you allow it, I would still like to court Helga."

"Over my dead body!" Wulf raged.

"Calm yourself, brother," Hagar soothed, then turned to Rannulf. "If we allow you to court and wed Helga, Rannulf, we will expect you to give up raiding and rapine and turn to trading, just as we did."

Stroking his chin, Rannulf considered Hagar's stipu-

lations. "You would still let me court Helga if I agree to your terms?"

"Hold on," Wulf injected. "We would also require you to remain faithful to my sister, promise that you will take no other woman to your bed during your marriage."

Rannulf's gaze shifted to Hagar. "You are the elder brother, what say you? Are you a faithful husband? Was Wulf faithful to his wife while she lived?"

"Aye, to both your questions. The only way we will allow you to court Helga is if you agree to our terms. If you refuse, you had best seek a wife elsewhere."

"Let me add to that another condition," Wulf said. "You are to keep your hands and eyes away from Reyna. She is mine."

Rannulf sent Wulf a puzzled look. "I have never known you to be so possessive of a woman."

"Nor I," Hagar said, grinning. "Nevertheless, Reyna belongs to Wulf, and I confirm his final condition. If you do not agree to the terms put forth by us, I suggest you return to your farmstead."

"I agree," Rannulf said without hesitation. "Helga is worth any sacrifice."

"So be it," Hagar replied.

They clasped arms. But when Rannulf turned to Wulf, it took a good deal of prodding from Hagar before Wulf offered his hand to Rannulf.

Reyna was still sleeping when Wulf returned to his hall. He knew because Uma made it a point to mention Reyna's laziness.

"I am famished," Wulf said. "I will wake Reyna while you fix us something to eat. Where is Lorne?" he asked when he noted the thrall's absence.

"Gathering firewood," Uma replied.

Wulf nodded as he strode toward his sleeping alcove

and slipped through the curtain. He was surprised to see that Reyna was up, dressed, and sitting on the edge of the bed, staring at her hands.

"I was hoping you'd still be abed," Wulf rasped, his expressive silver eyes hinting at his reason for wanting her in bed again. "Disrobe for me."

Reyna's eyes widened and she glared up at him. "No, I refuse to become your whore." She rose and swept past him. She had almost reached the curtain when Wulf grabbed her arm.

"When I give you an order, I expect you to obey."

"I will obey when it pleases me to do so. You cannot force me to your bed."

Wulf scratched his head. "What has gotten into you, woman? You were amenable last night."

"Last night was an aberration. You caught me at a weak moment. 'Tis bad enough that I am a slave. The only way you will bed me again is by force. That will make you no better than Rannulf. Is that what you want?"

Wulf scowled. He hadn't anticipated this kind of defiance from Reyna, though he should have expected it. But after her passionate response to his lovemaking last night, he'd thought they would move forward, not backward. What had changed in the span of a few hours?

"I want you in my bed willingly," Wulf said tersely. "But if you continue to resist me, I may change my mind." He held the curtain open for her. "Come, we will break our fast together and discuss this later. I am starving."

Though Reyna doubted Wulf would accept her refusal easily, she swept past him into the hall. Wulf wasn't the only one who was hungry.

Reyna had thought long and hard this morning about the passion they had shared last night. Her first thought had been that she had willingly bedded the man who

had sold her for profit. She supposed she'd been so grateful that Wulf hadn't been the man who had taken her on the hard ground the day of the raid that she had lost control of her emotions.

But upon awakening this morning, Reyna had realized Wulf wasn't guiltless. In the space of two summers, terrible things had happened to her. Wulf had led the raid on her farmstead, and for all she knew he had slain her entire family save for her brothers, who had been off on a trading voyage. And she laid the blame for those deaths at Wulf's feet.

Reyna still had a modicum of pride left, and that pride was telling her not to add insult to injury.

Clasping her elbow, Wulf led Reyna to the table. She sat on a bench, trying to ignore the sullen glances Uma slanted her. When Uma slammed trenchers of eggs, bacon and thick slices of toasted bread down on the table, Reyna dug in, ignoring the thrall's obvious hatred.

"Ale for me and buttermilk for Reyna," Wulf ordered as he filled his plate. The ale and buttermilk appeared almost immediately.

"Is there anything else you desire, master?" Uma asked with a hint of sarcasm.

"Not right now," Wulf replied curtly, "though it would serve you well to change your manner. I do not find it pleasing. Mother, Olga and my sisters plan to smoke meat and fish today. I give you permission to join them. You may leave now."

Uma stormed off, grabbing her cloak from a hook beside the door before leaving the hall and slamming the door behind her.

"Uma is in a bad mood this morning," Reyna ventured.

"Aye," Wulf agreed. "She has no reason to be jealous,

but she hates you for my attention to you. I plan to sell her to a new master soon."

Reyna continued eating. Though she shouldn't care about Uma's fate, she did. They were both in the same situation, thralls dependent upon their master's whim.

Reyna swallowed and cleared her throat. "I hope you don't sell her to a cruel master."

"Forget Uma. She does not deserve your consideration. She has been cruel to you since the day you arrived. I would rather talk about your duty to your master."

Reyna pushed her empty plate away. "Not everyone is rich enough to eat off of pottery plates and bowls," she said, abruptly changing the subject.

"We are not talking about pottery and such," Wulf growled. "We were discussing your disobedience."

"You were discussing it, not I. If you will excuse me, I promised to help Lady Thora today. There is a great deal of preparation necessary for the long winter months ahead."

Reyna pushed her chair from the table. She didn't like the expression on Wulf's face; he looked like a child deprived of a favorite toy. But her hopes of escape evaporated when he grasped her arm and pulled her hard against him.

"You are not getting away that easily."

Reyna watched his eyes kindle and burst into silver flame as he lowered his head, claiming her mouth with hungry thoroughness. Relentlessly his tongue probed against her lips, forcing them to open beneath his. His tongue searched for hers, found it and sucked it into his mouth. Reyna felt her insides melting, felt heat infuse her bones.

Stiffening her spine, she fought her own body's response to Wulf's sensual attack. Her body was betraying

her in the worst possible way and she vowed to resist. When Wulf's hands found her breasts with unerring accuracy, Reyna knew she had to put a stop to this or end up in his bed, enjoying every minute of his attentions.

Hardening her heart, Reyna bit down on Wulf's tongue, wringing a yelp of pain from him. He lifted his head and glared at her. "Why did you do that?"

"I know where your kisses will lead. I succumbed to your seduction once, Wulf, but never again. Just because your family is kind to me it does not mean I have forgiven you for what you did to me and my family. The boundaries between right and wrong became blurred for a time, but after Rannulf arrived and I had time to think, I still hold you responsible for destroying my life.

"I no longer know if I have a father or mother, or if my farmstead is still standing. I am a slave to a ruthless Norseman with no possibility of freedom or escape."

Her chin went up. "You can order me to your bed, but you will have to use force to get me there."

Spinning on her heel, she stormed off.

Wulf stared after her. Most thralls would be shaking in their boots at the thought of defying Wulf the Ruthless. But not Reyna the Dane. He couldn't decide whether she was ridiculously foolish or excessively brave. Wulf was utterly befuddled by Reyna. Should he force her to obey him or let her have her way? Either course had its drawbacks. Forcing Reyna to his bed would not be a pleasant experience, despite his newfound knowledge of her passionate nature. On the other hand, if he let her have her way, he would become the thrall and Reyna the master, leading him around by his cock.

Wulf's resolve hardened. Reyna was his thrall and she had to obey him. Mayhap not today, or tomorrow, or the next day, but he vowed that soon she would

come willingly to his bed. Confident of his ability to manage his thrall, Wulf left the hall.

He strode with purpose toward his brother's hall to speak to Hagar about preparing and storing their ships for the winter months. They would still have two small rowboats available for fishing when weather permitted. Norsemen were born sailors. The sea was their life; it held no fear for them, and Wulf was more competent than most.

As Wulf reached the front entrance, the door opened and Reyna dashed out, straight into his arms. Wulf's protective nature roared to life. "What is wrong? Has someone hurt you?"

Reyna's face was colorless, her mouth open in a mute scream. Wulf glanced behind her and saw Rannulf standing in the open doorway. "What did you do to her?"

Rannulf shrugged, his expression inscrutable. "I merely wished your thrall a good morning. Reyna has no reason to fear me. I will not harm her."

Wulf grasped Reyna's shoulders. "Look at me, Reyna." She raised her eyes to his. "Is Rannulf telling the truth? Did he merely wish you a good morning?"

"I cannot be in the same room with him. Every time I see him, I want to kill him."

Her words were spoken so fiercely Wulf did not doubt her sincerity. "If Rannulf hurts you again, *I* will kill him. Do you believe me?"

Reyna stared into his eyes with such intensity that Wulf wondered what was going through her mind. Did she hate him with the same intensity that she hated Rannulf? He could scarcely credit it after their passionate night together. With Reyna, however, anything was possible.

"Do you believe me?" Wulf repeated harshly.

After several interminable moments, Reyna gave an affirmative nod.

"Then listen to me. No one here is going to hurt you. You belong to me, I am the only one who can punish you, and right now punishment is the last thing on my mind." His silver eyes burned into the green depths of hers. "You do understand what I want, do you not?"

Reyna gave a jerky nod.

"Return to what you were doing."

Reyna turned and sidled past Rannulf. When Rannulf started to follow her inside, Wulf stayed him with a hand on his shoulder. "What did you do to frighten her?"

"I neither threatened nor hurt your thrall, Wulf," Rannulf denied. "I am determined to obey your brother's rules and court Helga. She is old enough to be a bride, and I truly want to wed her."

"Do you swear you have no designs on Reyna?"

"Aye, my sights are set on Helga and no other. I will not poach on your territory. Even a blind man can see you have feelings for Reyna beyond those of thrall and master."

Wulf went still. "You are wrong, Rannulf. Reyna is a Dane; her people killed my wife and unborn son. Any feelings I have for Reyna are centered below the belt. You above anyone should know about lust. Dane, Swede or Finn, my cock makes no distinction when it comes to pleasure."

Laughing, Rannulf slapped Wulf on the back. "Fear not, I consider Reyna beyond my reach."

Eyes narrowed, Wulf watched Rannulf stroll off. Mulling over Rannulf's words, Wulf wondered if what he felt for Reyna was lust and naught more. When had his attitude toward her changed? When had Reyna the Dane ceased to be the enemy? The day she saved his life or the day she had stepped off his brother's dragonship, faced him defiantly and spat at his feet? Confusion

muddled his brain. Did his entire family know he yearned so intensely for his thrall?

During the following days Reyna moved like a shadow about the farmstead, keeping well out of Wulf's way and avoiding Rannulf altogether. She continued to spend a great deal of her day in the stillroom, processing the herbs and roots she had gathered. Not only did she enjoy the solitude, she was honing her skills. A fortnight passed before the idea of sleeping in the stillroom occurred to her. She already took her meals in her private sanctuary. Helga brought food to her three times a day and thus far no one had insisted that she join the family or eat with the thralls.

She still feared that Wulf would lose patience with her and order her to his bed. She couldn't allow *that* to happen again. She had enjoyed it too much. As long as Reyna remained a slave, there was no future for her and Wulf. And Wulf wasn't likely to free her any time soon. He enjoyed the role of conqueror too much. That was why she tried to avoid him. Out of sight, out of mind.

One day, when Helga arrived with her midday meal, the girl appeared reluctant to leave.

"May I stay and help you?" Helga asked shyly.

"I've placed some leaves in a bowl," Reyna said, gesturing toward a crockery bowl resting on the worktable. "You can grind them into a paste with a pestle, if you'd like."

Helga took her place at the table and picked up the pestle. After a lengthy pause she said, "Why do you not like Rannulf?"

Reyna went still. "Is it that obvious?"

"It is to me. Did you know he is courting me?"

"Aye," Reyna muttered. "How do you feel about him?"

Helga shrugged. "I have known Rannulf for years and I am of an age to wed. I could do worse."

"Do you like him enough to spend the rest of your life with him?"

"If it does not work out, 'tis simple enough to divorce him. Is it not the same in your land?"

"Aye, a woman has but to walk out the door of her husband's hall, declare herself divorced and return to her father's home. Any children born from the union go with her."

"It is the same here." Helga cocked her head. "Will you tell me why you go out of your way to avoid Rannulf?"

"I prefer to keep my own counsel. It is you who must decide if Rannulf is worthy of you."

Both women turned contemplative as they performed their tasks. At length, Helga said, "Rannulf is not the only male you are avoiding. What has Wulf done to you? He asked me to see to your welfare while he and my brothers prepare the farmstead for the coming winter."

Reyna felt herself flush. "Wulf is inordinately possessive of his property."

"I think it is more than that."

"I am Wulf's enemy."

"I do not think so."

"He is my enemy."

Helga sent her a look of utter disbelief. "I do not believe that either."

Reyna dropped the subject. It was beginning to make her uncomfortable. "I have a favor to ask of you, Helga."

"Ask away. I will do whatever I can to help you."

"Will you arrange to have furs brought to me so that I can sleep here in the stillroom? The bench is wide and

will serve me well, and there is a hearth to keep me warm if I am supplied with wood."

"Why do you wish to sleep in the stillroom when Wulf's hall is where you belong?"

"I feel at ease here with my herbs. Besides, Uma hates me. I prefer to keep out of her way."

"Out of my brother's way too, I assume," Helga stated sagely.

Reyna ignored her comment, no matter how astute. "What say you, Helga. Will you help me?"

"Aye," Helga agreed. "I will bring sleeping furs myself and ask Eric to provide you with firewood and fresh water for as long as you remain in the stillroom. And I will continue to bring your meals."

"Thank you; I appreciate your kindness." She hesitated. "About Rannulf, if I were you, I would think long and hard about wedding him."

True to her word, Helga brought a stack of furs later that day and Eric carried in firewood and built a fire in the hearth. Now all Reyna had to do was avoid a confrontation with Wulf when he learned about her new sleeping arrangements.

Later that day, after she finished the evening meal Helga had brought, Reyna prepared her bed on the bench, stripped to her shift and sat down to brush her hair. Both Helga and Inga had kindly provided her with items that made life easier for her, including a brush, comb and scented soap. She was also allowed to use the volcanic pool and did so often.

Reyna was still brushing her hair when the door burst open and Wulf stormed through the opening.

"What is the meaning of this?" he roared.

Reyna knew precisely what he meant but pretended otherwise. She was shaking inside, so she remained sit-

ting lest her legs fail to hold her upright. "To what are you referring?"

Wulf's gaze strayed to the bench, already laid out with sleeping furs. "You did not ask my permission to camp out in the stillroom. Taking your meals and spending your days and nights in the stillroom tries my patience. Gather your clothing; I am taking you home, where you have a perfectly good bed."

"I prefer to stay here," Reyna defied.

Wulf prowled toward her. Reyna flinched; she didn't know what he intended. Would he strike her? Most masters would not hesitate to punish a disobedient slave. But Wulf was not most masters.

He snagged her about the waist, scooped her into his arms and carried her out the door.

She pounded his chest. "Put me down!"

"Cease!" Wulf roared. "Have you forgotten that you belong to me? You will do as I say whether you like it or not."

Wulf kicked open the door and carried her across the yard to his hall, not stopping until he reached her sleeping alcove. He shoved the curtain aside and set her down on her feet.

He bared his teeth at her. "This is where you belong. Never pull a stunt like that again."

Reyna took a step backward. He was too close, too aggressively male; too feral with his teeth bared as if he wanted to devour her. The alcove was too small. All he had to do was reach for her, and he did, bringing her against his aroused body.

"You know why I cannot stay with you, Wulf. We cannot be together. There is too much enmity between us."

He caressed her breast through her shift. "Enmity is not what I am feeling right now."

"I know you are angry with me but it will pass. We do not belong together."

"Why not? I have not harmed you, nor have I forced you."

"No, you have not, but you still do not understand. I do not trust myself with you. You have but to look at me and I am lost. You know we have no future together as long as I remain a slave. Our situation as it stands is unbearable for me."

"How does living in the stillroom help?"

She looked away.

He grasped her chin, forcing her to look at him. "Answer me, Reyna."

"I do not have to contend with temptation if you are not around to tempt me."

A grin stretched Wulf's lips. "I tempt you?"

She changed the subject. "Uma hates me. Moving into the stillroom keeps peace in your household."

Wulf knew she was trying to avoid the issue she had just raised. "You did not answer my question. Do I tempt you?"

"You know you do. But as long as I am your thrall, naught will come of it. I am too proud to play the slave for any man, especially Wulf the Ruthless."

"This is no game, Reyna. You are in truth my slave. Until I give you leave to do otherwise, you will sleep in my hall."

When Reyna tried to push him away, Wulf tightened his hold. She felt too good in his arms with naught covering her charms but a thin shift. He ground his hips against the soft place between her thighs, his randy cock wanting more than she was willing to offer. He stared at her lush lips. Could he tempt her beyond control? A wary light glowed in her green eyes as he slowly lowered

his head to her. He claimed her lips just as she opened her mouth in protest. He ignored the tiny squeak that escaped her throat as his tongue swept past her teeth into her mouth. He kissed her thoroughly, savagely, determined to break down her barriers.

He nearly crowed when he felt her mouth soften, felt her body melt against his. Reyna *was* his! Despite her protests, she all but admitted she couldn't resist him. One hand found her breast while the other began to slowly raise the hem of her shift.

He was wrong. Reyna *could* resist him. She proved it by scrambling away and putting the narrow bed between them.

"I will not become your bed slave, Wulf. You can force me but I guarantee you will not like it."

Frustration colored Wulf's words. "I do not know why I bother when there are countless women willing to accommodate me. I can have any thrall I wish in my bed, with little effort on my part."

Reyna had no idea why Wulf's words should hurt but they did. Though she knew denying him was denying herself, she refused to think of herself as a slave to her master's whims. If Wulf admitted she was a woman with a choice, she might be tempted to lie with him, for she knew he was capable of giving her great pleasure.

Wulf had shown her that not all men were brutes like Rannulf, who selfishly used women, disregarding their unwillingness or pain. And Reyna was grateful to Wulf for that much. She could easily learn to care for him if he treated her as a woman and not a possession.

Reyna cast a wary glance at Wulf. Why hadn't he left to find a willing woman? Why was he staring at her, devouring her thinly clad body through hooded eyes?

Crossing her arms over her breasts, Reyna tried to shield herself from his probing gaze.

"Why are you still here?"

"Thor's hammer, woman, I do not want just any woman. To my everlasting regret, I want you."

Without warning, Wulf reached out a long arm, snagged Reyna about the waist and dragged her across the bed. Then he fell on top of her, effectively pinning her beneath him. For Reyna, Wulf's unexpected attack was far too reminiscent of Rannulf's assault. She began to struggle in earnest, to strike out, recalling the raid with vivid clarity.

"No!" she cried, thrashing her head from side to side. "Do not hurt me, I beg of you."

Wulf gathered her flailing wrists in his hands and held them above her head as he rose to his knees and stared down at her as she continued to struggle.

"Rayna, I am not going to hurt you. Look at me. I am Wulf, not Rannulf."

He released her wrists and slid off her.

Slowly Reyna's wits returned. Disoriented, she glanced around, suddenly aware that she was lying on a bed of furs and not on the hard, blood-soaked ground.

"I . . . I thought . . ."

"I know what you thought and it pains me that you consider me a ravishing beast. I won't bother you again."

Whirling on his heel, he stormed from the alcove. Tears blurred Reyna's vision. The flashback to that terrible day of the raid had undone her. Though she knew in her heart Wulf wouldn't hurt her, she couldn't prevent the fear and panic that had gripped her.

Reyna swiped at the tears rolling down her cheeks as she came to a decision. She had to leave Wulf and return to her own country. She desperately needed to know if her parents still lived. Had her brothers returned safely

from their travels to find their parents dead, their sister gone and everything they held dear destroyed? Remaining here as Wulf's slave would bring her nothing but heartbreak.

Chapter Eight

Reyna had no idea why she couldn't stop crying after Wulf had departed, assuring her he wouldn't bother her again. That was what she wanted, wasn't it? Wulf was a Norse savage. A plunderer. A killer of innocent people.

Yet she could not deny there was something between them. Something irresistible and compelling. Then reality cut into her thoughts. There was too much painful history between them to ignore, too many obstacles, too much distrust. And their situation as master and slave was intolerable to her.

A tentative smile chased away the tears as Reyna's imagination ran amok. What if she were the master and Wulf the slave? Oh, how she would enjoy that, even though she knew it would never come to pass. Wulf was a dangerous man. He would make a terrible thrall. However, the pleasant image of Wulf doing her bidding soothed her rattled nerves and she drifted off to sleep.

Wulf attempted to ignore Reyna during the following days. He and his brothers worked tirelessly to prepare the farmstead for winter, when snow would likely reach the roof and the wind would howl through the trees. Unfortunately, the image of Reyna lying beneath him on the bed, her pale gold hair spread over the pillow,

haunted his mind and kept him in a constant state of arousal. He should take her as his body demanded. The only thing stopping him was the paralyzing fear he had seen in her green eyes. He couldn't abuse her as Rannulf had done, but his willpower was ebbing by the day . . . no, by the hour.

Wulf entered the main hall and looked around for Hagar. Today he intended to help his brother and the male thralls stack firewood they had gathered. Wulf suspected Hagar wanted to remain close to home during the next few days. Olga's time was near and Hagar didn't want to wander far from the hall.

The hall was in an uproar when Wulf entered. Thralls were running hither and yon; his mother and Hagar were nowhere in sight. Helga spotted Wulf and hurried over to him.

"What is going on?" Wulf asked.

" 'Tis Olga," Helga replied, wringing her hands. "She went into labor last evening and is suffering terribly. Mama doesn't know how to help her. The babe does not want to be born."

Thora stepped out of Olga's sleeping alcove, a frown worrying her brow. She spotted Wulf and visibly relaxed. "Thank the gods you are here, son," she said. "The birth is more than I can handle. We need Reyna. Would you please fetch her? Tell her to bring her medicinal chest."

"Why did you not send for Reyna immediately when you knew Olga was in trouble?"

"Olga did not want Reyna touching her. I will explain later; just fetch Reyna. You will probably find her in the stillroom. Tell her that her skills are desperately needed."

Nodding, Wulf ran from the main hall and raced across the yard to the stillroom. He opened the door and charged inside. Stunned by his abrupt entrance, Reyna assumed a defensive stance.

"What are you doing here? Can you not see I am busy?"

"Olga went into labor last night and it is not progressing well. Mother fears Olga and the child will die. She asked me to fetch you. Bring your medicinal chest."

"Why did Thora wait so long to send for me?"

"Olga did not want you touching her. That does not matter now. You may be the only one who can save Hagar's heir."

Reyna added a small vial to the chest, slammed down the lid and handed it to Wulf. Then she sped out the door with Wulf following close behind. When they reached the hall, Thora was waiting for her, pacing before the hearth and wringing her hands.

"What seems to be the problem?" Reyna asked in a hushed voice.

"The babe won't come. Olga is too exhausted to push and there is too much blood."

"I will go to her. Please send in a basin of hot water so I can cleanse my hands. Have you assembled clean cloths and the usual things necessary for birthing a babe?"

"All is in readiness," Thora replied. She glanced at Wulf. "Take your brother outside and keep him occupied. The sleeping alcove is small; he will be in the way."

Suddenly Hagar burst from the alcove, his face creased with worry. "Where is Reyna?"

"Right here, son," Thora replied.

"Go to her, Reyna. Her life and that of our babe depends on your skill. Ignore her ranting, for she knows not what she says. She needs you, even if she does not want you."

Reyna hurried toward the sleeping alcove. When Hagar started to follow, Wulf grabbed his arm, stopping him in his tracks.

"Let Reyna handle the birthing, brother. You are not needed. In truth, you can best serve your wife by coming outside with me and stacking wood, just as we planned."

Hagar looked longingly at the alcove before allowing Wulf to lead him out the door.

Reyna pushed through the curtain and assessed the situation with a single glance. A naked Olga, her belly heaving, her face a mask of pain, was covered with perspiration and moaning softly. Reyna approached the bed and placed a hand on Olga's belly. Reyna wasn't new at this. Her mother was a midwife and Reyna had assisted at several births, some of them difficult. Now, her innate sense of healing kicked in, and she knew immediately that Olga was in trouble. The next contraction made Olga arch violently, her scream a piercing cry for help.

Reyna whispered soothingly in Olga's ear. "Relax, Olga, try taking deep breaths. I'm going to help you bring your babe into the world."

The sound of Reyna's voice seemed to increase Olga's agitation. Opening her eyes wide, she spat, "Get her away from me! I don't want that witch touching me."

Thora hurried to Olga's side in an effort to placate her. "Calm yourself, Olga. Reyna is here to help."

"Can you not see Hagar wants her in his bed? I do not trust her."

"You are wrong, Olga," Reyna insisted. "Hagar wants only you. He anxiously awaits his heir. Please calm yourself lest you harm your child."

Olga was in no mood to listen to reason as she began to struggle against Reyna's ministrations. Reyna moved away to the medicinal chest, searching for and finding the vial she had placed there earlier.

"Is this laudanum?" Reyna asked Thora. "I found it in the stillroom."

Thora frowned at the vial filled with dark liquid. Then her face cleared with sudden comprehension. "Aye, 'tis laudanum, a concoction made from the poppy plant to relieve pain. Hagar brought it back from Byzantium on one of his voyages. My sister used it sparingly to ease pain."

Reyna nodded and set it aside. "I thought so. Though my mother had no such concoction, we knew of it. I am going to examine Olga and need your help to calm her."

Thora followed Reyna to the bed, her face a mask of anxiety. "Will she live?" she whispered.

"She will if I have anything to do with it. Something is keeping the babe from being born and I need to find out what it is before I can help her."

"What are you two whispering about?" Olga cried. "I am going to die—I know it."

"No, you are going to live, and so is your babe," Reyna said fiercely. "Unless you continue to fight me."

Olga looked desperately at Thora. "Do not let her touch me. I do not like her. Have you forgotten that her people killed Astrid?"

Reyna realized helping Olga wasn't going to be easy. Her hostility was making her unreasonably fearful. If Olga and her child were to be saved, Reyna would have to take extraordinary measures.

"You will find some dried raspberry leaves in the medicinal chest," Reyna said to Thora. "Place them in a mug and brew them into a strong tea for me, please. Add no more than two drops of laudanum to the tea and steep it until the liquid is the color of tree bark. The raspberry leaves will aid Olga's labor and the laudanum will calm her enough for me to conduct my examination."

While Thora rushed off to brew the tea, Reyna did

her best to calm Olga, softly talking her through her contractions, which had coalesced into one unending pain. When Thora arrived with the tea, a thirsty Olga sipped the entire cup. A short time later, laudanum took effect and Olga's body relaxed, though she still moaned and cried out with each contraction.

Reyna washed her hands thoroughly, then proceeded with her examination. A few minutes later, her expression grave, she glanced at Thora and said, "The babe is stuck in the birth canal. He needs to be turned before he can be born. If the babe is not turned into position, both Olga and her child will die."

A look of horror crossed Thora's face. "Can you do it?"

"With Freya's help, I will try. Keep Olga calm while I do what is needed."

Despite Olga's lethargic state, she screamed like a banshee when Reyna used one hand to begin turning the babe into the correct position for birthing.

The curtain parted and Hagar poked his head inside. "What in Thor's name is happening?" He glanced at Reyna and turned deathly pale when he saw her kneeling between Olga's spread thighs, her hands bloody.

"Leave us, son," Thora ordered. "Let Reyna do what must be done to save your wife and child."

After casting an anguished look at his wife's heaving body, Hagar withdrew.

Meanwhile, Reyna slowly but surely turned the babe, until he was in position. She withdrew her hand and washed thoroughly before returning to Olga.

"Olga, can you hear me?" Reyna asked.

Her head lolling, the other woman nodded.

"I want you to push with your next contraction. Can you do that? It will not be long now. Your babe is anxious to be born."

Though Olga seemed to rally, she had little strength left to push. Reyna silently railed at Olga's reluctance to summon her at the first sign of trouble. Now Olga was too weak to do what was required of her and she might still die.

An idea formed in Reyna's mind. "Lady Thora, send for Hagar. He may be the only one who can help Olga."

"Are you sure? Men do not belong in the birthing room."

"We have no choice. Hurry, Olga is fading fast."

Thora hurried off. Hagar couldn't have been far, for she returned with him almost immediately.

"Tell me what to do, Reyna," Hagar said. Though he appeared willing to do whatever it took to help his wife, his face had gone from pale to an odd shade of green.

"Sit at the head of the bed and support Olga's back. At the next contraction, you must encourage her to push your babe into the world. Olga is exhausted from her long travail and needs support."

Hagar obeyed instantly. When Reyna alerted him to the onset of the next contraction, he lovingly urged Olga to push, to gather her strength and bring forth their child. Two more strong contractions racked Olga's body before the babe slid into Reyna's hands. She quickly cut and tied off the cord and handed the babe to Thora. The new grandmother let out a cry of joy when the babe gasped and gave a lusty wail.

"You have a healthy son, Hagar," Reyna said. "You did what you needed to do. Please wait in the hall while I finish up here. You will be summoned when Olga is clean and ready for visitors."

"Thank you, Reyna, for my wife and son's life," Hagar replied with heartfelt honesty. "When I brought you home, I never knew how important you would become to us."

Reyna was touched by Hagar's words. Tears blurred her vision as she worked over Olga, delivering the after-birth and stanching the bleeding. Once satisfied that Olga and the babe were out of danger, Reyna rose and stretched the kinks out of her back.

"My thralls and I will clean and dress Olga and tidy up the alcove," Thora said. "Go now and take your ease. You have earned your rest as well as our eternal gratitude."

Reyna nodded, washed her hands and arms with strong soap and stepped into the hall. Helga hurried over to her. "Come join us. The midday meal is on the table. You must be famished."

Reyna joined Helga, Hagar, Wulf and Inga at the table. Olaf, Eric and Rannulf were conspicuously absent from the family group. Reyna subsided wearily onto a bench, almost too tired to eat.

Someone filled her plate and she ate without tasting a single morsel. Reyna had done something today she had never done before. She had known instinctively that the babe must be turned and had done it. If she had failed and Olga had died, Reyna would not have been able to face Hagar or Thora. Thank the gods that had not happened.

Reyna glanced at Wulf. He was staring at her strangely. A prickle of unease settled at the base of her neck. Their eyes met and held. Tremors of sensation ran down her spine. No one else seemed to notice the sizzling tension between them; it was as if they were the only two occu-pants in the room. Wulf was the first to look away.

Reyna returned her attention to her food, eating me-chanically until her plate was empty. No one stirred un-til Thora appeared from behind the curtain. Hagar leapt up but Thora dashed his hopes of seeing Olga when she shook her head.

"Reyna, Olga wishes to speak with you." She smiled at Hagar. "You will have to wait a few moments longer, Hagar."

More than a little puzzled, Reyna rose and followed Thora into the alcove. Olga's eyes were closed, the babe nestled in the crook of her arm. She appeared to be sleeping.

"Shall I come back later?"

Olga opened her eyes. "Nay, do not go."

Reyna moved closer to the bed. "Can I do something for you?"

"Aye, you can accept my apology. I let jealousy poison me against you. When Hagar brought you home, all I could think about were all those days and nights you were aboard his dragonship, and what might have happened between you. I was wrong. You saved my life and that of my son. Please forgive me."

"There is naught to forgive. Your condition made you distrustful of your husband. It happens. Think no more on it. Rest now, Olga. I will check on you later." Reyna turned and went out through the curtain.

Hagar, who was pacing nearby, rushed into the sleeping alcove the moment Reyna left. Reyna smiled at his eagerness, imagining what Wulf would be like if she presented him with a baby. Would Wulf welcome a child by her? Would he care about her welfare as Hagar cared about Olga's, or would he remain aloof about the whole process?

Apparently Wulf had genuinely cared about Astrid and their unborn child. He must have loved his wife dearly for he had wreaked terrible vengeance in her name. Reyna and her family had been made to pay dearly for the sins of Dane raiders with whom they had no connection. It wasn't right.

"Reyna." Wulf's voice jerked her back to the present.

Reyna was surprised to see that she and Wulf were alone at the table. "Where has everyone gone?"

"My sisters are with Olga and the babe."

"Where are Olaf and Eric? Do they not want to see their new nephew?"

"They accompanied Rannulf to his farmstead yesterday. Rannulf wanted to help his father and their thralls prepare for the winter months and my brothers offered to go with him. They should return within a fortnight."

Reyna suppressed a shudder. "Is Rannulf serious about courting Helga? Are you and Hagar going to allow it?"

"We are going to wait and see how the courtship progresses. In the end, it will be up to Helga. I know Rannulf hurt you, but he is a Norseman, and Norsemen raid and plunder. 'Tis our way of life."

"What about you, Wulf? Will you continue raiding and plundering?"

"No, I plan to become a trader like Hagar. We will sail to Byzantium next summer. Trading pig iron and amber for luxury items has made our family prosperous."

"I am glad," Reyna whispered.

"You should rest. You look worn out. I will stay here for a while in case I am needed."

Reyna nodded, grabbed her cloak and headed out the door. She was halfway across the yard when a cold drizzle began to fall. Thralls scurried here and there to get out of the rain. She saw Uma duck into Hagar's hall. Reyna had hoped to bathe in the volcanic pool, but now she would have to make do with a basin of water.

The hall was deserted when she entered. She shook out her wet cloak and hung it on a nail beside the door. Reyna walked to the hearth, pleased to see a kettle of water warming on the hearthstone. She picked the kettle up by the handle, carried it into her sleeping alcove

and poured water into a crockery basin sitting on a small table. Then she replaced the kettle on the hearth-stone and fetched a drying cloth, a washcloth and soap from a cupboard in the hall, bringing all the items back to her alcove. Grimacing at her bloodstained clothing, Reyna quickly stripped and began to wash.

Wulf paced the length of the hall. He felt restless and strangely unsettled. He vividly recalled the day he had learned Astrid was expecting his babe and how happy he had been. He had given up raiding for Astrid's sake and had been looking forward to being a father. A jolt of jealousy ripped through him. If Astrid hadn't been slain, his child and Hagar's would have been as close as siblings.

Wulf shook the morbid thoughts from his head. He had no child. He had no wife. He had naught but a Dane thrall who drove him mad with wanting.

A short time later Hagar joined Wulf. He carried his sleeping babe in the crook of his arm, waxing poetic about the boy, whom he had named Rollo after their fa-ther. Wulf voiced his admiration and chucked the lad under the chin like a doting uncle.

A sudden flow of thralls into the hall, all of them drip-ping water, alerted Wulf to the rain pounding outside. He rose, deciding it was time to return home. He briefly looked in on Olga before bidding Hagar and his new nephew good-bye and dashing out the door into the pouring rain.

As Wulf sprinted across the yard, his thoughts re-turned to Reyna. Would he find her asleep? he won-dered. She certainly deserved a rest after her heroic deed today. Reyna had endeared herself to his entire family. What was he going to do with her? The gods were con-

spiring against him. If he had a shred of decency, he would return immediately to Hagar's hall and leave Reyna in peace. He flashed a wicked grin and kept walking. Promises were made to be broken.

Wulf entered the hall and shook the water off himself like a large dog, sending droplets in every direction. All was silent. Was everyone sleeping? He strode to Reyna's sleeping alcove. The devil inside him urged him to push aside the curtain and peek inside.

He froze when he saw a nude Reyna, bending over a small trunk, the round globes of her enticing bottom tempting him beyond endurance. His body went instantly hard, his rigid cock standing nearly upright. Wulf regarded the shape of her bottom like an artist studying a piece of priceless art. So white, so perfect, he couldn't repress the groan that sounded in his throat. Reyna could tempt one of those statues made of stone he had seen in Byzantium, and he most definitely was not made of stone.

Wulf didn't move, could scarcely breathe. His chest felt constricted; his blood surged hot and ravenous through his veins. His reaction was immediate and spontaneous. He was a Norseman; it wasn't in his nature to deny himself when he wanted something as fiercely as he wanted Reyna.

Reyna must have heard him groan for she whipped around. Her lush lips fell open when she saw him standing just inside the curtain. She dove for the bed, pulling a wolf fur up to her chin.

"What are you doing here?" she demanded.

"I wanted to make sure you were all right."

"As you can see, I am fine."

"More than fine," Wulf said in a strangled voice. He moved closer to the bed, dripping water on the floor.

Reyna eyed him nervously. "You are soaked. You should get out of those wet clothes before you catch your death."

Wordlessly, Wulf began to remove his clothing, tossing the wet garments on the floor. He glanced at Reyna; she was biting her lip and frowning. Cool air hit his heated skin and he shivered, more from anticipation than from cold.

"Stop! Why are you undressing?" Reyna gasped.

"You advised me to get out of my wet clothes, and I am."

"Not here! Go away. You promised you wouldn't attempt to seduce me again."

Wulf shrugged his shoulders. "I lied."

Reyna found it impossible not to stare at Wulf. She tingled with the thrill of his nearness, and her resolve to resist faltered slightly, for he radiated soul-gripping power. He was breathtaking, tall and commanding and powerfully built from head to toe. The flowing swell of his chest muscles, the flat brown circles of his masculine nipples, the rippling tendons of his abdomen and trim waist mesmerized her. Not to mention the size of his sex; it grew and thickened as her wayward gaze settled on that part of his body.

"You want me, Reyna."

Gripped by the compelling potency of his silver gaze, Reyna gulped hard and closed her eyes. "No, I do not want *that* to happen again. Go away. I do not trust myself, and I trust you even less."

"Why are you deliberately denying us what we both want? Relax; I will not do anything you do not want me to do."

Her eyes flew open. "I have heard that before, Wulf

the Ruthless, from your own lips. You know how *that* ended."

His fire and ice eyes gleamed with an unholy light. "Aye, I dream of it often."

Reyna recognized his determination and struggled desperately to control her wayward body. She didn't want to be Wulf's slave, obliged to obey his commands. But she didn't know how long she could keep on fighting. Right now she was so physically exhausted and so weary of fighting both Wulf and her own body's desire that she could scarcely summon the strength to resist. So she decided to try a new approach.

She tossed the fur aside, baring her body, and went limp. "Go ahead, take what you want. Whatever you do will be accomplished without my compliance. I will not respond, nor will I give you any pleasure."

The possessive gleam in Wulf's eyes should have warned her that she was doomed to failure. His voice had never sounded so confident. "I vow you will scream for me to take you, no matter what you say now."

"I will hate you afterward."

"You hate me now."

Not true, Reyna wanted to shout, but she wouldn't give him the satisfaction of a reply.

Reyna gasped as she realized he had moved and was kneeling between her legs. It had happened so swiftly, she didn't have time to roll off the bed. "Stop," she said, sounding weak and ineffectual even to her own ears. "Do not . . ."

But there was no stopping him. When Wulf leaned in and kissed her, she imagined flames shooting from the top of her head.

So much for resisting the ruthless Norseman, Reyna thought as she tasted Wulf's tongue and explored his

mouth with her own. Her resolve had been trampled beneath his fierce determination. Even as he kissed her, his hands were working magic on her body.

She could feel him parting her slick folds, sliding his fingers inside her, working them in and out. And then he scooted down and opened his warm, moist mouth over her, drawing her sensitive, swollen bud into an intimate kiss that made her world spin on its axis.

"Do you really want me to stop?"

"Aye. I will hate both of us if we continue. Why do you torment me like this when you know I cannot resist you?"

"Because you are mine, and I want you."

His answer did not please her. Instead, it reminded her that she was Wulf's slave. If they could change places, she would prove to him that belonging body and soul to another person was humiliating and demeaning.

Her thoughts scattered when she felt his tongue, pleasantly rough, delving deep inside her core, then rubbing over the most sensitive part of her, moving faster, deeper, even as his hands fondled her breasts and teased her nipples.

At this particular moment, hating Wulf was a dim memory. She felt an undeniable urge to raise her hips and wrap her legs around him. Abruptly Reyna recalled her vow to lie unmoving beneath him as a way to thwart his seduction. With Herculean effort, she relaxed her body, willing her mind anywhere but on Wulf's ravaging mouth and agile hands.

It didn't work. Wulf would have none of it. Even as his tongue worked its magic, he plunged two fingers deep inside her, sliding them in and out, raising her level of passion without a shred of shame on his part. When he began moving his tongue in tight circles around her swollen bud, the darkness behind her eyeballs exploded

into sparkling white stars and she spiraled upward to touch them.

Wulf surged over her, impaling her on his rigid staff, pumping vigorously, again and again. He filled her in strong surges. He touched the deepest part of her, sending fire straight to her womb. She heard him groan in an agony of need, of desperation, and then felt him shudder.

His groans escalated as he drove hard, pushed deep, filling her to bursting. Then she felt herself spiraling upward again, reaching higher and surrendering to another climax even more explosive than the first.

Holding her thighs in his big hands, lifting her, pounding inside her, he cried out as his staff jerked, riding her all the way to completion.

Silent tears rolled down Reyna's cheeks. Wulf had done it again. Despite her vow to resist, despite her promise to lie woodenly beneath him, she had allowed him to carry her to Valhalla, that place of eternal bliss. A sob escaped her throat as she pushed him away. He pulled out willingly enough, but when his arm came around her to draw her against him, she lashed out at him.

"Leave me! You got what you wanted. You broke your promise, Wulf the Ruthless."

Wulf sighed heavily. "I could not help myself. What can I do to make it up to you?"

"Free me! Let me return to my family."

"Never!" Wulf growled with fierce determination.

"One day, Wulf the Ruthless, you are going to regret enslaving me. I wish . . ."

"What do you wish?"

"I wish our situations were reversed, that one day you will understand how it feels to be a slave."

Laughing, Wulf rolled off the bed and snatched up his

wet clothing. "Wish all you like, Reyna the Dane, for that will never happen." Then he was gone.

Reyna stared at the curtain through which Wulf had disappeared. There were times when she truly hated the big Norseman, and this was one of them.

Chapter Nine

The rain continued for two days, a harbinger of the bleak winter days that Reyna dreaded. Being cooped up with Wulf in his hall during the long days and nights to come did not bode well for her peace of mind. Even more depressing, escape would be impossible with snow piled up to the roof, and rescue even less likely. Though Reyna held virtually no hope of escaping, to give up wasn't in her nature. She had come a long way from Constantinople and was so close to home she could almost taste freedom.

Almost . . .

So near yet so far. Wulf stood squarely in the way of her returning to her homeland again. And though she knew he wouldn't physically hurt her, her heart was bound to suffer if she let him continue to make love to her. She would not allow herself to care for Wulf while she was suppressed under the yoke of slavery. Wulf cared only for the pleasure she brought him in bed, not for her as a person. If he truly cared, he would free her.

Reyna spent long hours in the stillroom, processing herbs and roots into ointments, salves and potions. She also spent time in Hagar's hall caring for Olga, who was not recovering as rapidly as she should. Thora had asked Reyna to sleep in Hagar's hall until Olga regained

her strength, and Reyna readily agreed. If nothing else, it thwarted Wulf's plans for using her to slake his lust.

When Reyna thought of Wulf bedding Uma, however, a mysterious pain in the region of her heart gripped her. Nevertheless, Reyna remained determined to guard her body and protect her heart from her arrogant Norse master.

The rains finally ceased and the sun came out; though the air was chilly, it was still pleasant compared to the past dismal days. Reyna had processed all the herbs, roots and bark in the stillroom and decided today would be a perfect time to gather the plants that had been left behind during her earlier excursion.

Wulf frowned when Reyna explained her intention to venture forth into the forest again. "I will accompany you, of course."

When Reyna protested, Wulf reminded her of the wild boar they had encountered previously. "Very well. Can we leave immediately, before the weather turns?"

Wulf fetched a variety of weapons and they hiked off across the fields, a basket swinging from Reyna's arm. Despite the sunshine, the air was cool and invigorating. Reyna found a patch of red clover, used to calm colicky babies, and stooped to dig it out. Farther on, she came across some burdock and plucked off the leaves and flowers. When they entered the damp darkness of the forest, Wulf kept a hand on his sword while Reyna knelt beside a patch of mint.

Wulf stared moodily at Reyna as she worked. He had seen little of her these past few days. She had gone out of her way to avoid him, and his mother hadn't helped when she asked Reyna to sleep in Hagar's hall to care for Olga during her slow recovery.

Did Reyna really hate him? He supposed she had

every right to dislike him. Despite his promise, he had seduced her . . . and enjoyed every minute of it.

Wulf didn't understand Reyna's persistent pleas to be released. She had no onerous duties, she was virtually free to come and go anywhere on the farmstead she pleased, and his family was fond of her.

If she were free, Reyna might leave him or choose another man to protect her. It did not occur to Wulf to wonder why he felt so possessive of Reyna. His mind refused to delve into the reason he was so attracted to her. He only knew he would not let her go. Dane or not, Reyna pleased him in every way.

Wulf was so caught up in his troubling thoughts about Reyna that he didn't hear the whisper of footsteps behind him. Only when the hair on the back of his neck prickled in warning did he whip out his sword and spin around. But by then it was too late. The last thing he recalled was an explosion of pain in his head and then blackness.

Reyna sniffed the fragrant mint, placed it in her basket and rose. "My basket is full, Wulf. We can leave now."

Silence.

"Wulf?" No answer was forthcoming. She spun around, shocked to see Wulf lying unconscious on the ground. She opened her mouth to scream, then clamped her mouth tightly shut when her gaze rose from Wulf to settle on three men standing nearby. She gave a cry of gladness and ran into the outstretched arms of her eldest brother Borg.

"Borg, you came for me," Reyna sobbed into his neck.

"Did you think we would not, little sister?"

It was her youngest brother, Dag, who spoke.

"Dag, you are here too!"

"Aye, and Ragnar. We brought sailors and warriors with us in case we were forced to do battle. They are hiding in the forest, waiting for our signal to move on the farmstead. But you have made it easy for us, little sister. You came to us."

Reyna smiled at her brothers through a veil of tears. "How did you know where to find me?"

" 'Twas not easy," Borg replied. "We had all but given up on you. When we embarked on a voyage to Constantinople this past summer, we learned about the beautiful Dane slave girl who had just recently been sold on the auction block. After a little persuasion, the slave trader gave up your name and the name of the Norseman who bought you. He also said that Hagar the Red bought you for his brother, Wulf the Ruthless. We already knew that Wulf the Ruthless was the Norseman who'd raided our home. So here we are. We came prepared to attack the farmstead once we learned for sure that you were there."

Ragnar, her betrothed, stepped forward and briefly hugged Reyna. All three men had long dark hair and were big and brawny, though not as brawny as Wulf, Reyna noted.

"I almost gave up on you but your brothers convinced me you were alive and persuaded me to come with them," Ragnar explained. Their gazes met and then his slid away. "Are you well?"

"Aye, I am well, Ragnar."

Ragnar poked Wulf with his boot and raised his spear. "Shall I kill him for you?"

Kill Wulf? No, she did not want Wulf to die. "No, leave him be."

"He hurt you, Reyna; he deserves to die," Dag pointed out.

"He did me no physical harm," Reyna asserted.

Ragnar sent her a skeptical look. "Is he not Wulf the Ruthless, the same Norseman who raided your farmstead, ravished you and sold you in Byzantium? Are you not his thrall?"

"Wulf did not assault me. 'Twas another. You will be happy to know I refused to be subjugated to his will and never considered myself his thrall. We should leave before he awakens. He is a formidable warrior."

"I agree with Dag and Ragnar," Borg said. "Kill him."

Ragnar raised his arm again, aiming his spear directly at Wulf's heart. Reyna's own heart nearly stopped. She hadn't saved Wulf's life only to see it taken away by her former betrothed. She stepped in front of Ragnar. "Stop! I . . . I want the Norseman for my slave. I want him to learn how demeaning it is to be owned by another person. Death is too easy an end for him."

Borg laughed. "So my sister wants revenge, does she? What say you, Dag? Shall we let her have the Norseman? It will not be easy for him to assume the yoke of slavery and bow to the wishes of a woman."

Dag shrugged. "If that is what Reyna wants, then let her have him."

Wulf woke to find himself bound hand and foot, lying in the bottom of a ship. Rain pelted his face with icy pellets as the ship skipped before the wind at a furious pace. His head felt as if it had been split in two and he could feel the sting of blood in his eyes.

It occurred to Wulf that he was in a very precarious position. A dozen or more armed men sat in the ship, taking him only Thor knew where. Then he remembered Reyna. Had she been taken captive too? He could see little save for angry gray skies above him and men seated on either side of him as the wind carried the dragonship through the choppy water.

Who were these men who had captured him? Had they come to his homeland seeking slaves? Had they raided his farmstead, murdered his family? Not knowing was killing him. Never had he felt so helpless.

"Are you cold, Reyna?" he heard one of the men ask, in the language of her people. Fortunately Wulf could understand the Dane tongue.

"I am fine, Dag. The furs you brought along are keeping me warm."

"Father and Mother will be happy to see you, little sister."

"They are alive?" Reyna asked joyfully.

"They are, but for a time we all thought *you* were dead, or out of our reach. The gods have favored us."

Sister?

These men had come for Reyna? Questions crowded his mind. Why had he been kept alive?

"It appears your thrall is coming around, Reyna."

Thrall? Were they referring to him? *He* was Reyna's thrall?

Her voice came from behind him. His position prevented him from looking at her no matter how he twisted his head. All he got for his effort was a sharp pain behind his eyes.

"Reyna," he croaked.

She was beside him instantly, kneeling near his head. "Are you all right, Wulf?"

"What happened?"

"I warned you my brothers would find me."

"Are these savages your brothers?"

"Two of them are. Ragnar, my betrothed, came with them. The others are my brothers' friends. They came along to man the oars and fight if needed."

"You are unhurt?"

"What do you take us for?" Borg growled. "Reyna is

our sister; we would never hurt her, unlike you, Wulf the Ruthless. You are a vicious despoiler of innocents. You would be dead now if not for Reyna. She wanted you for her thrall and Dag and I were inclined to grant her wish."

Wulf stared up at Reyna, a fierce scowl darkening his brow. "Is that true, Reyna? Am I your thrall?"

"So it would seem," Reyna replied. "Do not complain, Wulf—'tis better than the fate my brothers intended for you."

"I am not so sure of that," Wulf growled in a tone that promised dire retribution. "You will not find me a willing thrall, or an easy one to handle."

"I am confident one of us can 'whip' you into shape," Dag quipped.

Another voice joined in. "You took from Reyna what rightfully belonged to me. I would have slain you without a qualm had Reyna not asked that you be spared and bound to her in slavery. 'Twill be a far crueler fate than death."

Wulf made a gurgling sound in his throat, aware that the man who had just spoken must be Reyna's betrothed. He had never felt so powerless in his life. His head was pounding and all this talk of slavery was just beginning to sink in.

"You are wrong, Ragnar," Reyna protested. "Wulf is guilty of many things, but ravishing me is not one of them."

"Enough of this," Borg ordered. "We will sort everything out when we reach our farmstead. But no matter what, Wulf the Ruthless will be punished for his insult to our sister."

The dragonship hugged the shore of Norway, following natural landmarks of mountains, fiords and burial mounds as navigational aids. When darkness fell, they

beached the ship for the night at a secluded spot and made camp. Not daring to light a fire, they ate a meal of smoked fish, cheese and bread before curling up in their furs for the night.

Borg refused to untie Wulf, so Reyna fed him. Then Borg led Wulf into the woods to relieve himself. Humiliation rode Wulf. Never had he felt so shamed.

At first light they returned to the ship and headed due south across the sea to the land of the Danes. Once they reached open water, the stiff breeze carried them forward. The men laid down their oars and raised the square red-and-white-striped sail.

The wind held, and four days later Wulf spotted the Danish coast. The ship sailed into the fjord and docked at a sandy landing. Wulf was unceremoniously hauled from the ship and forced to walk inland, to the farmstead he recalled raiding two summers earlier. Though Reyna walked at his side, he refused to look at her. Not only was he a thrall, but his mistress was a woman who had once been his to command.

The situation was intolerable.

"Oh, the farmstead still stands," Reyna cried when the many outbuildings of the farmstead came into view.

Borg poked Wulf in the back with his spear. "We rebuilt the buildings that this Norse bastard burned." He paused, then said, "Reyna, I did not tell you that Father was wounded during the raid. He is well now but still limps from a leg wound that healed badly."

"And Mother? You did not mention how she fared."

"Mother fled through the back door. She and our thralls hid in the woods until the raiders left. They looked everywhere for you but you could not be found. Then one of our wounded told them he had seen you lying on the ground, and that a Norseman scooped you up and carried you off."

"I am sorry we were not there to protect you, little sister," Dag apologized. "The Norseman will suffer for assaulting you."

Reyna darted a furtive glance at Wulf. His blond hair was matted with blood and his silver eyes, sweet Freya, his eyes were boiling cauldrons of rage. Did he not realize she had saved his life? If not for her, he would have been slain where he lay, within sight of his farmstead.

"Wulf did not . . . hurt me," Reyna choked out. It was still difficult to talk about the act that had taken her innocence.

"I do not believe you!" Ragnar spat. "Doubtless the Norseman has raped countless innocent women."

"I am not lying, Ragnar," Reyna huffed. "Why would I lie about it?"

"Do you deny the Norseman took you to Byzantium and sold you into slavery?" Dag asked.

"No, I cannot deny Wulf sold me to a slave trader," Reyna admitted.

"Things are not what they seem," Wulf growled. "Did the Danes care when they raided my farmstead and killed my wife and unborn child? I think not. I but sought revenge for my terrible loss."

"We are a family of farmers and traders," Borg shot back. "Did you even care who you were attacking before you raided our farmstead?"

Wulf shrugged. "Danes are Danes. At the time it did not matter who we were raiding. Your farmstead was close to where we happened to beach our ships. You would have done the same in my place."

"Your excuses are meaningless, Norseman," Ragnar growled out. "You took my betrothed and used her as your bed slave. Does she carry your bastard in her belly?"

"Ragnar, please stop!" Reyna pleaded. "The past cannot be undone."

"Quit badgering her," Wulf growled.

Ragnar sent him a poisonous glare. "Think you I want to remember what you did to my betrothed? But I must know. A Norseman's bastard will never become my heir."

Reyna sucked in a sharp breath. Though she could very well be carrying Wulf's child, she wouldn't allow herself to think about that possibility now. Apparently Ragnar was as angry at her as he was at Wulf.

"Enough!" Borg shouted. "We will speak of this later. We are home now. Father is standing outside the long-house to greet us."

A smile curved Reyna's lips when she saw her father. His face was glowing with joy as he ran toward her, his limp slowing him down not at all.

Reyna lifted her skirts and raced to meet him. Her father caught her in his arms and held her tight. "Reyna, sweet Reyna, we feared we would never see you again." He held her away from him and searched her face. "Are you well? Did they hurt you?"

"I am fine, Father, truly. Wulf's family treated me like one of their own."

"Wulf the Ruthless?" His sharp green eyes found Wulf. A feral growl burst from his throat. He removed a dagger from his belt and started toward Wulf, intending no less than murder.

"Father, no!" Reyna cried.

"Tell me why I should not kill him."

"Wulf is my thrall. Borg and Dag said I might have him."

Harald Fairhair pulled up short. "Your thrall? Is that why he is here instead of in hell?"

"Aye," Borg answered. " 'Tis Reyna's right to name the Norseman's fate and she chose a life of slavery for him."

Harald stroked his bearded chin. "Are you sure of this, daughter? The man looks dangerous."

"You do not know how dangerous," Wulf muttered. "Release me now and I will spare your lives."

"I say we kill him before he kills us," Ragnar persisted.

Borg searched Reyna's face. "What say you, sister? Shall we kill your tormentor?"

"Wulf did not torment me," Reyna insisted. "Leave him alone. He is my thrall. 'Tis my right to say whether he shall live or die."

Borg sent her a strange look but said no more. Reyna studied her father as she walked alongside him. Though he appeared older, his hair a little grayer, he was still vigorous despite his limp. She had imagined all kinds of dire circumstances since the raid, but after two summers, the farmstead and it occupants seemed to be prospering.

The front door opened and a tall woman with graying blond braids stepped out. She gave a cry of gladness and rushed forth, arms opened wide. Moments later Reyna was enveloped in her mother's fierce embrace. "I have prayed to the gods for this moment," Maida cried. "Oh daughter, we have missed you! I never dared hope your brothers would find you and return you to us."

"I missed all of you so much," Reyna said in a choked voice.

"Our daughter is finally home, Maida," Harald said joyfully.

Maida's gaze slid past Reyna to Wulf. Her eyes hardened as she released her daughter and poked a finger at Wulf. "Is that the Norseman who carried you off? What is he doing here?"

"Wulf is my thrall," Reyna explained. "Borg, Dag and Ragnar captured him."

"They should have killed him," Maida spat. "That Norseman is trouble. One has but to look into those cold eyes to know he will not submit easily."

"I have a better solution," Reyna said in sudden inspiration. "Why not demand danegeld for him? His brother is a wealthy jarl and will pay any ransom we name for his safe return."

"Reyna's idea merits consideration," Borg said, stroking his chin thoughtfully. "It is a way of regaining what we lost in the raid."

"I am not convinced," Maida replied. "Wulf the Ruthless carried off some of my most prized possessions and burned our crops. We had to sell most of our thralls to provide food that winter."

Harald listened to his wife and sons before making his decision. He was, after all, a jarl and head of the family. " 'Tis in our best interest to demand danegeld for the Norseman, but it will have to wait until spring. Winter is nearly upon us, and the open water is too dangerous to traverse now. Until the demand can be delivered, Wulf the Ruthless will serve as Reyna's thrall."

Wulf had listened to the exchange with growing anger. He was no slave. He was the son of a jarl and brother to one. He was known far and wide as a fierce warrior. Not only had he successfully fought off raiders among his own countrymen seeking to expand their lands, but he'd also battled both Finn and Dane marauders. He had sailed to Byzantium and back without mishap or loss of life or limb.

Wulf knew his brother would pay the danegeld gladly; that did not worry him. What did concern him was submitting to slavery until the ransom arrived. How had he gotten himself into such a degrading situation? How

had it come to this? He had been so intent upon his thoughts of Reyna that the enemy had caught him off guard. Never would he forgive himself the lapse.

The shame, the embarrassment of being a thrall made him furious. He glared at Reyna, his fire and ice eyes ablaze with the promise of retribution.

"So be it," Borg approved. "We will demand danegeld for the Norseman."

"Aye," Dag agreed. "Come spring, we will sail across the sea to deliver our demands."

Maida regarded her daughter thoughtfully. "We should leave it up to Reyna. She was the one abused by the Norse brute."

"Mother, I was not abused by Wulf, truly. Wulf's family treated me well, and I grew to care for and respect them. I also came to know Wulf. He was not an easy master, but he did not mistreat me. He raided our farmstead as a random act of revenge for the death of his wife and unborn child at the hands of our countrymen."

Wulf gave Reyna credit for telling the truth, though he did it grudgingly. He had raided two other farmsteads that summer and Reyna's had been the last. All the farmsteads had been within easy reach of where his flotilla of ships had landed. His brothers at arms had returned home loaded with loot and thralls, except for Wulf, who had sailed on to Constantinople with Reyna. He had gained more from her sale to the slave trader than all the loot combined.

Wulf's expression must have been fierce for Harald said, "The Norseman is a danger to us. We should lock him up until he comes to terms with his fate."

"I have ears," Wulf growled. "If you think you can keep me locked up and fettered like an animal, you are wrong."

"Wulf," Reyna intervened. "Listen to me. If you give your word that you will not try to escape or harm anyone in my family, I will not let them lock you away."

"Now see here, Reyna," Borg protested, "the Norseman cannot be trusted. He will kill us all in our beds."

"Not if he gives his promise. I believe Wulf is a man of honor."

"Ha!" Maida mocked. "The Norseman has no honor."

Wulf drew himself up to his full height. "I have more honor than the marauding Danes who kill women and children."

"Do you give your word?" Reyna pressed, ignoring his outburst. "If you do not, you may have to spend the entire winter in a windowless hut, locked away from human contact."

Wulf considered Reyna's words. He would go mad if he could not see the sky or smell the freshness of new-fallen snow. He needed to exercise his muscles and keep his mind agile. But agreeing to subjugate himself to slavery infuriated his considerable pride. Norsemen did not make good thralls.

However, the alternative of imprisonment was not attractive. Could he submit to slavery until spring, when his ransom was demanded and the danegeld arrived?

"I am waiting for your answer, Wulf," Reyna prodded. "If you agree, your bonds will be removed immediately."

"Now wait a minute," Borg interrupted. "I am not sure that is wise. He should be kept in bonds until he learns humility."

Wulf threw back his head and laughed. "Like your sister learned humility? She never behaved like a thrall. Instead, she ingratiated herself with my family and was given a sleeping alcove of her own. How many thralls earn that kind of trust from their masters?"

"Is that true, Reyna?" Harald asked.

"Aye, my healing skills found favor with Wulf's family and I earned their respect as well as favors not normally given to thralls."

"Reyna refused to acknowledge her status as a thrall," Wulf continued, "yet I did not punish her for her disobedient nature."

"Also true," Reyna admitted.

Reyna's brothers grinned. "Our sister has not a submissive bone in her body. We are happy to hear she has not changed despite her suffering at your hands," Borg said.

Wulf winced. True, Reyna had suffered enslavement because of him. But he had not sexually abused her. Their coming together had been a pleasure that both wanted.

Until now, Ragnar had neither interrupted the homecoming nor the discussion about Wulf's fate. Apparently he could hold his tongue no longer.

"I will wed Reyna and take her home with me. Though the Norseman has had her in his bed, I will overlook her sins and make sure my parents welcome her in our hall."

Wulf stiffened. Reyna had committed no sins. He shot a glance at her and saw something in her expressive green eyes that kept him silent.

"I thank you, Ragnar, but under the circumstances, I release you from our betrothal contract. As you so aptly put it, I am used goods. I do not expect you to sacrifice yourself on my account."

Wulf would have clapped had his hands been free. Ragnar was not worthy of Reyna.

"Daughter," Harald reprimanded, "think about what you have just said. Ragnar is willing to wed you despite your . . . er . . . well, you know what I mean."

"I know what I am about, Father. I am sure Ragnar can find a bride less tainted than I."

Wulf felt like cheering even though he bristled when Reyna claimed she was tainted.

"Is that your final word, Reyna?" Ragnar asked. "Because Jarl Otto's daughter has hinted that she would be happy to have me as a husband. You were gone so long, I started courting her last year."

"Wed her with my blessing," Reyna replied without a hint of remorse.

Ragnar stared at Reyna a full minute before turning and stalking off.

"You were not kind to him, daughter," Maida chided. "He may be your only hope of marriage."

"It is over, Mother. Let it be. Ragnar would never let me forget I once belonged to a Norseman, or that I resided in a harem. I am home with my loved ones— that is all that matters. I hope you have prepared something good to eat, for I am famished."

"Lock the Norseman in the grain shed until he agrees to our terms," Harald ordered. "After a few days of isolation, he will be more amenable to our offer."

Wulf glanced at the tiny shed Reyna's brothers were prodding him toward and balked. How terrible could it be to pretend to be Reyna's thrall? Surely it was better than moldering in a tiny, airless shed with no windows.

"Wait!" Wulf said. Whipping around, he directed his gaze at Reyna. "Tell me again what I must agree to."

Borg answered in Reyna's stead. "You must vow on your honor as a Norseman . . ."

"Ha! He has no honor," Maida repeated.

"You must promise," Borg continued, "to become Reyna's thrall, to do her bidding without complaint and to make no threat to anyone on the farmstead until your danegeld arrives."

"And once it arrives, will I be free to return home?"

"Aye, on my honor as a Dane."

"Such as it is," Wulf muttered.

Borg bristled. "We do not kill and plunder, Wulf the Ruthless. We are farmers and traders. You would already be in Valhalla if Reyna had not begged us to spare you. Do you agree to serve our family as she served yours until you are returned to your homeland?"

What choice did Wulf have? Though submitting to slavery shamed him, he would swallow his pride and agree to the terms.

"Very well, I agree. You have my word as a Norse warrior to abide by the terms you have set forth. But once the danegeld arrives, you must return me to my homeland."

Borg nodded. Wulf extended his bound arms to Borg. "Cut me free."

When Borg hesitated, Wulf growled, "Why do you hesitate? Do you fear me? I have nowhere to go. With winter coming, I would be stupid to attempt a sea crossing without sailors to man a ship, even if by some miracle I were to escape."

Borg slashed the ropes binding Wulf's wrists. "I fear no man, Norseman. Remember that and act accordingly. If you fail to obey my sister or attempt to harm her, you will face instant death."

"A warrior's death is a good death," Wulf shot back, "but fear not, Borg the Dane, no harm will come to your sister at my hands."

Wulf had been bound several days; the lack of circulation to his hands had caused him a great deal of pain. Though that pain now radiated from Wulf's numb hands to his shoulders, his expression showed no emotion save disdain for his captors.

"Inside, all of you," Maida said, holding the door open. "First we will eat and then we will learn more about Reyna's time away from us. Perhaps she will tell us of the wonders she encountered in the harem. 'Tis the one place

her brothers have not visited in their travels to Byzantium."

Reyna cast a surreptitious glance at Wulf before following her mother into the hall. He met her gaze with an inscrutable look she could not decipher. But it didn't take a genius to know that although their circumstances might be reversed, Wulf would not bend beneath the yoke of slavery.

Chapter Ten

Wulf sat on the bench Borg had indicated and waited to see what would happen next. As the family gathered around Reyna, hugging her again and again, Wulf took note of his surroundings. It was a large hall, but he saw only two thralls, both women. A tall, blonde young woman caught his eye immediately. She appeared Nordic in looks, and he wondered if she was from his own country.

The lack of thralls appeared to confirm Maida's words that the family had been forced to sell its thralls in order to survive after the raid. The hall itself was snug and warm but without the ornamentation and rich furnishings of Hagar's hall.

The delicious smell of food coming from various iron pots hanging over the hearth made Wulf's mouth water. He watched as the family members seated themselves around the table and wondered if they intended to starve him. It seemed not, for after the family had been served heaping bowls of savory stew and thick slices of bread, the blonde thrall carried a bowl of stew, a spoon, and a slice of bread spread with yellow butter to him and set them down on the bench beside him.

"Are you Norse?" the girl asked in a hushed voice.

"Aye, and so are you if I am not mistaken."

"Aye, I was taken in a raid last summer and sold to Jarl Harald at the slave market in Rika. My name is Haley."

"Have you been treated well, Haley?"

"Aye, but the work is hard. Once Harald buys more thralls, things will get easier." She sighed. "Had the gods favored me, I would still be home with my parents and sisters. I was the only one of four sisters unlucky enough to be caught by the raiders."

"Haley," Borg called, "fetch us some ale. And fill a horn for our new thrall."

Haley hurried off to do Borg's bidding. Wulf dipped a hunk of bread into the stew and popped it in his mouth. The stew was as delicious as it smelled and he dug in with gusto. It was a plain but filling meal and Wulf was satisfied with the fare. It didn't take a seer to know that the family had suffered reverses since the raid and he felt a pang of guilt. But at the time he had been too consumed with grief to care about the farmstead or its habitants.

Maida rose to help the thralls clear the table and put away the food. Wulf began to relax when he heard Maida say, "Reyna, tell your thrall to fetch water from the well. The water barrel is empty."

Wulf met Reyna's gaze. The challenge in his eyes collided with the determination in hers.

Reyna rose gracefully from the bench. "I will show him where to find the well. Follow me, Wulf."

Wulf waited to see if Reyna's brothers would intervene, and when they did not, he followed her out the door. The well was not in the center of the yard but behind one of the outbuildings.

"It will take several bucketfuls to fill the water barrel," Reyna said as Wulf lowered the wooden bucket into the well.

Scowling, Wulf sent her a dismissive look. "I suppose you are happy now that you can order me to do your bidding."

Reyna returned his scowl with a satisfied smile. "I am supremely happy. Give thanks that you are still alive. Being a thrall does not seem so bad when you consider the alternative. Now you know how I felt. Does it hurt your pride to serve me? Does it shame you? Make you feel less a man?"

Wulf felt all those things and more. Helpless. Enraged. Yet still hungry for the Dane vixen standing beside him, looking smug and far too lovely for his peace of mind. How would he manage an entire winter in her company without acting on his impulse to toss her to the ground and thrust himself inside her?

"The bucket is full, take it inside," Reyna said, interrupting his lustful thoughts.

Wulf's temper rapidly reached the boiling point. Knocked unconscious, carried across the sea to the land of the Danes and forced into slavery, he wanted to rail against the gods. How had his life gone awry in so short a time? He glared at Reyna, aware that there was nothing he could do about his current situation . . . except persevere until his ransom arrived.

Forgetting his lowly position, ignoring the danger in acting impulsively, Wulf snared Reyna around the waist, pulled her hard against him and kissed her.

Reyna felt the anger in his kiss, the frustration, and understood those emotions from personal experience. Though she fought her reaction, his kiss aroused feelings she had tried to keep tightly under control. She recalled his lovemaking and her avid response. She remembered how frightened she had been at first, for she had let no man touch her after she had been cruelly ravished.

But despite his size, despite his gruff exterior, Wulf had not hurt her. He had been an ardent lover, demanding a response that she had willingly given. She had enjoyed their mutual passion far too much.

Wulf's kisses grew frenzied, his tongue slipping between her teeth to explore her mouth. A small cry gurgled from her throat when she felt his hands on her breasts, kneading the soft mounds and pinching her nipples into hard points.

This should not be happening, Reyna silently raged. Her brothers would kill Wulf if they knew what he was doing. Reason made her break off the kiss and push him away.

"Why did you do that?" she demanded.

"I want you, Reyna. Being a prisoner has not changed that. How many times must you save my life before you realize you want me as much as I want you?"

"You are mad!" Reyna spat. "My brothers will kill you if they find you kissing me."

Wulf shrugged. "Perhaps death is preferable to wearing the yoke of slavery."

Still feeling the effects of Wulf's kiss, Reyna backed away from him. "Carry the water to the hall. Now that you know where the well is located, you can fill the barrel without my direction."

"Are you afraid of me?" Wulf taunted.

"No, I am not. Be careful, Wulf the Ruthless. I may not be around to save your life the next time. Or"—she paused for effect—"I may not care enough to save your hide yet again."

Head held high, Reyna walked away on shaky legs, still reeling from Wulf's kiss. As she reentered the hall, determination stiffened her spine. She was the mistress and Wulf the slave. Before he returned to his homeland,

she wanted him to know, as she had known, how slavery strangled one's soul.

Reyna joined her parents and brothers, who were gathered around the hearth, surreptitiously watching Wulf make several trips to the well to fill the barrel. When the barrel was full, he looked at Reyna. She gestured toward the bench and he returned to his former place. A short time later the thrall named Haley joined him. Reyna watched them closely, well aware of how females reacted to Wulf's blatant masculinity. She was not surprised to see Haley and Wulf, heads together, engaging in intimate conversation.

Wulf glanced at Reyna. Then, catching her eye, he smiled blandly and returned to his conversation with Haley.

"Where did Haley come from?" Reyna asked her father.

"I bought her in Rika after your brothers returned from Byzantium. Their successful trading voyage returned some of our former prosperity to us. The other thrall's name is Alice; she is Saxon. We bought them at the same time."

"Haley is a beauty," Dag said, ogling the young Norsewoman.

Borg laughed. "Wulf the Ruthless seems to think so. We had better keep him busy; the female thralls seem quite taken with him."

"Take him out to cut wood tomorrow," Harald suggested. "He is our only male thrall; his services are needed to prepare the farmstead for the winter months."

One by one, the family drifted off to their sleeping alcoves, leaving Reyna sitting alone, staring thoughtfully into the fire. The two thralls removed wolf pelts from a cupboard and made their beds on wide benches against the wall. Wulf waited to see what Reyna would do. He

remained watchful as she rose and lit a rush in the hearth. Then she plucked her cloak from a hook, strode over to him and said, "Follow me."

Wulf followed her outside. She strode purposefully toward a small hut, opened the door and walked inside. Wulf entered behind her.

"The stillroom. My mother and I used to prepare our herbal remedies here. It was partially destroyed during the raid and rebuilt. It needs a great deal of work before I can use it."

She gestured with the rush toward a small hearth. "You can begin by bringing some of the wood you gather tomorrow and stacking it beside the hearth. The table needs repairing and lines need to be strung up to dry the plants I collect."

Wulf gestured toward a stack of folded wolf pelts on the table. "What should I do with those pelts?"

"Leave the pelts; they may be of some use in here. After you chop wood with my brothers in the morning, you can work in here in the afternoon. I will inform my brothers of your work schedule."

Wulf studied the room with a critical eye. Could he convince Reyna to let him use it as his private sleeping chamber? He would prefer sleeping on a pallet of furs rather than in a crowded hall. Privacy was important to him.

"Wulf, did you hear me?"

"Aye, I heard," Wulf muttered. "I hope you do not expect me to bow down to you, *mistress*," he emphasized sarcastically.

Reyna stared at him. "Wearing the yoke of slavery is not an easy burden for a proud man to bear, is it, Wulf the Ruthless? I suspect slavery is as humiliating for you as it was for me. I do not expect you to bow, but I do expect you to obey my orders."

"I will restore your stillroom and do it willingly if you grant me a boon."

Reyna eyed him with suspicion. "You just arrived and already you are begging for favors?"

"How long was it before you began taking liberties, helping yourself to food, asking to keep your silver girdle?"

He had a point. "What do you want?"

"I want your permission to sleep here instead of on a bench in the hall."

"Why?"

"I built my own hall because I like my privacy. Sleeping in the stillroom would afford me the privacy I seek."

"You are a thrall."

His temper flared. "I do not consider myself a thrall."

"So it was for me. How do I know you will not try to escape?"

He ground his teeth in frustration. "Where would I go? Besides, I gave my word, and the word of a Norseman is his bond."

Reyna considered Wulf's request. Though it was outrageous, it made sense in a curious way. First of all, it would keep the female thralls away from him, especially Haley, who seemed quite taken with Wulf. And it would keep Wulf away from them. Anything could happen between Wulf and the women in the middle of the night, when everyone was sleeping. While Wulf's sexual activity shouldn't bother her, it did. She knew him to be highly sexed.

"Very well, I will inform my family of my decision and you can sleep here once you complete the improvements I require. Meanwhile, keep your hands off of Haley. She is not here for your pleasure."

Wulf's grin sent Reyna's temper soaring. "What are you grinning about?" she demanded.

"You are jealous."

"Jealous? Me? You are mad, Wulf. I am merely warning you away from Haley for your own good. If you get her with child, it will complicate her life. Father will sell her to someone willing to take on her and her babe."

When she tried to walk past him to the door, Wulf plucked the rushlight from her hand and tossed it into the hearth. It landed on dry wood in the grate and flared into flames.

Reyna rounded on him. "Why did you do that?"

He hauled her into his arms, his voice rough. "Listen well, Reyna. Since I am being held for ransom, I consider myself a guest, not a thrall. I will lend a hand on the farmstead because I am not a man to sit around while others toil. But never again refer to me as a thrall."

His mouth came down on hers . . . hard, giving her no time to protest. Her feminine scent wafted up to him, and his head filled with it. It drove him wild with wanting. He felt her tense and then slowly soften, her body melting against his. He brought his hands down, shaping them to her, as he renewed his acquaintance with every prefect curve: the slender shoulders, the lush fullness of her breasts, the sweet indentation of her waist and the roundness of her hips.

Wulf wanted her.

Reyna couldn't help herself. Even as her hands rose to push Wulf away, she pulled him closer. The heat of his body singed her, melting her resistance. She felt him drag his hands over her breasts, belly and hips, and then around to cup her bottom, dragging her closer.

She knew she could end this any time she wanted, but kissing Wulf was far too pleasant to stop now. She wanted more, and opened her mouth to his probing tongue, savoring his taste. It occurred to Reyna that

since she was no longer Wulf's thrall, she could do as she wished without her pride suffering. Taking Wulf as a lover for as long as he remained with her family was a thrilling concept.

Since Reyna was no shy virgin, she had nothing to lose and much to gain by letting Wulf make love to her, and that seemed to be where he was headed. When he pushed his knee between her thighs, Reyna rode him eagerly, letting the pleasurable sensation wash over her. Reason and logic fled as his mouth ravished hers and his hands molded her breasts and rolled her swollen nipples between his fingers.

Panting, Reyna forced herself to break off the kiss. "Wait, we both are in need of a bath. Everyone is abed; we will have the steam hut to ourselves." She grasped his hand. "Follow me."

"I did not know you had a steam hut."

She led him out the door into the cool air. "Aye, 'tis over there," she said, pointing to a small hut across the yard.

She gave a squeal of surprise when Wulf scooped her into his arms and strode toward it. He set her down at the door and they entered together. The room was warm and steamy, the hot rocks in the middle of the fire pit still glowing. Wulf added more wood to the pit, then turned toward Reyna.

"Shall I undress you?"

Reyna swallowed hard and nodded. She wasn't a slave, she kept telling herself. She had the power to deny Wulf. Aye, the power but not the will. Come spring he would be gone, ransomed back to his family, and she would have naught but these memories to sustain her. It was unlikely she would ever have a husband. Though Ragnar would have accepted her as she was, it would not have been a happy union.

Reaching out, Wulf removed her cloak and released the fastenings at her shoulders. Her tunic dropped to her waist. She removed her belt, tossed it aside, pushed her tunic down and stepped out of it. Then he released her undertunic. It slid down her body into a puddle at her feet. Wulf stood back and stared at her, his eyes kindling with desire.

Wanting Wulf as naked as she was, Reyna pushed his vest over his shoulders. He shrugged out of it as she undid the strings of his tunic. He pulled it off in one smooth motion, revealing a massive chest rippling with muscles. Reyna nearly lost the ability to speak. Wulf was magnificent, everything a warrior should be and more. She gasped aloud when he removed his boots and shrugged out of his hide breeches. He was fully aroused, his staff rigid, the tip purplish blue and weeping.

Instead of reaching for her, Wulf turned toward the water barrel, removed a bucketful of water and threw it onto the hot rocks. Steam rose up in thick clouds; humid air swirled around them. Wulf grasped Reyna's hand and led her to a bench. He sat down, pulling her onto his lap.

"What has changed?" Wulf murmured into her ear. "Why are you not denying me? When you lived in my hall, you avoided me like poison."

"I am no longer your thrall," Reyna replied. "You cannot order me to your bed. What I do now is not forced upon me. I can do what I wish without surrendering my pride."

Wulf frowned. "Do not think you are forcing this upon me. I am not your thrall, so making love to you will not offend *my* pride." He lowered her to the wide bench and followed her down. "Even if it did, I would still make love to you."

Lowering his head, he licked the sweat that pooled between her breasts, then laved her nipples with the roughness of his tongue. Their bodies were slick and hot and beaded with sweat. Wulf sipped the moisture from her navel. When the combined warmth from the steaming rocks and their heated bodies became unbearable, Wulf rose, fetched a bucket of water from the barrel and poured it over Reyna. Then he cooled his own body with a second bucket of tepid water.

When he returned to the bench, Reyna sat up and ran her fingers through the wet strands of his blond hair. Then she pulled his mouth down to hers.

His mind thickened and darkened. Need to be inside Reyna shot through him like a bolt of lightning. His loins swelled and his cock filled with lust. Hunger rode him but he fought for control. He wanted so much more than a quick tumble. He wanted to taste her, to bring her to climax with his mouth and hands before thrusting his cock inside her. He wanted to hear her cry out his name while he watched her break apart. What was wrong with him? He had never felt this way before, not even with Astrid.

Wulf groaned against her mouth, their lips clinging as he shifted until he was lying between her spread thighs. Grasping her ankles, he raised her legs until her feet were flat on the bench on either side of him, her knees wide apart. He broke off the kiss and looked into her eyes. She returned his gaze, her green eyes heavy-lidded and unfocused.

His eyes shifted downward, to the pale fleece between her legs and her pouting nether lips, rosy and inviting. His hands slid from her ankles upward, skimming over the sensitive flesh of her calves and inner thighs to her weeping center. He caressed her, opened

her, and pushed two fingers into her. When she arched against the pressure of his fingers, he began moving them in and out.

Her sheath was incredibly tight and wet, gripping his fingers hungrily. He nearly lost it then, and had to force himself to concentrate on Reyna's pleasure rather than his own.

He lowered his head and whispered into her ear, "Come for me."

"I want you inside me," Reyna panted.

He ignored her, his fingers pushing harder, faster, in and then out, her juices spilling over his hand. He felt the pulse of her wildly beating heart. His heart beat with hers, harder, faster. And then she was there, her body tensing, her muscles tightening against his fingers. He took her cries into his mouth, his fingers moving inside her until her climax eased.

"Why did you not come inside me?" Reyna gasped once she caught her breath. She glanced down at his thick cock. "You did not . . ."

"In good time," Wulf choked out. He had almost lost it. How long could he endure? He was determined to find out. "We have the whole night ahead of us."

Reyna shook her head. "I must return to the hall before someone notices my absence."

"Your family has retired for the night."

Her eyes still fixed on his erection, she said, "My brothers oftentimes roam during the night."

It was as if he hadn't heard her. "I need to taste you."

Leaning in, he softly sucked on her earlobe. Her hands trailed up his chest to wind around his neck. His hands found her breasts, molding them, covering them completely with his palms. Then he lowered his head to suckle her nipples, making her cry out with renewed desire as she grasped his head and arched her back for

more. When both her nipples were hard and throbbing, he moved down her body, to her spread thighs. With his mouth just inches from her exposed sex, he breathed against her. He felt her shiver. Emboldened, he pressed his open lips to her, his tongue delving into her feminine folds, finding them slick and tasting like honey.

He spread her with his thumbs, his tongue finding the sensitive button above the opening of her sex and suckling it gently into his mouth.

She cried out, her fingers clutching hard at his hair. "Wulf, you are driving me insane!"

"I want you to come with my tongue inside you. Do not hold anything back," he mumbled against her swollen flesh.

He kissed and laved, licking and devouring her while his hands clutched and molded her breasts. When his tongue thrust deep inside her wet sheath, she gave a sharp cry, undulating her hips, abandoning herself to his greedy mouth and the emotional impact of her climax.

Wulf was beyond arousal, beyond any other sexual experience in his entire life, and he was no novice when it came to women. He was also hard as stone, thick and aching . . . and at the end of his endurance.

Spreading Reyna's legs wide with his hips, he pushed his cock hard and deep inside her. He groaned. Her quivering sheath felt hot, wet and welcoming. Holding nothing back, he began thrusting and withdrawing. He was far too aroused to be gentle, but Reyna did not appear to want gentleness. When she began responding, meeting him thrust for thrust, he became even more aroused, if that were possible.

"Hurry, Reyna, I am almost there," Wulf groaned into her ear.

He needn't have worried. Reyna was with him all the way. He felt his climax begin down in his toes and travel

up to his groin. Then he erupted; shouting her name, he emptied himself inside her, thrusting again and again until he had no more to give. Reyna was still quivering in the aftermath of her own climax when he collapsed on top of her.

They lay without moving a long time, sweat plastering their bodies together. Though the fire had burned down to embers and the steam had long since dissipated, their wild coming together had produced a fiercer heat.

At last Wulf shifted his weight off of her and rose. He walked to the water barrel, dipped a bucket inside and splashed water over his head and body. Then he refilled the bucket, carried it to Reyna and dumped it on top of her. Reyna yelped and sat up, sputtering.

"You could have warned me."

"We both needed cooling off."

Wulf set the bucket down and pulled on his clothing. Then he found Reyna's discarded garments, including her cloak, shoes and stockings, and tossed them to her. "Don't bother putting them on, I intend to carry you back to the guest hut and take you again there."

"I will freeze," Reyna protested as Wulf scooped her off the bench and into his arms. Her protests went unheeded as he carried her out the door.

Hugging her clothing against her chest, Reyna felt cold air hit her and sucked in a startled breath. But she needn't have worried, for Wulf sprinted across the yard and had her inside the hut before she could form a protest. He set her on her feet, tossed some wolf pelts on the floor and left her there while he built a fire in the hearth with the last of the wood.

Then he stalked back to Reyna and lowered her onto the furs.

She started to rise. "What are you doing?" she asked. "I should leave." She peered up at him beneath golden

lashes. "I cannot stay here with you, Wulf. You are a thrall and it would not be fitting."

Wulf's body tensed and his expression darkened. He looked so fierce, Reyna sidled away from him.

"What must I do to convince you I am a guest and not a thrall?" Wulf growled. "Once my danegeld arrives, I will be free to return to my home."

"You will have to convince my brothers of that," Reyna huffed. "You would be dead had I not intervened. I asked them to give you to me as my thrall instead of killing you. They know you took me to Constantinople and sold me. I told them about my time in the harem. They believe you used me as your bed slave after Hagar brought me to your farmstead, and I fear they will not forgive you for that. They will never treat you as a guest. My mother would rather see you dead than ransomed."

"I did not use you, Reyna. Our enjoyment was mutual. You know in your heart you were never my thrall, no matter how many times I insisted otherwise. You saved my life and that of my brother. Even Olga came to appreciate your skills."

Reyna bit her lip. Everything Wulf said was true. Except for the first few days after she'd arrived at Hagar's farmstead, she had been treated like one of the family. Still, her brothers were protective of her and angry at Wulf. If not for the danegeld he would bring to their coffers, he would be dead.

"I will try to convince them to treat you as a guest, but it will not be easy. It may cost your brother more danegeld."

"Hagar will pay whatever is demanded of him for my safe return." He pushed her down and rolled on top of her. "I want to love you again, and I know you want me too."

She pushed at his chest. "Arrogant Norseman. Get

up. This cannot happen again. What if my brothers catch us?"

Reyna had to admit that making love with Wulf this time was different from how it had been when she was his thrall. Before, she had felt degraded, embarrassed, powerless. But now that Wulf was the powerless one, she felt redeemed and emboldened.

Making love with Wulf tonight had been her choice. She had wanted it. She could have screamed and her brothers would have come running to her rescue, but she didn't want to be rescued. She wanted Wulf to love her without the yoke of slavery hanging over her, and it had been an unbelievable experience. But she now realized she could not let it happen again. Birthing a Norseman's babe after he was ransomed back to his family would bring new shame to her.

Wulf reached for her. Reyna pushed him away and leapt to her feet. Plucking her undertunic from the floor, she tugged it on, keeping a wary eye on him.

"You cannot sleep here tonight without my family's permission."

"I care not about your brothers. I am sleeping here tonight," Wulf persisted.

"Our thralls sleep on benches in the hall."

"Has naught I've said gotten through to you? I am not a thrall. Go find your bed, if that is what you want. I will hash this out with your family on the morrow."

Well aware of Wulf's stubbornness, Reyna saw no way to change his mind without using force. And since she had no weapon and would not have used it against him even if she had one, she shrugged on the rest of her clothing, threw her cloak over her shoulders and returned to the hall.

As luck would have it, both her brothers were pacing the hall, waiting for her return.

"Where have you been?" Borg growled.

"And where is the Norseman?" Dag added, pointing to his empty bench.

Reyna raised her chin defiantly. "I gave Wulf permission to sleep in the stillroom."

"Are you mad?" Borg demanded. "The Norseman is a thrall, not a guest, and should be treated accordingly."

"Are we not demanding danegeld for his ransom?" Reyna asked.

"You know we are."

"It occurred to me that since he is a jarl's brother and we intend to ransom him back to his family, we should treat him as a guest. Therefore, I gave him permission to sleep in the stillroom."

"I knew letting the Norseman live was a mistake," Dag complained to his brother. "Now he is demanding guest privileges."

"Wulf has agreed to do his share of work until his ransom arrives," Reyna explained. "He has also promised not to attempt an escape."

"And you believe him?"

"Aye, I do. Where would he go? He cannot sail a ship without sailors. Who here would help him?"

"I do not like it," Borg rasped.

"Wulf is mine," Reyna persisted. "You have no say over where he sleeps or does not sleep."

The brothers exchanged knowing glances. "You were with him tonight. Did you let him . . ." Borg stumbled over the words.

Reyna bristled. "I merely showed him what I want done in the stillroom."

Obviously neither brother believed her. "Fetch your weapon, Dag. 'Tis time we paid our 'guest' a visit. Stay here, Reyna," Borg ordered.

Reyna watched helplessly as her brothers fetched a

variety of weapons from their sleeping alcoves and strode out the door.

"Do not forget how much he is worth to us alive," Reyna called after them.

Chapter Eleven

Wulf had just dozed off when the door burst open. He was fully awake in an instant, reaching for Blood-Seeker; unfortunately he no longer had his trusty sword. Cursing, he glared at the open door. Two brawny men stood illuminated by the dying fire, fully armed and poised for battle.

Tossing off the wolf pelt, Wulf rolled to his feet, his fists clenched, his body a mass of bulging muscles and flexing tendons. "What do you want?"

"You do not belong here," Borg growled. "Thralls sleep in the hall on benches. They are given no special favors."

"I do not consider myself a thrall." How many times had he heard Reyna say those very same words? "Your sister gave me permission to sleep in the stillroom."

"How did you convince her?" Dag asked with a snarl. "I say we kill him, Borg. He used our sister's vulnerability to get what he wanted."

"Kill me and you can forget about the danegeld my brother will pay for my safe return."

Dag whipped out his sword and advanced toward Wulf. Wulf braced himself. Naked and weaponless, he had never felt more vulnerable.

Borg grabbed Dag's arm, stopping him in his tracks. "No, brother, you cannot kill the Norseman. We need

the danegeld to buy more thralls and help the kraalls repair their huts. We suffered a major loss during the Norse raid. They stole our valuables and scattered our livestock. The Norseman's life is valuable to us."

"Can't we rough him up a bit?" Dag asked. "He has to learn to keep away from our sister. 'Tis still possible that Ragnar will wed her."

"Would you rough up a valuable guest?" Wulf asked.

"Though you may be valuable, you are not a guest," Borg growled. "Nor are you allowed to dally with our sister. She is off-limits to you, Norseman."

"I will fight you for my status as a guest," Wulf challenged. "Give me a weapon."

"Nay, we are not stupid. Putting a weapon in your hands would be dangerous as well as unwise."

"I will fight him with my bare hands," Dag said, dropping his sword and the other weapons he was carrying. Then he advanced toward Wulf. Wulf met Dag halfway, wrapping his arms around the Dane as they tried to wrestle each other to the ground.

It didn't take long for Wulf to gain the upper hand. Reyna's brothers were strong, but they were traders, not warriors. Wulf had been fighting his whole life against one enemy or another.

Both men were pretty well bruised by the time Reyna burst onto the scene. "Stop it!"

The sound of her voice put a damper on the fight and the men fell apart.

"What are you doing here?" Borg growled. "I thought I told you to remain in the hall."

"Why? This involves me as much as it does you. I gave Wulf permission to sleep in the stillroom. You should both be ashamed of yourselves. You came here fully armed to fight a weaponless man."

Dag rose to his feet. "Why are you defending the

Norseman? He has openly defied us and insulted you with his unwanted attention. When you asked us to spare his life and make him your thrall, Borg and I thought you intended to punish him for his foul treatment of you. Granting favors is not punishment."

"Do you have feelings for the Norseman?" Borg asked. "'Tis the only explanation I can think of for your preferential treatment of our enemy."

Reyna glanced at Wulf, refusing to answer. Instead, she said, "I am of an age to live my life as I please. I need not answer to you."

Borg shook his head. "I do not understand you, Reyna. Consorting with the Norseman will not gain you a husband. Once he leaves, you will never see him again."

Wulf listened carefully to the interchange. Did Reyna have feelings for him? They certainly bore a great deal of lust for each other, judging from their explosive bouts of lovemaking. The thought of never seeing Reyna again caused an odd pang in the vicinity of his heart.

"I know I will never see Wulf again once he leaves," Reyna admitted, "and have accepted it."

Was that a catch Wulf heard in Reyna's voice? he wondered.

"Is it your wish to treat the Norseman as a guest instead of a thrall?"

"Aye, that is my wish. If you recall, I already told you Wulf has agreed to do his share of work on the farmstead, and that he's agreed to remain with us until his danegeld arrives. Whether you call him thrall or guest makes little difference, except in Wulf's mind. The Norseman is a prideful man, though no more prideful than I was in his position."

She glared at Dag. "Fighting will gain you naught. Though I love you and Borg dearly, Wulf is the superior warrior."

While they bickered among themselves, Wulf pulled a pelt from the bed and wrapped it around his waist. He looked longingly at the sword that Dag had tossed aside but decided to wait for the outcome of the argument between brothers and sister before taking any action.

"Can we all agree on Wulf's status as a guest so we can seek our beds?" Reyna asked.

"I do not like it," Dag complained. "How can you forgive what he did to you, to all of us?"

"I forgave him for selling me and have naught else to forgive him for. His raid was in retaliation for a raid by our own countrymen that killed his wife and unborn child. Grief can change a man and drive him to commit grievous misdeeds."

Borg glared at Wulf. Wulf glared back. "What say you, Norseman? Is my sister right? Will you work beside us and not try to kill us in our sleep?"

"I have already said I would."

"Will you keep your hands off our sister?" Dag growled.

"Do not answer, Wulf," Reyna replied in his stead. "Your promise to work and remain with us until your danegeld arrives is all that is required of you."

"You are being deliberately willful, Reyna," Dag warned. He slanted a look at his brother and said, "We will agree to treat your Norsemen as our guest if you agree to wed Ragnar."

"Nay!" Wulf shouted. "Do not agree to those terms, Reyna. Ragnar is not worthy of you."

Reyna sent Wulf a speaking glance. "I agree to wed him if he will have me." she said. "But Ragnar wants me no more than I want him, so I have naught to fear on that score."

"We shall see about that," Borg gloated. "Meanwhile,

'tis time we were all abed. Come, sister, our 'guest' needs to be up early to chop wood."

"Aye, and to make the improvements to Reyna's still-room," Wulf added. "Sleep well."

Reyna turned and preceded her brothers out the door. Wulf didn't relax until the door closed behind them. Even then he remained alert, until enough time elapsed for them to have returned to the hall. Then he lay down and went over in his mind everything that had been said.

Obviously Reyna's brothers knew that he and Reyna had gone far beyond what was proper. And Wulf knew those same brothers would do all in their power to see that Reyna wed Ragnar once he crossed the sea to his own home. Envisioning Ragnar and Reyna together left a bitter taste in Wulf's mouth. Why had she agreed to wed the Dane? Wulf fell asleep wondering how soon he and Reyna could be alone again.

Wulf was out of bed and in the hall breaking his fast long before the family was up the following morning. Haley waited on him personally, placing a variety of mouthwatering foods before him. Wulf dug in, unaware of Haley's shy glances.

"You did not sleep in the hall last night," Haley said. "I saw you and Lady Reyna leave the hall together after the family sought their beds. When neither of you returned, I alerted the lady's brothers. I feared something was amiss. Fortunately she returned shortly thereafter."

Wulf glared at her. "*You* told Reyna's brothers that Reyna was missing?"

"Did I do something wrong, Wulf?"

Her answer was forestalled when Reyna's brothers emerged simultaneously from their sleeping alcoves. They stopped short when they saw Wulf.

"You are up early, Norseman," Borg said.

Wulf shoveled the last bit of ham into his mouth and rose. "I am ready to chop wood."

Dag glanced at Wulf's empty plate and gave Haley a sour look. "It appears you fed our 'guest' well, Haley."

"Guest?" Haley squeaked. "I thought . . ."

"You thought wrong, Haley," Reyna said from behind them. "Wulf is our guest and will remain so until his ransom arrives."

Haley's face fell. "Wulf will be leaving?"

"So it seems," Dag complained, "though I like it not. Bring us food, Haley. We are anxious to be off."

"I am going with you," Reyna said. "I want to see if there are any plants left to gather."

"It is warmer here than in the north," Wulf offered. "In my homeland the ground would already be frozen. Our wood has already been cut and stacked against the longhouse."

Dag sent him a sour look. "Wait outside for us, Norseman. We will join you after we break our fast."

Wulf returned his look with one of his own, then turned and stormed out the door. Haley followed him, calling his name. Wulf stopped and turned toward her.

"What do you want, Haley?" Wulf wasn't too pleased with her right now.

"Is there anything I can do for you, Wulf? I could bring linens for your bed and an iron pot to heat water in, if you like."

"Both would be appreciated, Haley." He sent her a curious look. "Speak freely, what do you want from me?"

Haley licked her lips nervously. "I want to return to my homeland and you can help me."

"How?"

"Once your danegeld arrives, you could persuade your brother to buy me from Harald Fairhair." Her face

crumpled. "I . . . I am Norse, like you, and miss my home and family."

Wulf felt immediate empathy with Haley. His arm went around her and he patted her back clumsily while she sobbed against his jacket.

" 'Tis cold out here. You had better go inside. I will do my best to see you returned to your farmstead."

"Return to your duties, Haley!" Borg barked from behind them.

Wulf's arms dropped from around Haley when he saw Reyna and her brothers watching them. The betrayed look on Reyna's face did not bode well for him.

Haley gave a yelp of fright, scurried past him and the others and disappeared inside the hall.

"Making conquests already?" Dag sneered. "Keep away from Haley. Is my sister not enough for you?"

"Dag!" Reyna scolded. "Mind your tongue. I am ready to leave when you are."

Grumbling to himself, Dag led the way to the forest that lay beyond brown fields whose dying vegetation had been nipped by frost. Reyna and Wulf followed. Borg brought up the rear. Dag carried an axe in his belt and Borg carried two, apparently loathe to give an axe to Wulf before they reached the forest. Reyna bore a basket over her arm with a short blade resting inside.

The air was cold and clear. The men wore fur-lined jackets and high boots with fur on the outside. Reyna was dressed warmly in the fur-lined cloak Wulf's mother had given her and her own fur boots. Wulf still wore the leather breeches and fur-lined jacket he had worn when he was captured.

Once they reached the forest, Borg reluctantly handed Wulf an axe. "Dag and I will cut the wood. Your job will be to chop the logs into pieces small enough to be carried back to the farmstead."

"I shall wander off on my own," Reyna said.

"Do not go far," Wulf warned. "If you meet up with a wild boar, scream as loud as you can and I will come running."

Dag glared at him. "We can take care of our sister without your help. Besides, there are no wild boars in these woods. Go, Reyna, just don't wander off too far. Hakkon the Raider's warriors could be lurking nearby."

"Who is Hakkon the Raider?" Wulf asked.

"He rules the territory to the south and has harassed us for years, stealing livestock and sometimes a thrall or two caught away from the farmstead. He seeks to enlarge his territory by adding our farmstead to his holdings."

Wulf scowled. "You should not let Reyna wander off by herself if Hakkon is a threat."

"He usually confines his raids to summertime. Only rarely has he trespassed on our land at this time of year. Forget Hakkon and get to work."

While the brothers cut down saplings and Wulf chopped them into manageable pieces, Wulf kept an eye on Reyna. Whenever she wandered out of sight, he grew anxious. He didn't like the idea that an enemy might be lurking nearby and kept a wary eye out for trouble.

When the weak winter sun rode high in the sky, Borg called a halt to the wood cutting and gave a shout for Reyna. She appeared a few minutes later, her basket holding nothing but roots.

"The frost has already ruined most of the plants," she lamented. "I hope we have enough medicinal supplies on hand to last through the winter."

Each of the men grabbed an armful of wood to carry back to the hall. Reyna walked beside Wulf. "I am sorry about last night. My brothers are protective of me."

"No harm done," Wulf replied.

"What are you two talking about?" Dag asked from behind them.

"I am apologizing for your behavior last night," Reyna replied.

Dag muttered grumpily.

"Haley appears taken with you," Reyna said, tossing her head.

"I do not want Haley."

Reyna snorted. " 'Twas not how it looked to me. Haley was falling all over you earlier."

Wulf gave her one of his rare grins. "You are jealous."

Reyna shrugged. "Bed whom you want. I care not."

Borg walked up to join them, effectively halting their conversation. Leaning close, Wulf said, "We will continue this discussion later."

Wulf carried an armload of wood to the stillroom, washed up at the well and joined the family for the noon meal. Though no one protested when he sat at the table, Wulf could see Maida struggling with his presence. Apparently Reyna and her brothers had spoken to their parents about Wulf's status as a guest.

Immediately after the satisfying meal of bread, cheese and meat, Wulf, Harold, Dag and Borg returned to the forest to fetch the rest of the wood, stacking it up against the outside wall of the longhouse for use during the winter. Darkness came early. When the men quit for the day, Wulf returned to the stillroom to find Reyna covering his pallet of furs with clean bed linens. She had also made good use of the broom, started a fire in the hearth and brought an iron pot, which now sat on the hearthstone.

"All I need now is a woman to share my furs," Wulf said, moving up behind her. He surrounded her with his arms and dragged her against him.

"Shall I summon Haley?"

"I have what I want right here in my arms."

She turned slowly, until she was facing him. "Only until your danegeld arrives," Reyna shot back. She was still annoyed at Wulf's apparent closeness to Haley. "Will you wed again after you return home, Wulf?"

"No, I swore never to wed again after Astrid's death."

"Will you continue raiding?"

"No. I plan to join Hagar on his trading ventures. My two younger brothers are old enough to defend the farmstead while we are away. But soon they, too, will want to go a-Viking. 'Tis in their blood."

He searched her face. "Will you wed Ragnar after I leave?"

She shook her head. "I spoke the truth when I said he wants me no more than I want him."

"Your brothers seem to think otherwise."

"They can think what they will. By now they should realize I have a mind of my own and know how to use it."

"I admire strong-willed women. If you were a Norsewoman . . ." His sentence hung in the air, permitting Reyna to interpret it as she would.

"If I were a Norsewoman I would never have met you," Reyna said, finishing his sentence. "I would not have been your thrall or you mine."

"You talk too much," Wulf said, lowering his head for a taste of her lush lips.

The door opened. They drew apart as Maida's tall figure filled the doorway. "Return to the hall, Reyna," Maida ordered. "You do not belong here."

Reyna looked as if she wanted to protest, but in the end did as her mother asked. Maida waited until the door closed behind her daughter before rounding on Wulf.

"Leave my daughter alone. She has suffered enough at your hands."

"Hurting Reyna was never my intention. I did not harm her during or after the raid. 'Twas another."

"So Reyna told me, but that knowledge does not make you any better than the Norseman who violated her. Reyna will wed Ragnar as planned. She is not for you."

"I . . ."

Maida gave Wulf no time to reply. "I will tolerate you at my table as long as you remain with us, but I do not have to enjoy your presence." So saying, she whirled about and stomped out the door.

Wulf slumped down onto a bench. Maida feared for her daughter's feelings and he did not blame her. Had he a daughter, he would protect her from men like himself. Men who wanted, took and gave nothing in return.

The meal that night was an uncomfortable one for Wulf. He ate quickly and left. Before seeking his bed, he visited the steam hut, reliving in his mind every detail that had happened the previous night.

The ritual of chopping and stacking wood continued for several days, until the entire winter supply of wood was stacked up nearly to the roof of the longhouse. Once that chore was completed, the men drove the livestock down from the hills to the winter pasture and stacked hay into piles for the animals' use. The first snow had fallen by the time the men got around to repairing some of the outbuildings and fences, though it was much lighter here than in Wulf's homeland.

Though Wulf wished it otherwise, Reyna had not returned to the stillroom. He saw her only at meals, beneath the glare of her wary family. When Dag, Borg and Harald left the hall to go hunting one morning, Wulf asked to accompany them.

"I would not trust the Norseman with weapons,"

Maida advised. "He will kill you all when your backs are turned."

Wulf merely sighed and busied himself elsewhere, even though he was an excellent hunter.

Reyna railed at her mother after Wulf left the hall. "Why do you hate Wulf, Mother? He is a skilled hunter and could help our men provide food for the table. Not long ago, he killed a wild boar that charged me while I was gathering herbs."

"I know you are taken with the Norseman, daughter, but I beg you not to mistake attraction for more than it is. Admittedly Wulf is an attractive man, but he took advantage of you and enthralled you. I pray you will come to your senses and wed Ragnar as planned. Ragnar is a good man. He will take care of you."

"Ragnar is weak. He thought me dead and courted another."

"You promised your brothers you would wed Ragnar."

"So I did, but Ragnar wants me no more than I want him."

Maida led Reyna to a bench and urged her to sit. "Tell me, daughter, do you have strong feelings for the Norseman?"

Glancing down at her folded hands, Reyna hesitated before saying, "I do have feelings for Wulf, but I do not know how strong they are. I know I will miss him when he leaves, and that few men can match him in strength and courage. I saved his life and would do it again."

"He will use you and leave you; he has no conscience. You may have forgotten that he carried you off and sold you, but I have not."

"Mother, I . . ."

Before Reyna could finish her sentence, Haley flew in through the front door, out of breath and panting. "Mis-

tress, I saw a strange warrior lurking behind a haystack in the field and I fear there are more of them hiding in the woods to the south."

Reyna jumped to her feet. "Hakkon! 'Tis just like him to raid our farmstead while our men are away."

"Run and fetch the men, Haley," Maida cried.

"No, 'tis too dangerous. She might be caught and dragged off. We must make a stand here. Perhaps we can hold them off until Father and my brothers return. I will find Wulf. Thank Freya he remained behind."

Wulf found her before Reyna located him. He burst through the door, his expression frantic as his gaze swept the hall. "Are all the women inside?"

"We are all here," Reyna replied, taking note of the thralls huddled together in a far corner. "Haley alerted us to danger. We believe it is Hakkon."

"I noticed warriors observing the hall but did not know who they were. I counted a dozen or more men. Where are the weapons?"

"You cannot hold them off by yourself," Reyna cried.

Wulf sent her an impatient look. "The weapons, Reyna, I must arm myself if I am to protect you. I will need a shield, spear, battle-axe and sword."

Reyna moved with alacrity. "I will help you. I can wield a weapon as well as my brothers."

"We will all arm ourselves," Maida exclaimed. "I can fight as well as any man."

Reyna ran to a cupboard and threw open the door. Inside were a variety of weapons. Wulf chose his weapons first, then Reyna and her mother.

"We should remain inside until we learn what they are about. Mayhap they are after your livestock," Wulf said.

" 'Tis more than that," Maida spat. "Hakkon covets our

land. He will not be satisfied with livestock. He must have been watching our farmstead, waiting for the time when our men left for the day. He believes we will be easily conquered without our men to defend us." She sneered. "Hakkon does not know whom he is dealing with."

"If he and his warriors try to breach the hall, we will surprise them. Stay behind me; let me take out as many as I can before you join the battle."

Maida stared at him. "Why would you defend our farmstead when we are holding you for ransom? How do I know you will not betray us?"

Wulf shot a glance at Reyna. "Reyna saved my life when she could have just as easily let me die. I can do no less for her. If it is within my power, no harm will come to you or your thralls."

Wulf crept to the narrow window and peered out. He spotted men stealthily creeping closer to the hall. He crossed the hall and looked out the window on the opposite side of the longhouse.

"They are closing in from both sides," Wulf said. "It appears you are right, Lady Maida; they intend to break inside and loot. I count between ten and twelve men, all moving toward the front entrance."

"They do not only want loot," Maida bit out. "I believe they intend to take us as prisoners and launch a surprise attack on our men when they return. Once our men are dead, they will claim our lands and all our belongings and enslave us and our thralls."

Haley and the other female thrall started wailing.

"I will not let that happen," Wulf promised with more assurance then he felt.

As if to disprove his words, the first thud upon the door sent shock waves through the hall.

"They are trying to break down the door with a battering ram," Reyna cried.

The door shuddered again but held. "Stay here," Wulf ordered. "They do not expect to be met at the door by an armed Norseman. I will make them rue the day they tried to take a defenseless farmstead."

Suddenly Wulf realized this raid by Hakkon was similar to the surprise raid he had made upon this very same farmstead two summers ago. Borg and Dag had been on a trading voyage, leaving their home virtually defenseless against his onslaught. His defense of their farmstead now would repay them for all he had taken from them.

Wulf strode to the door, shield held high, sword at the ready. Reyna feared for his life. There was no way he could fight off twelve heavily armed men bent on death and destruction. When it appeared as if the door was about to give, both Reyna and her mother took their places behind Wulf, ready to battle the enemy alongside him.

"I told you to stand back," Wulf hissed.

Reyna snorted. " 'Tis our right to defend our home."

The time for arguing passed as the door burst beneath the weight of the battering ram. Wulf quickly skewered the first warrior who came through the door then prepared himself for the horde of men stepping over their comrade's body.

The battle was fully engaged as Wulf pushed the men backward through the door and into the open, a sword in one hand and battle-axe in the other. Soon he was fighting outside in the cold air, deflecting blows from warriors bent on killing him. No sooner had he dispatched one Dane than two others took his place.

Wulf didn't allow himself to consider defeat, for it meant the women would be at the mercy of the raiders. He couldn't allow that to happen.

Wulf cut down a man who had rushed at him with a

raised battle-axe, and when he turned, he confronted a hulking warrior he strongly suspected was Hakkon himself.

"Who are you?" Hakkon roared, swinging his battle-axe at Wulf.

Wulf used his shield to take the brunt of the blow. "I am a Norseman, your worst enemy."

"I will kill you, Norseman. Name yourself before you die."

"Wulf the Ruthless, brother to Jarl Hagar the Red."

Hakkon seemed to falter before he renewed his attack. "I know your name, Norseman. My warriors and I raided your farmstead two summers ago. Prepare to die!"

Rage consumed Wulf. "You killed my wife! Die, Dane bastard!"

Determination gave Wulf superhuman strength. He dropped to one knee, and when Hakkon lunged at him he thrust his sword upward, finding a target in Hakkon's belly. When he freed his sword, Hakkon's blood flowed freely. Hakkon stopped in his tracks, looked down at the wound and began a slow spiral to the ground, not yet dead but severely wounded.

From the corner of his eye Wulf saw a Dane approaching on his left. He could do nothing about it at the moment, for another warrior had taken Hakkon's place, hacking away at Wulf with the strength and determination of three men. Though Wulf's blood was seeping from several minor wounds, he handily dispatched the warrior. Then he spun around to his left to confront the warrior that had been charging at him. He was shocked to see the Dane lying on the ground with Reyna standing over him.

Then, horrors of all horrors, he saw another of Hakkon's warriors run up behind Reyna and slice a deep groove down her left arm. The wound would have been

much worse if Maida hadn't called out a warning so that Reyna moved aside at the last minute. With a mighty roar, Wulf threw his battle-axe at the warrior, burying it in his forehead. The Dane fell dead at Reyna's feet.

Unfortunately, not even the combined efforts of Wulf, Reyna and Maida could prevail against the sheer number of raiders closing in on them for the kill. Wulf stood in front of the women, determined to fight to the death.

Just when everything looked hopeless, a war cry pierced the din around them. Wulf spared a glance over his shoulder, issuing his own battle cry when he saw Borg, Dag and Harald running toward him, fully armed, their clothes bloody from the hunt.

The men had returned!

The raiders saw Harald and his sons at the same time Wulf did and immediately started backing away. Then they were in full rout, carrying their dead and wounded with them as they headed south toward their own lands. Harald and his sons gave chase but stopped at the edge of the forest. By the time they returned, Wulf had gathered Reyna in his arms and carried her into the hall with Maida close on his heels.

"Take her to her sleeping alcove," Maida said, "while I gather what I need to treat her wound."

"Don't fuss," Reyna said. " 'Tis a shallow wound."

"Which sleeping alcove is yours?" Wulf asked, ignoring her protests.

"The first one on the right. You can put me down now."

"Not a chance." He shoved the curtain aside and entered the sleeping chamber. Two long steps brought him to the bed, where he placed Reyna on the soft furs.

"My heart nearly leapt out of my chest when I saw that warrior wound you. I told you and your mother to stay back, not throw yourselves into the heat of battle."

With great care he lifted her arm and tore away the

sleeve, wincing when he saw blood spilling out of the wound. Grabbing a drying cloth from a narrow night-stand, he pressed it against the wound to stanch the blood.

Then, because he couldn't help himself, he lowered his head and brushed her lips against hers. He would have leaned in for more if Maida hadn't pushed through the curtains and brushed Wulf aside. Reluctantly he re-linquished his place beside Reyna to her mother.

Chapter Twelve

Wulf retreated to the back of the alcove as the female thralls entered behind Maida. Haley carried a basin of hot water and Alice bore the medicinal chest. The thralls set their burdens down on the nightstand and left. The alcove was too small to hold more than two people and Wulf wasn't budging. He had seen Reyna's wound. It stretched from shoulder to elbow in a long narrow gash.

Maida set to work immediately, first thoroughly washing the wound and then inspecting it closely.

"Is it serious?" Wulf asked. "She looks so pale."

Maida glanced up at him, as if surprised to see him still there. "No, 'tis a shallow cut, but she has lost a great deal of blood. As long as you are still here, you can hold her down while I stitch the wound."

Wulf moved with alacrity, placing his hands on Reyna's shoulders.

"There's no need," Reyna said weakly. "I will not move."

"This is going to be painful, daughter. Let the Norseman lend you his strength."

Wulf watched Maida thread a slim needle, his expression grim. The thought of the sharp instrument piercing Reyna's tender skin made sweat pop out on his forehead.

Though Reyna sucked in a breath and slowly released it, she did not move.

Maida sprinkled dill seeds into the wound, then took the first stitch, pushing the needle in and out of Reyna's tender flesh. Though no sound passed Reyna's lips, pain was clearly visible in her wide green eyes. As Maida's needle pierced her skin a second time, Reyna shuddered and went still.

"She's passed out," Wulf said.

Maida spared Reyna a quick glance. " 'Tis for the best. Your help is no longer needed, you can go now."

"I will stay. Will there be a fever?"

"Most likely, though I will brew a concoction to prevent it."

Wulf watched stoically as Maida took small, neat stitches in Reyna's arm. When she was done, she applied a salve and wrapped the wound in a clean cloth.

"Send Haley and Alice to me, Wulf. We need to get Reyna's clothes off and put her into a sleeping shift."

Had Wulf heard right? Maida had addressed him by his name, the first of the family to do so besides Reyna. Smiling, he left the alcove to pass on Maida's orders to the thralls. Once that was done, Harald approached and asked Wulf how his daughter fared and if her wound was serious.

"Lady Maida is the healer—she can tell you better than I. But I believe the wound is not life threatening and that Reyna will recover."

Harald slapped Wulf on the back. "My daughter is strong; she will survive. Join us in a victory toast."

Wulf joined the three men at the table. Borg poured him a horn of ale and all three men raised their horns to Wulf. "We owe our thanks and mayhap our lives to Wulf the Ruthless," Borg toasted. Then they drank to Wulf's courage, strength and honor.

"My sons and I have decided to change your name," Harald said.

"What have you decided to call me?" Wulf asked warily.

"Henceforth you shall be known as Wulf the Defender," Borg said. "'Tis a fitting name for the man who saved our home this day. Did you really kill Hakkon?"

"I have never seen Hakkon, so I cannot be sure he was the man I slew. Reyna and Lady Maida saw me skewer him—mayhap they can verify his identity."

"Saw what?" Maida asked as she joined them.

"How is Reyna?" Harald asked in a voice tense with anxiety.

"Our daughter will recover with no lasting ill effect save a scar," Maida assured him. "She may develop a fever, but I will do what I can to prevent that from happening." She glanced at Wulf. "What were you talking about?"

"We were discussing changing Wulf's name. We think Wulf the Defender more fitting than Wulf the Ruthless."

A tentative smile curved Maida's lips. "'Tis a good name for the man who killed Hakkon the Terrible."

"So 'tis true, then," Harald said.

"Aye, I saw the man fall. His son, Elgar, carried him off, but no man can survive a wound such as Wulf delivered to our enemy. Hakkon is dead."

"We have been trying to kill that devil for years," Dag crowed. He clapped Wulf on the back. "Forgive my initial hostility toward you. 'Tis difficult to forget or forgive the havoc you inflicted on our farmstead and family."

"Just as it was impossible for me to forget or forgive what a Dane raiding party did to me and mine. 'Twas Hakkon, you know. He admitted raiding my farmstead before I thrust my blade into his gut."

"He knew you?" Borg exclaimed.

"He wanted to know whom he was about to kill and I gave him my name. He laughed and said he had led a raid on my farmstead. Rage lent my sword arm strength. 'Twas my destiny to kill Hakkon the Terrible."

Harald held up his arm for silence. "You have earned your freedom this day, Wulf the Defender. We will not accept your brother's danegeld."

"Father, we need the danegeld for Reyna's dowry," Dag objected. "Ragnar will expect it."

A nerve in Wulf's jaw twitched. "She will not have him."

"Wulf, I do not want to argue with you," Dag began, "but Ragnar is Reyna's last chance for a husband. No one else will have her after you . . . after . . ." He flushed and looked away.

"She will not have him," Wulf repeated.

"Why not let Reyna decide her own future," Maida said, joining in the discussion.

"What makes you think Ragnar will marry her, Dag?" Wulf asked. "Have you been in contact with him?"

"Aye, we visited him today, while we were out hunting. His farmstead lies but a short distance to the west."

Wulf had no answer for that. No matter what Dag believed, Reyna would never wed Ragnar. The man had no backbone. "I am going to the steam hut; does anyone want to join me?"

"Father, Dag and I must return to the forest for the game we bagged today. We dropped everything when we saw that the farmstead was under attack." Borg said.

"I will help you," Wulf offered.

"No, we can manage. You must be sore after the fierce battle you fought today. Go soak your muscles, Wulf the Defender."

Wulf the Defender. Wulf liked that. He also liked be-

ing a free man. If not for Reyna, he would confiscate a small boat and risk the winter sea to return home. But he couldn't leave Reyna until he was sure she would recover. By that time, it would be too late to cross the sea in a small boat, though it might be possible in a dragonship.

Wulf left the men to their ale. He strode toward the door, where Haley was waiting for him. "You will need this," she said, thrusting a drying cloth into his hands.

Wulf grunted his thanks and left the hall. A blast of cold air met him as he walked across the yard to the steam hut. He was sore and stiff from wielding his sword and battle-axe and eagerly looked forward to hot steam easing his cramped muscles.

Reyna awoke slowly to weak sunshine peeking through her small window. What was she doing in bed so late in the day? She tried to sit up and fell back when a sharp pain wrung a cry from her. Then she remembered: the battle, Wulf fighting for their lives and her own entrance into the fray, and then being wounded. She recalled Wulf carrying her to her sleeping alcove and little more after that.

A head poked through the curtain, then Maida walked into the small chamber. "How do you feel, daughter?"

"My arm hurts but 'tis bearable, and I am a bit lightheaded."

"'Tis no wonder. Though the wound is shallow and should heal quickly, you lost a great deal of blood. I am brewing an herbal tea to fight infection. I will bring it as soon as it is steeped. Make sure you drink it all."

"What about Wulf the Ruthless? Is he well?"

"You mean Wulf the Defender," Maida said, smiling.

Reyna's brow wrinkled in confusion. "Are we talking about the same man?"

"Aye, your father gave Wulf a more appropriate name and freed him. He is no longer being held for ransom."

Panic seized Reyna. "Is Wulf leaving?"

"Aye, he will leave, but not until spring. There is something else you should know." Reyna's attention sharpened. "Your brother said Ragnar intends to ask you to wed him. That he regrets being harsh with you."

"I do not want Ragnar."

"Wedding Ragnar is for the best, daughter. Wulf is not the man for you. Come spring, he will leave and eventually wed one of his own kind. Consider Ragnar's proposal carefully while you are confined to your bed."

Two days later Reyna was out of bed and joining the family for meals. Due to Maida's healing skills, Reyna remained free of infection and fever. She still favored her wounded arm but that was to be expected. Much to Reyna's chagrin, she had no time alone with Wulf. Her brothers were always underfoot, as if guarding her from Wulf's attentions.

The following days were spent smoking meats for winter consumption, gathering rushes and performing other chores necessary to get them through the winter. The men visited the cottages occupied by kraalls and their families, providing them with the necessities they lacked to see them through the winter months.

Wulf went out with the hunters nearly every day to see to the traps they had set, and one day he sent his spear through the heart of a deer. He carried it home, to the delight of everyone. Venison was tasty and highly valued.

One evening Wulf and Reyna finally found themselves alone after the family had sought their beds.

"How is your arm?" Wulf asked solicitously.

"Nearly back to normal except for some pain when I raise it above my head. That too will pass in time."

"You will probably bear the scar for life."

Reyna shrugged. "It matters not. How does being a free man feel?"

"My mind and heart have always been free." He searched her face. "I miss you, Reyna."

"I have not left, Wulf. I am here."

"Not where I want you." Very gently he cupped her shoulders and brought her into his arms. "This is where I want you. Do you know how frightened I was when I saw you fall? You could have been killed."

"But I wasn't. Instead I am here, in your arms."

"I am surprised your brothers left us alone."

"They expect me to wed Ragnar."

"Will you?"

"No, not if he were the last man on this earth."

"Come with me to the stillroom," Wulf whispered. "Be with me tonight. I have a feeling your parents will not let you refuse Ragnar."

Reyna was tempted. She had no intention of wedding Ragnar, no matter how persuasively her parents argued for the match. She wondered what inducement her brothers had offered him to wed her. It mattered not; nothing would convince her to become Ragnar's wife.

"What say you, Reyna? Will you come to my bed tonight?"

How could Reyna refuse such an invitation? She wanted to be with Wulf again before he left her forever.

"Wait here while I get my cloak."

Reyna returned shortly, wrapped in her fur cloak. She preceded Wulf to the door, uncaring that someone might be watching. She opened the door, but before she

could step outside, Wulf swept her into his arms, closed the door behind them and strode through the cold air to his hut.

" 'Tis snowing," Reyna said, catching large, wet snowflakes on the tip of her tongue. "I wonder if Ragnar . . ."

"Forget Ragnar," Wulf ordered. "This night is for us."

When they reached the stillroom, Wulf opened the door, stepped inside and kicked the door shut. Then he set Reyna down on her feet.

"Keep your cloak on while I build up the fire."

Reyna sat on the bed, her gaze wandering over Wulf's body, watching the play of muscles in his legs and buttocks as he bent to his task. His leather-covered legs were sturdy as twin oaks, his buttocks taut. If any fat existed on Wulf's virile body, she had yet to see it.

The fire caught; light filled the hut. Wulf watched the shooting flames a moment, then turned toward Reyna, his face taut with desire. His eyes never left hers as he shed his jacket and tunic and beckoned to her.

Reyna stood, threw off her cloak and walked into his arms. It felt like coming home. How could she wed a man who was not Wulf? The question went unanswered as Wulf lowered his mouth to hers, his tongue thrusting between her lips to taste her. She returned his kiss eagerly, stretching on her toes to meld her body to his.

She clung to him sweetly, wildly, yielding her heart and soul to him, if only for this one night. Making love with Wulf might mean nothing to him but sex, but it meant a great deal more to Reyna. Their mouths were still joined as he slowly undressed her, his large hands roving over her body. Then he laid her down on the bed of furs.

Reyna felt his loss when he left her to remove his own clothing. Her gaze roamed over him slowly, checking his

body for bruises or wounds sustained in the raid. She saw a few minor cuts already healing and a large bruise on his left hip. When he knelt on the pallet, she caressed his bruised hip.

He trembled beneath her touch. Her hand slid down his thigh. He grew hard as a rock. Her gaze moved to his erection; her fingers followed. He groaned. Her touch was pure torture. When her fingers slid up and down his sex, he jerked and cried out.

A wildness seized them both. Her hands were everywhere on him, caressing, grasping. His mouth devoured her, laving her breasts with his tongue, suckling her nipples. He kissed his way down her body. She writhed, grasping his head. He stroked into her cleft and caressed the sensitive petals. She raised her hips to meet his touch.

Then he lifted her legs to his shoulders and lost himself in the musky sweetness of her scent. She writhed, she cried out, arching into each flick of his tongue. Then suddenly she grasped his shoulders and pushed him away. Startled, he gazed up at her, his lips glistening with the evidence of her arousal.

"Lie down," she whispered. "I want to taste you."

Wulf's heart began to pound. Did she mean what he thought she meant? Eager to find out, he stretched out on the furs and waited, his breath locked in his chest. She gazed at him a long moment before her tongue flicked out, lapping up a dewy pearl at the tip of his sex. Wulf nearly jumped out of his skin.

Reyna reared back. "Am I hurting you?"

"Nay, do not stop."

His words spurred her on. She grew more aggressive, taking him fully into her mouth as her questing fingers sought the sacs below and squeezed them. Somehow he found the strength to watch her. Her pale hair, spread

out over his stomach and thighs made the muscles of his stomach clench. Then his thoughts shattered as she licked down the rigid length of his cock and back over the tip.

Several heartbeats later, Wulf could take no more. "Enough!" He barely got the word out. Grasping her waist, he dragged her on top of him, spread her thighs to straddle him and thrust upward, impaling her. He watched her closely. Her eyes sparkled like emeralds, full of mysterious facets and sparks in the flickering firelight.

Lust roiled through Wulf. He was hot, so very hot. He couldn't think beyond satisfying the painful demand of his loins. He withdrew nearly all the way. Reyna made a mew of protest. He thrust again, hard and deep. Her breasts, lush and swollen, rose and fell provocatively before his face. He caught a nipple in his mouth. Reyna was his; no other man deserved her. The thought that Ragnar might have the right to bed this majestic woman made him furious. Could he stop the match? Would he?

Wulf thrust wildly into her hot center, and then he reached down between them to rub her sensitive nub, already erect and throbbing. She rose and fell upon him unceasingly, taking him deep, her inner muscles caressing his rigid length.

She rode him to ecstasy. When he felt her body spasm and begin its rise to glory, he pressed his fingers hard against the tight knot of flesh between her thighs and felt her body explode beneath his touch. Her climax set off his own. They came together, their cries filling the silence around them. A long time passed before Wulf lifted her off of him. When he turned his head to look into her sweet face, her eyes were closed and she was smiling.

"What are you thinking?" he asked.

She rolled toward him. "Take me with you when you return to your farmstead."

"Do you mean that?"

She looked away, her lip caught between her teeth. "I don't know."

"Would you really leave your family after all they risked to bring you home?"

"Mayhap. Would you promise to wed me and remain faithful?"

Wulf sat up, his expression unreadable. "You want us to wed?" He held up his hand. "No, do not answer. You must know I cannot wed you."

Raw pain pierced her. "Why? Is it because I am a Dane?"

"Wedding a Dane would dishonor Astrid's memory."

Reyna's stomach clenched. "Astrid has been dead two summers and longer. You must have loved her dearly."

Now it was Wulf's turn to look away. "Astrid and I were well suited. She carried my child."

"Life goes on, Wulf. You above anyone should know that."

"I have spent two years of my life avenging her death."

" 'Tis past time to let it go."

"Will you be my mistress? We can live together in my hall and I will make sure everyone treats you with respect."

Reyna shook her head. She wanted more than Wulf offered. "No, never! I could not bear it. If Ragnar still wants me, I will wed him," she lied.

"You will not wed Ragnar," Wulf roared.

"You have no say over my life, Wulf. Wed me or let me go."

Wulf was torn. Thor's hammer, what was he to do? Could he wed a Dane after what her countrymen had done to Astrid and his aunt? How could he ever forget

what he had been told about the raid? Astrid had tried to run but the size of their babe in her belly hindered her. She had been caught, raped, and left to die in the dirt, her belly ripped open.

He violently shook the image from his mind, fearing that it would never leave him. But what was he to do about Reyna? Could he wed her with hatred for Danes still alive in his heart? True, he had become friendly with her family and had killed Hakkon, the man responsible for the raid that had killed Astrid and his aunt, but his enmity toward most Danes was as strong as ever.

"Wulf, what are you thinking?"

"I want you as my mistress. And in time, when Astrid's memory fades, mayhap I will feel different about making you my wife."

"I am in your bed, Wulf. We made love tonight, and not for the first time. Have you no guilt?"

"We give each other pleasure. There is no guilt in that."

Reyna shoved him so hard that he rolled off the narrow pallet onto the cold floor. Then she leapt to her feet and struggled into her clothes.

"Where are you going? The night is still young."

"The night is over for us, Wulf the Ruthless, and all the nights to come until you leave our shores."

"My name is Wulf the Defender, remember?"

She pulled on her cloak and rounded on him. "My family got it wrong. You are still Wulf the Ruthless to me. What you did for them was completely out of character for a Norseman."

So saying, she turned and stormed out the door. Groaning, Wulf rolled onto the pallet and pulled the furs up to his neck.

Why did Reyna have to bring up marriage? Everything was going so well between them. He had no reservations about making her his mistress. They were good

together in bed and compatible in other ways. The more he thought about never seeing Reyna again, the more he began to questions his feelings for her.

Did his hatred for Danes prevent him from wedding Reyna? Was he mad to let her go? With his mind in turmoil, Wulf surrendered to sleep.

Wulf awoke later than usual the next morning. He didn't hurry to the hall to break his fast but spent time in the steam hut first. Borg joined him and they spoke of various things that had nothing to do with Wulf and Reyna. When he finally arrived in the hall, Reyna was nowhere in sight.

The thralls set food before him and Borg. Wulf was hungry and ate with relish, waiting for Reyna to appear from her sleeping alcove. Normally she was an early riser. Maida sat down to join them.

"Is Reyna being a slug-a-bed this morning?" Wulf asked.

"Reyna left with Ragnar a short time ago to visit his family. They are expected to return by nightfall."

"Alone? When did Ragnar arrive?" Wulf asked with a calmness that belied his inner furor. What was she thinking to go off alone with Ragnar?

Maida gave him a puzzled look. "Dag is with them. Besides, Ragnar is Reyna's friend and possibly a husband-to-be. Why should she be afraid to be alone with him?"

"Has she decided to wed him, then?"

"I do not know. They spoke in private before they left, but I have no knowledge of their conversation. Nor did I refuse her permission to visit Ragnar's family. The distance is not so great that they cannot return by nightfall."

Wulf glanced out the window. "The weather looks threatening."

Maida shrugged. "Reyna and Dag will be welcome to

spend the night in Ragnar's hall. She is well loved by his family."

"Where is Ragnar's farmstead located?"

Borg sent Wulf an assessing look, but Maida apparently saw no harm in divulging that information.

"Ragnar's farmstead lies but a short distance to the west. About a two-hour walk from here."

Wulf nodded, finished his breakfast and rose. "I am going hunting."

"I planned to spend the day in the smokehouse, else I would accompany you," Borg said.

Wulf left the hall and went directly to the stillroom for his weapons. He strapped on a sword, pushed a battle-axe beneath his belt, pulled a wolf pelt over his shoulders for added warmth and picked up his spear. Once he was armed for whatever danger he might encounter, he left the stillroom and headed west at a brisk pace. If he were lucky, he would catch up with Reyna.

Reyna had no idea why she had agreed to accompany Ragnar to his hall. She supposed she was angry enough at Wulf to want to spite him. How dare Wulf refuse to wed her after leading her to believe he cared for her! Did he think so little of her that he believed he could bed her and leave her without a care for her feelings?

Worse yet, he had asked her to be his mistress. What gall! What arrogance! Better she wed Ragnar, she thought, than become mistress to a man who could bed her with impunity but refuse to wed her because she was a Dane.

They hadn't walked far when Dag stepped into a rabbit hole that had been covered with a fresh layer of snow. He fell heavily to the ground, twisting his ankle.

Reyna dropped to her knees beside him. "How badly are you hurt, Dag?"

Dag shrugged. " 'Tis naught but a turned ankle."

"Shall I find you a sturdy limb to lean upon?" Ragnar asked.

Reyna helped him to his feet. "Aye, that would be helpful."

Ragnar hurried off while Dag tested his ankle. "Try to put weight on it," Reyna said.

Dag's ankle refused to hold him up. Apparently the injury was more serious than he'd thought.

"Sit on that fallen log and remove your boot so I can look at it," Reyna said.

Dag shook his head. "Not a good idea, Reyna. If I take off my boot, I might not be able to put it back on and my foot will freeze."

Ragnar returned with a sturdy limb. "This should do," he said.

"Since our farmstead is closer than Ragnar's, we should return home," Reyna advised. "I need to take care of that ankle."

Supported by the limb, Dag found he could stand and even walk, albeit slowly. "I am capable of hobbling home, no need for you to return. Mother can take care of me without your help." He glanced at Ragnar. "I trust Ragnar to see you safely to his hall."

"I will protect Reyna," Ragnar bragged. "Return home, Dag. You look like you are in pain."

"I cannot let you return home alone, Dag," Reyna protested.

"I am a warrior, Reyna, armed and capable of defending myself. Go with Ragnar. You two have a great deal to talk about."

With a jaunty wave of his hand, Dag limped off in the direction from which they'd come.

Frowning, Reyna said, "I do not like it."

"There is naught to fear, Reyna. Hakkon is dead; he cannot hurt you or your family."

Reluctantly Reyna turned and trudged after Ragnar. Ragnar's land was more than an hour away on the shores of a branch of Limfjorden Fjord.

As they continued along, making their way across the wet snow, Reyna felt a strange prickling sensation on the back of her neck. Were they being watched? Glancing about, she saw nothing to arouse suspicion. The trees bordering the path they followed were bare of leaves and the shrubbery withered.

"Ragnar," Reyna began, "I have a strange feeling that we are being watched."

Ragnar looked around him. "There is naught to be frightened of, Reyna. I am glad you decided to accompany me instead of returning with Dag. This gives us a chance to be alone. I have something to ask you."

Reyna feared she knew what was coming, but she had no idea what she would say if Ragnar asked her to wed him. She had no reason to reject him, not after Wulf had tossed her aside. Wulf didn't want her because she was a Dane. It was just as well, she told herself, for she couldn't bear to be with a man whose mind was consumed with his dead wife.

"I know we parted on less than cordial terms, but I have come to see the error of my ways. Wed me, Reyna. Wed me and come to live with me. My parents adore you and so do I."

Why not? Reyna thought. Wulf didn't want her and she wanted a home of her own and children. The sudden thought occurred to her that she might already be carrying Wulf's child. She touched her stomach beneath her cloak. If she were increasing, the babe would need a father. Was Ragnar the right man?

"Reyna, say you will wed me."

"I will think about it."

Ragnar grasped her shoulders, his fingers digging

through her cloak into her soft flesh. " 'Tis the Norseman, I knew it!"

"Ragnar, I . . ." The words died in her throat when she saw several armed men materialize from behind some nearby trees.

Ragnar noticed where she was looking and spun around. To his credit, he drew his sword, preparing to defend himself and Reyna. "Norsemen! Run, Reyna!" he cried.

One of the men stepped forward and removed his helmet, revealing himself to them. "Olaf!" Reyna exclaimed.

"Aye, Reyna, I have come for my brother. Where is he?"

"You know this Norseman?" Ragnar bit out.

"Aye, 'tis Olaf, Wulf's younger brother. Put your sword away, Olaf will not hurt us."

Wulf was slogging through the snow when he saw Dag limping toward him. His heart thudded painfully in his chest. Had something happened to Reyna? Dag saw him and waved. Wulf ran to meet him.

"Are you injured? What happened? Is Reyna all right?"

"Reyna is fine, Wulf. I stepped into a rabbit hole and injured my ankle. Since we had traveled but a short distance from home, I decided to turn back. Reyna is safe with Ragnar."

"I am not sure about that, Dag. Can you manage on your own?"

"Aye, 'tis not far."

"Then I shall make sure Reyna reaches her destination safely."

"Wulf, Reyna is in no . . ." He might have been talking to the wind, for Wulf had already sprinted off. Dag continued his slow journey home.

They cannot be far, Wulf thought as he followed footprints in the snow. He came to an abrupt halt when he

heard voices up ahead. He sensed danger and un-
sheathed his sword. He didn't know what or who was
ahead, but he would fight to the death to protect Reyna.
Taking cover behind a thick tree trunk, Wulf crept from
tree to tree until he came close enough to make out
what was happening.

The first thing he saw was Ragnar, sword drawn, taking a fighting stance. Then he saw Reyna, who didn't
seem frightened in the least. Gazing beyond them to the
enemy, Wulf nearly lost the ability to speak when he recognized his brother Olaf and the crew from his dragonship standing behind him.

Wulf stepped out from behind a tree, calling Olaf's
name. "Olaf, what do you do here?"

Olaf crouched and whipped around, smiling widely
when he saw Wulf approaching him. Relaxing his stance,
he waited for Wulf to reach him. Then they came together,
clasping arms and patting each other on the back.

"I am here to rescue you, brother," Olaf replied.

Chapter Thirteen

"Have you naught to say to me after I've come all this way to save your worthless hide?" Olaf chided.

"I cannot believe you are here."

Finally their arms fell away and they merely stared at each other.

"You are looking well," Olaf said. "Captivity must agree with you."

Reyna moved to join them. "Wulf is no longer a captive. My family planned to return him to his home in the spring."

Olaf's eyebrows shot up. "How did that come about?"

"Wulf defended our farmstead against invaders. His courage earned him a new name and his freedom. He is now known as Wulf the Defender."

"You have done well for yourself, brother," Olaf praised.

"While you," Wulf charged, "risked your life and those of our friends by crossing the sea during this uncertain time of year."

Olaf shrugged. "It was either me or Hagar and he was needed at home. I left before Hagar could stop me. One of us had to rescue you, and I preferred it to be me."

Wulf's attention sharpened. "Something is amiss at home. What is it?"

Olaf glanced at him, then looked away. " 'Tis mother; she is unwell." His gaze settled on Reyna. "There is no one in our land with Reyna's healing skills."

"What is wrong with Thora?" Reyna asked.

"We do not know. She coughs and has grown weak and listless. I hoped to rescue you and bring Reyna home with us."

Reyna stiffened. "How did you intend to convince me to return to your farmstead?"

Olaf's face reddened. "I was prepared to use force, if necessary."

"Abduction would not have worked, Olaf. I am with my family again after a long absence; I would not have gone with you willingly, and my brothers would have fought to the death to keep me safe."

Olaf sighed. "I anticipated that but I had to try."

Reyna looked up as a snowflake hit her forehead. The sky had darkened and the wind had risen. "A storm is brewing. We should return to the farmstead. My family will provide food and shelter for you and your warriors until the weather allows you to return to your homeland."

"How did you know where to find me?" Wulf asked. "Anyone could have taken me."

"We searched for you everywhere. If some of the villagers had not seen a Dane ship in the fjord, we would not have figured it out. I still was not sure until we saw Reyna."

"Is your dragonship secured?" Wulf asked. "We will need it for the return voyage across the sea."

"We found a landing in a nearby fjord. Luckily it wasn't frozen over. We stopped at a village first and asked directions to Jarl Harald's farmstead. We made it known that we were friendly. Our trading expeditions served us well for we speak the Dane language well enough to make ourselves understood."

"Summon your men and follow me," Reyna said. "The weather worsens."

Ragnar had simply stood by and listened during the conversation. Frowning, he asked, "Are you sure you wish to bring Norse warriors into your home, Reyna?"

"I vouch for my brother and his crew," Wulf snarled. "We do not bite the hand that feeds us."

"Do you trust the Norseman's word, Reyna?" Ragnar continued, ignoring Wulf.

Reyna gazed up at Wulf, his forthright gaze meeting hers. "I trust Wulf. If he vows there will be no trouble, I believe him."

"Then I had best return to my farmstead before the weather closes in." He turned and strode off.

"We should leave too," Reyna said as she noted the snow swirling around them. "If this develops into a full-blown blizzard, finding our way home will become extremely difficult."

Holding the hood of her fur cloak down with her gloved hands, Reyna trudged through the snow toward the farmstead. Wulf fell into step beside her while Olaf and the others followed.

By the time they reached the farmstead, the hall was barely visible through the heavy curtain of snow. Reyna's feet and hands were nearly numb and her nose had turned red. She led the large group to the front door, opened it and motioned everyone inside.

Everyone in the hall froze in place as more than a dozen Norsemen filed through the door. Harald, Dag and Borg reached for their swords. The Norsemen looked to Wulf for direction.

"Hold!" Wulf said, striding forth. "My countrymen are no threat to you, Jarl Harald." He pulled Olaf forward. "This intrepid fool is my brother, Olaf, who ventured across the sea to rescue me. The rest of these

equally foolish Norsemen blindly followed my brother into danger. We wish you no harm. But now that they are here, they beg your hospitality until such a time that we can return home together."

Harald strode forward to greet the unexpected visitors. "I have to agree with Wulf the Defender. You are foolish men who risked your lives for naught. We would have returned Wulf to his home when the weather permitted. But you are all welcome to remain until you are ready to journey across the sea to your homeland. Olaf can stay with Wulf in the stillroom and the others can bed down on benches and the floor. We have plenty of fur pelts to go around."

He turned to his wife, who had come up to join him. "As for food, I will let my wife decide if our winter stores are sufficient to feed everyone."

"We have food aplenty, husband," Maida offered. "The harvest was good this year and the Norsemen can hunt for meat when the need arises."

"Thank you," Olaf replied. "I am happy my brother proved himself worthy of freedom, for he is needed at home. Our mother is ill and a large part of her illness stems from worry over Wulf's disappearance."

Reyna looked away. She felt guilty for refusing to return to treat Thora, but this was her home. This was where she intended to stay.

It was settled, then. The Norsemen huddled around the central hearth to soak up the warmth, and later sat down to a hearty meal, their first hot food since they'd left their homeland. After, one of the Norseman, a talented storyteller, enthralled everyone with his sagas of ancient battles. It was full dark when the visitors were provided with sleeping furs and Wulf and Olaf headed out to Wulf's sleeping hut.

"How is it that you were given your own sleeping space?" Olaf asked once they entered the small hut.

Wulf immediately walked to the dying fire and fed wood onto the grate. "This is Reyna's stillroom, as you can see by the herbs hanging from the ceiling to dry. I asked for permission to use it as private sleeping quarters. Later, I was freed for helping to defeat the attack on Harald's farmstead. During the battle I learned that the attack was led by the Dane who raided our farmstead, the same one who took the lives of Astrid and our aunt."

"You killed the bastard, I hope."

"Indeed I did." He hesitated, then said, "Reyna saved my life during that battle."

"Sounds like you've been leading an active life in the land of the Danes. I hope you have no qualms about returning home with us."

Reyna's face rose up before Wulf. He shook her image away. "No qualms whatsoever, brother. Tell me about our mother. Is she truly as ill as you say?"

"Aye, but I am sure that seeing you again will revive her flagging spirits somewhat. She began to fail shortly after you and Reyna disappeared. She started coughing and her condition only grows worse. We need to convince Reyna to return home with us."

Wulf sat heavily on a bench. "Reyna has only just been reunited with her family, Olaf. She has a fiancé waiting to wed her. Good luck convincing her."

Olaf's shoulders stiffened. "Then we must kidnap her. Bringing Reyna to the farmstead is imperative if we wish to save our mother."

Wulf shook his head. "I cannot allow you to do that, brother. Harald has been good to me. I will not betray his trust in such a manner. If Reyna returns with us, she must do so willingly."

"That will never happen." Olaf rested his head in his hands. "I'm tired. 'Twas a difficult journey across the sea."

"You will find sleeping furs in yonder cupboard. Take what you need and make your bed before the fire. Tomorrow we will visit the steam hut if we can wade through the snow to reach the door."

Wading through the snow was exactly what they had to do the following morning to find the steam hut. And it was still snowing.

"It looks like we're going to be stranded here for a while," Wulf remarked. "At least you will be fed and have a warm bed until the weather breaks."

"I am grateful the weather held until we reached land," Olaf said. "Thor was looking out for us."

"The gods favor children and fools," Wulf muttered.

The two brothers spent an hour in the steam hut, running out naked into the snow once, then returning posthaste. Invigorated, both men dressed and walked to the hall to break their fast.

Men were milling around everywhere in the hall. Wulf wondered how the family was coping with the crowded conditions. He looked around for Reyna and saw her near the hearth, conversing with her mother. She must have felt him looking at her for she turned her head in his direction. Their gazes met, clung, and then Reyna quickly looked away.

"Is Reyna angry with you?" Olaf asked.

Wulf shrugged. "With Reyna 'tis hard to tell."

"She is coming this way," Olaf whispered. "I'll make myself scarce while you make peace with her. Do not forget, brother, we need her skills. Do your best to convince her to return home with us."

Olaf wandered off toward a group of Norsemen as

Reyna joined Wulf. "Were you and your brother talking about me?" Reyna asked.

"Olaf was commenting on your father's generosity. It was good of him to extend his hospitality to my countrymen. Not all Danes would welcome Norsemen into their home."

"My father is a good-hearted man. Do not betray his trust."

"I would not do that," Wulf said, looking directly into Reyna's eyes.

She looked away first. "The thralls are setting food out on the tables. Come break your fast with us."

The food was plentiful and hearty. Wulf ate his fill and joined a group of men who had volunteered to do chores and hunt. Hindered by falling snow, the hunting party soon returned to the hall to while away the time dicing and spinning tales.

Wulf was rarely alone with Reyna during the following weeks and he missed the closeness they had once shared. Watching her move about the hall made him go hard with wanting. Her lithe body held an attraction for him he had felt for no other woman, not even Astrid, whom he had loved dearly. How could he leave Reyna behind when he departed?

The cold and snow continued unabated, trapping too many people in one place. Sometimes tempers grew short and the warriors would bicker among themselves. Chores still needed to be performed and animals had to be fed, breaking up the monotony of white days and black nights.

Weeks turned into months as the winter slowly passed by. Finally, a break in the weather sent excitement through the hall. The warriors decided it was a perfect day for hunting and divided into two groups, each setting out in a different direction.

Reyna watched the warriors leave, with Dag and Borg leading one group and her father leading the other. When she saw Wulf join Harald's group, she decided to visit the stillroom to process some of the herbs her mother had gathered last summer before she had arrived.

Trudging through the snow, Reyna entered the stillroom, removed her outer clothing and began gathering bunches of herbs hanging from a line strung across the low ceiling. Suddenly the door opened and a cold breeze swept into the room. Reyna spun around and saw Wulf standing in the doorway, his shoulders blocking out the light. He stepped inside and closed the door.

"What are you doing here? I thought you went hunting."

Wulf glanced toward his pallet, where a wicked-looking blade rested on the furs. "I left my hunting knife and returned to retrieve it. What are *you* doing here?"

"I decided to work in the stillroom today. Some of the herbs are ready to be processed."

Wulf removed his outer wear, tossing the heavy furs on a nearby bench. "I am glad to find you alone. Privacy is hard to come by in the crowded hall."

"I did not know we needed to be alone," Reyna shot back.

"Do you still intend to wed Ragnar?"

"Naught has changed my mind since last we spoke. If you recall, you refused to—"

Before she could finish, he hauled her to him, clamping her against the hard length of his body and lowering his mouth to hers. She squirmed in his arms, but he held the back of her head firmly in his large palm so she could not turn away. Then, to her mortification, she did not want to turn away. As always, Wulf's kisses made her knees tremble and she clung to him, aware of the

stimulating scent of aroused warrior and the compelling taste of his mouth.

His mouth moved over hers, hard, hungry and desperate. She felt utterly consumed by him, appalled by his easy seduction of her. Had she no pride? When would she learn the handsome Norseman wanted only one thing from her? He did not want a Dane for a wife; he wanted a bed slave.

She pushed against his massive chest. "No, Wulf, I cannot let you do this to me again."

"You want this, Reyna. Your eyes and body do not lie."

"I am female and human, Wulf. No flesh and blood woman could resist your kisses. But that doesn't make it right."

Wulf's eyes devoured her, his hunger for her ravenous. "No matter how long and loud you protest, you are mine, Reyna. You will never wed Ragnar."

"You are wrong, Wulf. Ragnar is my last chance for a husband and family. No other man will want me, not after all that has happened to me."

Wulf's silver eyes darkened as he lowered his head and claimed her mouth. He kissed her like a man starved for the sweet taste of her, his tongue slipping into her mouth to explore her more fully. He groaned into her mouth. He had been denied this pleasure far too long. He kissed her until her breath seized and his head began to spin with heady pleasure. At length he broke off the kiss and gazed into her eyes.

"Return with me to my homeland, Reyna."

She lowered her eyes. "I cannot do that. I will be neither your thrall nor your bed slave."

"You will be treated as one of the family; why can that not be enough for you?" His eyes blazed into hers. "My mother needs you, Reyna."

"Your mother needs me, but you do not," Reyna charged.

"I do need you. We can be . . ." he searched for a word and seized on the only one that came to him, "partners."

"Partner is a pretty word, Wulf, but not as pretty as wife. Ragnar does me honor by asking me to be his wife."

"You know my feelings. Wedding a Dane would dishonor the memory of Astrid and my unborn child."

"How would bedding me without marrying me be a more honorable choice? Your wife is dead. You cannot live in the past forever."

"I do not want to argue with you, Reyna; I want to make love to you. This may be our only chance to be alone before I leave, unless you change your mind and accompany me."

Reyna was torn. She had missed the closeness she had shared with Wulf these past weeks. Soon he would be leaving and she would never see him again. She glared at him. A man as stubborn as Wulf did not deserve her love. His wife had been dead two years and more. Did he intend to mourn Astrid the rest of his life? Wulf was a man of mysterious contradictions. He wanted to be with her even though vengeance still filled his heart and mind.

"I am staying with my family, Wulf. Even if I do not wed Ragnar, I will remain here, where I belong. You should leave if you wish to catch up with your hunting party."

Reyna thought he was doing as she asked when he turned and headed for the door. But instead of leaving, he bolted the door and began shedding his clothing.

"What are you doing?" Reyna exclaimed.

He reached for her and pulled her against him.

"This," he murmured, seconds before he claimed her mouth.

The kiss stirred Reyna clear down to her toes. The tingling began where their mouths were joined and traveled down, down, down. This was madness. She had no resistance where Wulf was concerned. His will took over, molding her to his needs, his desires, which in truth were her wants, her desires. Freya knew she had tried to resist, but this stubborn warrior owned her soul.

Wulf felt Reyna stir in his arms, felt her mouth soften and her body cling sweetly to his. Her response seemed to unleash a caged beast inside him. He growled low in his throat and began savaging her mouth. After several long, wild kisses, his control snapped and he began tearing at the ties on her tunic and undertunic.

"Wulf, I did not say . . ."

"You do not need to," Wulf growled. "Your body tells me all I need to know."

He stripped her to her linen shift. The sight of her pink nipples pushing against the flimsy material made his cock jerk and stiffen. If he didn't have her soon, he feared he would explode. Sliding his fingers into her hair, he cupped her head to hold it in place and plied her mouth with deep, consuming kisses that made her body tremble and her mind reel.

Unable to resist her warrior lover, Reyna opened her lips to take his tongue deep into her mouth. Pushing her fingers into the silk of his sun-streaked hair, she slid her hands downward over his cheeks in a gentle caress. Groaning, Wulf grasped the soft globes of her bottom and pulled her against his hardening body, making her aware of the thick ridge of his erection. The fever inside her grew as her hands grasped his remaining clothing, pulling at the fabric in order to leave him naked and accessible to her hands and mouth.

Tightening his hold on her, Wulf hoisted her higher, walked her to his pallet, tossed aside his hunting knife and laid her down on the furs. Before joining her, he stripped naked, strode to the hearth and built up the fire. His groin stiffened painfully when he noticed her gaze roaming greedily over his bare flanks as he bent to his task.

A low growl rumbled in his throat as he stalked back to her. "You drive me mad, woman." Then he joined her in the furs.

The wildness inside Wulf could only be sated in one way. He needed to be inside Reyna and it had to be now. "You have too many clothes on," he muttered in a voice roughened with need.

Lifting the hem of her shift, he pulled it over her head and tossed it aside. Her thick, woolen stockings and boots followed quickly. Reaching for her, he caught her hips in his big hands and lifted her astride him. With an impatient groan, he held her in place and entered her in one strong thrust.

Reyna marveled at the fullness inside her as she pushed herself down, taking even more of him, her body instantly wet and ready for his possession. They moved together as one, their hunger for each other unstoppable and urgent. She ground her loins downward, rocking against him in wild abandon as he held her hips steady for his deep penetration.

Reyna hadn't realized how much she had missed Wulf, how desperately she still wanted him. Needed him. Her thoughts skittered away as Wulf raised his head, took her nipple into his mouth and suckled her, first one breast and then the other. She felt the pulling sensation clear down to her womb. Blood pounded in her temples, building to a climax as fierce heat danced through her. Moments later, violent tremors ripped her apart.

His fingers digging into her thighs, Wulf drove fiercely upward, raw, frantic sounds echoing from within his chest as he raced toward his own climax. She heard him shout her name as he gave up his seed. Moments later she collapsed against his chest, aware of the harsh rasp of his breath mingling with hers.

Reyna made no move to climb off him since she had no idea what to say to this forceful warrior who held her heart even though he did not want it. Trying to deny him what they both wanted had been a waste of time.

"When will you tell your father that you are journeying to my homeland with me?" Wulf asked in a voice still breathless from his exertions.

Reyna reared up. "What makes you think I am leaving?"

"How can you deny that you want to leave after what just took place here?"

"I shall not be your bed slave, Wulf. Never again will I be a man's thrall."

Wulf lifted her off of him. "I did not ask you to be my thrall. You will become our healer and will be treated as one of the family."

"So you said before. Will you expect me to warm your bed?"

"Is that not what we both want?"

Reyna shook her head. "You are a stubborn man, Wulf. Hakkon is long dead. Why are you still seeking vengeance for your wife's death? Why can you not let that loss go and get on with your life? If you opened your eyes, you would see what is in front of you."

Wulf frowned. "What is that supposed to mean?"

"If you cannot figure it out for yourself, I am not going to tell you. You are neither dense nor stupid. What is it that keeps you from seeing me as anything but a thrall or bed warmer?"

Wulf looked perplexed. "I see you as a healer and a warrior woman, a beautiful Valkyrie."

Reyna ground her teeth in frustration. "Do you see me as your wife?"

Wulf's silence spoke volumes.

Reyna rose and searched for her clothing, feeling suddenly cold. "You should rejoin the hunting party. They will wonder what happened to you."

Wulf gained his feet and began dressing. "I won't be missed."

They dressed in silence. Reyna finished first and waited for Wulf to retrieve his hunting knife and leave.

Wulf walked to the door, stopped and looked back at her. "I won't take no for an answer, Reyna. You heard Olaf. My mother needs your skills and I need . . ." The words stuck in his throat.

Reyna hardened her heart. "Good-bye, Wulf. I doubt we will be alone again before you and your countrymen leave. Already the ice is melting on the fjord and the air holds a promise of spring."

After a long, hard look, Wulf opened the door and stormed out. Reyna's body went limp. How long could a man hold a grudge? How long would vengeance rule his life? Though she would miss Wulf desperately, she would not leave her family for an uncertain future with a man who still considered her the enemy.

Reyna was helping the women prepare the evening meal when Wulf and the hunters returned. Luck had been with them. They had bagged an assortment of rabbits along with several deer. The hides and meat would be welcome during the waning days of winter.

Reyna searched out Wulf among the men, found him and quickly looked away when their eyes met. That was the last time Reyna sought Wulf's attention until he ap-

proached her one day a few weeks later. "The ice is melting on the fjord," he announced. "Olaf and I will be leaving soon."

Reyna had been aware of the changing weather for some time. The air wasn't as harsh, and blades of green were pushing up through the bare spots in the ground. She had known this day was coming but had tried not to think about it. Once Wulf left she would never see him again.

"It is time to pack your things," Wulf continued.

"How many times must I tell you I am not going anywhere with you," Reyna snorted. "I wish you a safe journey, Wulf."

Though Wulf said nothing more, Reyna liked neither the possessive look in his silver eyes nor the oblique smile curving his lips. Whatever he planned wasn't going to happen, she vowed. She was smart enough to be wary of the determined Norseman's tricks.

"We shall see, Reyna," Wulf replied as he stalked off.

The next few days fled in a flurry of activity. Most of the Norsemen were off readying their dragonship while Maida and the thralls prepared food for their voyage. Reyna tried not to dwell on Wulf's leaving. Though she knew she would miss him, she refused to return to his farmstead on his terms. It would happen on her terms or not at all.

Reyna avoided Wulf until the morning he told her father they would be leaving in a few hours. All the Norsemen had gathered around her parents and brothers, thanking them for their hospitality and bidding them farewell. Reyna remained in the background, pretending indifference while all the time her heart was breaking.

She watched warily when Wulf approached her father and said, "Reyna is coming with me."

Both her parents spun around to look at her. "Is that true, Reyna?" Maida asked. "Why did you not say anything to us about your intention to leave?"

Reyna strode toward Wulf, her chin jutting in open defiance. She didn't stop until they stood nose to nose. "Wulf is mistaken, Mother. I am going nowhere with him. This is where I belong."

Hands on hips, legs spread wide, Wulf glared down at her. "I beg to differ. You are coming with me."

Harald stepped forward and pulled Reyna behind him. "My daughter does not wish to go with you. Though I appreciate everything you have done for my family, you cannot take Reyna without her consent."

Reyna glanced around her. All the Norsemen, including Olaf, were poised with their hands on their swords. Fear snaked through Reyna. Her family was badly outnumbered should a fight ensue. Would Wulf really go so far?

Harald did not back down from his confrontational stance despite the odds against him. "Why do you think my daughter should leave her home?"

Wulf raised his eyes to Reyna and said, "She could be carrying my child."

Both Borg and Dag, who had come up to flank their father, drew their swords.

"Hold!" Harald said. "I wish to hear what Reyna has to say about this. Look at me, daughter. Is what Wulf claims possible?"

"I . . ."

"Speak the truth, Reyna," Wulf warned. "If you carry my child, it is my right to raise him."

Reyna had no idea whether or not she was carrying Wulf's babe. It was too early to know. It was possible, she supposed, but unlikely. She hadn't conceived before, so why would she now?

"Well, Reyna," Harald prodded. "What say you?"

" 'Tis possible but highly unlikely," Reyna admitted.

Harald's penetrating gaze returned to Wulf. "If you have been enjoying my daughter's favors, Wulf the Defender, you shall wed her here, before her family."

"Father, no!" Reyna protested. "Wulf does not wish to wed me."

"If Wulf has bedded you, 'tis best that you wed him. A man should raise his son."

"But I am not . . ."

"But you could be," Wulf interrupted.

Reyna's mouth snapped shut. This was a tactic she hadn't counted on. "Father, Wulf does not want to wed me. He still blames our people for killing his wife. If he says he will wed me, he lies. He merely needs my skills to heal his mother."

Reyna didn't know why she was protesting so loudly. She truly wanted to be Wulf's wife, but not under these circumstances. She couldn't understand why he was insisting so vigorously when he had refused to wed her time and again. She glanced at Wulf. His mouth was set, his fists clenched at his sides.

Wulf glanced at the Norsemen flanking him with weapons at the ready. "I could take Reyna by force if I wished to."

"But you will not," Harald replied. "You are too honorable to kill your host."

Wulf grimaced. Harald was correct. He glanced at Reyna, saw her smug expression and realized she was expecting him to refuse to wed her. She was wrong.

"Well, Wulf the Defender, what say you?" Harald asked.

He straightened to his full height. "I, Wulf the Defender, vow before you and my countrymen that I take Reyna the Dane as my wife."

" 'Tis done, then," Harald said.

"What?" Reyna exclaimed. "But you do not want to wed me."

"I just said I did, did I not?"

"Then allow me to state my terms before I agree to this match," Reyna said, folding her arms across her chest.

"You have terms?" Wulf growled.

"Aye, I do. If I am not increasing, you must agree to return me to my family if that is what I wish."

"That sounds fair," Borg said. "In fact, we will visit Wulf's farmstead when we set out on our trading voyages in the summer to see if all is well with her. If she wishes it, we will take her home. Is that agreeable, Wulf the Defender?"

"I agree," Wulf said with supreme arrogance. If Reyna wasn't with child now, she would be soon. And his mother would have a skilled healer to cure her. The only drawback was having a Dane for a wife. But for his mother's sake, he would make the sacrifice.

Chapter Fourteen

Luck was with the Norsemen. A brisk wind at their backs made rowing unnecessary as Wulf steered the dragonship across the choppy sea. The men had erected a shelter on the ship to protect Reyna from the worst of the elements and her parents had provided them with fur pelts to keep them warm and food to eat during the journey.

Having departed from the narrowest point between the two countries, the longboat, propelled by the wind, made the journey in four days. Though somewhat uncomfortable, Reyna remained cozy and protected inside the shelter. She had seen blessed little of Wulf during the sea voyage. She was still angry with him for tricking her into returning to his homeland and had refused to speak to him when he made the attempt.

It wasn't as if Reyna didn't want to help Thora; she did. It was the underhanded way Wulf got her father to agree to her leaving that bothered her. Wulf had deliberately lied about wanting her for his wife. She knew without a doubt that Wulf had wed her only to help his mother and please her father. What kind of marriage was that?

If she wasn't breeding, and Reyna felt certain she wasn't, she would hold Wulf to his promise to allow her

to return to her parents' farmstead. After she nursed Thora back to health, she would wait for her brothers to arrive, divorce Wulf and return home. Remaining unwed was preferable to loving a man who could not return her love.

Reyna was still brooding over Wulf's contrariness when she heard someone yell, "Land ahead."

She peeked out from her shelter, saw land in the distance and joined Olaf at the railing. "Have we reached your homeland?" Reyna asked.

"Aye, but we still have a distance to go. We will follow the shore until we reach Boknafjord. After that, 'tis only a matter of sailing up the fjord to our farmstead."

Olaf walked away when Wulf arrived. Wulf stared at her, thinking she looked like a Viking queen with her hair braided and wrapped around her head like a crown; a pale gold halo reflecting the afternoon sun. Lust sucked the breath out of him, and his loins grew heavy at the sight of her. It had been weeks since he and Reyna had made love. He couldn't wait to have her in his hall and in his bed.

"We will be home soon," he said.

"*You* will be home soon," Reyna corrected. "My home is across the sea."

Wulf shrugged. "My homeland is now your home."

Reyna gave a snort of disgust. "Admit it, Wulf, you wed me for your mother's sake. You lied to my father about wanting me for your wife."

Wulf's silver eyes narrowed dangerously as he leaned in toward her. "I do want you, not just for my mother but for myself."

Hands on shapely hips, Reyna held her ground against the impressive warrior. "What happens after I cure your mother and we learn I am not carrying your child? Will you still want me?"

The intensity of Wulf's gaze sent shivers racing down her spine.

"I will always *want* you; that was never in doubt."

Reyna forged on. "Aye, but will you honor our vows?"

"I stand by my word."

"Even if being married to a Dane repulses you?" Reyna charged. "Remember, Wulf the Defender, if I am not breeding, I intend to return to my own country with my brothers when they visit in the summer."

Wulf laughed. "You will be breeding long before your brothers arrive." Turning, he walked away.

Reyna frowned at his departing back. Why didn't Wulf understand what she wanted from him? His vow meant naught to her without his love. Even as Wulf's wife she would forever wonder if a thrall or freewoman or new captive would capture his interest next. Being his wife would be meaningless without his esteem and love.

As the dragonship hugged the coast, Reyna could see patches of green amidst the melting snow, a sure harbinger of spring. Wulf steered the dragonship into Boknafjord, sailing around patches of ice that hadn't yet melted. They pulled up to shore for the night and resumed the journey the following morning.

Reyna stood at the railing, watching for familiar landmarks. When they passed the village of Sauda, nestled on the bank of the fjord, she recognized it immediately.

"It won't be long now," Olaf said as he joined her. "Hagar will be frantic with worry after our long absence. 'Tis doubtful he expected me to reach the land of the Danes much less find Wulf and return him to the bosom of our family. Bringing you with us is an unexpected bonus."

"I hope we find your mother well on the way to recovery when we arrive," Reyna said.

"If not, I am sure you will heal her with the herbs and cures your mother sent along with us."

Reyna glanced at the medicinal chest beneath her shelter, filled with everything her mother thought she might need to treat whatever ills were visited upon Wulf's family. "I pray my skills are sufficient."

"Your skills are considerable," Wulf said as he came up to join them.

Reyna started at the sound of his voice. "I remember the last time I arrived at your farmstead," she reminisced. She glared at him. "It was not a happy occasion, if you recall."

Olaf glanced between the two antagonists and walked away.

"You endeared yourself to my family and to me," Wulf murmured in her ear. "We all grew fond of you."

She glared up at him. "Fond? Fond? Forgive me for wanting more from you, Wulf."

Turning on her heel, she entered her shelter and pulled the curtain across the opening. She didn't reappear until she heard cries of shock and anger. She shoved aside the curtain and rushed out on deck. One look at Wulf and Olaf told her something unexpected was causing havoc among the crew.

"What is it? What's happened?" Reyna cried.

Wulf pointed toward the landing. "There is a foreign longboat beached where only our dragonships should be. We know not whether they are friend or foe."

"Foe," Olaf said through clenched teeth. "Finn raiders by the look of their longboat. Something is amiss."

Immediately the Norsemen took their places on the benches, grabbed up the oars and rowed toward the shore. They beached the dragonship beside the longboat.

Wulf lifted Reyna from the dragonship and set her down on the ground. "Stay here until I return for you. I

don't know what mayhem we will find . . ." His sentence fell off at a shout from Olaf.

"Listen!" Olaf exclaimed, placing a constraining hand on Wulf's arm. "Do you hear that?"

The blood froze in Wulf's veins when he heard the familiar sounds of a battle being waged. The clash of swords and battle-axes, voices raised in rage and cries of pain all mingled to provide an ugly picture of what was taking place at the farmstead.

"To arms!" Wulf shouted as he raised his sword and battle-axe, and prepared to rush to his family's defense.

"Wait!" Reyna cried. "If I'm to remain here, give me a sword or dagger, something with which to defend myself."

"Find Reyna a sword," Wulf ordered Olaf moments before he raced off toward the farmstead.

Olaf returned to the dragonship, pulled out a sword from under a canvas and thrust it into Reyna's hands before running off to join his comrades.

Wulf's fear escalated when he thought of the too few warriors left to defend the farmstead; Hagar and Eric and a handful of kraals. Without sufficient warning, they would be badly outnumbered and their women in danger.

The Norsemen burst upon a scene of utter chaos. One glance told Wulf that a few kraals had indeed joined the fight to repel the raiders but not in sufficient numbers to make a difference against the murderous horde of marauding Finns bent on gaining plunder and slaves.

Wulf let out a Viking war cry loud enough to pierce the sounds of battle then waded into the fray, wielding a sword in one hand and battle-axe in the other.

Reyna paced the shore, listening to the din of battle and wondering what was taking place. Remaining behind

while Wulf and the others fought for their lives was not to her liking. She waited for as long as she could then, clutching her sword, she advanced resolutely toward the farmstead.

Her first glimpse of the battle raging violently outside the hall revealed just how desperately the returning Norsemen were needed. A second glance revealed Helga and Inga, true Norsewomen to the core, standing shoulder to shoulder near the front entrance of the hall, armed and ready to defend their home against enemy raiders.

Eric appeared to have suffered a sword cut to his arm and blood was streaming down Hagar's temple from a head wound. But from the look of the Finns, they appeared to have fared no better. Now, with the returning Norsemen joining in the fray, the tide seemed to be turning.

Reyna kept her distance, waiting to see where or if her sword arm was needed. After a few moments of observing from the sidelines, she decided to lend her help to Helga and Inga. But as she made her way around the perimeter of the battlefield, she saw two Finns converge on Wulf, one from the front and one from behind. Wulf immediately reacted to the frontal attack.

Reyna, however, saw what Wulf did not. She screamed his name, but could scarcely hear her own voice above the din of battle. Without a thought for her own safety, Reyna ducked and dodged swords and battle-axes to reach Wulf before it was too late. Then, horrors of all horrors, just as Wulf handily dispatched his opponent, the warrior behind him thrust his sword into Wulf's back. Wulf staggered a few steps, then spiraled to the ground.

"Reyna," he gasped, raising himself slightly when he saw her leap out of nowhere, lift her sword over his attacker's head and bring it down.

Outrage lent strength to Reyna's arms as she swung her sword at the cowardly Finn raider and struck him down with one vicious slice. Ignoring the bleeding Finn at her feet, Reyna stepped over him and dropped to her knees beside Wulf. He met her concerned gaze before his eyes glazed over and his head dropped down on the hard ground. Her fear for Wulf's life escalated when Reyna saw the blood pooling beneath him. Then Hagar and Olaf were beside her, lifting Wulf between them and dragging him into the hall.

The Norsemen had broken the back of the raid. Outnumbered and reeling in defeat, the Finns began retreating toward the fjord and their longboat. The Norsemen gave chase, determined to slay them before they reached the fjord. Reyna paid little heed as she followed Hagar, Olaf and Wulf into the hall.

Helga and Inga parted to let them pass, then followed them inside.

"Is Wulf all right?" Helga asked anxiously.

"I won't know until I examine him," Reyna threw over her shoulder. "Place him on his stomach on a bench and send someone to the ship for my medicinal chest," she ordered crisply. Olaf passed the order on to a thrall and rejoined them.

"We need to get him out of his blood-soaked clothing so you can inspect his wound," Hagar said, handing Reyna his short blade. "Olaf and I will lift him while you cut away his tunic and fur vest."

Once that task was completed, Reyna bent over the jagged wound in Wulf's back.

"Is the danger over?" The question came from Olga. She stood outside Thora's sleeping alcove, holding her son protectively in her arms. After assessing the situation, she rushed over to where the family was gathered around Wulf. "Olaf, you have returned! And you brought

Wulf and Reyna with you." Her gaze settled on Wulf, ly-ing prone on the bench, still bleeding from his wound. "What happened to him? Will he be all right?"

"Wulf has been wounded," Hagar explained. "We don't know how badly yet."

"Have the Finns been driven off?"

"Aye, thanks to my brothers' timely return," Hagar said. "If not for the additional men, we would not have prevailed."

Olga's gaze rested on Reyna. "Thank you for coming, Reyna. Thora's condition has worsened. We desperately need your healing skills. And now this," she said, ges-turing toward Wulf. "Can you save him?"

Wulf's muffled words startled them. "I am not dead yet."

"You are conscious," Reyna breathed. "Thank Freya. Lie still, Wulf. The bleeding has slowed; that's a good sign. As soon as my medicinal chest arrives, I will give you something for the pain." To Helga she said, "I will need hot water and clean cloths."

Helga raced off.

"Reyna, you . . . you looked like a Viking warrior woman, swooping down to slay the enemy," Wulf said in a voice laced with pain. "You should have stayed where it was safe."

"I could not. I had to know what was taking place and lend help where I could. I am sorry I did not reach you in time."

Wulf grunted as Reyna examined the wound more closely. "How does it look?" he asked.

" 'Tis not life threatening. I will know more once the wound is cleaned."

The thrall returned with the medicinal chest at the same time Helga arrived with a bowl of hot water and a stack of clean linen cloths.

"What is happening?" asked Thora, her voice barely audible through the thick curtain of the sleeping alcove.

"I had best go to her," Olga said. "She will want to know what is happening. She is too weak to leave her bed."

"I will go with you," Hagar said. "Mother will be pleased to know her wayward sons have returned. Olaf, you and Eric take charge of the cleanup outside. The girls can help Reyna. No sense all of us hovering over Wulf while Reyna does what is necessary to heal him."

"You are wounded, and so are Eric and Olaf," Helga cried.

" 'Tis naught compared to Wulf's wound," Hagar replied. "You can wash away the blood before I go in to see Mother. My brothers are capable of caring for themselves. Their wounds and mine are minor."

Reyna paid little heed to what was going on around her as she carefully cleaned Wulf's wound and sprinkled dill seeds from her medicinal chest into the open slash.

"I will need to close the wound," Reyna muttered to herself.

"Do it and get it over with," Wulf groaned.

Turning toward her chest, Reyna saw that Inga had already threaded a needle that one of Reyna's brothers had brought back from Byzantium.

"Thank you," Reyna said, taking the threaded needle from Inga.

Concentrating on Wulf's wound, Reyna pierced his skin with the needle, glanced once at his face and then began making small neat stitches, until the wound was closed and the bleeding contained. Once she had finished, she sat back on her haunches and inspected her work.

"Are you finished?" Wulf asked weakly.

"Aye, are you all right?"

"I have been better."

"Do not move while I spread a healing salve over the wound and apply a bandage."

Reaching into her chest, Reyna removed a small jar of salve made from dried marigold mixed with lard. Once the salve was spread to her satisfaction, she made a thick bandage out of linen, placed it over the wound and wound strips of linen around Wulf's chest to hold it in place.

Reyna stood, rummaged in her chest until she found a small sack, and then handed it to Helga. "Brew this into a strong tea, let it steep until the color is a deep brown; then bring it to me."

"What is it?" Helga asked.

"Valerian. It will ease Wulf's pain."

"I don't need anything for pain," Wulf mumbled.

"Do not argue with me," Reyna said sternly.

"Is my brother misbehaving?" Hagar asked as he rejoined them.

"He needs to learn that I am the healer and he is the patient," Reyna said impatiently. "Help him to sit up, Hagar, so he can drink the brew Helga is preparing for him."

Hagar eased Wulf into a sitting position. Wulf wobbled a bit, but with his brother's help managed to remain upright.

"How long do I have before fever sets in?" Wulf asked.

"I hope my herbal salve will prevent infection. If a fever does develop, I will fight it with proven herbal remedies. How is your mother, Hagar?"

"The news that Wulf and Olaf have returned, and that you were with them, cheered her considerably. After you work your magic on Wulf, perhaps you can look in on her."

" 'Tis why I am here," Reyna replied.

Wulf turned his brooding gaze on Reyna. "Have you forgotten the words we spoke before your family? We are husband and wife."

"You and Wulf are wed?" Hagar asked, looking to Reyna for confirmation.

"For now," Reyna muttered.

"But Wulf just said . . ."

His words fell off when Helga returned with a cup of steaming tea and handed it to Reyna. "Does this look right to you?" Helga asked.

"Perfect," Reyna declared as she held the cup to Wulf's mouth. "Drink it all, Wulf. Then Hagar can help you to bed."

"I wish to return to my own bed in my own hall," Wulf said.

"No," Reyna was quick to reply. "If I am to treat both you and Thora, I will need the two of you in the same place."

"Olaf and Eric can stay in Wulf's hall and Wulf can occupy their sleeping alcove as long as needed," Hagar offered. "Now drink the tea, Wulf."

Though Wulf's hands were unsteady, he grasped the cup from Reyna and drank, handing the empty cup to her when he finished. "Perhaps you should help me to my bed now, Hagar," Wulf said groggily.

Reyna watched with trepidation as Hagar half carried, half dragged Wulf to the sleeping alcove he was to occupy. Once he was safely inside, she collapsed onto the bench, rested her head against the wall and closed her eyes. When she had first seen Wulf struck down, her emotions had had been pulled between rage and fear. Rage sent her flying into the fray to slay Wulf's attacker, and fear that he would die gave her the strength to react. Now Reyna was exhausted, but she had no time to rest. She still had to wash Wulf's blood from her hands and check on Thora.

"What do you need?" Helga asked anxiously. "You look so weary. Inga is preparing a bed for you."

"First I want to check on your mother. A basin of hot water and soap would be appreciated. I cannot go to your mother with blood on my hands."

Helga left and returned with a basin of hot water, a pot of soft soap and a drying cloth. Reyna smiled her thanks and thoroughly scrubbed and dried her hands and arms. Then she walked to Thora's sleeping alcove, parted the curtain and stepped inside. Shock lanced through Reyna. Once robust, Thora looked a mere shadow of herself. Her complexion was too pale, her cheeks sunken and her eyes appeared too big for her face. Reyna hurried to her bedside and took her hand.

Thora opened her eyes, saw Reyna and smiled. "Are my sons truly safe?" Thora asked.

"Aye, Olaf has returned hale and hardy. Wulf was wounded while fighting the raiders but I expect him to make a full recovery. The rest of the family is fine but for a few minor wounds."

"So Hagar said, but I wanted to be sure. Will you tell me what happened when you and Wulf disappeared? Hagar almost had a fit when he learned that Olaf had sailed across the sea to rescue Wulf in the middle of winter. We were all afraid we had lost two sons instead of one."

Then Thora launched into a paroxysm of coughing that left her weak and wheezing for breath.

"Do not exert yourself Thora, I beg you," Reyna pleaded. "I will tell you everything you wish to know after I prepare an infusion of herbs to ease your cough and help you relax."

Reyna left Thora's sleeping alcove and sent Inga in to sit with her mother while she removed what she needed from her medicinal chest. Working on a table near the hearth, Reyna measured out portions of two different dried herbs and tossed them into a kettle of boiling

water. While the infusion steeped, she returned to Wulf's bedside to check on him.

She found Wulf lying on his stomach, a fur pelt thrown over the lower half of his body and his eyes closed. She sidled closer and placed a hand on his cheek, checking for fever. He was still cool to her touch. Just as she started to withdraw, Wulf's eyes snapped open, and he grasped her arm.

"Do not go."

"You are still awake."

"Aye, barely. Why do you do it?"

Puzzled, Reyna asked, "Do what?"

"Make a habit of coming to my defense."

Reyna shrugged. "I thought the Finn had killed you and I wanted to avenge your death."

"You thought me dead?"

"I did not know but feared the worst."

"I live a charmed life." He tugged on her arm. "Lie down with me."

"No, I merely came to check on you. I am brewing an infusion to ease your mother's cough and cannot linger."

"How is she?"

"I am not sure yet. I plan to examine her thoroughly soon. Close your eyes and rest, Wulf. When you awaken, I will bring you a restorative to help you regain your strength. You've lost a great deal of blood."

Wulf wanted to say something more but his sluggish mind could not form the words. Nor could he recall precisely what he wanted to say. His grip on Reyna's hand loosened and his eyes closed. Then he knew no more.

Stubborn man, Reyna thought as she left him to his rest.

By the time the evening meal was announced, Thora had been told about Wulf and Reyna's abduction and their

triumphant and timely return. Thora was now resting easily, her cough subdued for the time being. Now that her loved ones had returned, Reyna suspected that Thora would recover, though it would be some time before her lungs were completely clear of congestion. Reyna knew of several cures she could try on Thora, and she wouldn't give up until one of them worked.

When Hagar suggested that Reyna should seek her bed, she didn't argue. She excused herself immediately after the meal and fell into bed, pulling the fur pelt over herself. Sleep claimed her the moment she closed her eyes.

Reyna's sleep was not restful. Wulf's moaning awakened her during the night and she went to his alcove to check on him. When he felt feverish to her touch, she decided to brew him red clover tea, which was good for fever and infection. While she was waiting for the tea to steep, she checked on Thora. Wolf's mother appeared to be resting comfortably, though she was still wheezing.

Once the tea was ready, Reyna carried it to Wulf's alcove, surprised to find him awake and lying on his side instead of his stomach. She touched his forehead, but before she could remove her hand he grasped her wrist and pulled her forward.

"Lie beside me," he said in a low growl.

"You're feverish. I've brewed an infusion to bring down the fever and help you to sleep."

"I don't want it." He sounded like a petulant child.

"Drink it, Wulf, so we can both go back to sleep."

"I will drink it if you sleep beside me."

Reyna sighed. If that was what it would take to get him to drink the tea, then she would lie beside him until he fell asleep.

"Very well. Rise up a little and I will hold the cup to your lips."

Wulf obeyed and drained the cup. Then he eased back down and moved over so she could join him.

"Come, you promised," he said when she hesitated.

Rather than argue, Reyna lay down beside him, intending to leave as soon as he fell asleep. As luck would have it, she fell asleep before he did. She didn't awake until the sun was high in the sky.

Both Reyna's patients began to recover with proper treatment. Wulf was up and about before his mother, for he was eager to regain his strength, even though Reyna had advised bed rest. Reyna continued to treat Thora with her herbal remedies, until her cough and congestion all but disappeared. Little by little Thora's strength returned and she gradually rejoined her family in their daily activities.

During this time Reyna learned she was not expecting Wulf's child. If she were honest, she would have to admit that she didn't believe herself capable of conceiving. With spring full upon the land, the family was engaged in planting crops and making plans to attend the *althing* in midsummer. It was to be held in an empty field near the port city of Kaupang.

Reyna decided she would wait for a time when she and Wulf were alone to tell him she wasn't with child. She planned to divorce him and return home when her brothers arrived.

That day came when Wulf unexpectedly joined her in the steam hut.

"What are you doing here?" Reyna exclaimed as she grabbed a drying cloth and wrapped it around her. "I thought you were with your brothers."

"I saw you come in and decided to join you. I wanted to tell you that I am well enough to return to my hall, and that I expect you to accompany me. You are my

wife and I want you in my bed. Mother is sufficiently recovered, so there is no need for you to live in Hagar's hall."

"There is no reason for us to remain wed, Wulf," Reyna replied, inching away from him. "I am not carrying your child. I was waiting for the right time to tell you."

Wulf's silver eyes narrowed and the look on his face grew almost fierce. "You are well-versed in herbal remedies. Admit it; you took something to abort my babe!"

Reyna blanched, shocked at being accused of such a terrible deed. Hands on hips, she faced him squarely. "How dare you accuse me of using my skills in such a vile manner! If I had not conceived your child during all the times we have been together, what makes you think I would now? You should be happy," she charged. "There is no longer any need for you to remain wed to a hated Dane. Please leave now so I can get dressed."

Reyna's outburst stunned Wulf. What did she want from him? He had wed her before her family. Dane or no, with child or no, a Norseman's vow was his honor.

"You are my wife. I will instruct one of the thralls to carry your medicinal chest and the trunk with your belongings to my hall. I will hear no more on the subject."

"Do you love me, Wulf? Is that why you wish to keep me?"

Stunned, Wulf stared at her. "You know my feelings on that subject. We are speaking of vows here, not love."

"Why did you wed me before you knew whether or not I carried your child?"

Wulf had no answer that made sense to him. Except that she was a healer and his mother had needed her. Instead of providing an answer, he merely shrugged.

Reyna pressed on. "Did you love Astrid when you married her?"

"What a stupid question. Of course I loved her."

Annoyance colored Reyna's words. "Is loving a Dane abhorrent to you? Is loving *me* abhorrent to you?"

Wulf drew himself up to his full height, leaning forward until they were nose to nose. "Love has naught to do with us, Reyna. We have enough lust between us to last a lifetime. When we are together we burn. And right now I am burning for you. Forget all else. We are wed and in lust with each other. Love is unnecessary."

Reyna took a step backward, hurt beyond description. "Speak for yourself, Wulf. Was lust enough between you and Astrid?"

"Why are you challenging me like this? I told you I loved Astrid. Lust had no place in our marriage."

Reyna clutched her heart as if she'd been dealt a lethal blow and spun away. Wulf stared after her for the length of a heartbeat before snagging an arm around her waist and tossing her over his shoulder. Reyna kicked and screamed as he carried her out of the steam hut and across the yard to his hall. If her flailing fists caused pain to his wound, he did not show it. Nor did anyone who saw them make a move to stop him.

Chapter Fifteen

Wulf opened the door to the hall and strode inside with Reyna still slung over his shoulder like a sack of grain. Uma and Lorne, Wulf's thralls, stopped what they were doing and stared.

"Out!" Wulf shouted, leaving no doubt what he wanted. When they continued to stare at him, he rasped, "Now! Find something to do outside until I summon you."

Both thralls made a hasty exit.

Wulf stormed into his sleeping alcove, pulled the curtain across the opening and set Reyna on her feet.

"You are mad!" she charged.

"Aye, mad for you." He reached for the ties on her tunic. She slapped his hands away.

"I am not your thrall, Wulf. I do not have to do your bidding. Move away, I am leaving."

Truth to tell, Reyna wanted Wulf as intensely as he wanted her, but she had yet to hear the words she needed to surrender herself completely to him. And likely she never would.

"Submit, Reyna, you know I will get my way. We are two passionate souls who want each other. You are my wife; we can indulge our desire all we want."

This time when he reached for the ties on her tunic,

his efforts to undo them succeeded. Reyna sputtered a protest when he removed her silver girdle, for all the good it did her. The tunic slid down past her hips. When she made a grab for it, he released the ties on her undertunic and both garments slid down her body and pooled around her feet. Then he grasped her waist and lifted her onto the bed so he could remove her stockings and shoes.

Reyna gathered her strength to leap off the bed, but when she looked up and saw Wulf tearing off his own clothing, all thought of leaving fled. Her eyes caressed his virile body. He was magnificent in his nakedness. Broad chest, arms like tree trunks and narrow waist. Despite the recent wound he had suffered, he looked remarkably healthy. Her gaze lowered to his loins, where his rampant manhood rose hard and massive between his thighs.

Her gaze returned to his face. He was grinning at her, apparently aware of her close inspection of his body.

"Am I to your liking?"

Reyna gave a snort. "You know you are. Are all Norsemen as arrogant as you?"

"We Norsemen have a right to be arrogant." He crawled onto the bed beside her, half covering her body. "Shall I prove it to you?"

In truth, he did not need to prove anything to Reyna. She already knew. If he weren't so dense, he would realize she needed no convincing, even though he wasn't ready to give her the words she wanted from him. Then Wulf's mouth covered hers and her thoughts skittered away. All she could do was respond.

She parted her lips and tilted her head back to receive his burning kisses, returning them with all the love in her heart. There was no gentleness in his lips, no tenderness, only a hunger he couldn't disguise. She met him measure

for measure, tongues dueling, breaths mingling. When her breath was nearly gone, he broke off the kiss, his eyes following the path of his hands as his callused palms slid over her breasts and the aching peaks of her nipples.

Resisting such a virile man was impossible. Freya help her, but he looked so fiercely handsome, hovering over her like a Viking warrior on the verge of plundering a village.

"I need to taste you," Wulf growled as he bent to lick one nipple; it stiffened in response. He gave the same attention to the other; it was just as quick to respond. He licked and suckled until Reyna wanted to scream in frustration.

A blast of pleasure scorched her. She arched up against him, offering more of herself to him. Long minutes later, his mouth left her breasts, kissing a path to her naval . . . and lower. He made a low, deep sound of satisfaction as he buried his mouth in her wet center, his tongue and teeth working her into a wild frenzy. She shivered uncontrollably, waiting for him to claim her fully. But apparently Wulf was in no hurry. Suddenly she wanted him to burn for her as she burned for him.

She surprised him by shoving him away, pushing him down and straddling him. His eyes glittered like hot ice as he gazed up at her. When he took her hips in his large hands and attempted to lift her onto his straining cock, she slid away and shifted down his body. Crouching over him, she lowered her head and kissed the engorged head of his sex.

"Thor's axe!" Wulf shouted as he arched his loins upward.

She took him deeper into the scalding heat of her mouth, swirling her tongue and teeth around the head, tasting his saltiness and the earthiness of his essence. Then she licked his length, up and down, enjoying the

feel of his hardening sex in her mouth. Experimentally she sucked. He muttered a strangled curse and buried his hands in her hair, holding her head in place, urging her on.

She continued to torment him until he gave a shout and rolled her off him. She landed on her back. With one fluid movement he flipped her onto her stomach. "On your knees," he growled.

Reyna flashed him a puzzled look but did as he asked. Her body was thrumming, her nerve endings tightly coiled. If he didn't take her soon she would go mad. When Wulf rose up on his knees behind her, Reyna glanced askance at him over her shoulder.

"Wulf, what . . . !"

His body was tense, the hard planes of his face stark with need as he grasped her hips, pulled them hard against him and thrust into her hot core. Reyna cried out as he filled her with his massive length and strength. The act was incredibly erotic. It felt wonderful, *he* felt wonderful inside her. And then he began to move, pounding into her, probing deep as his hands slid around to fondle her breasts, tugging and rolling her nipples between his fingers as his mouth caressed her neck.

Their bodies were so in tune, so violently ready that they came simultaneously. She called his name as rapture streaked through her. She rode the waves of ecstasy from climax to climax, first one and then another and yet another. Each flung her higher, until she reached the summit and shattered. She heard Wulf shout and felt his hot seed fill her. Then her knees gave way and she collapsed beneath Wulf's shuddering body.

Wulf rolled away so as not to crush her, his chest heaving, his breath rasping in and out of his lungs in great gulps. Never had Wulf been so lost in mindless, overwhelming pleasure. Each time he and Reyna came

together was more intense, more satisfying than before. Earthshaking was a better word. What in Thor's name had she done to him?

He glanced over at her. She was lying in a boneless heap, a beautiful smile on her face. His chest swelled. *He* had put that smile on her face. Suddenly he thought of his beloved Astrid and a nagging memory rattled him. Why had he never seen that smile on Astrid's face? Though Astrid loved him, he had never seen her smile in blissful satisfaction after he made love to her. Nor had he ever found this kind of bliss with his beloved wife.

Pulling Reyna into the curve of his body, Wulf listened to her even breathing and then joined her in sleep.

The weather continued to improve as spring warmed the air, and trees and flowers burst into bloom. The men were busy preparing their dragonships for their summer voyages and supervising the planting. This was also a busy time for the women and thralls.

Thora's cough had all but disappeared and everyone appeared to be in good health. Olga and Hagar's son had prospered and grown during Reyna's absence. Reyna was fascinated with the babe and played with him as often as possible. It saddened her to think she would never have a babe of her own.

She was also disheartened because she had heard nothing from Wulf to change her mind about divorcing him. She wanted love but got lust instead. Any bed slave could give Wulf what she gave him. Reyna knew Uma was eager for Wulf to invite her to his bed. Though Reyna tried to be kind to the thrall, Uma did not treat her like someone whose good will she depended upon.

When Reyna tried to make friends with Uma, she was rebuffed with the words, "Though Wulf has wed you, he will never forgive you for being a Dane."

"What lies between Wulf and me is none of your business, Uma," Reyna answered.

"You were once one of us," Uma reminded her, "until you used your wiles on the master. We will see what happens when he tires of you."

Reyna didn't intend to stay around that long. She feared that Uma was right about Wulf's feelings for her and didn't want to wait until he grew bored with her. Though they were wed in the eyes of their families, there was no longer a reason for Reyna to stay with Wulf. It was apparent to her that she was barren and could never replace the child Wulf had lost when Astrid died. She would rather wed Ragnar than be held in contempt by the man she loved.

There was a great deal of excitement about the *althing* as the weather grew mild and the season progressed. The time approached for people to bring their grievances before the lawspeaker. Lawbreakers would be punished, property disputes settled, and men and women would announce marriages and ask the lawspeaker to sanction their union.

New clothing fashioned from silks, satins and brocades that Hagar had brought back from Byzantium was being made by the women. The *althing* was also a social occasion, where friends gathered and exchanged gossip and news of births and deaths.

Until her brothers arrived, Reyna bided her time, waiting for Wulf to declare his love to her. How could he make love to her with such intensity, such wild abandon and not care for her?

Did his love for his dead wife still burn in his heart? Was that why he couldn't love her? If so, then he would never love her and she was wasting her time with him. Loving a man who could not return her love was hopeless.

Some weeks after Reyna returned to Wulf's farmstead, she was rudely awakened in the middle of the night by someone softly calling her name. A light sleeper, Reyna answered at once, keeping her voice low so as not to awaken Wulf.

"Who is it?" Reyna asked.

" 'Tis Hagar."

Reyna reached for her tunic. Hagar wouldn't be summoning her if it weren't an emergency. "Is someone ill?"

"Aye, 'tis my son. He's gasping for breath. Please hurry."

Already dressed by now, Reyna stepped through the curtain. "Rollo seemed fine yesterday," Reyna mused. "But with babies, one never knows. I'll fetch my chest and be there directly."

"Let me carry that," Hagar said after Reyna removed the chest from a nearby cupboard. "Perhaps you should tell Wulf where he can find you."

"I will tell him," Uma said, rising from a nearby bench, where she had been sleeping.

"Thank you," Reyna replied as she sailed out the door without giving Uma's offer a second thought. A baby was ill and she was needed.

Hagar's hall was ablaze with light. Reyna followed him inside and heard the baby's harsh breathing followed by several gasps, as if he were struggling for breath. She hurried over to Olga, who was doing her best to comfort her son.

"Thank Freya you are here," Olga said, holding the child out to Reyna.

"How long has he been like this?" Reyna asked. She placed the babe on a table and removed his swaddling clothes to examine him. Rollo was a sturdy child who, according to Olga, had had few illnesses in his short life.

Reyna's brows furrowed when she saw his tiny chest heave with each breath he took.

"Can you help him?" Hagar asked anxiously.

"I have seen children heaving and gasping for breath like this before," Reyna said. "It happens most often during the spring and summer, when plants are growing and flowers are blooming. I will brew red clover tea; you and Olga can try to get some of it down him while I boil burdock root and mash it into a paste for a poultice."

Reyna set to work immediately. When daylight arrived, Rollo was beginning to breathe easier. Reyna spent the day with him, treating him with various cures. That evening Reyna told Wulf she intended to stay the night in Hagar's hall in case she was needed.

"Are you deliberately abandoning my bed?" Wulf growled.

"Your nephew is ill, I am trying to cure him," Reyna retorted.

Wulf stomped off. He didn't like Reyna sleeping anywhere but in his bed. Now that Reyna was his, he was jealous of her time away from him. He knew her brothers would arrive one day, and that she might leave him. He tried to tell himself she didn't matter all that much to him and that he would survive her leaving, but he knew it was a lie. Reyna had become an important part of his life and vital to his family.

Would opening his heart to Reyna be such a bad thing? he wondered. Would he ever get past the fact that she was a Dane? He would have to if they were to live in harmony as husband and wife.

Wulf returned to his hall in a sour mood and sat down at the table, calling for a horn of ale. Uma hurried to do his bidding. When she returned, she hovered over him while he drank deeply from the horn.

"Is there something you need, Uma?" Wulf asked.

"When is Rey . . . the mistress returning?" Uma asked.

"She will remain in Hagar's hall as long as it takes to cure my nephew."

Uma raised her head, smiling beguilingly into Wulf's eyes. "You must be lonely. A virile man like you needs a woman's comfort. I would be happy to serve you in any way you wish."

"You want to take Reyna's place in my bed," Wulf repeated tonelessly.

Uma brightened. "I would be honored to serve you in such a fashion."

Wulf heaved a sigh. He wasn't even tempted. Uma was attractive enough but she wasn't Reyna. "I must decline your offer. Had I wanted you, I would have taken you to my bed long before now. There are male thralls aplenty on the farmstead. Choose one of them to bestow your favors upon for I am not interested."

Bowing her head, Uma shuffled off. Wulf stared after her, wondering why she didn't appeal to him, had never appealed to him. Was it because Wulf wanted Reyna with an unquenchable passion? The more he thought about it, the more he wanted Reyna in his life. Despite his hatred for Danes, Wulf realized he needed Reyna in his home and his bed.

That night after eating the evening meal with his family, Wulf retired to his own hall, wishing he could take Reyna with him. She appeared weary and in need of rest when he had bid good night and sought his bed alone. Sometime during the night he felt Reyna slide beneath the furs and cuddle next to him, her body warm and inviting.

"I am glad you decided to join me," he murmured into her ear. "You must be exhausted."

When she did not reply, he pulled her into the curve of his body and promptly fell asleep, thinking of how

nice it would be to make love to her upon awakening in the morning. Morning sex was a delightful way to charge the body for the coming day's activities.

Reyna stepped away from Rollo's cradle, allowing herself to relax for the first time in two days. The child was breathing easily and sleeping peacefully. There was nothing more she could do for him tonight.

"You should return home," Olga advised. "You have cured my son and I am grateful. You look exhausted. I will send for you if you are needed but I doubt it will be necessary. Take a torch with you, 'tis dark outside."

Reyna took one last look at the sleeping babe and nodded. She was tired and looked forward to joining Wulf in his bed, where she would be warmed by his big body.

She threw a cloak over her shoulders, removed a torch from a wall sconce and quietly left so as not to awaken the sleeping household. The air outside was brisk as she crossed the yard to Wulf's hall. The room was dark but for the dying fire in the hearth. Reyna placed the torch in an empty sconce, hung her cloak on a wooden peg and stumbled to Wulf's sleeping alcove. Stifling a yawn, she pulled the curtain aside . . . and froze.

Enough light filtered into the alcove to reveal two bodies entwined in the furs. A large male body all but covered a smaller female one. Wulf and . . . She crept closer, peering through the dim light at the woman occupying her place in Wulf's bed.

Uma!

"Devil take you, Wulf!" Reyna shouted loud enough to wake the occupants entwined cozily in the furs.

Wulf jerked upright, a puzzled expression on his face. "Reyna?"

"Apparently you did not expect me to return tonight,"

Reyna spat. "Is this the kind of marriage I can expect from you? Well, I will have none of it. Keep Uma as your bed slave for all I care."

"Uma? What are you talking about?"

Uma rose up beside Wulf, her naked shoulders gleaming seductively in the pale light. Wulf turned his head and stared at her, as if seeing her for the first time. Reyna scoffed at his show of innocence.

"Thor's hammer, Uma! What are you doing in my bed?"

"Don't act the innocent with me, Wulf," Reyna charged. "Any woman will do for you. You do not need me."

Rising to his knees, Wulf grasped Uma's arms and hauled her from his bed.

Reyna stared at Uma's naked body. Without the shapeless tunic covering her form, she was generously curved in the right places. What man could resist her? Not Wulf, apparently.

"You made no objection when I climbed in bed with you," Uma pouted. "I only wanted to comfort you."

"Get out! We will speak of this on the morrow."

"Do not kick your bed slave out on my account," Reyna said sweetly. "I will find a bed in Hagar's hall."

"Go!" Wulf shouted when Uma lingered.

As Reyna turned to follow Uma through the curtain, Wulf grabbed his wife's arm and pulled her across the bed. "I did not invite Uma into my bed," he growled.

"I do not believe you, Wulf. Let go of me. I am returning to your brother's hall. I would rather sleep on a bench than take Uma's place beside you."

"I told you, I did not invite Uma into my bed," Wulf repeated through clenched teeth.

"Don't tell me Uma was bold enough to come to you of her own accord," Reyna scoffed, "for I find that difficult to believe."

"Come to bed. We will work this out in the morning. I've missed you, wife."

"No, I mean naught to you. I am merely your family's healer."

"Reyna, be reasonable. Did I not wed you before your father? Why would I do that if I did not want you as my wife?"

"You needed my skills."

"That, too, but I wanted you for myself."

Reyna slid off the bed. Wulf reached for her and missed. Finding herself free, she raced through the curtain and into the hall. She was out the door and across the yard before Wulf could stop her. Chancing a glance over her shoulder, she saw him standing in the doorway, a naked god in all his magnificent glory.

Wulf turned away. He had done nothing to warrant such treatment from Reyna. Then his glance lit on Uma, cowering in the corner, and he advanced toward her, his silver eyes glinting with barely contained anger.

"Explain yourself, woman!" he roared.

"Reyna does not deserve you," Uma whimpered. "When you welcomed me into your bed, I thought you wanted me."

"Thor's hammer! I was asleep. I thought you were Reyna. At the first opportunity I will find you a new owner."

"No, master, I beg you. I do not want to leave. I will behave, I promise."

"We will discuss this later," Wulf growled, offering little hope for her future as his thrall.

Wulf strode to his sleeping alcove, dressed quickly, lit a torch from the dying embers in the hearth and stormed from the hall. He would be damned if he would take the blame for something not of his doing. This time

Reyna was being unreasonable. He had done nothing to earn her contempt.

All was quiet when he entered Hagar's hall. Holding the torch high, he searched for Reyna and found his wife huddled beneath a wolf pelt on a bench near the door.

Stiffening his impressive form, he marched to the bench and stopped, arms folded over his chest, legs wide apart. She appeared to be sleeping but Wulf wasn't fooled. "I know you are awake, Reyna."

"Return to your bed slave," she hissed.

"You judge me wrongly," Wulf returned gruffly.

Reyna sat up, her green eyes glittering fiercely. "I know what I saw."

"I did not invite Uma to my bed. You know how soundly I sleep. She crawled in beside me without my knowledge. Naught happened between us in my bed tonight."

"Tell that to someone who will believe you," Reyna spat.

He grasped her arm, roughly pulling her to her feet. "You are returning with me to my hall, where you belong."

A light flared from behind them. "What is going on here?"

Both Reyna and Wulf spun around to face an angry Hagar. "Take your fight outside. 'Tis late and the household is sleeping. Or they were until you two started carrying on. What is this about?"

"Ask Wulf," Reyna muttered.

"I did naught," Wulf barked.

"He took Uma to his bed. I found them together."

Hagar's eyebrows shot up. "Is that true, brother?"

"No, 'tis *not* true." A long silence ensued. "I did not invite Uma into my bed. She crawled in while I was sleeping."

"To the volcanic pool; I feel like a long soak this morning."

Wulf grinned at her. "If I hadn't joined Hagar in the steam hut this morning, I would go with you." His eyes glittered provocatively. "And if I did not have chores to do, I would join you anyway."

Reyna flashed him a grin and said, "Thank you for bringing Gerta to your hall. She is a definite improvement over Uma."

"I told you Uma would never find her way into my bed again. Go enjoy your soak. You earned it. Hagar said his son is cured of his ailment, thanks to your skill. And do not worry about being interrupted; I will warn the men away from the pool."

Leaving Wulf to his breakfast, Reyna fetched a drying cloth and soap from a cupboard and left the hall. The short walk in the bright sunshine reminded her that soon the family would leave to attend the *althing*.

Reyna's thoughts turned to Wulf. She was torn. Could she live the rest of her life with a man who lusted after her but did not love her? Indecision weighed heavily upon her as she undressed and stepped into the pool, sinking down until the water rose up to her neck. She reclined on a ledge, rested her head back against the side of the pool and closed her eyes, letting the heat cleanse her body and soul.

Reyna wasn't sure how long she had lain there, enjoying the hot water and sun upon her face before she heard someone say, "I changed my mind. Joining you is far more enjoyable than performing chores that can wait until later."

Reyna gazed up at Wulf as he hastily removed his clothing. Then the water rippled as he slipped into the pool and sat down beside her.

"You appeared lost in thought when I arrived," Wulf said. "What were you thinking?"

She hesitated, then said, "I was wondering when my brothers would arrive."

Wulf sent her a sharp look. "What are you trying to tell me, Reyna? Have you decided to leave me?"

"I have decided naught . . . yet."

"I told you I did not invite Uma into my bed. What more do you want from me?"

"I want what you cannot give me, what you refuse to give me. Astrid is buried too deep in your heart; there is no room for me. If I cannot have all of you, I want none of you."

Wulf's silver eyes darkened. "You had a great deal of me last night."

Exasperated, Reyna snapped, "That is not what I mean and you know it."

He reached for her. "I am willing to give you more now."

"Wulf, I do not . . ."

That was as far as she got before Wulf's mouth came down hard on hers. After that she had no will to resist. Her body and mind were totally consumed by Wulf as he made love to her in the pool.

Wulf spent the next few days observing Reyna. Though he knew she might leave him when her brothers arrived, he couldn't bring himself to utter the words she wanted to hear. What did Reyna want from him? Women were a puzzle, he decided, and Reyna was more puzzling than most. Surely she knew he cared for her. Why else would he go out of his way to convince her father that she belonged with him?

Wulf was a warrior not a skald who could spew tales of romance and poetry. As for love, he had known love

once, and Astrid now lay in a cold grave with his un-born child. If Reyna left him, Wulf swore by the war god Odin that he would not chase after her. His pride would not allow it. Even so, he wondered each time she wandered down to the fjord to gaze toward the North Sea if this was the day her brothers would arrive and carry her off.

The following days were busy ones for Wulf and his family. The men spent long hours preparing the dragon-ships for their summer voyages and supervising the thralls who tended the crops, which were just beginning to shove their green heads above ground.

The women were excitedly preparing Helga for her joining with Rannulf, filling her chest with linens and other necessities a new bride was expected to take to her husband's hall. Since Reyna did not approve of the marriage, she participated as little as possible. Even if Rannulf's despicable act had been committed in the heat of bloodlust, Reyna could not like him.

The day finally arrived when the entire family was to visit Rannulf's hall and discuss the final marriage terms with his parents. When Reyna announced her intention to remain behind, Wulf, after a long hesitation, seemed to understand her unwillingness to accompany them and did not press her to change her mind.

Reyna waved the family off, then set out for the steam hut, knowing she had the entire day to do as she pleased.

Reclining on a bench with hot steam misting around her, Reyna closed her eyes and relaxed, letting her mind wander. Wulf had appeared torn about letting her remain behind this morning. Did he worry that her brothers would arrive and she would leave him? If he wanted her to remain, why hadn't he said the words she needed to hear?

Another thought plagued Reyna. If she left him, would he come after her? Something told her Wulf would not follow her across the sea. When it came right down to it, Reyna wasn't sure she could leave him. She could talk about it, think about it, but actually leaving the man she loved would not be easy.

When Reyna left the steam hut she felt invigorated and decided to work off some of her energy. Though a gray fog hung in the air, she decided to gather some of the early blooming herbs she had noticed growing along the bank of the fjord.

She returned to the hall to fetch her cloak, basket and knife and walked the short distance to the fjord. Reyna tramped along the shore, searching amid the sea grass and water plants for herbs and roots. When her basket was full, she looked up and noticed two dragonships advancing up the fjord through the mist. Her heart thumped against her chest when the ships drew close enough for her to recognize the cut of the sail and the markings on the hull.

Danes!

Her brothers had finally arrived, but on a day the family was away. Now she had a difficult decision to make. Could she live with a man who refused to bend, who couldn't admit to loving her, who clung tenaciously to the past?

Reyna waited anxiously near the bank of the fjord, hoping to identify one of her brothers. The fog was so thick that it wasn't until both dragonships scraped ashore that Reyna realized the ships were not those of her brothers. The armed warriors that leapt into the surf and beached the ships were obviously raiders. Worse yet, they had seen her.

Though she knew there was no hope of escape, Reyna turned and fled. To no avail. A massive Dane grabbed her from behind and literally swept her off her feet.

"What have we here?" the Dane growled in her ear.

Reyna answered in her native tongue. "I am Reyna the Dane, daughter of Harald Fairhair. Put me down."

"What do you here at the farmstead of Wulf the Ruthless?"

Reyna went still. It occurred to her that her countrymen were looking for more than slaves and plunder.

"How do you know this is the home of Wulf the Ruthless?"

"I have been here before with my father. And I have returned to avenge his death."

A chill swept down Reyna's spine as she looked into the warrior's face. She recognized this man. "Elgar?"

"Aye, I am Elgar, son of Hakkon the Terrible. You remember what happened to him, do you not? Wulf the Ruthless killed him. Now I shall kill the Norseman." His hand tightened on the hilt of his sword. "Revenge will be sweet."

At Reyna's cry of distress, the Dane shook her into silence. "What is the Norseman to you? Speak, woman!"

"Wulf is my husband," Reyna said through clattering teeth. She noted that Elgar's warriors were gathering around him, awaiting his orders. "If your plan is to kill him, you are wasting your time. He and his family are not at the farmstead."

"Then we will do as we always do. Take slaves, plunder and burn," Elgar growled. "I will return another day to slay the man who killed my father."

"No!" Reyna cried. "Do not burn the longhouses. Destroying them will gain you naught. Take me instead. The ransom my father and brothers will pay for my safe return will make you rich. They have had two successful years of trading and will gladly share their wealth with you."

"Do not tell me what to do, wench. Put her on the ship," Elgar ordered brusquely.

Though Reyna resisted, it did little good. A warrior grabbed her and dragged her through the water to the ship as Elgar motioned to the rest of his men to follow him.

Reyna's mind worked furiously. She had to do something . . . anything. "Wait!" she screamed. "You were probably seen as you traveled up the fjord. As we speak, Norsemen from nearby villages and farmsteads could be preparing their ships to attack yours."

Elgar sneered at her. "A few paltry Norsemen do not frighten me. I have come a long way to kill Wulf the Ruthless."

"As I said before, Wulf is not here," Reyna argued desperately.

"The wench is right," Elgar's right-hand man pointed out. "We should take her and leave before we find ourselves surrounded by Norse dragonships. I say we let the Wulf come to us so we can kill him on our own ground. If Reyna the Dane is Wulf's wife as she claims, he will surely come for her."

A chorus of "ayes" followed the man's words.

Elgar seemed to consider the suggestion. "How will Wulf know who has taken his wife?"

"Send word to my father," Reyna suggested hopefully. "Wulf will go to him when he finds me missing."

Though Reyna was not sure Wulf would consider her worth rescuing, she must try to convince Elgar that he would.

"Perhaps you are right," Elgar admitted. "The longer we remain in hostile territory, the greater the risk of facing opposition. Much as I relish a rousing battle, getting you to my farmstead will increase my chances of luring the Wulf out of his lair."

He waved his arms in the air. "Back to the ships, men."

* * *

Uma had been gathering watercress by the fjord and had hidden herself in the dense brush when Reyna approached. Now she observed what was happening. Though the words were foreign to her, she assumed the warriors were Reyna's brothers, despite the fact that they did not look friendly.

She watched from her hiding place as the foreigners returned to their ships and shoved off into the fjord. When the oarsmen rowed toward the sea, Uma crept away. Excitement swept through her. Reyna had returned to her homeland with her brothers without bidding Wulf as much as a good-bye. Well aware of Wulf's pride, Uma knew he would not go after his wife. Perhaps he would turn to her for solace, Uma thought gleefully. She wished she could have understood what Reyna's brothers were saying for there seemed to have been some sort of argument. It mattered not, Uma thought, shaking her head. Reyna was gone and only Uma knew what had happened.

The family returned to the farmstead in time to partake of the evening meal. The mood all around was light and happy. Hagar and Rannulf's father had agreed upon the marriage terms to everyone's satisfaction. Afterward, a sumptuous feast had been laid out and a copious amount of mead and ale consumed. Late in the afternoon, the family, except for Helga, who would remain with her new husband and his family, had trekked back to their own farmstead.

Wolf returned to his hall, expecting to find Reyna waiting for him. But as he approached, he was struck by a strange premonition that all was not as it should be.

Wulf looked for Reyna the moment he walked through the door, frowning when he did not find her. It

was growing dark; where could she be? After he questioned his thralls, his apprehension multiplied. Neither Lorne nor Gerta had seen Reyna since she'd left the hall this morning.

Concerned but not overly worried, Wulf left the hall and walked to the volcanic pool. Reyna was not there. Nor was she in the steam hut. Concern turned to fear. What had happened here today? How could Reyna have disappeared without a trace? Wulf hastened to Hagar's hall, chiding himself for not checking there first. She was probably with his family, helping with the evening meal.

Wulf began to worry in earnest when he learned Reyna was not there either. His family expressed concern and offered to help Wulf look for her. Hagar, Eric and Olaf left the hall immediately while Thora questioned the thralls. Wulf was headed out the door when Uma timidly approached him.

"Master, I know what happened to the mistress," she confided.

"If you know something, speak freely," Wulf replied.

"I was collecting watercress growing near the water's edge when I spotted foreign ships approaching the landing. Not knowing what to expect, especially with the family away, I hid in thick foliage. Then I saw Reyna standing on the bank of the fjord, watching the ships. When they scraped ashore and fierce warriors jumped from the ships, I became frightened."

Wulf's lips flattened. "What happened next?"

"I heard Reyna speak to the leader. Their conversation seemed friendly enough, so I naturally assumed your lady's brothers had arrived. They conversed for a time, and then a warrior helped Reyna board one of the ships. Finally, all the warriors returned to their ships and sailed away, taking Reyna with them."

Wulf cursed so violently, Uma shrank away from him. "Do you know what was said?"

"No, I was not familiar with the language. Reyna, however, spoke to them with ease."

"Return to your duties," Wulf growled. He needed to think. He hadn't for one minute believed Reyna would actually leave him. What a fool he'd been.

"What is it?" Thora asked as she joined him. "What did Uma say to you? Does she know what happened to Reyna?"

"Uma claims Reyna's brothers arrived and she left with them."

"I find it difficult to believe she would leave you," Thora scoffed. "She loves you. Could she have been taken by force?"

"Uma says Reyna spoke their language and conversed easily with them." His fists clenched at his sides. "I can only assume that Reyna has divorced me and left without so much as a farewell to anyone."

"Will you go after her?"

Wulf's mouth turned downward into a scowl. "No, I will not chase after a woman who does not want me."

Wulf shared the evening meal with his family and returned to his hall immediately afterward. He found it difficult to believe that Reyna had left so abruptly. Why hadn't Dag and Borg stayed to greet him? Was Reyna that desperate to leave him?

Once inside his hall, Wulf went directly to his sleeping alcove, where Reyna's scent still lingered. Then he saw her trunk sitting in a corner and realized she had left without her belongings. It struck him as odd that Reyna would leave everything she owned behind. The more Wulf thought about it, the angrier he became.

Good riddance, he thought. She had made her decision. So be it.

The days following Reyna's disappearance passed slowly for Wulf. He still planned to attend the *althing* with his family but no longer looked forward to it. Obviously there would be no marriage announcement. Disgusted with himself for missing Reyna, he shook his head. Marrying a Dane had been a mistake, despite their attraction and compatibility in bed. Determined to forget Reyna, Wulf began making plans for his summer travels. Perhaps this time he would sail to England, where great riches could be taken from monasteries protected by monks who were forbidden the use of weapons. Sounded like easy pickings to him.

The day before the family was to leave for the *althing*, visitors arrived at the farmstead. Wulf and Hagar had just left the steam hut when they saw two men trudging up from the fjord. Wulf stiffened with outrage the moment he recognized Reyna's brothers. How dare they return to taunt him! He reached for his sword, recalling too late that he carried no weapons.

"Brother," Borg greeted, reaching out to clasp arms with Wulf and then Hagar. "How fares our sister?"

Wulf's silver eyes glittered with malice. "I was going to ask you the same question."

"What do you mean?" Dag asked. "Why would we know anything about Reyna's welfare? We have not seen our sister since she left our farmstead."

"You lie!" Wulf sneered. "You came and took her away from under our very noses."

"We did no such thing!" Borg denied vehemently. "We sailed to Ireland, exploring the coast. 'Tis a good land, a fertile land. Perhaps we will settle there one day, like many of our people do. We have come to visit our sister as we promised."

Fear rose up in Wulf's throat, nearly choking him. "If

you did not take Reyna away and she is not here, then . . ."

"An enemy took her," Hagar concluded.

"I do not understand," Dag growled in a voice rife with menace. "How could an enemy spirit Reyna away without your knowledge?" He took a threatening step toward Wulf. "Why did you not protect her?"

"Everyone but Reyna was visiting the family of the man my sister Helga married," Wulf explained. "Reyna does not care for Rannulf so she remained behind. When we returned and found her missing, we naturally assumed you had arrived and she'd decided to return to her homeland with you. One of the thralls swore that the dragonship Reyna left on belonged to Danes, and that she spoke with the men in your language. What else were we to think?"

Hand on the hilt of his sword, Dag advanced on Wulf, until he and Wulf stood toe to toe. "What reason would my sister have for leaving you? Were you a cruel husband?"

"I was not a cruel husband. Reyna's reasons for leaving me, if she did indeed leave me, were personal. But now that it seems she was carried off by an unknown enemy, I will find her and bring her back where she belongs."

"How do you propose to do that? Do you know who carried her off?" Dag challenged. "It could be Finns, or Swedes or even Russians."

"The thrall, Uma, witnessed the entire exchange between Reyna and the men with whom she left. She said the dragonships belonged to Danes. Come with us to the hall. I will question her again and translate anything you do not understand."

Dag and Borg agreed with alacrity, and they followed Wulf and Hagar to the hall. After introductions were made to the rest of the family, Wulf summoned Uma.

"Uma, these are Reyna's brothers. Do they look familiar to you?"

Uma studied the two Danes, her eyes wide with fear. "No, master, I do not recognize these men."

"Look carefully, Uma. 'Tis important."

"These are not the warriors who carried Reyna off," Uma vowed.

"You said 'twas Danes who took Reyna away. How did you identify them as Danes?"

"The cut of their ships and the markings were identical to those of the Danes who attacked the farmstead before and killed your wife and aunt. And though I recognized some of the words they spoke, I could not put them together. The ships belonged to Danes, master, I am positive."

"Did you understand that?" Wulf asked Borg.

"Most of it. We will return home immediately and find the bastard Danes who took our sister. Perhaps Father has already received a ransom demand."

"My ship is ready to sail," Wulf said. "Give me two days to gather sailors and warriors and we will leave together. No one steals my wife and gets away with it."

Driven by a feeling he could not name, a madness he could not shake, Wulf implored Odin to help him find his wife and bring her home safely. Life without his warrior woman would never be the same.

Suddenly Wulf went still.

"What is it?" Hagar asked.

"Uma said the enemy ships and markings resembled those of the raiders who attacked the farmstead. I know Hakkon is dead because I killed him, but what if someone close to him seeks revenge?"

"Elgar," Borg bit out. "Hakkon's son."

Chapter Seventeen

From the moment Wulf realized that Reyna hadn't left him willingly, his feelings underwent a complete reversal. He was relieved that she had not left him by choice, fearful that she might be in danger.

Wulf cursed himself for not realizing how much he cared for Reyna, how much losing her would impact his life. How could he have been so stupid? Why hadn't he been able to embrace the love she offered him and return it? Did he love Reyna? His heart did an erratic flip flop. It appeared so. Was he ready to admit to loving a Dane? Aye, he was.

Worry, however, chased the fleeting pleasure of his realization from his mind. Reyna could be in grave danger. If Hakkon's son had taken her and Elgar knew Reyna was Wulf's wife, would the Dane exact revenge on her in Wulf's stead?

With that thought in mind, Wulf set out immediately for the village, seeking warriors and sailors to man his dragonship and fight the Danes who had kidnapped Reyna. By day's end, he had recruited thirty-two warriors and sailors, all eager to flex their muscles in battle. They were to meet at the landing on the fjord and leave in Wulf's dragonship the following morning along with Dag and Borg.

Meanwhile, Olaf and Eric were readying the ship with provisions for the voyage across the sea. Only Hagar would remain behind to protect the women.

The following morning, on an overcast, windless day, three ships sailed down the fjord to the sea. Since the wind refused to cooperate, the men rowed, hugging the coast and then using a sun stone to turn south toward the land of the Danes.

The next day the wind picked up and the ships scudded across the waves toward their destination. Four days later, Borg's ship led the way into the fjord that would eventually take them to the landing closest to their father's farmstead.

The moment the ships scraped the bottom, men jumped into the shallows, pulled them onto the sandy shore and began making camp on the grassy bank. They would provide their own meals from the provisions they had brought with them, supplemented by the wild game available in the nearby forest.

Wulf and his brothers accompanied Dag and Borg to the farmstead. As they entered the yard, Harald came bounding out of the hall to meet them.

"How did you know?" Harald asked.

Fingers of icy dread crept up Wulf's spine. "Know what?"

"Hakkon's son has Reyna. A ransom demand was delivered by one of his people just yesterday." He turned on Wulf, his anger palpable. "You were supposed to protect my daughter, Wulfric the Defender. What happened?"

Wulf explained why Reyna had been left alone on the farmstead in a few concise words. But Harald still wasn't satisfied.

"How is it you arrived with my sons?"

There was no help for it. Wulf had to tell Harald the whole of it. "When Reyna first disappeared, I assumed

Dag and Borg had arrived while the family was away and that Reyna had returned home with them."

"Without telling you she was leaving?" Harald barked. "Was Reyna not happy with you?"

Wulf shrugged. "I do not know. As I said, we all assumed she had left with her brothers. And then your sons arrived and disclaimed any knowledge of Reyna's disappearance. Fortunately, one of the thralls saw what had happened. Uma said two ships arrived while Reyna was walking along the bank of the fjord. When Reyna spoke in her own language to the warriors, she naturally assumed they were her brothers, since their arrival had been expected. When I questioned Uma further, she remembered that the markings on the ships and the cut of the sails were the same as those belonging to the Danes who raided our farmstead before.

"I knew Hakkon was dead for I killed him, but your sons told me Hakkon has a son named Elgar. Everything seemed to fall into place. We sailed here straightaway to see if you had heard from Elgar or received a ransom demand."

Harald snorted. "The bastard did not waste any time contacting me."

"I brought some gold and valuables with me to help with the ransom," Wulf said. "Together we should be able to meet Elgar's demands."

"You misunderstand, Wulf," Harald bit out. "Elgar wants something only I can provide. He desires my land. Our country is small; there is little room for expansion. He will accept naught less than my farmstead for Reyna's life."

Borg spit out a curse. "What will he do if you refuse?"

"Elgar will kill Reyna if we do not leave our farmstead," Maida said as she came up to join them.

"I've brought warriors, enough to defeat Elgar in bat-

tle, if it comes to that," Wulf informed him. "They are camped near the ships."

"Our own warriors will join Wulf," Borg vowed.

"We should have no difficulty defeating Elgar in a fair fight, but we cannot risk it," Harald replied. "I cannot endanger Reyna's life by refusing Elgar's ransom demand."

"Let us go inside," Maida suggested. "You can eat and drink and ponder a solution that will not harm our Reyna. What about your men? Their numbers will not fit in our hall."

"The men will hunt to supplement their stores. Worry not about them; they but await orders," Wulf said.

"Our men will make camp alongside yours," Borg said.

They all tramped inside the hall, taking seats around the table while thralls served them food and drink.

Wulf's mind searched furiously for a resolution to the problem, one that would not endanger Reyna. At length, he asked, "How does Elgar plan to return Reyna to you, Harald? Did he send instructions?"

"Elgar and his warriors will arrive by way of the fjord, where Reyna will be handed over to me. After that, we are to depart aboard my dragonship for whatever destination we choose."

"When?" Wulf asked.

"In three days," Harald lamented.

"Elgar wants more than your land, Father," Dag growled. "He wants your life. He will keep Reyna for himself and kill you and Mother."

"There has to be a way to beat Elgar at his own game," Wulf said, pondering the dilemma placed before him.

Reyna sat on a crude pallet on the floor of the dark hut that had become her jail. Since her arrival at Elgar's farmstead, she had seen no one but the male thrall who

delivered the two unpalatable meals a day she was allowed.

Reyna had no idea what was to become of her, or what plans Elgar had for her. She knew he intended to ransom her, but to whom—her father or Wulf? Which man would pay more for her safe return? Elgar was merely a minor jarl who aspired to greater riches and power.

Reyna stiffened when she heard the door latch rattle. Someone had removed the bar from outside the door and was about to enter. Was it mealtime already? It took a moment for her eyes to adjust to the sudden burst of light, and when they did she saw Elgar leering at her through a circle of torchlight.

Reyna rose to her feet. "What do you want?" she asked, refusing to be cowed by his threatening stance.

Elgar advanced into the hut. His bulk seemed to suck the air from the small room. "I thought you would like to know your fate."

Reyna's chin rose defiantly. "Even if I do not, I suppose you are eager to tell me."

Elgar scowled at her. "Your defiance will get you nowhere. It would serve you well to listen to me. 'Tis no secret my father coveted your family's land. I sent a messenger to deliver my ransom demand to your father. He was told that your life is forfeit if he does not adhere to my demands."

"My father is not easily frightened, not by the likes of you, anyway. Besides, when Wulf arrives . . ."

"Forget your husband. He has no idea what happened to you. He will not show up any time soon. Nor will your brothers. They went exploring and have yet to return."

Disbelief colored Reyna's words. "My father can command an army to defeat you in a matter of days."

Harsh laughter filled the small hut. "Think you your father will let you perish at my hands? I seriously doubt it. He knows I will kill you if he refuses to comply."

His next words made Reyna's breath seize in her throat. "Once Jarl Harald abandons his land, he expects me to hand you over to him and let you all sail away unharmed. But I am no fool. Once he leaves, he will gather an army and retaliate."

"How dare you make such demands!" Reyna cried, when she realized Elgar's evil plans.

"I would dare much for land," Elgar growled. "Your family will not leave their farmstead alive. After we kill your family, I will claim their farmstead and you will become my bed slave."

"When is all this to take place?"

"I have given him three days. We are to meet at the fjord near your farmstead."

A coil of fear snaked through Reyna. Like his father Hakkon, Elgar was an evil man. "You have forgotten my brothers," Reyna reminded him. "They will punish your foul deeds when they return."

"Oh, fear not, Reyna, we have plans for them too. They will be slain the moment they return from their travels."

"Why are you telling me this?" Reyna spat.

"I thought if you knew you would be sharing my bed, it might soften your attitude toward me. Since your life depends on my good will, it behooves you to treat me with kindness."

"Kindness? Ha! Never! Like your father, you have been dredged up from the pit of the deepest, darkest hell. I think it is you who should ponder your fate. Wulf will not let your depravity go unpunished."

Actually, Reyna had no idea how Wulf would learn what had happened to her and her family across the sea.

Nor did she know if he would even care. He did not love her, so why should he care that she had disappeared from his life? The only hope for her and her family's survival was her brothers. And even that was doubtful. Somehow she needed to escape and warn her father. Once he knew she was safe, he could raise an army to fight Elgar without fear of endangering her life.

"Forget Wulf the Ruthless," Elgar boasted. "He cannot possibly reach you in time, even if he figures out where you are, which is highly unlikely."

He leaned in closer to her, until she could smell the foul odor of his body. "My wife divorced me and I am in need of a bed slave. I am eager to see how good you are beneath the furs."

"Come any closer and you will be sorry," Reyna threatened.

Elgar threw back his head and laughed. "I am twice your size, wench. Naught you can do will hurt me."

He placed the torchlight in a nearby sconce and reached for her. Reyna ducked. Wulf had called her a warrior woman and she intended to live up to the name. Elgar wouldn't take her without a fight, she vowed. He reached for her again. This time Reyna was ready for him. Bracing herself against the wall, she kicked out with all her strength, her booted foot catching him square in the groin. Elgar let out a roar and fell back, his hand protecting his privates against further assault.

"Bitch!" he cried, once he recovered enough to speak. Then he backhanded her across the face. "You will die if you try that again. As soon as I am recovered, I will beat you until you beg me to take you."

Limping to the door, he opened it and let himself out. Cupping her bruised cheek in her hand, Reyna heard the bar scrape across the opening, sealing her inside. She slid down the wall to the floor, shaking uncontrollably.

Elgar was going to kill her family and there was nothing she could do about it. Or was there?

Suddenly Reyna became aware that Elgar had left the torchlight. She was no longer in the dark. Removing the torch from the sconce, she held it aloft. This was the first opportunity she'd had to examine her prison. The one narrow, shuttered window, barred on the outside, did not let in enough light for her to tell night from day.

Reyna's hopes fell when she realized the hut was bare except for her pallet and a slop bucket. It was also sturdily built with no visible loose boards or weak walls. After replacing the torchlight in the sconce, Reyna sank to her pallet to think. A short time later the door opened, admitting a male thrall carrying a bowl of stew, a hunk of bread and water to wash it down. Reyna glanced at the door, hoping to make a break for it, but the thrall wasn't alone. A warrior stood at the door, guarding the only exit.

Once she was alone again, Reyna picked up the spoon and tried to eat, but the stew was tough and her bruised jaw pained her too much to chew. But the pain was nothing compared to what Elgar would do to her when he returned. She prayed that his injury would prevent him from coming back any time soon. Or that a miracle would save her. Without a miracle, she would die with her parents.

Giving up had never been Reyna's way. As long as a breath was left in her body, she would fight to return to Wulf. Her hand fluttered to her stomach. In one way a miracle had already taken place. Freya had heard her prayers. She wasn't barren after all. Her courses, due about the time she had been abducted, had not arrived. If the gods were kind, she would live to bear Wulf a son.

While the household slept that night, Wulf came up with a plan to rescue Reyna. He laid out his scheme the

following morning when the family gathered to break their fast. Though it wasn't perfect, any plan, no matter how flawed, was better than no plan at all.

Harald was skeptical at first, but since no one had offered a workable substitute, the consensus was to go with Wulf's proposal. After a lengthy discussion, Dag and Olaf set out to apprise the warriors camped on the bank of the fjord of the upcoming battle and their part in the surprise attack.

"Be prepared to shove off at nightfall," Dag instructed the eager warriors. "We will row our ships along the fjord and beach near Elgar's farmstead. Then we will make our way through the woods to the farmstead and hide there until we receive Wulf's signal. Make no mistake—victory will be ours."

Battle cries filled the air in response. All the warriors would welcome an honorable death in battle.

Meanwhile, Wulf prepared to walk the distance to Elgar's farmstead and hide in the woods until dark. It was his job to locate and rescue Reyna before the warriors arrived by ship. If he could not remove her from her present situation, he would be forced to call off the attack for fear that Elgar would kill her once the attack began. Since Wulf did not know the way, Borg accompanied him.

Wulf and Borg left the farmstead after a hearty morning meal. Borg led the way through a gray, misty day well suited to their mission. They walked for several hours, meeting no one along the way. Once Elgar's longhouse was in sight, they took to the woods, sidling from tree to tree lest they be spotted by anyone who happened to be out and about.

Motioning silently, Borg pointed to a group of warriors camped in the yard near the longhouse. Wulf nodded. He had already noticed them. Inching closer to the

longhouse, Wulf spotted a large maple tree with a profusion of branches and leaves that overlooked the yard. Using sign language, he indicated that he intended to climb the tree in order to gain a complete view of the longhouse and surrounding outbuildings.

Wulf easily ascended the tree, climbing from branch to branch until his view of the farmstead was unrestricted. Borg followed close behind. Comfortably ensconced on sturdy branches, they watched the comings and goings of Elgar and his people.

Wulf tensed when he saw Elgar leave the hall and limp across the yard. Wulf glanced at Borg and shrugged, wondering how Elgar had acquired his limp. So far Reyna had not made an appearance, which not only worried but frustrated Wulf. If she were being held in the longhouse, his chances of freeing her were not good. Darkness was closing in when Wulf noticed a male thrall leave the longhouse carrying a bowl and cup. What struck Wulf as strange was the armed warrior following the man.

Wulf watched closely as the thrall stopped before a hut and waited for the warrior to unbar the door before entering. The thrall reappeared shortly and returned to the longhouse while the warrior replaced the bar and joined a group of men milling in the yard. Wulf and Borg exchanged knowing glances and settled down for a long wait. Hours later, when the household and men camped in the yard had bedded down for the night, and the darkest part of the damp, cloudy night had closed in, Wulf and Borg left the safety of the tree.

Stiff from long hours perched aloft, both men stretched their cramped muscles. "Wait here," Wulf mouthed to Borg, "while I see about freeing Reyna."

Before Wulf moved off, he heard an owl hoot. "'Tis Dag," Borg whispered. "Our men have arrived and are in place."

Wulf nodded. So far everything was going as planned. Leaving Borg behind, Wulf circled around to the hut, approaching it from behind. A window would be helpful, but he couldn't count on finding one, so he mulled over different scenarios as he stealthily crept around to the rear of the hut.

To Wulf's surprise and pleasure, a window did indeed exist. The shutters were closed tight and barred from the outside. Though the window was narrow and high up, Reyna was slim enough to squeeze through it. Fingers of dim light pierced through a slit in the shutters.

Carefully Wulf slid the bar from the window and set it on the ground. Then he opened the shutters. Though the torch was nearly extinguished, enough light remained to afford Wulf an unrestricted view of the tiny hut. He saw Reyna immediately. She was lying on a straw pallet not far from the window.

What had that bastard Elgar put her through? Wulf wondered. If one hair of Reyna's golden head had been harmed, he would make sure Elgar died a slow death. One woman he loved had been taken from him; he wouldn't let Reyna suffer the same fate. Aye, Wulf thought, he loved Reyna, and nothing short of death would take her from him. She would live to hear him say the words she yearned to hear.

Softly, Wulf called Reyna's name, but she was so deeply asleep she didn't hear him. Fearing that someone would hear him if he spoke louder, he searched his mind for a way to wake her. If she cried out, all could be lost.

Dropping to his knees, he searched the ground for small pebbles. Once he found what he needed, he stood and threw the pebbles at Reyna through the window, one at a time. The first two missed her. The third hit her cheek. Wulf held his breath as Reyna swiped at her cheek with her hand and opened her eyes.

"Reyna, wake up," Wulf softly called.

Reyna stirred but did not waken.

"Reyna, 'tis Wulf. I am here, at the window."

Reyna started violently and glanced toward the window. She blinked and looked again. "Wulf? Is that really you or am I dreaming?"

"'Tis no dream, sweet."

Reyna rubbed her eyes. "How . . . I do not understand. How could you be here? Are you alone?"

"I will answer all your questions later. We must move swiftly or risk discovery. Come close to the window and give me your hands; I will lift you out."

Reyna gave the window a skeptical look. "The opening is too narrow. I am not sure I can squeeze through."

"You are slender enough to do it. Quickly, give me your hands."

Reyna approached the window and held up her hands. The moment their hands touched she felt confidence surge through her. If Wulf said she could squeeze through the window, then she knew she could do it.

The opening was indeed narrow, but with Wulf's help Reyna managed to scrape through. Once he had her on the ground beside him, he pulled her into his arms and hugged her as if he never intended to let her go.

Reluctantly he released her. "Did Elgar hurt you?"

"No, but he tried. I did him a grave injury when he attempted to assault me."

Wulf chuckled softly. "So that's why he was limping when I spied him earlier in the yard. That will teach him to leave my warrior woman alone. Come, I need to get you safely away from here."

He grasped her hand and led her through the darkness into the woods. "Where are you taking me?"

"To the ship; you will be safe there. Your brothers and mine will lead our warriors in a predawn attack. Sur-

prise and superior numbers are on our side. We will not be defeated."

"My brothers are here?"

"Aye. We do not have time for lengthy explanations but I will tell all when this is over."

"I am happy you cared enough to come for me."

"Before I knew what happened to you, I feared you had left me for good. Then once you were gone, I realized how much you meant to me. I want you in my life forever, Reyna."

Reyna couldn't believe what she was hearing. Wulf wanted her in his life? She'd never expected to hear those words from him.

"I could not have left you even if I'd wanted to. You are my life, Wulf. I . . . I love you."

Wulf stopped in midstep, turned toward her and dragged her hard against him, seizing her mouth in fierce possession. "I love you, Reyna," he whispered against her lips. "I humbly beg you to forgive me for my sins against you. I did not want to love you. I fought a hard battle, but in the end I lost my heart to you."

He kissed her again, his mouth hard and hungry as his tongue delved between her lips to taste her sweet essence. The kiss would have gone on forever if the hoot of an owl hadn't interrupted. Wulf broke off abruptly and looked around.

"Come, we are not alone. The woods are teeming with our warriors. The fjord is just ahead. You will be safe aboard my ship." He guided her through a clump of trees to the fjord. "Here we are, and there are the warriors left behind to guard the ships."

The three warriors saw them despite the darkness and reached for their weapons. Wulf called softly to them and they relaxed.

"I have my wife with me," Wulf said. "Once she is

safely aboard my ship, you are to guard her with your life. She is not to leave the ship no matter how she begs." He turned toward Reyna. "The lives of these men are in your hands, sweet. If you manage to escape, they will be severely punished."

"Wulf, let me come with you. I can be useful."

"No, obey me in this, my love. I need my warrior woman alive and well."

He led her to his ship and helped her aboard. "Rest while I am gone. Use the wolf pelts to make a bed on deck and get some sleep."

"Sleep?" Reyna squeaked. "Are you mad? How can I sleep when you are risking your life on my behalf?"

He touched her cheek in a gentle caress. "I will return, I promise you."

He kissed her hard and then left her staring into the darkness, wondering if she would ever see Wulf alive again.

The gods wouldn't take him from her so soon after he'd declared his love, would they? She hadn't even told him about their child.

Chapter Eighteen

Fear and anxiety rode Reyna. Sleep was out of the question. When she located the wolf pelts, she wrapped one around her and paced the deck of the ship, pausing from time to time to peer into the darkness toward Elgar's longhouse.

When Reyna heard war cries, followed by screams and the sound of clashing weapons, she knew the battle had begun. Remaining behind was unbearable. Forgetting Wulf's strict orders, she searched the deck for a weapon, pleased when she found a battle-axe. Throwing off the wolf pelt, she loped along the deck, leapt to the ground and came to an abrupt halt against a solid wall of hard flesh.

A pair of strong, male hands seized her and held her in place while a second warrior grabbed the weapon from her hands. Reyna glanced up into the faces of her determined guards.

"Where do you think you are going, my lady?" the warrior holding her asked. "You heard Wulf. You are to remain with the ship."

"But I want to help," Reyna cried. "I can protect Wulf's back."

"He does not need your help. His orders were to keep

you safe. Back aboard you go," he said, lifting her bodily onto the ship.

It didn't take long for Reyna to realize she wasn't going anywhere. She sank down on the deck, pulled the wolf pelt around her again and listened to the sounds of battle as dawn broke around her.

The battle had begun scant minutes before dawn, when the sky held but a promise of daylight. Wulf had nodded to Borg, Borg had cupped his mouth and imitated the sound of an owl. A moment later the call was returned.

"Everyone is in place," Borg whispered.

Wulf grasped his sword in one hand, his battle-axe in the other and let out a war cry loud enough to wake the dead. Immediately men crashed through the woods toward the longhouse and the warriors sleeping in the yard.

To their credit, Elgar's warriors had woken quickly and armed themselves, but it was soon evident that they were badly outnumbered. The overwhelming numbers and surprise attack had worked in Wulf's favor.

When Wulf saw Elgar emerge from the hall, he hacked and fought his way to the man who'd dared to steal his wife. Elgar must have seen Wulf advancing toward him for he paused, a stunned look on his face. Then he changed directions and headed for the hut where Reyna had been imprisoned. Wulf didn't break stride as he charged after the Dane.

Elgar threw back the bar securing the door, flung it open and turned to confront Wulf. "Your wife is a dead woman, Wulfric the Ruthless. You cannot reach her in time to save her."

So saying, he disappeared inside the hut. Wulf had just reached the door when he heard Elgar roar out a curse. "Where is she?"

"Where you cannot hurt her," Wulf said. He stood in

the doorway, feet wide apart, weapons at the ready. "You have lost, Elgar, son of Hakkon. No one steals what is mine and lives to tell the tale. Prepare to die."

His face a mask of fury, Elgar attacked. His weapons flashing, he thrust and hacked at Wulf. Wulf met the attack with equal fury, maneuvering Elgar in the small hut until he had the advantage. The fight for power and superiority lasted long after the sounds of battle outside the hut had abated. Wulf had received a shallow slash across his upper arm while Elgar was bleeding from several places on his body.

Growing tired of Elgar's feeble attempts to kill him, Wulf struck out with his battle-axe, sending Elgar's sword flying. Before Elgar had time to react, Wulf pressed his sword to Elgar's throat, pushing him against a wall.

"Kill me," Elgar growled. "Send me to Valhalla to frolic and feast with the Valkyries."

Poised on the verge of thrusting his sword into Elgar's throat, Wulf suddenly had second thoughts. Why should he send Elgar to an honorable death when the man did not deserve it?

Borg and Dag pushed their heads through the door to see what was going on. "Is all well in here, Wulf?" Borg asked.

"Aye, though I am undecided what to do with this scum. He does not deserve an honorable death. Is everything under control? Have our warriors prevailed?"

"Aye," Dag replied. "Elgar's warriors are defeated, and those that still live await their fate."

"My brothers?"

"Alive and well. They guard the prisoners."

"Move," Wulf ordered, prodding Elgar in front of him.

"Kill me," Elgar goaded.

The point of Wulf's sword pressed into Elgar's neck,

drawing blood. "No. Move, I say. I am taking you to join your comrades."

Grudgingly, Elgar obeyed. With his men beaten and his hostage gone, he was left with no choice.

Olaf greeted Wulf gleefully. "Shall we kill the bastards, Wulf?"

"What think you, Borg, should we kill Elgar and his comrades?" Wulf asked Reyna's brother.

Borg rubbed him chin as he pondered Wulf's words. Before he could make a decision, Dag forestalled him. "Banish Elgar from his land. Give him and his people time to gather their belongings and women and leave in their dragonships. Once Elgar is gone, I will occupy his holdings. I have no land of my own, and Elgar's farmstead will serve me well."

"Will sparing Elgar's life satisfy you, Wulf?" Borg asked.

"Aye, as long as Elgar settles far away, somewhere like Scotland or Iceland."

"'Tis settled, then," Borg decided. "Dag and I will remain here to make sure Elgar and his people leave for foreign parts."

Wulf nodded his approval and motioned for his brothers and warriors to follow him to their dragonship. It was time to take his wife home. But first they would return to Harald's farmstead to let her parents know what had transpired this eventful day.

The wait and worry was getting to Reyna. Dawn had given way to daylight and the sounds of battle had ceased long ago. When no one appeared immediately after the shouts and cries had ended, Reyna became a tangle of raw nerves, waiting to learn the fate of Wulf and those she loved.

The sound of feet pounding through the woods brought her thoughts to a halt. Throwing off the wolf pelt, she

clambered down from the ship and ran toward the woods. She didn't get far, for the guards held her back, ready to defend her with their lives, as Wulf had ordered.

The sight of Wulf emerging from the cover of the trees was the sweetest thing Reyna had ever seen. Her knees buckled and she would have fallen had Wulf not reached her and snatched her up into his arms.

"Are you ready to go home, sweet?" he asked against the warmth of her neck.

She pulled back and looked at him. "Are you well?" Her eyes widened in panic when she noticed his bloodied sleeve. "You are wounded!"

He grinned. "'Tis a mere scratch."

Suddenly his grin darkened into a scowl. He reached out and tenderly touched her bruised cheek with a fingertip. "Did Elgar do this to you?"

"It does not hurt anymore," Reyna said in an effort to calm his building rage.

"What happened?"

"Elgar struck me after I kicked him in the groin. Think no more on it, Wulf. I want to leave this place. The men are taking their seats at the oars as we speak. My father will be frantic with worry if we do not return soon." She glanced about, suddenly aware that her brothers were missing. "Where are Dag and Borg?"

"Do not worry, they are safe. I will explain once we board the dragonship. But now, after seeing what Elgar did to you, I should return and put an end to his miserable life instead of sparing him."

"Do not return, I beg you. I injured him more than he injured me. Let it go, my love."

For a moment Wulf looked torn between punishing Elgar and doing as Reyna asked.

"Are you coming aboard?" Eric called to them.

Eric's words must have convinced Wulf, for he

shrugged and lifted Reyna aboard the dragonship. They sat side by side while Wulf's brothers took charge of the crew.

The moment the ship glided into the fjord, Reyna said, "What do you mean you spared Elgar's life?"

Gathering Reyna into the shelter of his arms, Wulf told her what had transpired during and after the battle. "Elgar is smart enough to heed my warning. He will leave these shores and never return. Your brothers remained behind to make sure he obeys orders. Dag is excited about owning his own land. I am sure he will make a success of it."

" 'Twas generous of you to let Elgar live," Reyna praised. "I am sick of war and killing. If I had my way, you would never go a-Viking again."

"I am of the same mind, sweet. I will go to sea because it is in my blood, but like Hagar, my travels will be for the purpose of trade and exploration, not plunder and killing." His gaze wandered past her, toward the open water. "One day I hope to settle on my own land, to farm and live in peace. I have heard a great deal about Ireland. Norsemen have settled on the Isle of Man and the Orkneys and I would do the same, but only if you are agreeable, of course."

"Anywhere you choose to settle is fine with me, but not right away. You see, I am . . ."

"We have reached the landing adjoining your father's farmstead," Wulf interrupted as the oarsmen inched the dragonship toward the sandy beach.

Reyna slumped in disappointment. Apparently this wasn't the time to tell Wulf about their child. But soon, she vowed, very soon; before they crossed the sea to his farmstead.

"Look." Reyna pointed. "Father awaits us on the shore."

Sure enough, Harald stood on the bank of the fjord, awaiting the return of his family. His face lit up when he saw Reyna stand and wave as the ship pushed through the surf and scraped to a stop. He waded out to meet them, though his gaze swept past the ship, searching for the vessels belonging to his sons.

Wulf jumped ashore and handed Reyna down. She flew into Harald's arms and he hugged her tight. "Have you been keeping a vigil, Father?" Reyna teased.

"Aye, 'tis what fathers do." His gaze swept over her, searching for signs of abuse. When he saw her bruised face, his mouth hardened. "Did Elgar do that to you, daughter?"

"Aye, but he did not escape unpunished. I am fine, Father. Thanks to my husband, I have returned safely." She grinned up at Wulf. "Wulf was magnificent. He found me before the battle was engaged and took me away to safety."

Harald's gaze drifted past her again to the fjord. "Where are your brothers? Never say they . . ."

"They are well," Wulf interjected. "Once we return to the hall, I will explain what happened and why they remained behind. Reyna is exhausted and needs to rest."

"Forgive me," Harald said. "Maida has been supervising the preparation of food since everyone left yesterday. You, your brothers and your warriors are invited to the hall to share a meal with us."

Everyone trooped up to the hall, crowding inside behind Harald, Wulf and Reyna. Maida ran to meet them, her arms closing tight around her daughter. She studied Reyna's face, frowning when she saw the purpling bruise.

" 'Tis naught, Mother, truly."

Though Maida looked skeptical, she did not question Reyna further. Instead, she asked, "Where are my sons?"

"They are fine, Mother. Wulf will explain when everyone is settled and has eaten."

Maida nodded and invited everyone to sit. Soon afterward, thralls began placing platters of food on the table and pouring mead, ale and buttermilk into mugs and horns. Once everyone had eaten, Harald looked at Wulf and said, "I am eager to hear what has happened to my sons. Speak, Wulf the Defender."

Wulf cleared his throat and began his explanation. When he finished, Harald appeared stunned. "You let Elgar live? I cannot believe it."

"Wulf is finished with killing, Father," Reyna revealed. "When he goes to sea it will be strictly for trading. I commend him for allowing Elgar to seek new lands."

"Hmmm," Harald said, stroking his chin. "Still, the man should not have struck you."

"His punishment was defeat and loss of land, not to mention Reyna's own brand of retribution."

"I think Wulf was wise not to kill Elgar," Maida revealed. "Our Reyna has no stomach for brutality. I approve, Wulf."

"Aye," Harald added grudgingly.

"Will you bide with us a while?" Maida asked hopefully.

"We will remain until your sons return. Then my brothers and I must return home. Hagar and my mother will be anxious to know if our mission to rescue Reyna succeeded. They are more than fond of her."

"As I am of them," Reyna returned.

When Wulf, his brothers and her parents began a lively conversation, Reyna excused herself, telling Wulf she planned to rest in the stillroom that had once been Wulf's sleeping hut.

While Reyna was eating, she had begun making plans for the coming night. Before she left the hall she col-

lected wolf pelts, candles and clean linens and asked a thrall to help her carry them to the hut. Then she set the thrall to cleaning the place while she collected a variety of sweet-smelling herbs and wildflowers. Tonight, when she told Wulf about the baby, she wanted everything to be perfect.

Wulf was becoming anxious. He hadn't seen Reyna since she'd left the hall to rest. He'd expected she would return later to join the family, and when she didn't, he could scarcely wait to join her. He ached to hold her soft body against his, kiss her and make love to her. His love for his wife was such a new thing that he still marveled at it. He knew now that Astrid and their unborn child belonged to his past; Reyna was his future. It didn't matter that she couldn't give him a child; all he needed was Reyna.

He sighed wistfully. Though a girl child with Reyna's pale gold hair, courage and loving heart would be wonderful, children weren't necessary for his happiness. The more he thought about Reyna's sweet body, the more he wanted to rush off and join her. When the conversation lagged, he excused himself for the night and strode from the hall.

"Sleep well," Olaf called after him. His brothers' snickers followed him from the hall. Wulf paid them no heed. They were just jealous because they did not have a woman like Reyna in their lives.

"I thought you would never get here," Reyna said when he entered the stillroom.

Wulf sniffed the air. The fragrant scent of herbs wafted to him through the air, teasing his senses. Torchlight cast a golden glow through the hut and the scent of wildflowers mingled with the aroma of herbs. A thick pallet of wolf pelts covered with pristine linen had been laid out.

"Did you do all this for me?" Wulf asked, in awe of what Reyna had done. "Were you working here when you were supposed to be resting?"

"I have a lifetime to rest. Do you like it?"

"Aye, but I do not need embellishments when I make love to you." He sent her a lusty grin. "I am humbled that you would go to such lengths to please me, wife." He reached for her.

She tactfully avoided him. "No, not yet, come join me in the steam hut. When we return, I have something to tell you."

Wulf went still, fearing she would tell him that Elgar had done more to her than bruise her face. Not that it would matter. It might, however, convince him to return to kill Elgar before the bastard sailed off to parts unknown.

"Tell me now."

"No, first the steam hut. Relax, 'tis something that can wait till after we bathe."

Though Wulf feared the worst, he hadn't the heart to press Reyna. They walked to the steam hut together and undressed. She sat on the bench while Wulf poured water onto the hot rocks. Steam rose up to engulf them. Wulf had to admit the steam felt good on his sore body. Though the battle had been brief, it had been intense and the hot steam soothed away his stiffness.

He glanced at Reyna. Her eyes were closed, her head thrown back. He wondered if she was thinking the same thing he was. Reaching out, he turned her toward him. She sighed and leaned into him.

"I have never felt such happiness," Reyna sighed.

"I intend to make you happier very soon," Wulf growled.

Then he kissed her. Her mouth opened beneath his, inviting his tongue inside. She drowned in the scent and

taste of him as his hands roamed the hills and valleys of her naked body. When he started to lay her down on the bench, she placed her hands against his chest and pushed.

"Not here," she said. "I want everything to be perfect."

"I hunger for you, my sweet. How long must I wait?"

"Not long—I am as eager for you as you are for me. Fetch soap and warm water."

Reluctantly Wulf did as Reyna asked. He could deny her nothing, even though he was hard as stone and aching. They washed each other with tender care, rinsed the soap off their bodies and wrapped themselves in drying cloths. Then they gathered their soiled clothing and walked hand in hand to their cozy bower.

The moment the door closed behind them, Wulf took Reyna into his arms and kissed her wildly, abandoning all pretense of control. A thrall had started a fire in the hearth while they were gone and the hut was warm and sweet smelling. With their mouths still fused, Wulf removed the damp drying cloths from their bodies and tossed them aside. Then he scooped Reyna into his arms and carried her to the pallet, following her down onto the furs.

The kiss went on and on. When Reyna feared she would die from lack of breath, his mouth left hers, sliding down her cheek to the tender hollow beneath her ear, and then to that sensitive place where her neck met her shoulder. After he teased and nibbled to his heart's content, his mouth blazed a trail of fire to her tender nipples. Reyna let out a gasping sigh when his mouth closed over the tip of one breast.

Her fingers bit into his shoulders as he fed hungrily on her nipples. His hunger only served to heighten her desire as she arched beneath him, asking, begging for more. Wulf obliged, kissing a burning path down her

midriff and over her stomach, to the patch of golden fleece between her thighs. Reyna let out a long, shuddering breath, yearning for the scorching pleasure of their joining.

Parting the moist petals of her sex with his fingers, Wulf placed his mouth over her wet center, flicking his tongue in and out of her honeyed sweetness, drawing a low, keening wail from her. When he sucked the erect bud of her femininity into the hot well of his mouth, Reyna jerked wildly and exploded. While her body still thrummed with the force of her climax, Wulf rose up over her and sank into her, his sex piercing deep. In and out, he thrust, increasing the pressure with each powerful stroke, igniting a renewed burst of fire in her blood. She arched up. Wulf's hands unerringly found her breasts, stroking them, teasing her taut, puckered nipples with his fingertips.

"Come again for me, sweet," he urged.

She rocked against him. He met her stroke for stroke, driving his engorged shaft into her again and again. His face grew hard with need, his lips compressed as he drove upward with ever increasing urgency. Her moans seemed to inflame him. Grasping her bottom in his cupped palms, he raised her so she could take him deeper. Her inner muscles clutched around him as he lowered his head and kissed her, his tongue plunging into her mouth to mimic the driving rhythm of his flesh moving deep inside her body.

Overwhelming need built and swelled; the fire nearly consumed her. Moments later Reyna cried out, convulsing wildly, overcome by relentless waves of raw bliss.

As he relinquished control, guttural groans came from Wulf's throat and his climax burst from his powerful body into hers. His strong arms came around her as he buried his face in the hollow of her neck and whis-

pered her name. Still panting from his exertions, he lifted his body weight off of her and rolled to his back, bringing her against him.

"I waited a long time for that, sweet. Do you have any idea how bereft I felt when I thought you had carried out your threat and left me? Your leaving made me realize how desperately I loved you, how empty my life would be without you."

Reyna snuggled against him. "My threats were empty ones. All I ever wanted was for you to love me. There are so many reasons I should *not* love you, but one by one you destroyed them all. You were a bitter man bent on revenge when I came to you, but I came to love the person you are beneath all that bitterness and hate."

Wulf rolled her on top of him, his expression watchful as his silver eyes gazed deeply into hers. "You said there was something you wanted to tell me. Whatever it is will not change how I feel for you."

Reyna chuckled. "Oh, my love, I fear what I am about to tell you will change our lives forever."

"No," Wulf denied. "Just tell me so we can put it behind us."

A nagging fear that Wulf would not want their child gave Reyna pause. But Wulf's tender smile dissolved her fears. If he loved her, he would love their child.

"I am with child," she said.

Wulf went still beneath her; Reyna could not read his closed expression. Did he not want their child?

"By Odin's sword!" he swore. "Now I know I should have killed Elgar. All the time you were under his control you were carrying my child. What if you lost our babe? What if he had harmed you? What if . . ."

Relief flooded through Reyna. She touched his lips. "Hush, my love. Naught happened to me. Our child is safe beneath my heart. I did not realize I was with child

until after Elgar took me away." She smiled down at him. "You want our child, truly?"

He gave her a puzzled look. "How could I not? I love you, Reyna, and I will love any and all the children you give me."

They made love again, so slowly and with so much meaning it brought tears to Reyna's eyes. Their troubled past no longer mattered. Wulf had proved his love in so many ways that she could not find it in her heart to blame him for what had gone before. The future stretched before them, endless and shining brightly.

Several days later, after Borg and Dag had returned to the farmstead, Reyna boarded Wulf's dragonship and waved good-bye to her family as they sailed up the fjord to the North Sea. Reyna felt only happiness, for her parents had promised to visit in time for the birth of her child, their first grandchild.

Everything was right in Reyna's world.

"Do not be sad, sweet," Wulf said. "You will see your family again."

"I am not sad, Wulf. I have everything I need right here beside me."

"As do I, sweet, as do I." Then he kissed her, sealing their pledge of eternal love.

Epilogue

Reyna stood on a sloping hillside overlooking the ocean, a misty rain dampening her hair and clothing, clothing that was lovelier than anything she had ever worn before. Wulf had purchased the silk material and other equally luxurious items during his summer trading voyages to Byzantium.

They had found a new life in this lush, green island called Ireland. Wulf had claimed the land six years ago and built a home for them before bringing her and their one-year-old daughter Aleta to their new home. Wulf's brothers, Olaf and Eric, arrived a year later and had claimed land for themselves. Helga had divorced her husband and was now living with them. Reyna was happy Helga had learned Rannulf's true nature and had the good sense to leave him. Olaf had married the village blacksmith's daughter and settled down, but Eric wasn't ready yet to become domesticated.

The three brothers still went adventuring but no longer for the purpose of gaining plunder or slaves. Hagar had even brought his family and Thora for a visit last summer and her parents and brothers had visited twice.

Life was good here. The land was lush and welcoming, perfect for raising sheep and crops. Even now their flocks of sheep grazed contentedly on nearby hillsides.

Their cottage was different from their old hall on Hagar's farmstead. Wulf had built it with his brothers' help and had even added a few embellishments that their old hall had lacked. At Reyna's urging they had built separate sleeping chambers with leather hinged doors instead of the less private curtained sleeping alcoves. Their cottage had four such chambers in addition to the main hall and kitchen. It also had more windows than the old hall. Reyna never tired of looking out the window at their lush, new land when weather kept her inside.

Reyna lifted her face to the cool misty rain drifting down from a charcoal sky. Sighing in contentment, she dashed the rain from her face and gazed one last time at the sea before returning to the cottage and her beloved family. Besides five-year-old Aleta, there was three-year-old Deter, a small replica of his father. And now there was another babe resting beneath her heart.

"You should not be here in the rain," Wulf said from behind her. His arms came around her, pulling her into the curve of his body, sheltering her from the fine drizzle misting her clothing and hair. His hands drifted to the slight swelling of her stomach. "I would not have you sicken and endanger our babe."

Reyna turned in his arms and smiled up at him. "You worry too much, husband. I am healthy as a horse. This child will be born as easily as the first two."

"Come into the house, sweet. I will help you strip off your damp clothing." He grinned at her, his eyes twinkling mischievously as he urged her toward the house, one arm clasped tightly around her waist.

She returned his smile with one equally mischievous. "And then what, my fierce Viking warrior?"

He leaned down to whisper into her ear, "Then, my courageous warrior woman, while the children play with the wooden toys I carved for them, I will lock our

bedchamber door and join you in our bed, where we will while away the rainy afternoon making mad, passionate love."

And so they did.

SHIRL HENKE

Sky Brewster's heart cries out for justice, and she will not be satisfied until she sees her husband's murderer dead at her feet. To get the job done, she'll leave her Sioux people to make a devil's bargain with a man whose talent as an assassin is surpassed only by his skills at seduction.

Max Stanhope is an infamous English bounty hunter who always delivers—dead or alive. But now he must take a wife to claim his birthright. When his newest client turns out to be as delectable as she is passionate, he figures he'll mix business with pleasure.

The beautiful widow and the Limey make a deal: her hand in marriage for his special skills. But an old Cheyenne medicine man has seen the Great Spirit's grand design, and True Dreamer knows Sky Eyes of the Sioux is destined to love the...

PALE MOON STALKER

ISBN 13: 978-0-8439-6112-6

DAWN MACTAVISH

The battle that won Robert Mack his scars was lost in the cradle, and thus the third Laird of Berwickshire wore his silver helm not for personal protection but the sake of others. While the right side of his face was untouched—handsome, even—the left lay in ruin. No man could look upon him without fear. Nor could any woman. Such a life was worse than any prison, so Robert set out for Paris and the great healer Nostradamus.

The powerful young Scot reached a land in conflict. With a boy on its throne and her people at war, all of France was shadows, intrigue and blood. All except for Violette Cherier, a blind flower girl with honey-colored hair, as beautiful and fragile as her namesake. Soon enough, what at first seemed Robert's unwise act of kindness proved sage. The fires of civil war were rising, and Violette was the only one who could free the...

Prisoner of the Flames

ISBN 13: 978-0-8439-5982-6

PAMELA CLARE

MacKinnon's Rangers: They were a band of brothers, their loyalty to one another forged by hardship and battle, the bond between these Highland warriors, rugged colonials, and fierce Native Americans stronger even than blood ties.

UNTAMED

Though forced to fight for the hated British, Morgan MacKinnon would no more betray the men he leads than slit his own throat—not even when he was captured by the French and threatened with an agonizing death by fire at the hands of their Abenaki allies. Only the look of innocent longing in the eyes of a convent-bred French lass could make him question his vow to escape and return to the Rangers. And soon the sweet passion he awoke in Amalie had him cursing the war that forced him to choose between upholding his honor and pledging himself to the woman he loves.

ISBN 13: 978-0-8439-5489-0